Truly, Madly,

WHISKEY

The Whiskeys

New York Times Bestselling Author

MELISSA FOSTER

SPENCER
HILL
PRESS

ISBN: 978-1-63392-106-1

TRULY, MADLY, WHISKEY

Published in the United States by Spencer Hill Press.
This is a Spencer Hill Press Contemporary Romance.
Spencer Hill Contemporary is an imprint of Spencer Hill Press.
For more information on our titles visit www.spencerhillpress.com

Distributed by Midpoint Trade Books
www.midpointtrade.com

Cover Design: Elizabeth Mackey Designs
Cover Photography: Sara Eirew

Printed in the United States of America.

A Note to Readers

I'm thrilled to bring you Bear and Crystal's steamy and emotional love story. I hope you fall in love with them, as well as all their warm and wonderful family members and friends, each of whom will be getting their own happily-ever-after.

Remember to sign up for my newsletter to make sure you don't miss out on future Whiskey releases: www.MelissaFoster.com/News

For more information about my fun, sexy romance novels, all of which can be read as stand-alone novels, or as part of the larger series, visit my website: www.MelissaFoster.com

Melissa Foster

CHAPTER ONE

CRYSTAL MOON'S STOMACH knotted as she drove through the gates of West Millstone Estates Wednesday evening. *Estates.* She scoffed, her eyes darting to a group of scraggly looking guys smoking beside the rusted chain-link fence that surrounded the trailer park where she'd grown up. The "gate" hadn't functioned since she was ten, when a stoned neighbor had driven his truck through it. Doing her best to ignore the lascivious stares coming from another group of guys standing by the run-down trailer on her right, she focused on the road, mentally ticking off the only names she'd ever associated with the people who had lived in the trailers as she passed each one.

Hateful. Creepy. Sweet. Staythefuckaway.

With the exception of her mother, she no longer had any idea who lived in each trailer, but the names she'd given them when she was a kid would stick forever, like the dirty feeling that clung to her like a second skin every time she returned.

She parked behind her mother's old Toyota. Decomposed leaves lay like skeletons on the hood. Dirt caked the wheel wells and lower half of the door. She'd made the mistake of giving her mother money to get a new battery ages ago, but her mother had spent it on alcohol. She scanned the street for her older brother Jed's truck. Uttering a curse, she pulled out her phone and called him.

He answered on the first ring. "Hey, you."

"Don't 'hey, you,' me. I'm sitting in front of Mom's. Did you forget? Third Wednesday of the month."

"Oh, shit. I'll get a ride and be there in ten."

The line went dead. She'd forgotten his driver's license had been suspended for too many unpaid tickets. Mike McCarthy, a local cop, had a personal vendetta against Jed, and pulled him over every chance he got, doling out the highest points possible. Jed swore the guy had a homing device to keep track of him, but Crystal knew their hatred went back to their high school days, when Jed had slept with every girl Mike had dated. She had a feeling it hadn't stopped after graduation, but that was one confirmation she didn't need. She loved Jed to the ends of the earth, but he was a bit of a hoodlum and had spent his teenage years in and out of trouble, and as an adult he'd spent a few months in jail for stealing. He said it was in his blood, but Crystal could attest to the fact that, unless she was born from different parents, it wasn't. It was simply *Jed*.

She zipped up her hoodie and glanced at the stack of designs she'd been working on for Princess for a Day, the boutique where she worked with her best friend, Gemma Wright. She'd met Gemma at a café shortly after escaping from her *second* bout with hell. When she'd left the dregs of the trailer park, she'd thought she'd left that nightmare behind. A few years later she found out that hell came in many forms, and the trailer park hadn't looked quite so bad. She hadn't returned, though. She'd been broken, not stupid.

Pushing those dark thoughts away, she cut the engine.

Untrusting of the cachectic, shirtless dude standing across the street, holding the chain of a vicious-looking barking dog, she shoved the designs into her bag and slipped the strap over her head and across her body. A barrier. As small as that thin strap was, anything separating the person she'd become from the mother who bore her was worth its weight in gold.

She made one last sweep of her car, searching for anything theft-worthy. The 2010 Ford Fusion might not be much, but it was hers. Her eyes caught on the colorful worry doll hanging on her rearview mirror, a gift from her father. He'd made it out of twigs, fabric, and yarn when she was eight, and he'd given it to her the first week they'd moved into the trailer park. He'd been making her dolls for years, but this time he'd given her a reason. *Give these dolls all your worries, and then you'll be free of them. Like magic.* Her eyes drifted to the smaller doll hanging from her key chain. Little reminders that she'd once had a parent who'd loved her. She snagged the doll from the rearview and stuffed it in her bag. It would piss her off if it got stolen. She'd hang it up again when she left.

She stepped from the car and locked it up, bracing herself for the visit. *It's only once a month. One hour, twelve times a year.* She could suck it up for an hour. Then she'd return to her life in Peaceful Harbor, Maryland, forty-five minutes away. Just far enough to allow her to pretend that this part of her life didn't exist.

Her phone vibrated with a text, and she pulled it out, ready to give Jed a hard time for whatever excuse he might use to skip dinner. *Him* flashed on caller ID. She rolled her eyes, trying to keep her body from heating up from head to toe. It didn't work. It never did. She'd listed Bear Hot-as-Fuck Whiskey as *Him* in her contacts in an effort to fool her mind into thinking of him in generic male form. The problem was, there was nothing generic about the six-three, bar-and-auto-mechanic-shop-owning, tattooed biker.

She opened and read the text. *Bear.*

One word was all it took for fire to ricochet through her body like lightning. *Traitorous body.* The guy was relentless. He'd been acting as if she were *his* ever since she'd met him more than eight months ago, when Gemma had first met her fiancé, Truman Gritt, who was Bear's best friend. The harder she'd pushed Bear away, the more determined he'd become. He'd been texting her his name for weeks, always out of the blue. It wasn't like he knew she'd changed his name in her phone. He was just being *Bear*. Did he really think texting his *name* would change her mind?

There wasn't much changing necessary. She swallowed against that reality. She was not only hot for the guy, but she couldn't stop thinking about him. The hardest part was that over the past eight-plus months, he'd grown on her like a third arm—exciting, reliable, and uncomfortable all at once. He was cocky and arrogant when it came to pushing himself into her life, which should have made her wary of him, but she was drawn to him like a moth to a flame. Because he was also a loyal, generous friend and funny in ways that made her wonder what it might be like to experience all those attributes tangled together—*in her bed*.

Ugh. She really needed to stop thinking about him.

Her phone vibrated again with a text from Gemma. She opened it and found a picture of Bear painting. Great. Now she'd never stop thinking about him. His muscular, tattooed arm was over his head as he painted along the edge of the window. His shirt clung to his broad back, tapering down and disappearing into a pair of low-slung jeans that hugged his frustratingly hot ass. Another text rolled in. *Enjoying watching my man paint. Thought you might want to see yours.*

Crystal rolled her eyes. Gemma knew she wasn't *with* Bear in that way. She was meeting Gemma and Truman after dinner to help paint their living room in preparation for their backyard wedding, and she knew Bear would be there. Their close-knit group included all four Whiskey siblings, so Bear was always around, like an itch she shouldn't scratch. Her stomach fluttered, and she groaned. The last thing she needed in her busy, not-living-in-a-trailer-park life, was to be lusting after a man. Especially one who *assumed* he owned her.

She shoved her phone in her pocket, inhaled deeply, and faced her mother's mustard-yellow trailer, wishing she could climb back into her car and return to her normal life.

Each of the trailers had a tiny plot of land out front. Most had turned to dirt over the years from being trampled or driven over. But before her father had been killed in a car accident, he'd set enormous rocks around the perimeter of their lot, where he and Crystal had planted a garden. Now that tiny plot of land was overgrown with long grass and the type of prickly bushes she'd always given a wide berth, as if the branches were gnarled claws that could capture her as she walked by.

The whole complex feels like that.

She stepped onto the musty indoor-outdoor carpeting beneath a green awning that hung from the side of the trailer. Jed had put it up when they were teenagers. The stench of cigarettes and sweat hung in the air. Two ancient lawn chairs and a plastic table sat at the far end of the carpet. *Outside living at its finest.*

She hesitated, wishing Jed would hurry up, and finally reached for the metal handle of the screen door, which had no screen.

"Jeddy? That you?" Her mother's raspy voice might sound sexy if her speech weren't slurred and the raspiness weren't clearly the sandpaper sound of a throat worn down by too many cigarettes.

Crystal stepped inside, assaulted by the earlier stench, only a hundred times stronger. Habit had her breathing through her mouth, which seemed less repulsive than smelling the rancid air with every inhalation. Her eyes skirted over the dark paneled walls, low-pile carpeting, and plaid sofa, hallmarks of her youth. The same green-and-yellow curtains that were there when they'd moved in hung from metal rods, darkening the windows. The two wooden chairs Crystal and her father had painted bright aqua the first summer they'd lived there were now chipped and marred. They were the last project she and her father had worked on together. Two empty beer bottles sat on the coffee table beside an empty carton of cigarettes, the top of which was torn off. *Welcome home.*

"Chrissy?" Her mother stood by the stove stirring something in a big pot. A cigarette hung from her lips, as if it had grown roots. "I was expecting Jeddy." Ashes floated to the floor as she spoke. Pamela Moon was a blond, drunken Peg Bundy lookalike, from her overly teased hair, pink tank top, black leggings, wide white belt, and high heels to the way she carried herself with one hand constantly waving.

Crystal cringed at the name she'd given up when she'd gone off to college. It had been years, and her mother hadn't noticed. Either that or she simply hadn't cared. Crystal imagined it was a little of both.

"Sorry, Mom. Just me."

She hoped her mother remembered they were supposed to have dinner. Sometimes she forgot. Crystal used to bring dinner for their monthly visits, but her mother complained about everything, and she'd given up trying.

Her mother grabbed a beer bottle from the counter and took a long swig. Crystal gauged her unsteadiness, tallying the five empty bottles in sight and knowing it probably wasn't the day's total count. Her mother had gone downhill after they'd lost their father to a drunk driver, which made no sense to Crystal. Her father's death had had a profound effect on her in too many ways to count, but most importantly, Crystal was careful not to drink too much. At first she'd thought her mother's drinking was a coping mechanism, but as the months, then years, had passed, she'd realized she had a problem and had encouraged her to go to AA and seek help. Her mother had ignored her efforts, turning cold and bitter. Crystal had no idea how she functioned with the amount of alcohol she consumed.

Crystal peered into the dark mass in the pot. "What are you making?"

"Chili. You hungry?" More ashes drifted to the floor.

"Yeah, sure." She'd push the food around on her plate and praise her mother's cooking. Then she'd wrap it up and leave it for her mother to eat tomorrow. She set her bag on the coffee table, settling in for the next hour, hoping it would race by.

"How are you, Mom? Is your job okay?" Her mother worked at a convenience store three blocks away.

She nodded, inhaling loudly as she plucked the cigarette from her mouth, and waved a hand. "Twenty, thirty hours a week. They're still talking about making me a manager, but you know." She winked and stuck the cigarette between her painted lips. "I'll find me a good man before that happens."

"Sure." Crystal had long ago stopped believing her mother's stories about being promoted, and had also given up trying to convince her that a man would never be the answer to her troubles.

She set the table, listening to her mother rattle on about a woman she worked with. Just once, she'd love for her mother to ask how *she* was or what was new in *her* life, the way her mother had before her father had lost his job and they'd been forced to move from their home in Peaceful Harbor. But her mother hadn't been that woman for years. She had changed when they'd moved, and she'd gotten even worse after her father was killed.

The door flew open and Jed stepped into the room, making the tight quarters feel even smaller. At six two, with dirty-blond hair, a beard that came in a shade darker, and piercing blue eyes, he was the spitting image of their father.

He kissed the top of Crystal's head. "Hey, shrimp. Still doing the goth thing?"

She rolled her eyes. She'd dyed her hair black right after she'd moved to Peaceful Harbor. That had been more than four years ago. She'd thought he'd be used to it by now.

"Still doing the stealing thing?" She nodded at his leather jacket as he dipped his head to kiss his mother's cheek.

He flopped down on the couch and kicked his feet up on the coffee table. "Nope. I helped a guy fix his car." He brushed an invisible speck of dirt from the dark leather. "Earned the money for this legally."

"Uh-huh." Crystal pushed his feet off the coffee table and went to fill water glasses for dinner. "I can't remember the last time you earned money the hard way. Where are you living these days?"

"Crashing at a friend's place. Basement apartment."

"Got my cigarettes?" their mother asked.

"Oh, crap." Jed winced. "I knew I forgot something."

"Christ, Jeddy," their mother said as she dished the chili onto three plates. "What have you been doing? I've waited all day."

"Ma. I've been working. Don't worry," Jed said. "I'll get them after dinner."

Crystal's ears perked up. "Working? Really?"

"I'm trying to pull my shit together. Finally putting that mechanics training to good use and picking up a few hours here and there at a restaurant."

Their mother scoffed. "Right. Get on up here and eat."

They sat at the table, the silence broken only by the clinking of silverware on plates. Crystal pushed her food around, watching her mother smoke and eat. She had vague memories of her mother without cigarette-stained teeth, yellowed fingers, and the bitterness of someone who the world had wronged. Memories of a woman who would send her off to elementary school with a paper-bag lunch and greet her with a smile when she'd stepped off the bus at the end of the day. In a sense, her father's death had stolen both of her parents.

"Where are you working?" Crystal asked, taking a longer look at her brother. He wasn't a big drinker, and he'd never been a drug user. Unfortunately, there weren't any outward signs for a thief.

"My buddy runs a gas station. I'm helping him out."

"How much do you pocket?" his mother asked.

"Mom!" Crystal might not buy that her brother was suddenly trying to clean up his act after a lifetime of trouble, but she didn't like her mother's condescending attitude. It was bad enough that she'd never believed a damn thing Crystal said, but at least she could understand her mother's anger toward her. She'd left home at eighteen with a Pell Grant to attend college and had never looked back. But Jed had stuck by their mother, put her to bed when she was too drunk to walk and done whatever she'd asked of him for years.

"What?" She took a drag of her cigarette. "You can't trust a liar's word. He's just like your father."

"Someone has to provide for you," Jed snapped.

"Jesus, Jed. Please tell me you are not giving her money." Crystal couldn't get lost in *that* right now; she was too pissed at what her mother had said. "Dad wasn't a liar." She crossed her arms, unwilling to fight the familiar battle. Her mother claimed her father had promised her a *good* life. It wasn't his fault he'd gotten laid off. Wasn't that what loving someone "for better or worse" meant? Sticking it out through the tough times? He'd given them all a good life, and he'd loved them. It wasn't his fault that at the first sign of trouble their mother had started drinking. She'd never understood what more her mother could have wanted, and at this point she simply didn't care.

Her mother pulled the cigarette from her mouth to speak, and Jed put a hand on her arm. "Mom, *don't*."

"Okay, you know what?" Crystal gritted her teeth. "I didn't come here to listen to you berate Jed *or* Dad."

"Why did you come here?" her mother challenged.

"I ask myself that question every time I visit." She looked away. "Some sort of warped sense of loyalty, I suppose."

Her mother rose to her feet, talking around her cigarette. "Don't be so stuck-up. You came from *my* womb. You have my blood in you, girlie. You're no better than me, so don't you dare judge me."

Crystal forced herself to dig deep and find the calm voice she used with overbearing parents at the boutique. "I'm not judging you, Mom. I just wish you'd stop judging Jed and Dad."

"Hey, how about we change the subject." Jed winked at Crystal. "How's your boyfriend?"

"What boyfriend?"

He laughed. "Uh-oh. Did you break up?"

She rolled her eyes. "With . . . ?"

"Bear? The guy who had his arm around you at Tru's Christmas party and again at the Easter parade? Did you forget I was there?"

"He isn't my boyfriend." *Although he's played a starring role in my dreams for months.* "There is no boyfriend. Same as last time and probably the same as next time."

Their mother scoffed. "She can't keep a man. A man touches her and she flips out."

The night of the attack, and the reason she'd left college, came rushing back. Why she'd thought she could confide in her mother was beyond her. *The hell with this.*

She stormed across the room and grabbed her bag. "Sorry, Jed. I've got to get out of here."

"That's it. Run away, just like always." Her mother waved a hand and picked up her fork, stabbing at her food.

"Whatever." She was so sick of the same old shit; her mother was barely worth the energy of her halfhearted response.

"Jesus, Mom. Give her a break." Jed pushed to his feet and stood between the table and Crystal, thankfully blocking her view of her mother. "Ignore her. She's blitzed out of her mind."

"You need a ride?" Crystal was dying to take a shower and scrub off the smoke and grime of her past.

"Yeah. I get my license back in six weeks, but can you swing me by my buddy's?" He looked at his mother, and Crystal saw the guilt eating away at him.

She rolled her eyes again. "I'll take you to get her cigarettes first, but I don't know why you cater to her."

"Same reason you're here every month. Good old-fashioned guilt."

CRYSTAL FLEW THROUGH Truman and Gemma's front door like wildfire, eating up everything in her path. Her raven mane was soaking wet, framing her beautiful, scowling face as she stormed into the living room. Her black hoodie hung open over a Rolling Stones T-shirt, and her piercing baby blues threw daggers. Her skintight black jeans had tears along her thighs and beneath her knees, revealing flashes of her tanned skin. Skin he'd like to touch and taste and have wrapped around him.

She stopped a few feet from Bear and set her hand on her hip. "Give me a paintbrush, or a roller, or a goddamn gun for all I care. Just give me something and get out of my way."

They'd finished painting ten minutes ago. Bear chuckled at her vehemence. She was sexy as sin no matter what mood she was in, but this tigress before him made him want to comfort her and fuck her at once.

"Hard night, sugar?"

She narrowed her eyes. "Not *hard* enough. And I'm not your *sugar*. I need to work out my frustrations." She thrust out a hand, obviously waiting for a paintbrush.

He grabbed that delicate little hand and hauled her against him. His entire body flamed. Several months of playing cat and mouse was way too long. Her eyes darkened and her breathing shallowed. Bear was done messing around. This brazen beauty not only wanted him, but she needed him. She just didn't know it yet.

"What do you think you're doing?" She spoke in a low voice and probably meant it to sound threatening, but she sounded sultry and hard to resist.

He cupped her chin, brushing his thumb over her lower lip, and the air rushed from her lungs. His hand slid over her hip. She had the sleek, sexy curves of a '61 Harley-Davidson Duo-Glide, and he couldn't wait to rev her up and make her *purr*. "Giving you what you need. A wild Whiskey night is the perfect remedy for your frustrations."

"Uncle Be-*ah*!" Three-year-old Kennedy ran into the room wearing a *Dora the Explorer* nightgown and clutching the Winnie-the-Pooh stuffed toy Bear's younger sister, Dixie, had given her. She squeezed between them. Truman had rescued his younger siblings, Kennedy and Lincoln, from a crack house after their mother overdosed. He and Gemma were raising them as their own.

Crystal smirked at Bear and arched a brow.

He reluctantly released her. *Cockblocked by a three-year-old.*

"Hi, pretty girl." Crystal gave Bear a snarky look as she crouched and hugged Kennedy. "This cuteness is all I need after a frustrating evening."

"Why are you fwustrated, Auntie Cwystal?" Kennedy still had a hard time pronouncing *r*'s, and the way she spoke turned Bear's insides to mush.

"I'm not anymore, thanks to you."

"I came to kiss you and Be*ah* good night." She gave Crystal a tight hug and kiss, then reached her spindly arms up to Bear and went up on her toes.

He lifted her up, and she wound her arms around his neck.

"Thank you for letting me help you paint." Kennedy yawned and rested her head on his shoulder. "The house will be *pwetty* for Mommy and Tooman's—I mean *Daddy's*—wedding." Although Kennedy and Lincoln were Truman's siblings, when Lincoln had begun talking, he'd called Truman *Dada*, and Kennedy had said she wanted to call him that, too. Sometimes she forgot and called him *Tooman*.

Bear ran his hand down her back. It was hard to believe it had been less than a year since Truman had found them. Kennedy had gone from a rail-thin, frightened little girl to a healthy, happy member of not just Truman's family, but Bear's, too.

"You're the best painter around, sweetheart. Thank *you* for helping me." He lifted his eyes, catching Crystal watching him with a warm—*interested?*—look in her eyes. He liked that a whole lot.

Crystal's eyes skittered away. "Hey, Ken? Where's Mommy?"

"She's giving Lincoln a baf."

Crystal smiled. "Want me to take you up to bed?"

"Yes," Bear and Kennedy said at once.

Crystal rolled her eyes at Bear and reached for Kennedy.

Bear put an arm around Crystal's waist, ignoring her glare. "I'm escorting two of my favorite girls upstairs. Deal with it." He guided her toward the stairs, where they ran into Truman on his way down.

Truman stood eye to eye with Bear, his dark gaze moving between the two of them. His lips curved up and he shook his head. He must have read the annoyed expression on Crystal's face, because he reached for Kennedy. "I think I'll intervene. Thanks, guys."

After he went upstairs, Crystal said, "You can let go of me now."

"No thanks." He kept ahold of her as she stalked back to the living room. "Want to tell me what happened tonight?"

"No. I want to paint." She squirmed out of his grip and he tugged her back.

"If you think I'll let this go, you're wrong. Talk to me. What's got you so irritated?"

"Jesus, Bear," she snapped. "I'm not *yours*. You don't have to protect me."

He ignored her comment because she knew damn well how things worked with the Whiskeys. More importantly, she knew *him* well enough to know he'd never sit idly by and let her get hurt. If someone had pissed her off, he'd straighten them out.

"You're not mine *yet*," he conceded.

"God, you're so arrogant and handsy and . . . *Ugh!*" She pushed away. "I just had a rough visit with my mom, that's all."

"What happened?" Her not wanting to go into specifics didn't surprise him. She'd always been cagey about her parents.

She grabbed the ladder and dragged it toward the far wall. He took it from her, and she glared at him again. She was the most stubborn woman he'd ever known. She was also sharp, confident, and possibly the most sensitive person he knew, though she'd never admit to it. Those were just a few of the things he found utterly entrancing about her.

Her arms were crossed, and he was pretty sure if it were possible she'd have steam coming out of her ears. "Can we just paint?"

"Sorry, sugar, but we're done for the night."

"Seriously?" She looked around the room, and her stomach growled. Her lips curved up at the edges as she spread a hand over her belly.

Perfect. He whipped out his phone, texting Tru and telling him he was taking Crystal out for a bite to eat. "Grab your bag. We're going out to eat." He draped his arm over her shoulder and headed for the front door.

"I'm not hungry."

He gave her his best deadpan stare.

Challenge rose in her beautiful eyes. "You don't *tell me* what to do."

"All right. Your stomach's growling. Obviously you're hungry. Let's go grab something to eat."

She folded her arms over her chest. "That's *telling*."

"Christ, woman." She had no idea how much he adored this side of her. They'd never been on an official date, but they'd gone to grab a bite to eat spur-of-the-moment like this plenty of times. "Are you hungry?"

"I could eat."

"Great," he said. "Let's go."

"Oh my God. Really? Didn't anyone ever teach you how to ask a woman if she'd like to go out to eat?"

"Are you telling me to ask you out on a date?" He slid his arm around her waist again and waggled his brows.

"No." She laughed.

He loved her laugh. It was brazen and loud, like her. "Damn. Thought I got lucky. Crystal Moon, would you like to grab a burger with me?"

She picked up her bag from the floor. "*Fine.* But I need to tell Gemma. You're so bossy."

"You totally dig bossy, and I already texted Tru and told him."

"Presumptive *and* bossy."

He pulled open the door. The starless sky made the night extra dark, and even with the streetlights it felt as though the night had swallowed the earth.

Crystal walked toward her car, and he tightened his grip. "We'll take my truck."

"I can drive. Then you don't have to bring me back to get it."

He opened the passenger door of the truck and said, "I also wouldn't have you with me on the way there. Climb in."

"Bossy." She stepped onto the running board and he smacked her ass. She glared over her shoulder.

"You know I like it when you glare at me." He circled the truck and climbed into the driver's seat, debating unhooking her seat belt and hauling her pretty little ass across the bench seat. But her expression turned serious, and he remembered she'd had a hard night. Empathy pushed his desires to the side.

They drove to Woody's Burgers in silence, which was how he knew there was probably more to this than a shitty visit with her mother. He also knew she wasn't going to tell him what was really going on. *At least not yet.* He came on strong, but they had a solid friendship that felt more like a relationship and went beyond his desire to finally taste her luscious mouth. He cared about her, and one way or another, he'd figure out a way to get her to talk. He had to, because knowing she was hurting and not being able to fix it made him want to tear someone's head off.

He parked the truck and reached across the seat, giving her hand a comforting squeeze. "Hey." He waited until she met his gaze. "Whatever's going on, you know you can talk to me."

Her eyes fell to their hands, and a hint of a smile lifted her lips. "Yeah, I know. Thanks."

Woody's was a low-key burger joint with brick walls that had been painted white and bright green tables and benches. Overgrown ferns and decorative iron lights hung from metal rods along the ceiling. The floor was a mismatched patchwork of wooden planks. It didn't look like much, but they had the best burgers and fries in Peaceful Harbor, and tonight Bear had the prettiest girl in the harbor on his arm, too. It was a good night, despite the cloud hanging over Crystal's head. He'd shelter her from whatever storm came her way.

He slid into the booth beside her.

"There are two benches for a reason," she pointed out.

"Oh, right." He kicked his feet up on the bench across from them, the tips of his black leather boots visible over the edge of the table.

She laughed.

"Your turn." He tapped her thigh, leaving his hand there as she lifted her feet beside his.

She pushed his hand from her thigh without a word, and he stretched his arm across the back of the bench.

"Are you always like this?" She picked up the menu and looked it over.

"You've known me for a long time. You tell me."

"I know how you are with me. I mean with other girls. I've never been out with you, like on a date."

He began kneading the tension from her shoulder. "Then maybe it's time to remedy that."

The waitress interrupted before she could respond, and they ordered burgers and fries, and Crystal ordered a milk shake. *Chocolate, vanilla, and strawberry mixed, please.* She was unique in everything she did, and he loved that about her. Their food came quickly, and they made small talk about getting ready for Tru and Gemma's wedding.

When he couldn't stand the edge in her voice any longer, he said, "Tell me about your mom."

She shrugged. "Nothing to tell. We're not very close."

"Why was tonight so rough?" He picked up a fry and dunked it in her shake as she lifted her burger to her mouth.

"Um . . . ?" She lowered her burger to the plate. "What are you doing?"

"Dunking my fry in your shake." He popped it in his mouth. "Haven't we done this before?"

"*No*."

"We've known each other for almost a year and we've never had fries and shakes? That's not true and you know it."

"You've never *dunked your fry* in my shake," she clarified.

He brushed his shoulder against hers. "Whose fault is that? I would love to bury my fry in your luscious milk shake."

She laughed. "Not happening." She took a big bite of her burger, her cheeks puffing out like a chipmunk, clearly trying to avoid talking about *that*.

He finished his burger and put his arm around her again, dipping another fry in her shake. He held it up for her, and she swatted his hand away, pointing to her full mouth. Her eyes were wide, but smiling, which he totally dug.

"Okay, I'll tell you what. Tell me why tonight was so rough, and I'll leave your shake alone."

She shook her head, and he dunked another fry. She whimpered, trying to swallow her burger as quickly as she could.

"My girl doesn't swallow well. *Noted*."

She laughed/snorted and choked on her burger. He patted her on the back, both of them laughing.

"I'll help you with that whole swallowing thing," he offered, which made her laugh harder, causing her to snort again.

She tried to catch her breath, and he dunked another fry.

"Hey!"

"Just try one. You'll like it. I promise."

She eyed the fry as if it were poison.

"One bite." He dragged the fry along her lower lip. Leaning closer, he said, "You'd better lick that off before I do."

Her eyes narrowed, and her tongue swept over her lower lip.

"Christ Almighty," he grumbled.

She laughed. "That's pretty good. Salty and sweet."

"Stick with me, baby. I'll make sure you get your fill of salty and sweet."

She shook her head, laughing softly. "You never answered my question about if you were this way with all women."

"You never answered mine about what really happened tonight." He dunked another fry and held it up for her.

Their eyes locked, unstoppable heat pulsing between them. She shifted her gaze to the fry, her fingers curling around her thigh. She didn't move, didn't say a word, just stared at the fry, as if that might cool down the inferno that followed them like a shadow.

He leaned forward to eat the fry at the same time she did, and they ended up nose to nose, their mouths a fry apart.

She licked her lips, and he lowered the fry, clearing the way for the kiss he'd been fantasizing about for months.

"I had to drive Jed all over creation," she said softly.

It took him a second to realize she was answering his question.

"I've got a ton of designs to work on for the boutique now that we're trying to make and sell our own costumes. And I haven't had time to get my car inspected, which I need to do before I get a ticket. Tonight was a total time suck. Not now," she clarified. "Earlier. With my mother and Jed."

She dressed and acted tough, but there were brief moments like this when she let her guard down just enough for him to catch a glimpse of the vulnerable woman behind the walls. He wanted to take her in his arms and protect her and love her at once. But she'd finally let him in, and he realized he still owed her an answer to her question.

The truth came easily. "You asked if I was this way with everyone. I'm this way because it's you."

He watched her assess his response with a skeptical expression. Did she sense the honesty in his confession? Seconds passed like minutes, minutes like hours. Months of pent-up sexual energy sparked between them. He slid his hand beneath her hair, drawing her closer. She was looking at him like she wanted to dissolve into him. *Finally*. He leaned in for the kiss, and just as quickly as their passion built, coolness descended over her face, lowering the sweet curve of her lips as she leaned back, putting space between them.

She turned her body toward the table, and lowered her feet to the floor, sitting up straighter and leaving him to wonder what the hell had just happened. He'd been *this close* to taking the kiss he'd been craving for months.

"Crystal . . . ?"

The shrill ringtone for the Dark Knights Motorcycle Club he and his brothers were members of, and his father headed up, broke through his confusion, and he whipped his phone out of his pocket. His heart thundered—from their almost kiss or the club alert, he couldn't be sure.

He answered the call, listening to his oldest brother, Bullet, relaying the information about Trevor "Scooter" Mackelby, a seven-year-old boy whose mother had caught the attention of one of the club members when she'd posted on Facebook about her son being bullied. The Dark Knights had "adopted" him into their club and had sworn to protect him. There had been an incident at school, and now Scooter was afraid to go to sleep. Tonight the club members would rally around Scooter's house, staying until morning, to ensure he felt safe.

"I need to drop Crystal at her car and grab my bike," he said to Bullet. "I'll meet you there."

He stepped from the booth and threw cash on the table, wishing he could delve into their *almost* kiss, but there was no time. "I'm sorry, sugar, but duty calls. I've got to take off."

Confusion clouded her eyes. "Duty?"

"Club business." They hurried out to the truck, and he explained about Scooter on the way back to Truman's to get her car. His great-grandfather had formed the Dark Knights, and his father, who went by the road name Biggs, for his six-five height, was the president. Bear and his brothers had been brought up to respect the brotherhood and honor its creed.

"'Love, loyalty, and respect for all' runs as thick as blood through our veins. A blessing and a curse." He went on to explain how they'd connected with Scooter and gave her examples of when they'd helped in similar situations in neighboring towns.

"So, if a kid or an adult is bullied—"

"Or abused," he corrected her.

"Or abused, you guys *all* sit outside his house until he feels safe?"

"Essentially, but not always. It depends on the situation. Schools, teachers, even the police, can't do much when it comes to bullies. The victims are left feeling weak and vulnerable. We empower them to *tell* and to *know* they have support. By getting involved and showing up in force—outside their house, for example, or around their block, or escorting them to school or work—the person who is hurting them realizes the victim is not alone and vulnerable. We're there to protect them."

"But what if they're abused and not bullied, by an adult?"

Bear ground his teeth together to ward off the anger the question incited. "We're there for those cases, too. And when they go to court, we escort them. The whole club, on our bikes, in front of and behind their parents' cars. And we line up in court to show our support."

"Intimidating the abuser?"

"That's a nice side effect, but our goal is to empower the victim and make them feel safe."

He pulled up in front of Tru's house and climbed from the truck, coming around to open Crystal's door and help her out. "Think of it this way. If they call a social worker at ten o'clock at night, they're not going to get an answer. Once they're 'adopted' by our club, they're a member for life, and we stand by them no matter what time of day or night. It all started a few years ago, when my father met a family who had lost their son to suicide after he'd been bullied. They were from Florida, but it opened his eyes. He brought the mission up to the members, and now it's part of who we are."

She dug in her bag for her keys. "That's impressive. I'm surprised there haven't been articles about you guys." Finally finding her keys, she unlocked her car door.

"We don't want press. It's all about helping the victims." He stepped closer, and she backed up, giving him a clear signal that whatever had scared her off in Woody's was still hanging around.

"I had a nice time tonight," he said. "Thanks for letting me dip my fry in your shake."

She smiled and shook her head, her eyes sliding to the ground. She looked adorably sexy. Another glimpse into that softer side of his tough girl.

With a finger beneath her chin, he lifted her face so she had to meet his gaze. "That goes for you, too. If you don't feel safe at any time, any hour, you know you can call me."

She looked at him for a long moment, as if she was struggling to decide if she should make a smart-ass remark, or go with the heat between them. It seemed to be the look du jour.

A smile crept across her face, and she climbed into her car. "And feed into that big head of yours? I don't need protecting, but I'm glad you're helping that little boy."

He leaned in and kissed her cheek. He'd snuck kisses like this a few times, but it always felt like the first time. His lips lingered on her warm skin, soaking in her feminine scent. "You haven't seen my *big* head yet, sugar. But I'm pretty sure you'll like it even more than the one you've been staring at all night. Drive safely."

She closed the door and rolled down the window. "Why do you keep texting me your name?"

He felt himself grinning. "I may have been out of sight, but I'll make damn sure I'm not off your mind. 'Night, sugar. Drop me a text to let me know you got home okay, and lock your doors."

She rolled her eyes. "I will if *I* want to."

"Oh, you *do*." He blew her a kiss, listening to the sound of her locks clicking into place and wondering how long it would be before his phone vibrated with a text.

CHAPTER TWO

CRYSTAL SPREAD THE designs she'd been working on out over the table at the boutique Thursday afternoon and stepped back, giving Gemma room to assess them. A few weeks ago Gemma had mentioned wanting to expand the boutique, and they'd discussed several options, including creating and selling their own costumes. Crystal had gone to college for business and fashion design, and she'd tinkered with designing her own clothes ever since. She had transformed her dining room into a quasi design studio when she'd first moved in and had been dabbling in making her own clothes ever since. Recently she'd begun playing around with a few new costume ideas. They purchased costumes in bulk from large suppliers, which allowed them to keep a nice variety in stock.

"Wow, you've been busy." Gemma tucked her brown and gold hair behind her ear, studying the designs.

Princess for a Day was Gemma's brainchild, and what Crystal loved most about it was that it had nothing to do with stereotyping girls as frilly little princesses and everything to do with enabling girls of any age to become whatever they wanted, at least for a few hours. They offered costumes for just about everything, from rockers and academic princesses to construction workers and goth princesses. Girls could dress up in leather or lace, tomboy outfits, and just about anything else they could dream up. As Crystal thought up new designs, she realized that with their own designs, the possibilities were endless.

Gemma and Crystal wore the costumes they offered, and Crystal loved when Gemma pushed her outfits beyond the proper confines of societal norms. Today Gemma wore a fancy Snow-White-meets-Lolita princess costume, complete with white thigh-high stockings, shiny black Mary Jane's, and a short dress similar enough to Snow White's for children to make the only connection they should. Even though they were best friends, Crystal's goth cheerleader outfit, complete with fishnet stockings and a black spike choker, underscored their differences. But while Gemma wore the outfits that rang true to who she was inside and out, Crystal's were only partially driven by who she was. They were mostly derived from the persona she needed to convey in order to feel safe.

"These are just sketches," Crystal finally responded. "But I think they'll add a unique flair to the princess realm. I took the warrior princess idea from *Game of Thrones*. You know that tall, sword-carrying blonde? She's my inspiration. I think lots of little girls dream of being that kick-ass. And the snow goddess is one of my favorites. We can make the boot covers out of white faux fur, and give the girls a choice of a long flowing dress accented with gold and sparkle appliqué to simulate snowflakes, or a knee-length outfit with tights. I *love* the nerd princess idea, and the banker princess, because, let's face it, some girls are number ninjas."

She fidgeted with the jagged edges of her skirt, anxious to hear Gemma's thoughts on her designs. In the silence, her mind drifted back to last night. She hadn't texted Bear when she'd arrived home, as he'd asked. She'd wanted to, but they'd been so close to kissing, she felt like they were on the cusp of taking their long history of excruciatingly hot flirting to the next level. And she wasn't ready for that. *Yet.*

For months his attention had had her insides whirling like a tornado, and working on these designs had thrown her right back to her college days, bringing an onslaught of both good and painful memories. The combination of both was overwhelming. Determined not to be defined by her dysfunctional family or where she'd come from, she had reinvented herself when she'd gone to college, and she'd done a hell of a job. She'd even gone by a different name. "Chrystina" had been everything "Chrissy" wasn't, and people had *liked* her. She was girly and proper and smart, of course, because her father had always drilled the importance of good grades into her head. And despite her mother's fall down the rabbit hole, she wasn't a stupid woman. But just over two years into her wonderful new life, one party, and one treacherously bad decision, had brought her world crashing down around her—and no-bullshit, hard-as-nails, don't-fuck-with-me "Crystal" was born. Creating a reputation for being into tough guys and having a penchant for one-night stands had made her emotionally untouchable, and that had kept her safe and sane.

"These are great," Gemma said, bringing Crystal's mind back to the moment. "But do you really think we can make them and still keep up with the business? Between the kids and the boutique, I have so little free time."

"I think so, if we start small. Maybe we make a few of *one* outfit so production is rote, and see how they sell. If they do well, we can recruit design students to work—"

"I can't afford a manufacturing staff," Gemma interrupted. "I guess we could see what it would cost to have them made overseas or something."

"I don't think we need to do that. Just hear me out." Crystal moved the papers over and sat on the table, getting more excited by the second. Never in her wildest dreams had she thought she'd find such a fabulous friend, much less have the opportunity to be part of something so exciting. "As I said, we can start by making a few costumes ourselves. I'll do it after hours."

"Says the girl who's going to get a big honking ticket because she doesn't have time to get her car inspected," Gemma reminded her.

"I know. I'll get to that this week." She knew that probably wasn't going to happen, given the limited hours of the inspection station, but hoping it was true kept her anxieties at bay.

"I have a sewing machine. I just need the production materials. If they sell well and there's enough demand, then we can recruit fashion design students and offer them a piece of the pie. I'd have given anything to have an opportunity like this when I was in school. They basically work for free for the first few months, until we get ahead of our costs. Then they get a commission off of each piece that sells. It's a win-win. They can use their experience on their résumés, like a commissioned internship."

"Or even better, maybe some of them stay on and we *can* build a staff." Gemma's green eyes glittered with enthusiasm. "I know how we can free up some of your time. I'll call the store where we ordered my wedding dress and set up a fitting instead of having you hem it and take it in." Gemma's dress wasn't a typical wedding gown. Two weeks ago she'd fallen in love with a knee-length white satin dress with a strapless crisscross bodice, a layer of chiffon over the skirt, and a jeweled sash. She looked gorgeous in it, but they'd had to order her size, and Jewel Braden, the manager of Chelsea's Boutique, where they'd found the dress, had warned her that that particular dress almost always needed to be fitted.

"Are you sure? Does Chelsea's even do fittings?"

"Yes, I'm sure. Jewel said they have a part-time seamstress. It's perfect. We can bring Dixie and look for your dresses at the same time. That is, if you don't mind going with me? That's a maid-of-honor thing, isn't it?"

Crystal laughed. "It's a *best friend* thing, and I'm totally on board with it. Let me know when they can do it." She'd never imagined being anyone's maid of honor, and when Gemma had asked her, she'd actually teared up. "There's so much you can do with the company if we make our own costumes. I know you weren't sold on taking the franchising plunge, and if this goes well, you can sell your designs to similar boutiques all over the country. No need to franchise. Then you'd just need to hire someone to manage the production."

"Wouldn't that be amazing? But while I think we can afford the material costs for a few costumes, if you're talking about making them in bulk, there are other associated costs."

"Right," Crystal agreed. "I've thought about that, too. Depending on how big you want to go at that point, we can either do some grassroots marketing or get a bank loan."

Gemma looked over the designs again. "Starting small is the way to go. If it takes off, we'll figure out the rest. You're really talented, Crys. You never told me why you stopped going to college."

"Sure I did." She slipped off the table and gathered the designs into a stack. "I ran out of money." She hated lying, but the last thing she wanted was pity, especially from Gemma. They'd met shortly after Crystal had returned to Peaceful Harbor, and she'd been barely holding her shit together. Gemma had been her saving grace. She'd offered friendship and a job Crystal adored, both of which she might not have given so readily had she known how broken Crystal had been back then.

Pushing those thoughts away, she went behind the register and put the designs in her bag to work on later that evening. "I'm going to start bringing out the costumes." She went into the back room, checked the costumes to make sure they had all their pieces, and tugged the tall metal clothing rack toward the front of the store.

Gemma looked up from where she was crouched beside the accessory bucket in the play area. "Are you going to tell me how last night went with Bear? Or should I pretend you didn't come over and leave without ever saying hello to me?"

Crystal laughed. "Jealous?" She set the rack by the dressing area and went back for another, passing Gemma on the way. "I forgot to tell you. The wedding cake tasting is set up for two weeks from Saturday. I requested several flavors because how often do you get to do a wedding cake tasting?"

Gemma was the closest thing to a sister she would ever have, and Crystal hoped she was doing enough to help her prepare for the wedding. She and Truman had wanted a simple backyard wedding. They'd ordered flowers from Petal Me Hard, a local florist, and Crystal had already arranged for the rental of tables and chairs. One of their customers had suggested they call Finlay Wilson, a caterer who had just moved back to Peaceful Harbor and hadn't yet reopened her business. Finlay was super sweet and so easy to work with. They'd instantly hit it off. She was also affordable *and* excited about catering the wedding.

"Sounds fun. I can't wait. But stop changing the subject and tell me what happened with Bear! I told you all about Tru when we started dating."

Crystal hiked a thumb over her shoulder. "I'm going to get the costumes. There's nothing to tell. We had burgers. He dipped his fry in my milk shake."

Gemma gasped. "He did? Was it amazing?"

"You are a filthy-minded princess," Crystal teased. "We went to Woody's. Can't chat any more or my boss will dock me for gossiping on company time."

"Sounds like a real bitch," Gemma called after her.

Crystal pushed through the doors to the back room, threw a few extra costumes on another rack, and headed back into the shop, dragging the rack behind her. The front door chimed, playing the boutique's special tune, and she was shocked to see Bear walking in.

His eyes locked on hers, and a wicked grin lifted his lips as he closed the distance between them like a lion on the prowl. He wore the same clothes he'd had on last night. His hair was tousled, his chiseled jaw covered in a thick layer of dark whiskers. Knowing he had spent a sleepless night to ensure a little boy felt safe brought a collision of overwhelming emotions.

He raked his eyes down the length of her body, awakening all the parts she was struggling to ignore as he placed a hand possessively on her hip and kissed her cheek.

Had last night's kiss on the cheek opened a door? He'd stolen two or three cheek kisses in the past, but this wasn't a stolen kiss. It felt like a kiss of ownership. Was this his new and improved greeting? She liked it a lot more than she probably should.

"Good afternoon, sugar," he said in a gravelly voice full of lust and fatigue. It slithered beneath her skin and settled in like steam from an iron.

Her heart melted a little every time he called her *sugar*, but hearing it in that voice made her wonder what it would sound like when their bodies were intertwined. She shifted her eyes away, pushing past the lustful thoughts that had been surprising her a lot more often lately. There had been a time when fear of being close to a man could swallow her whole. After years of therapy she'd finally gone out on a few dates, and surprisingly, she'd never felt *anything*. Not panic, not lust. *Nothing*. But when she played around with those thoughts about Bear, desire consumed her. She was sure that she was *too* attracted to him, and if they were close, she'd probably lose her mind.

"You didn't text last night. Next time send the text." His tone was somewhere between demand and concern. He brushed the back of his fingers gently down her cheek. "I worry about you."

She swallowed hard trying to regain control of her runaway hormones, but memories of last night drifted in. *I'm this way because it's you.* She wanted that *almost* kiss. He'd had her wanting more from nearly the very first time they'd met. She'd seen him snap into protective mode, and she'd seen him melt over Tru and Gemma's babies. He was as fierce and intimidating a protector as he was a gentle and kind friend, and she sensed that he'd love a woman with tenderness and devotion that she once thought only happened in storybooks.

It was those thoughts that had her fumbling to find her voice.

"Hi. What are you doing here? How'd it go last night?" An awful thought raced through her mind. What if he hadn't been at the boy's house all night? What if this was his morning-after-a-random-hookup look? A herd of elephants trampled through her stomach.

"It went well," he said, ignoring her first question in typical Bear fashion. "We escorted Scooter to school this morning, and he went right up to that bully and said, 'I'm not afraid of you anymore.' It was great to see him so confident."

She sighed with relief. He had been there all night after all. "I guess intimidation goes a long way." Catching her knee-jerk snarkiness, she added, "I mean that in a good way. Anyone would feel safe with burly bikers like you and your brothers on their side."

"Yeah?" He leaned closer. "Then how do *I* make *you* feel?"

Hot and bothered and scared of losing my self-control. "Like I need to get back to work."

"Hey, Bear," Gemma said as she walked by.

"Hi, Gemma. Sorry to take Crystal away last night, but her stomach was growling like she hadn't eaten in weeks. I was afraid for her life."

Crystal laughed.

"No worries." Gemma winked at her. "I'm still waiting on the details."

Bear put his arm around Crystal's waist. "You mean she hasn't told you we're a couple yet?"

"We are *not* a couple." She slipped from his grip and pushed the rack into place. "Nothing has changed."

"Don't be coy, sugar. Gemma's pulling for us."

He strutted behind the counter, and Crystal shot Gemma a what-the-hell look.

"What? He's sort of right," Gemma said.

Bear grabbed Crystal's car keys from the hook where she kept them.

"Hey. What do you think you're doing?" she asked as he came around the counter. "Give me my keys."

Bear shoved them in the front pocket of his jeans with a cocky grin.

She heard Gemma laugh.

"Hand them over." She thrust her hand out again, and he grabbed her wrist, pulling her against him as he'd done last night. He smelled earthy and manly, like Tarzan. Thoughts of playing in *Tarzan's jungle* rolled through her mind, setting off alarm bells, and she pushed away.

Confusion wrinkled his brow. He leaned closer and lowered his voice. "I'm taking care of that inspection you need, babe. No need to get all up in arms. I'll bring your keys back later."

"You're . . . *my inspection*? How did you know I needed one?" She looked at Gemma again, wondering if she'd told him, but Gemma shook her head.

"You mentioned it last night," he reminded her.

Holy cow. He remembered? "But you haven't slept, have you?"

"I caught an hour or two on the lawn. I'm good to go."

The bells chimed over the door, and a group of giggling girls walked in with their mothers in tow.

"Hi. Welcome to Princess for a Day," Crystal said to the group, then quickly returned her attention to Bear as Gemma went to greet the customers.

His eyes drifted down her cheerleader outfit again, making a purely male sound of appreciation loud enough for her ears only, and damn, her insides lit right up.

"Maybe you can cheer for me later." He blew her a kiss and headed for the door.

She watched him strut out of the boutique wondering how she was supposed to concentrate on a birthday party for seven little girls when her big-girl body was on fire.

BEAR PACED THE parking lot of Whiskey Automotive with the phone pressed to his ear, discussing last night's events with his father. Although his father no longer rode, he still ran the Dark Knights. Bear listened to his slow, slightly-hard-to-understand speech, a harsh reminder of the stroke he'd suffered shortly after Bear's high school graduation. The stroke had taken more than his father's once rapid and demanding verbal abilities. It had rendered his left side weak, his left hand clumsy, and had kept Bear from pursuing his dream of going to college to become a motorcycle designer. With Bullet out of the country on a military tour, Bones entrenched in medical school, Dixie a mere fifteen years old, and his mother, a nurse, caring for his father as he endured months of therapy, Bear had stepped in to run the bar. A few years later, his uncle Axel, who had run the auto shop and had taught Bear everything he knew about cars, passed away. He left the shop to Bear's family, and Bear had taken over running the shop, too.

"Sounds like it went well," his father said. "We need to meet to discuss the bar."

Both businesses were owned in equal partnerships between his father, Bear, and each of Bear's siblings. Since Bullet's return to civilian life, he'd taken over the day-to-day operations of the bar, while

Bear and Dixie handled the business management of both the bar and the shop. Dixie and their mother, who was now retired, worked part-time at the bar, and Bear took on bartending shifts as needed. They were all stretched for time, but their father refused to hire outside of the family. Bear was waiting for that decision to bite them in the ass.

"I think it's time to make some changes," his father said. "Can you come by the house tomorrow morning?"

Not if all goes well with Crystal tonight. "I'm not sure, Pop. Probably not, but I'll talk to Dixie and make sure she's there. She can fill me in."

His father was silent for a beat. A fucking annoying beat. Dixie was an equal partner in the businesses, but despite that, their father refused to give Dixie any say in them. Biggs had been raised by a hard-core biker with old-school beliefs that went back several generations. The men in their family bore the weight of all major responsibilities. It went hand in hand with the all-male motorcycle club mentality. Bear didn't have an issue with responsibility. He'd taken on more than his share over the years. But he took issue with excluding his sister, especially since she'd not only helped keep the businesses above water, but she'd made them even more profitable.

The struggle between family loyalty and the inequity of how their father treated Dixie left Bear harboring a nugget of resentment, like a festering wound that wouldn't heal.

"We'll do it another time," his father said, pushing Dixie to the side once again and leaving no room for negotiation.

Harley, Bear's favorite of the new litter of kittens that were born to Big Mama, the auto shop cat, rubbed against his leg. He bent down and picked her up, tucking her against his chest. She purred the loudest of the litter, and she stuck to Bear like glue. Her cuteness helped push away the familiar discomfort that accompanied business conversations with his father.

"Still trying to rope that little gal?" his father asked, as if he hadn't just rubbed Bear the wrong way.

Bear smiled at his choice of words. Trying to get together with Crystal often made him feel like he was trying to lasso a wild pony. It had bugged the hell out of him that she hadn't texted last night. He'd thought they'd broken new ground. But he wasn't about to give up. Eyes never lied, and Crystal's screamed, *I want you.*

"*Crystal*," he reminded his father. His parents had met Crystal in passing when she was hanging out at the bar with the rest of them, but his father was never big on names. "And yes, you could say that." He scratched the top of Harley's head. The little calico nuzzled against him.

"It's been a long time, son. Sure you're not barking up the wrong tree?"

At thirty-three, Bear had sown more than his share of wild oats, but he'd never met a woman who made him want more than a few hot nights. *Until Crystal.* She had a spark of rebellion that had captured his attention right off the bat, and a sweeter, more vulnerable side that she tried her best to hide. The combination had reeled him right in. He wanted to strip away all those layers and get to the heart of who she was. And after months of getting to know her, building a friendship that bordered on coupledom—without the physical side—he had a feeling they'd fall perfectly into sync.

"Definitely not," he said. "Listen, Pop, I've got to run. I've got her car, and I need to get it back to her before she gets off work." And he hoped to finally convince her to give in to the undeniable heat between them and give him a chance. He had to work at the bar tomorrow night, and he didn't want to wait another day. Not after they'd come so close to finally crossing the line from friends to something more.

They talked for another minute, and his father wished him luck with Crystal. He knew plenty of guys who couldn't stand their parents, and Bear considered himself lucky in that department, despite their differences. His father had always been hard on them, pushing them to be the best they could be. *When you think you're done with something, look it over again and see how you can make it better.* And his mother was as straightforward as a dart. There was a no-bullshit-accepted rule in the Whiskey household. But he knew without a shadow of a doubt that if he were in trouble, they'd always be there to back him up. Just like he was in his father's time of need. He'd never questioned their love or devotion to any of their children, including Dixie, despite his father's old-school ways with regard to business.

He went into the shop and headed for the playroom. When Truman had shown up with Kennedy and Lincoln the morning after he'd rescued them, he'd been afraid to leave them with anyone else. They'd renovated the shop to include a playroom with a fenced-in outdoor play area, and now he and Dixie helped care for them. Eventually they'd need to hire a babysitter, as it was getting more difficult and dangerous to get their work done with curious little ones underfoot, but Bear loved having them around.

Tru had taken Kennedy out on a father-daughter dinner date, and Dixie was watching Lincoln while Gemma went to the grocery store. Dixie looked up from where she sat on the floor with Lincoln in her lap.

The adorable tyke clutched a fistful of Dixie's flame-red locks and reached for Bear, yanking her hair. "Bababababa!"

"Ow. You little rascal." Dixie untangled his fingers from her hair and kissed his pudgy hand. "Now I understand why Bullet shaved his beard. This little man has a powerful grip."

Bear set Harley on the floor and reached for Lincoln. Spending time with Lincoln and Kennedy had fueled his love of babies. He'd always known he wanted a family, and watching Truman, Gemma, and the babies build their lives together had amped up that desire.

"He could be your son with that strawberry-blond hair."

"Babababa," Lincoln babbled as Bear kissed his cheek.

"Don't jinx me. I need a baby like I need a hole in the head." Dixie was the youngest of his siblings, and the mouthiest. At five nine, she was tall and thin, with colorful tattoos that rivaled her brothers'. She was the only one of them to take after their mother's side of the family. She shared her mother's red hair and green eyes, while Bear and his brothers took after Biggs, with dark hair and brown eyes. "You should really take Harley home with you. She wants to be yours."

"She can be mine here. I like having her at the shop with me. I'd miss her if she was at my house all day."

"You're such a softie," Dixie teased, petting the kitty. "Tru told me he dropped you at Crystal's work this morning and he was supposed to pick you up after you got her car inspected. But you still have her car . . . ?"

Of all his siblings, he'd always been closest to Dixie. Together they'd weathered their father's stroke, helped their mother cope, and brought both businesses to new heights. Dixie was as overprotective of him as he and his brothers were of her. "Our date got cut short last night. I'm hoping to make it up to her tonight."

"Did *she* know it was a date? Tru said you absconded with her."

He tickled Lincoln's belly and handed the giggling boy back to Dixie.

"You worry too much, and Tru knows me better than that. You've seen her with me, Dix. You know how she feels about me."

"You two *do* always look like you're going to rip each other's clothes off, but that doesn't mean you're a couple. You know I freaking love Crystal, but it's been months of this flirtatious game you're playing. I worry you're going to smother her and get your brawny heart broken."

"If I get lucky, I'll smother her all right." He made kissing sounds and went for the door, waving as he walked out.

He thought about what Dixie had said as he drove through town, but no matter how he turned it in his head, he couldn't shake the feeling that whatever this was between him and Crystal, it was worth the wait.

The door to the boutique was locked. The lights in the front of the store were off, but the back was lit up. He peered through the glass door and saw Crystal bent over a table. The skirt of her cheerleading outfit barely covered her ass, and her thigh-high stockings took his mind to dark places. He imagined a black lace thong riding high on her hips underneath that sexy little skirt, and taking it off with his teeth. His mouth watered at the thought.

Crystal stretched, arching her back and thrusting her magnificent breasts forward. Her red and black cropped cheerleading top lifted, exposing a few inches of taut flesh. His fingers itched to touch her. He longed to feel her hot naked flesh beneath him, to see her hair fanned out on his pillow while she cried out his name in the throes of passion. *Fuck.* He was hard as steel. He wasn't sure how much longer he could take this.

Who was he kidding? He hadn't gotten a hard-on for another woman in months.

As if she felt his presence, Crystal glanced up at the door, and his body thrummed. Jesus, what was he? A horny teenager?

No, jackass. A guy who has gone without for too fucking long and knows there's only one woman to satisfy him.

Crystal strutted up the center of the store with the confidence of a model on a catwalk. Her hips swayed, her shoulders squared, and that long black hair he wanted to wind around his fingers cascaded behind her, as if she were walking into the wind. Or maybe that was just his sex-starved mind working overtime, because he also imagined her completely naked, save for those sexy stockings and heels, beckoning him forward with a come-hither stare. *Come, baby, come.*

The sound of the locks turning snapped his brain into gear. He shook his head to clear his dirty thoughts as she pushed the door open.

"You okay?" She dragged her eyes down his body, lingering on the erection he had no chance of hiding. "*Hard* evening?"

He stepped into the boutique and turned the lock on the door. She had a badass reputation as a girl who was into tough guys. Bear wondered if he hadn't been aggressive enough with his playful banter. Tonight he'd step it up and give her what she seemed to find attractive in other guys. Or at least what she used to. He hadn't heard her talk about any other guys in months, and his gut told him it was because she was totally, one hundred percent into *him*. He just needed to get past whatever was holding her back.

"Baby, you have no idea what you do to me." He walked forward, backing her up until she hit the costumes hanging on a rack. "I'm not sure how I feel about you dressing like this in public."

"You have no say in how I dress."

He gathered her in his arms, and she squirmed.

"What are you *doing?*"

"More than eight months, baby." His hands moved down her back to the dip at the base of her spine. "That's a long damn time to be thinking about you the way I think about you."

"Then don't," she challenged.

He touched his lips to her cheek, feeling her heart hammering against his. "What are you waiting for, Crystal? You know I want you. I know you want me."

"What I know," she said in a firm voice, "is if you move your hands an inch lower, my knee is going to put a permanent end to your ability to have a *hard* anything."

"What's wrong, baby?" he asked softly. "What scares you so much that you have to toy with me?"

She clutched his chest, the color draining from her face. "Bear, please stop."

He stepped back, shocked by the conflicting emotions staring back at him, and fought the urge to pull her back into his arms and protect her. From *himself?*

"Crystal, you know I'd never *really* force myself on you. I was just playing around."

She rolled her eyes, scoffing as she walked away. "No shit."

"So, what's wrong? Shit, babe. The last thing I want to do is scare you."

"Your chick meter is off. I'm not scared. I'm just not in the mood for this. It's been a long day, and it's not nearly over."

"Christ." He let out a relieved breath. "You scared the piss out of me."

"Sure it was piss?" She glanced at his jeans and raised her brows. He'd gone soft at the fear he'd thought he'd seen in her eyes. "Looks like we took care of that mighty sword of yours."

"Not quite the way I had envisioned," he mumbled.

CHAPTER THREE

"REALLY, BEAR. I can drop you at your place before I go to the fabric shop." Crystal started the car, feeling more in control than she had inside the shop. She hated the way she'd frozen up when things had gotten hot between them. She wanted him. After putting herself through three years of therapy, dealing with not only the trauma of the attack, but the bullshit with her mother and the loss of her father, she was sure she could handle anything. She'd dated other guys since she'd left college without issue. Why did it have to be different with the only guy she *wanted* to be close to? It pissed her off that her past still owned a piece of her, and she needed to get over it before Bear got fed up and walked away for good.

"I have to go to the store anyway." He flashed one of his smiles. "We might as well go together."

"You need to go to the *fabric* store?" she said flatly, knowing he was bullshitting her. She realized her car smelled different, *cleaner*. The seats were shiny, the dashboard dust free. "Did you clean my car?"

"Detailed it," he said casually, as if he did this type of thing every day. For all she knew, he did. "Changed your oil, topped off your fluids. You really need to do those things every three thousand miles." He touched the doll hanging from her rearview mirror. "I dusted off this, too, even though I'm a little worried that it's a voodoo doll."

She wasn't about to tell him it was a worry doll that she loved more than life itself.

"Bear." She couldn't suppress her smile about the voodoo doll as she drove toward the store. "You really need to stop acting like you have to take care of me. I appreciate you handling the inspection, which I'm paying you for, by the way. But you don't have to do all these things for me. I already like who you are." *Even if I have a hard time showing it.*

"I know you do," he said, as cocky as ever.

Why is that such a turn-on?

"I didn't do it to get your attention. Shit, six three, two thirty." He flexed his biceps and winked. "You're sitting next to Peaceful Harbor gold, baby. I've *got* your attention."

She couldn't suppress a laugh. "That you do, and probably half the women in this town."

"Only half?"

He kept her laughing the whole way to the fabric store, and it was just what she needed. It really had been a long day. They'd hosted three parties, and one of the mothers was just about the most obnoxious woman on earth. She'd pushed her daughter toward pink frilly outfits for the first half hour, when all the little cutie had wanted was to dress up as a skateboard princess. Gemma realized Crystal was going to strangle the wench, and she'd calmly suggested the woman head down to Jazzy Joe's for coffee. The rest of Crystal's day hadn't been much better. Plus, she'd spent the morning overthinking everything about her relationship with Bear, which was probably why she'd freaked out when she'd really been dying to kiss him.

She parked in front of the fabric store. There were some things that just didn't fit in the world as Crystal knew it, and Bear Whiskey clad in a tight black T-shirt that said *Whiskey Bro's* across his massive chest, a pair of snug, low-slung black jeans, and leather boots strutting into Jennilyn's Fabric was on the top of the list.

She pulled her list from her bag as his eyes coasted over the store. What was he thinking, coming with her? That was dedication she could not ignore. The epitome of commitment.

That is Bear.

My Bear?

She toyed with that as he draped his arm over her shoulder. She wondered what had taken him so long. She'd expected him to do it the second she'd stepped from the car, but he was probably in shock that they were actually going to a fabric store. She smiled to herself as he leaned closer and rubbed his nose along her cheek.

"Can I help you?" she asked with a laugh.

"You smell like jelly beans, and I happen to have a thing for sugary goodness."

"You can't seriously have that good a sense of smell."

He pressed an unexpected, and deliciously warm, kiss to her cheek and reached into her purse, withdrawing a bag of jelly beans. "Hoarding? Or were we going to hide these later in your body and let me find them?" He moved his mouth beside her ear and whispered, "Blindfolded. With my hands tied behind my back."

He nudged her deeper into the store. *Holy crap.* She'd stopped walking. Was she breathing? And was that a *thing*? Blindfolded? Hands tied behind *his* back? Oh, the control that would give her. She'd be at no risk of being overpowered. But would she want that much control? She imagined herself lying naked on her bed, watching as his greedy mouth moved over her breasts, down her belly, and she felt herself go damp.

No, no, no.

Ice cream. Ice baths. Cow poop!

Her body continued vibrating from the inside out. *This is bad. Really, really bad.* Like a virus she couldn't shake. She needed an anti-Bear pill. *Stat!*

She focused on finding the items on her list and assessed the bolts of fabric against the wall. Bear held up a green jelly bean. When she reached for it, he pulled it away and shook his head, then held it up to her mouth. The man could make anything sexual. The look in his eyes when he placed that little green candy on her tongue was liquid fire, and it made her feel naughty and sexy.

Her expression must have given her away because a crooked smile dripping with wicked intent crept across his lips.

"Fabric." The word fell from her mouth like a rock. "I need fabric."

"Me too." He reached over her shoulder and fingered a bolt of red satin. "Something like this, maybe?"

Red satin sheets, his hands tied, eyes blindfolded, strategically placed green jelly beans. Her hands began to sweat. She wiggled out from beneath his arm.

"Burlap. Thick, ugly burlap." She walked away as quickly as she could, hoping the other side of the store had more oxygen.

Almost two hours, a long discussion about the costumes she was making, and several green jelly beans later, Crystal began unloading the cart at the cash register. She picked up several yards of red satin and black lace that were shoved between the bolts she'd chosen. He must have had them cut when she was busy talking with the saleswoman. *You sneaky thing. Sneaky sexy thing. Sneaky sexy thing in a fabric store.*

I'm in so much trouble.

"Ahem . . . ?" She held up the sinfully soft fabric.

Bear smirked. "What?"

"I am *not* buying these." She flipped her hair over her shoulder in a show of finality. "That material has no place in the costumes I'm making."

He took the fabric from her hands, and boy did it look good in his.

What is wrong with me? She'd turned into some sort of sex-starved vixen.

The jelly beans!

Wasn't that the joke in high school? Or was it green M&M's that were supposed to make a person horny? She looked at her burly biker boy's sinful smile and knew it had absolutely nothing to do with green *anything*.

"You're obviously making the wrong type of costumes." He ran the satin over his muscular, inked forearm.

She needed that fabric.

She snagged it from his hands and tossed it on the counter.

"That's my girl." His arm wound around her again.

She was pretty sure it had taken up residence there. "I'm not your girl."

She was so full of bullshit her blue eyes were probably brown. She might not be *his* in the sense he wished, but she was a fish on the line, and she was going nowhere without losing a piece of herself. Why was she fighting him so hard when she didn't really want to resist him? She'd kissed men since the attack, but she'd felt *nothing* for them. She felt so much for Bear she was freaking herself out about it. She needed to stop worrying and take that first step.

She toyed with the idea of taking a leap of faith and giving in to her feelings.

Bear put on a country music station on the way to her apartment, and when her favorite song came on, "Setting the World on Fire" by Kenny Chesney, Bear sang it word for word, chipping away her walls a little more. Every note brought a pulse of anticipation. She'd watched that video more times than she cared to admit. In fact, Bear resembled the hottie in the video—only Bear was hotter, bigger, and currently looking at her like she was the shake to his fry. *Steak* fry. The really big ones. She'd felt the heat he was packing, and that baby was *not* a puny McDonald's French fry.

She pulled into her apartment complex feeling happier, and more nervous, than she had in *years*. But it was a good type of nervous. They'd had so much fun, and he'd kept her body on edge all night. *Almost all year.*

He came around the car while she grabbed her purse, and he opened her door, helping her to her feet. He didn't step into her personal space as he had in the boutique, and she was even more drawn to him because of it. She didn't want to keep fighting the gravity between them, and there was no reason to. They were both single, they were good friends, and—

She was *done* overthinking. She stepped into the safety of his arms, drawn in deeper by his warm honey-colored eyes. His hands moved up her back, coming to rest on each shoulder, like the shoulder belts on roller coasters, binding them together.

"Sweetheart, you are incredibly beautiful."

Ohgod. I can't stop looking at your lips.

"You're funny and smart . . ."

His words floated into her ears, but she was mesmerized by his mouth, moving just out of reach. She'd watched it for so many months, dreamed about it night after night. His tongue swept across his lower lip, leaving it slick and enticing. She wanted to taste that tongue, to feel it move over hers. She hadn't even kissed a man in so long, she wasn't sure she remembered how. But right here, beneath the starless sky, within the arms of the man who had relentlessly pursued her, she didn't care if she did it wrong. She just needed to do it. She needed to kiss *him*.

"Please tell me, sugar. When are you going to let me kiss—"

She fisted her hands in his shirt and went up on her toes, pulling him down, and smothered his words with the hard press of her lips. The pit of her stomach whirred a flurry of heat and excitement. His hands moved over her back, pressing their bodies even closer together. His kiss was surprisingly gentle, exploratory, *delicious*. They kissed for a long time, there beside her car, in the middle of the parking lot. When they finally came up for air, Bear kept her close, which was a good thing, because she was pretty sure her legs had turned to noodles, and if he let her go, she'd slither to the pavement. He brushed his whiskers along her jaw, sending shivers down her spine.

"Jesus," was all he said.

Her hands were shaking as she reached up and touched his face. She'd been dreaming about it for so long, she thought she knew what his skin felt like, but she'd been way off. Despite how rugged and chiseled his features were, his cheeks were soft and smooth above his whiskers.

He covered her hand with his, keeping it there, and touched her lips again in a whisper of a kiss. And another. And another. Until he reclaimed her mouth, more demanding this time, delving deeper, taking her rougher, and somehow, still tenderly. He kissed like the waves rolled in, smooth and even, then powerful and pervasive, only to ease up again. Just when she met his rhythm, he intensified his efforts. Every wave was stronger than the one before, and when she was so high on him she thought she might pass out, he breathed air into her lungs, taking her to another level of intimacy she never imagined possible. All in a single incredible kiss.

My Lord.

If he could turn her inside out with his kisses, what would he do when he touched her, when he made love to her?

How would she survive Bear Whiskey?

Panic began as a swirl in the pit of her stomach, and she fought against it, refusing to let it take hold. It had been years, not days, not months. *Years* since that awful attack. She'd done all the right things. She'd reinvented herself, gone to therapy every fucking week.

She'd kept her secret from ruining her life—or at least she thought she had. But as Bear's hands moved lower, cupping her ass, and he ground his hips against her, making her dizzier, *drunk* on him, she felt herself slipping.

Losing her footing.

I'm not afraid.

I want to be with you.

Anxiety clawed up her limbs, making her rigid despite her desires. Her breaths came in fast, hard spurts.

"Crystal?"

Bear's voice sounded far away.

I'm okay. I'm okay. I want you so fucking badly.

"Crystal, look at me. What's wrong?"

The concern in his eyes nearly knocked her off-balance again. "Nothing," she finally managed. "I . . ." *Need to get a grip.* "I'm just tired, and that kiss. Damn, Bear. *That kiss . . .*"

He splayed his hands over her back, searching her eyes. "More than two hundred and fifty days of foreplay has its benefits." He nuzzled against her cheek again. "You sure you're okay? You don't look okay."

"I'm fine," she said, trying to ignore the heart palpitations determined to do her in. What the fuck was going on? She'd spent months keeping him at arm's length, and she didn't want to do that anymore. "It was the kiss." Damn, she didn't mean to say that out loud.

"Crystal," he said with a compassionate lilt. "You can talk to me."

She stepped from his arms, needing space to lower her invisible armor into place. She absolutely was *not* afraid to be intimate with Bear, and this panic was totally messing with her head. She grabbed the back door and flung it open, snatching the bags from the seat to give her hands something to do before they curled into fists she couldn't unfurl.

"I'm *fine*, okay?" She didn't mean to snap, but if he pushed, she'd disappear into her head, and she didn't want that. She didn't want *this!* This negativity between them, the fucking worry in his eyes. She wanted to kiss the man she'd longed to be closer to and not have her heart race, not have her mind rush back to the fucker who had taken her against her will. And not have *Chrystina* peek her weak fucking head into kick-ass *Crystal's* life.

She wanted *normal*.

He reached for the packages. "Let me help you with those."

"No," she said too quickly.

"No?" Confusion riddled his brow, and just as quickly it morphed to frustration. "What's going on, Crystal? You're hot one minute, cold the next. What's your deal?"

She rolled her eyes, a mannerism she'd mastered knowing it drove people nuts—the perfect way to keep people away. In full-on Crystal mode, she straightened her spine and met those honey-colored eyes, which melted her resolve and strengthened it at once. Self-preservation was to Crystal what breathing was to others. As she prepared to give him a snappy retort and storm off, she realized he didn't have his truck or his motorcycle. Damn it. She had to drive him home. What was the universe doing to her? She dropped her shoulders and tossed her bags back into the car.

"Get in. I'll take you home, and you can hit the bar and pick up someone to help you with those blue balls I'm sure you're packing." She bit back the bile rising in her throat. She hated saying something so vile and mean, but it was the only way. She needed to be alone to clear her head, and there was no stopping this runaway train except to completely derail.

Bear grabbed her arm and spun her around. "What the fuck are you talking about?"

She wrenched her arm free. "Just get in. I'll take you home."

Maybe some girls in her situation would tell him he could do better, or that they couldn't be what he needed, but she didn't believe that. Not for a single second. She was not going to let some asshole from her past ruin her chance at happiness. She was good and smart and strong. *So fucking strong.* She was more than good enough for whomever she wanted to be good enough for. Self-worth was *not* the issue here, and she knew that as wholly and confidently as she knew she had to get away from Bear to deal with the war raging inside her head. She just needed to figure out how to get past the anxiety brought on by being close to the first and only man she'd ever wanted.

He rubbed the back of his neck. "Crystal, what the—"

"Do you want a ride?" *Because you better get in now before I lose my head over the thought of you and another woman.*

"No." His voice was dead calm, his gaze locked on her.

"No? Bear, you're *not* coming upstairs." She sounded cold and distant. She fucking hated cold and distant, but she needed it. It was the only way.

His eyes narrowed. "You've driven that point home—it's as clear as those pretty cock-teasing eyes of yours." He rolled his broad shoulders back, his tatted-up biceps flexing as he pulled his phone from his pocket.

She watched him stalk away, his black boots eating up the pavement as he brought the phone to his ear, heading for the street.

CHAPTER FOUR

BEAR WIPED THE sweat from his brow, listening to the familiar sounds of the auto shop. After an entire week of frustrating days and restless nights spent debating showing up on Crystal's doorstep and insisting they talk their shit out, he'd finally had it. He'd woken up at the crack of dawn on Friday and decided this was it. He was *done* giving her space. Seven days was enough time for her to admit what she wanted. He didn't know what had happened the other night, but there was no way the kiss they'd shared was the kiss of a woman who didn't want him. She wanted *him*, and it was time for her to own up to it.

Decision made, and unable to go back to sleep, he'd gone down to his garage at five thirty, hoping to distract himself for a few hours. He'd spent the morning working on the motorcycle he was building.

Motorcycles were his first love. According to his parents, from the time he learned to walk and talk he'd been drawn to them. While his father had been happy to share the biker culture with his children, it was his father's brother, Axel, who had taken Bear under his wing and taught him everything he knew about mechanics, and more specifically, about motorcycles. From a young age, Bear had worked under his uncle's tutelage in the auto shop. By the time he was sixteen there wasn't anything he couldn't repair or build. At eighteen he was designing motorcycles.

He'd attended a technical high school, where he studied collision repair and automotive technology, and he'd done well enough to receive a scholarship to go to college for engineering and industrial design. But that had fallen by the wayside when his father had suffered his stroke. He'd thought his dreams would never come to fruition, but a few years later, Bear met Jace Stone at a rally. Jace was the co-owner of Silver-Stone Cycles, which were among the most sought-after custom motorcycles. At the time they'd just opened a new location in Pennsylvania, but Jace had been impressed with Bear's designs and said he'd be in touch when they were ready to expand again. It had given Bear a shred of hope that even without the degree, he might still have a chance at turning his passion into reality. But when they'd come back to him last month to discuss their expansion into Peaceful Harbor, they'd wanted him to commit to a full-time position. As much as he wanted to take his designing to the next level, he hadn't been ready to walk away from the family business completely. Two weeks ago they'd offered him a part-time position. It was exactly what he'd hoped for. The offer was on the table. They were just waiting for him to commit to a schedule before hammering out the final details.

He was waiting, too. And every day he vacillated on his decision. Working for them meant cutting back on his hours at the shop and the bar. He'd had his fill of the bar, but the shop was a whole different ball game.

He cleared his throat to wrench the frustrating thoughts from his head and did a quick visual inventory of the engine parts spread out on the floor and workbenches. After working in his garage at home for an hour and a half, he'd gone into Whiskey Automotive and had spent the day rebuilding an engine. It should have been the perfect remedy for a hard fucking night, but even after hours of work, as he'd removed the crankshaft, core plugs, brackets, pins, and went through the steps of checking valve heads, stems, and replacing worn keepers, his mind continually circled back to Crystal. He'd known her long enough to understand that no matter how frustrating it was for him, she needed space to work out her own shit. But it killed him that he had no idea *what* that shit was.

Harley brushed against his leg and meowed. He lifted her up and kissed her head, gazing into her innocent eyes. "Think you can have a talk with Crystal for me? Tell her what she's missing out on." Harley meowed again, and he tucked her against his chest as he pulled out his phone for the hundredth time since he'd walked away last week. He uttered a curse at the sight of the blank screen.

Tru sidled up to him. "Still no word?"

Truman had come a long way from the lost sixteen-year-old kid trying to keep his head above water Bear had met a lifetime ago. Like the good friend he was, Tru hadn't asked any questions when he'd picked Bear up and given him a ride home from Crystal's apartment complex. Other than a few supportive looks, Tru had kept his thoughts on Bear and Crystal's quasi relationship to himself. But he didn't have to say a word. Tru wore his emotions on his sleeves, as clear and present as the blue ink snaking up his arms. Bear knew Tru was just as baffled by this turn of events as he was. He and Crystal might not have so much as kissed before last week, but the magnetic pull between them could be felt around the world.

"Nope." He shoved the phone in his pocket and tipped his eyes up to the clouds rolling in. Frigging perfect. He'd hoped to go on a long bike ride after work to clear his head. He headed toward the back of the shop to wash his hands. It was after seven, and Gemma had picked up the kids an hour ago. He was dying to ask Tru if Gemma had said anything about Crystal. Girls talked, didn't they? Or did Crystal shut everyone out the way she'd shut him out?

He sure as hell hoped not, because that would suck for her. He had his family and Tru. He had the whole club if he needed them. One phone call and he'd have more support than he could ever want, and he took comfort in knowing that the same way he knew the other members did. But who did Crystal have? She'd mentioned a rough visit with her mother, and while he knew she and Jed were in contact, he didn't get the impression they were particularly close. She had Dixie and Gemma, but for obvious reasons she didn't seem to be reaching out to Dixie. The truth was, she had Bullet, Bones, and Tru, too, but he knew she'd never turn to them. Especially after how they'd left things last week.

He handed Harley to Tru and washed his hands.

"You're sure you didn't do something or say something to cause her to get riled up?" Tru handed him a paper towel. "I love Gemma to the ends of the earth, but, dude, women are wired totally different than we are. The wrong voice inflection can change the meaning of a sentence, and if you're like me, you could be clueless."

"No shit." He took Harley from him and scratched the kitty's head. "I grew up with Dixie, remember? I've been over it a million times." Was it possible that despite the hottest kiss he'd ever experienced, she wasn't into him the way he was into her? He couldn't believe it. He'd seen the heat in her eyes for months. "Tru, do you think she's done with whatever this is between us?"

"From the little bits and pieces Gemma has said, it seems like Crystal's been a mess all week."

He took far more pleasure in that than he should. "That's on her." As the words left his lips, he knew he didn't mean them. He wanted to know what was going on inside that beautiful head of hers.

"You're not thinking about giving up, are you?"

Bear, like Truman, was no stranger to physical, or emotional, pain. Bullet was impenetrable, Bones was practical, and Bear? Well, he felt pain for the people he loved as if it were his own. He'd endured emotional battles alongside Tru and his brother, Quincy, when Tru was sentenced to prison, taking the fall for a crime Quincy had committed. And again when Quincy got lost in drugs and disappeared. He remembered each instance with the ache of a fresh wound and had been pummeled anew when he'd learned of the conditions in which Kennedy and Lincoln had been living. This felt like that, only different. His gut was on fire, and for the second time in his life—the first being when his father had been in the hospital, his life hanging by a thread—his heart hurt like a motherfucker.

"When have you ever known me to give up on anything?" he finally answered. He'd sent Crystal a text this morning—*Bear*—hoping her radio silence didn't mean what he thought it did. She hadn't responded.

Tru cocked a smile. "There was that time when I was kicking your ass in darts."

"Shit." Bear laughed as he set Harley in the cat bed with two of the other kittens and they locked up the shop.

"I knew you were in deep when you told me you went to a fabric store." His eyes danced with mischief. "Dude, she probably lost all respect for you."

Bear wrenched his arm like he was going for a punch, and Tru fell right into the fake fight game they'd played too many times to count. Laughing, Bear patted his buddy's shoulder and walked him to his truck.

"Kiss those babies for me, will you? I didn't get much time with them today. And thanks again."

"For what?" Tru asked. "Giving you shit?"

Bear pulled his keys from his pocket and straddled his bike. "For hooking up with Gemma and introducing me to Crystal."

"You can't blame this shit on me." Tru shook his head as he climbed into his truck.

"Sure I can." He started the bike and pulled on his helmet, waving as Tru drove away. His phone vibrated in his pocket and he pulled it out. Crystal's name flashed on the screen and his pulse raced as he read the text.

I'm sorry about last week. I've got a lot of shit going on right now. Maybe we can talk this weekend?

"Fuck that." He sent off a response. *Where are you? I'll come over now.*

His phone vibrated seconds later. *I can't. I'm at Harbor View in a meeting.*

Can't wasn't in Bear's vocabulary. He shoved his phone into his pocket and took off.

He was good at biding his time. He'd been doing it for months. But standing outside Harbor View Professional Park waiting for Crystal made him antsier than a turkey on Thanksgiving. He paced the parking lot, wondering what type of a meeting she had in the medical office complex. As he mentally siphoned through possibilities, the front doors opened and Crystal stepped outside. His heart went wild as he headed in her direction, watching as she felt her pockets. For her keys? Her phone? The doors opened again and a tall man in dress pants and a stark white button-down ran after her, holding up her bag. Bear gritted his teeth as she took it—and embraced the guy.

"I WAS JUST looking for my keys. Thanks, David." Crystal hugged the man who had stuck with her for years, helping her get through the most traumatic events of her life.

"I'm here if you need me," he assured her.

His eyes sailed over her shoulder just as Bear's deep voice penetrated the air. "Crystal."

She turned, happiness bubbling up inside her. It took all her willpower to remain where she stood and not run to him. He looked rough and rugged in a pair of grease-stained jeans and a tight T-shirt, like he'd come straight from work. His eyes, which had haunted her dreams, were soft and hard at once. He was *beautifully intimidating*, eating up the pavement between them, his face a mask of strength and determination as he staked his claim with a kiss on her cheek.

"Hey, sugar." He lifted his chin toward David in a show of pure alpha dominance. "How's it going?" he said gruffly.

Lord help her. She felt herself smiling like a fool. She'd thought she'd lost him, and she'd longed for the assumptive, handsy man all frigging week.

"Fairly well, thanks." David glanced at Crystal.

She nodded. *Yup. This is the guy who has me tied in knots.* Between the possessive look in Bear's eyes and the newfound freedom stirring inside her, she fumbled for words. "I . . . um . . . Bear . . ."

David extended his hand. "David Lantrell. I'm an old friend of Crystal's."

Bear shook his hand. "Nice to meet you."

She went for levity to break the tension. "Now that we're past that awkward stage, thanks again for seeing me on such short notice, David. I'll be in touch."

David made a quick exit, which she was thankful for.

"Before you ask," she said to Bear, "I'm ready to tell you what's going on, but not here. Do you mind if we go someplace else to talk?"

"Thank fucking God, because there's only so much shit a guy can take before he loses his mind." He motioned toward his bike. "Climb on."

"I'm not getting on that thing."

"Why not?"

"You just want me wrapped around you." Old habits died hard. She'd done such a good job of selling herself as a hard-core biker chick, she knew he thought she had experience riding on a motorcycle.

His lips quirked up. "And that's bad because . . . ?"

He had a point. Wasn't that the reason she'd gone to see David? She glanced at the bike. *I guess this is as good a place to start as any.*

Inhaling a lungful of courage, she said, "You'll have to show me how to ride."

Goose bumps chased anxiety around her chest like a mouse in a maze, but she'd expected that. David had warned her. Nothing about tonight was going to be easy. But she wouldn't know what to do with *easy* anyway.

A deep V formed between Bear's brows. "Come again?"

"You have to teach me to ride. Now shut up and do it, or I'll change my mind."

He ran his eyes over the Harley-Davidson logo on her shirt, down the length of her black skinny jeans, to her chunky black leather biker boots.

I know. I have a lot of explaining to do. "Forget it. I can drive." She took a step toward her car.

He took her hand in his, walking toward the bike. "Are the eight piercings in your ear fake, too?"

"Maybe if you're not an ass I'll let you find out."

He placed his hands on her hips, tipping his face down with a serious expression. "Are you nervous?"

She opened her mouth to give him her usual snappy retort, and stopped herself. "There's nothing between me and the road. There are no airbags. It's freaking scary as shit."

"We don't have to do this. We can take your car, or you can take your car and I'll take my bike. I can teach you to ride some other time. No pressure from me. I'm just glad you're willing to talk, so it's your call."

She was done pretending, at least to herself. The truth was, she'd been dying to ride on the back of Bear's bike for months. She'd always had her car or he'd had his truck when they'd run errands or grabbed a bite to eat together. But it was like an extension of him, and she wanted to experience it. She might be putting herself into emotional overload, but what better way to rip off a bandage than to do it all at once?

"I want to ride with you on the bike."

His lips curved up as if he were pleased with her decision, but his eyes remained serious. "You're sure?"

She nodded before she could chicken out.

"Okay. After we get your helmet on, you're going to want to press your body as close to mine as possible. Arms around my waist, like this." He turned around, bringing his back flush with her chest, and took her hands, guiding them around his waist and placing her palms on his stomach. "Hold on as tight as you possibly can." Clutching both her hands in one of his, he reached his other hand behind her and pressed on her ass, bringing them even closer. "Got it?"

Got it? All those muscles pressed up against her? She got it all right. The problem was, she didn't want to let go.

"Yeah. I've got it."

He chuckled and helped her on with her helmet and then onto the bike.

"Okay?" he asked, visually assessing her.

"I'm surprised at how monstrous it is."

His eyes turned volcanic.

"Ohmygod. The *bike!*"

"If I have my way, this won't be the last time you feel something monstrous between your thighs."

He didn't pause long enough for her to think past the memory of how huge he'd felt when they'd kissed last week, and on its heels, the reason she'd come to see David.

Tone serious again, he said, "If you need me to stop, I want you to pat my stomach once. If you want me to slow down, then do it twice, okay?"

She nodded, getting more nervous by the second.

"You're safe with me, baby. I'll never put you in jeopardy."

She knew this, and more importantly, she believed it.

"We can take your car if you're not ready."

His expression was so serious, his concern so sincere, it took the edge off. "No. I'm good. Can you take me to the park on Eternity Lane?"

"At the other end of town? There's a park around the corner. Want to go there?"

"If you don't mind driving, I'd rather go to Eternity."

"Buzz Lightyear, at your service."

She laughed. How could a badass be so frigging cute? "I think he said 'to *infinity* and beyond,' not 'eternity.'"

"Seriously? Boy, I screwed that up." He climbed onto the bike, and before he put on his helmet, he said, "Try not to get too turned on."

He wrapped her arms around him and reached behind them, pressing his hand to her ass and hauling her so close she felt like they were glued together. The bike roared to life, rumbling between her legs like a supersonic vibrator. Not that she'd ever used one, but there's no way it'd have anything on this monster.

The bike rolled forward and she smacked his stomach. It must have been a reflex or something, because she didn't need him to stop, but he did. Immediately.

"What's wrong?"

"Nothing," she said. "Go ahead."

He waited until she was plastered against him again, her heart dancing a jig against his back. He drove across the parking lot and she slapped his stomach again.

He stopped and glanced over his shoulder without an ounce of irritation. "What's the matter?"

"Nothing. It's weird not being in control."

He torqued his body, holding her arm. "Sweetheart, you are in complete control. You say go, I go. You say stop, I stop. I'm your driver. That's all. But we can take your car—"

She shook her head vehemently. "No. I think I needed to *know* you'd stop."

That earned her a sexy smile. "Babe, there's nothing I won't do for you."

Swallowing hard, she motioned for him to turn around and snuggled up to him again.

Peaceful Harbor wasn't very big, and *across town* really meant driving only a few miles. Bear drove slowly, leaving plenty of room between them and the other cars, and checking on her at every stoplight. She was surprised at how freeing it felt to be on the bike, and how safe she felt with Bear. David had shed new light on the depth of her feelings, allowing her to acknowledge and feel them even stronger.

They drove down the winding side streets of her old stomping grounds toward Eternity Lane, passing houses she hadn't seen in years. When he drove up the steep road that led to the park, her nerves flared to life again.

He parked in the lot and cut the engine, but her body continued vibrating. He took off his helmet and stepped from the bike. His long legs made it look natural and easy, but as she slung her leg over the motorcycle, she pictured herself looking like a spider trying to dismount from a horse.

Bear wrapped his hands around her ribs, lifting her from the seat and planting her feet beside his. He took off her helmet and set it on the bike. "What did you think of your maiden voyage?"

"It was a little scary at first, but then it was exhilarating. I needed it tonight. Thank you." She looked up at the cloudy sky, glad it hadn't rained.

He draped an arm over her shoulder, as if last week's tiff had never occurred. It dawned on her that in all the time she'd known him, he'd put an arm over her shoulder or around her waist, keeping her as close as possible, rather than holding her hand like most couples did. Then again, they weren't a couple, and Bear was definitely not a typical guy. Most guys would have either pushed harder for more a long time ago, or given up and walked away.

"What did you have in mind when you asked me to come here? A little no-pants dance in the grass?"

She laughed, and he pulled her against him, gazing into her eyes. She expected to see heat, to have to fend him off so they could talk, but she couldn't have been more wrong.

BEAR TRIED TO keep things light and not let on about the worry mounting inside him. But he couldn't stop thinking about her short-notice visit in the medical building, and he was curious about her *friend* David. How many times had his brother Bones, an oncologist, told him that a person's health could change on a dime? Their father's stroke had given him proof enough. Now, as he gazed into Crystal's eyes, the spark of snark that usually glimmered back at him was dulled by worry, and that concerned him.

He touched his forehead to hers and his facade fell away. "I don't want to joke around. Let me in, baby. Let me help with whatever's stolen that spark from your beautiful eyes."

"Bear," she whispered.

In his name he heard a plea and a warning. He wanted to hand over the reins, let her lead, but he sensed that she was having trouble with that. "Tell me what you need," was the best he had to offer.

She moved from within his arms and took his hand. He didn't think that was a good sign, and he didn't like not having her where he could feel her emotions as clearly as he could see them, but he went with her to the crest of the hill, where they sat in the grass overlooking the street below.

They sat in silence for a long moment, and the uncertainty was eating him alive.

"This is what I know about you." Her soft voice broke through the silence. "You grew up in Peaceful Harbor with your brothers and sister and your parents, all of whom help run the bar. You and Dixie run the auto shop. You're a member of a motorcycle club, and I think you're the most loyal person I've ever met in my life, although Truman is right up there with you. You love Tru and Quincy as if they're your brothers, and when the babies and Gemma came into their lives, you loved them, too. And then there I was, practically joined at the hip with Gemma. And for some reason you opened your heart, and your family, to me, too. I feel like that's a *lot* to know about a person, even though there are a million things I don't know."

"I'll tell you whatever else you'd like to know."

"I know you would. We might have to go back and forth a hundred times before you got out of joking mode, but I know we'd eventually get there. The thing is," she said a little more confidently, "I realized that what *I* know about you doesn't matter as much as what *you* know about yourself. You obviously know that I'm attracted to you, but mostly, I'm attracted to what's *inside* you, that at your core, *you* know *who* you are. That confidence shines brighter than the moon and the stars and the sun put together."

She lifted her eyes to his, and for the first time in his life, he didn't have a snappy comeback. In fact, he didn't have any words at all.

"I know I sound crazy," she said.

"No. You sound saner than anyone I know. I'm just processing what you've said. It's a strange feeling to know you're attracted to the very thing that seems to make you push me away."

She nodded, a small smile lifting her lips, and she dropped her gaze to the house across the street. "Yeah, it's weird for me, too. But please hear me out, and hopefully you'll understand why. Everyone has a story. There's someplace where their life began and things that led them to where they end up. For most people, it's pretty clear-cut. And for people like you, who have lived in one small town, with a family who adores them, and parents who teach them how to handle life and love and all the things that make a person whole, your story is fairly easy to follow."

She paused, a haunted look hovering in her eyes.

He couldn't stand being separated by even the few inches between them. Everyone needed someone who would cross the lines they put up when they were too afraid to open a door. He'd never heard her so solemn and serious. He wanted to be there for her, to help her let go and to share the burden of whatever was weighing on her. He knew all about carrying the weight of the world on his shoulders, and it was a lonely place to be.

Scooting closer, he pulled her tight against his side. She went stiff for a second or two, and then the tension drained from her shoulders. This was better. This was readable, real. This was *safe*.

Her eyes drifted over the skyline, to the houses across the street, settling on the split-level at the bottom of the hill.

"Some people know where their stories begin," she said softly. "But like Truman, Quincy, Kennedy, and Lincoln, some stories have gaps and jogs and are pieced together with paste and tape. Those people choose a new starting point, and that's where their *new* lives, or their new story, begins."

Bear knew that everyone had their secrets, their private bouts with hell, and he could tell by her quickening breaths that she was about to reveal hers. He held her closer, feeling proprietary and grateful that she trusted him enough to share whatever it was with him.

"And my story is no different," she said just above a whisper. "This is where my story began, and after jogs and gaps and stitches that never held, this is where I chose to start over. David helped me. He's a therapist, and I've known him since I moved here. I saw him on a weekly basis for about three years, and then I stopped because I thought I'd moved past all the bad things that had happened."

She spoke fast, as if she feared if she didn't get the words out they might fester and rot inside her. He turned toward her, wanting to protect her, to hold her within the circle of his arms and catch the pieces of her spilling out between them. He shifted so her body was between his legs, his knees drawn up like barriers from the outside world.

"But then you came into my life," she said swift and soft. "Like a dragon-slaying prince on a mission, scooping up everyone's broken pieces and putting them back together again. You make me want things I long ago stopped hoping for, or even thinking about, and—"

She lifted her eyes, heaven and hell colliding within them. He tried to process what she'd said, but there were too many missing parts. *Jogs and gaps and stitches that never held.* He couldn't make sense of it. Though he desperately wanted to.

"I'm no prince, baby, but I want to understand. What happened in those jogs and gaps that led you to David?" *The guy that it sounds like I owe a whole heap of gratitude to.*

"We lived there"—she pointed to the house at the bottom of the hill—"in that house until I was eight, when my father lost his job. He was an insurance agent, and he traveled a lot, but when he was home, he tried, you know? He would do projects with me around the house, and sometimes, not often because he was gone so much, we'd go to flea markets together. He'd buy yarn and fabric that he used to make these dolls out of twigs and strings and yarn, and he'd leave them on my dresser before he left for a trip. I'd find them in the morning without a note or anything. Sometimes he'd make paella and hot grog, and we'd sit around the fire pit in our backyard, all four of us. We were a real family once." Her voice drifted off, and a look of longing came over her. "Those were good times, and those silly little dolls meant so much to me."

"They should, and I think they still do. The dolls in your car and on your key chain?"

"Yes, they do." The haunted look returned. "They probably always will. When we moved from the harbor to the mobile home where my mom lives, it was pretty awful. But that was okay, because I had school to focus on and those dolls to look forward to, which made it easier to ignore the awful neighbors. And then one day my dad didn't come home. He was killed by a drunk driver. That's where my story stumbled and eventually broke."

"*Christ.* I had no idea. I'm sorry, baby." He thought of the uncle he'd followed around from the time he was allowed inside the auto shop. Bear had been twenty-two when they'd lost him to cancer. That was the year he'd taken over managing the auto shop and the year he'd learned how differently people grieved. His father had gone through all the stages of grief in varying degrees of silence and anger, while Bear had needed to talk about his loss. Thankfully, his family knew he was a talker, and the rest of them had suffered through his long, emotional trips down memory lane. He wondered how Crystal had dealt with her father's death and who had been there to help her through.

She was watching him with a vacant look in her eyes, as if she were seeing memories unfold before her. "My mother and father used to drink occasionally, and for the life of me, I don't remember them being heavy drinkers. But losing him changed everything. My mother became hateful, drinking herself into a stupor night after night. I thought it was just her way of coping and that it would pass, but it didn't. And Jed started coming and going at odd hours, checking on me in passing. I think that's when he started stealing. So I focused on school, determined, even at frigging nine years old, not to lose myself in my mother's downward spiral. To control the one aspect of my life I *could* control. I spent hours in the library, like it was my second home. I have to admit, it was better than being home, so I sort of hid out there."

His heart ached for her. It sounded as though she'd never been given a chance to grieve.

He framed Crystal's face in his hands, wishing for the impossible. "I'm sorry, baby. I wish I could have been there for you."

"There were no dragon-slaying knights in my life. I took my senior English class over the summer and graduated high school a year early. My counselor helped me get a Pell Grant, and I went away to school. Not far, just to Lakeshore State, but it was far enough that no one knew me. And I reinvented myself." Lakeshore State was a small college about two hours from Peaceful Harbor.

Her strength and courage blew him away. "Crystal, you didn't need a knight. You kicked ass all on your own."

"I thought I did, but . . ." She looked away, but not before he saw tears fill her eyes.

His gut plummeted. "Missing your dad?"

"No," she said, swiping at her tears. "Yes. Always. But that's not it."

He moved her legs beneath his and pulled her closer, brushing away the tears sliding down her cheeks. "What is it, baby?"

"Part of reinventing myself was learning to fit in. I didn't want to be defined by my past. I wanted people to see me as just another girl who went to college because it was what most kids did after high school. The first couple years of school were great. I kept my head down, studied my ass off, and maintained top grades. I've always been good in school, and I made friends easily back then. I even had a few boyfriends, but I wasn't a partier. Truthfully, I was also trying to do well in school for my dad. He was always proud of my grades."

"He loved you." Thank God, because it sounded like his love had pulled her through an awful situation.

"He did." That earned a genuine smile. "But in my third year I lifted my eyes from the books and looked around." The edges of her mouth turned down, taking the pit of his stomach with them. "There was this whole world going on around me with parties and road trips and things I hadn't allowed myself to enjoy. I was afraid to drink because of my mom and because of what had happened to my dad."

"Which explains why you never have more than a drink or two when we get together with Tru and Gemma by the bonfire or hang out at the bar."

"Yeah. I'm careful. Anyway, one night a friend convinced me to go to this party. There was no alcohol there because it was in the art building to honor some kids who had qualified for a national award or something. But you know, it was college, so kids had alcohol in their soda cans and water bottles, and kids came from other parties where there *was* alcohol."

She looked away again, and the air grew thick around her. Bear touched her face, bringing her troubled eyes back to his.

"Sweetheart, take a deep breath with me." He breathed in and out slowly, and she did the same. "That's it. It's okay. I'm right here, and I'm not going anywhere."

"I'm afraid to tell you." Her voice trembled.

He ground his teeth together, sensing the darkness to come. "There is nothing I haven't seen, dealt with, or helped someone overcome through the club and bartending. We might not be an official couple—*yet*—but that doesn't mean we don't have a relationship. We've had months of close friendship. I care about you, and I haven't been with a woman since the first week I met you. I'd say that's a damn strong foundation, and I don't think you'd be sitting here with me right now if you didn't trust me."

"I *do* trust you," she said quickly. "Wait. Is that true? About you not being with any other woman since the first week we met?"

"Yes, of course. I might joke around a lot, but I don't lie. At least not to the people I care about, and definitely not to you. I haven't been with another woman and I got tested to make sure I was clean." He smiled. "Just in case. I'm *all in*, Crystal, and have been for a long time."

She looked at him as if she were weighing his honesty by the scent of the air. "Wow. I didn't expect to hear that."

"I didn't expect to say it, but it's true, and you need to know it."

"That's . . . thank you. I do trust you. It's just scary. I haven't told this to anyone. Not even Gemma."

That knowledge stopped him cold. They were as close as sisters.

"But I want to tell you."

He took her hand and pressed a kiss to it, holding on tight—for both of their sakes. "I'm here, and I'm listening."

She inhaled deeply, and when she spoke, her voice was shaky. "That night, my friend and I met these guys. They were older, and had come to visit one of their younger brothers or something. I didn't really care enough to listen to the details, although now I wish I had. Anyway, we were messing around in the halls, and you know how one minute you can be with a group and the next minute people are pairing off . . . ?"

His gut seized. He didn't like the direction this was going in. "Yes."

"Well, at some point the guy I was with led me up these dark stairs and we ended up in what I thought was a classroom. He said he wanted to show me sculptures his friend's brother had made that were being submitted to the next round of awards. It was dark, and I knew he was drunk, but there were so many people downstairs, and he'd come with a group of guys. I didn't worry until I realized there were no sculptures in the room. There were huge pieces of equipment and computers on every table, and it hit me that it wasn't right. But by then . . ." Her voice trailed off.

"He was all over me, and you have to understand. I had spent three years undoing everything I'd become in the trailer park. I dressed more proper, acted more feminine, and where I could have kicked anyone's ass when I first got to college, I had buried that girl in order to fit in."

Bear's muscles hardened to knots of rage. He clenched his teeth to keep those tight coils from unleashing a beast of vengeance.

Her hand was sweating, and tears spilled from her eyes. "And then he was on top of me, pushing my skirt up, tearing off my underwear, telling me I *wanted* him. It was like I was watching it happen from above, and then my brain kicked into gear. I fought back, Bear. I fought and punched, and I became *Chrissy* again, the girl from the trailer park, trying to kill him. I grabbed him by the hair at the same moment he slammed into me, and the pain . . ." Tears fell down her cheeks. "The pain was excruciating. I wasn't a virgin, but being taken against your will is nothing like consensual sex. It was over fast. I was horrified and hurt and so fucking angry I couldn't see straight. He pulled me up to my feet, and I'll never forget the look in his eyes when he said, 'Now you have something to write home about.'"

CHAPTER FIVE

CRYSTAL CLOSED HER eyes, waiting for Bear to react to her awful confession. When she looked at him again, interminable seconds pulsed and swelled like ticking time bombs as she waited for him to say something, *do* something. He shifted his eyes over her shoulder, the muscles in his face, shoulders, and arms flexing. She was tucked within the confines of his body, as if he wanted to swallow her up and protect her. But he couldn't protect her from the past, and she could see the pain that caused him written all over his face.

David's voice whispered through her mind. *Just because you're ready to share your past doesn't mean he's ready to hear it.*

"Bear," she said softly, wishing she could see inside his head. Would he move on to someone without such shitty baggage, without ghosts? Someone who had a normal, functional family like his? Sadness brought more tears. She forced them away, steeling herself for the worst. Sure, he'd been her friend for months, and he'd dropped everything to pick her up when she'd needed rides and showed up to help when she was babysitting for Kennedy and Lincoln. But no matter how much he flirted, or how good a friend he'd been, there was a world of difference between wanting to sleep with a person and wanting to bear their secrets. She'd been through hell and back, and she'd survived. She could survive this.

His angry eyes rolled from her forehead to her cheeks, her mouth, all the way to her chin, and back up again. When he finally met her gaze, the tension lines fanning out from the edges of his mouth eased, and compassion rose in his eyes.

"Is it okay if I hug you?"

Her heart tumbled inside her chest. The man who *told*, who *took*, who *possessed* had *asked* if he could hug her? "Yes."

As he gathered her in his arms, holding her with the strength of a hundred men and the tenderness of a thousand more, she thought of the day she'd tried to tell her mother, and pain sliced through her anew. *This* was what she'd needed all those years ago, when the woman who had raised her, who was supposed to love and care for her unconditionally, had only spat venom. And this man, this warm, wonderful man, who had known her for less than a year, knew exactly what she needed.

Bear held her tighter. "It's okay, sweetheart. I've got you."

He held her for a long, *long* time, comforting her and making her feel safe. Every word, every sweet, tender kiss he pressed to her head, chipped away more of the wall she'd constructed around her heart, unleashing years of unspoken fear and heartache. She clung to him, sobbing not only for the attack, but for the loss of her father and the descent of her mother, letting out all the sadness she'd kept locked up until she had no more tears to cry. And then she gasped for air, whimpering like a child coming to grips with an injury that no longer threatened to steal her life but stung like a paper cut—painful and sharp, but livable.

Within the safety of Bear's arms, his heart beating sure and steady against her own, her ghosts disengaged from some hidden dungeon deep within her, escaping through her confession and tears, and she found a sense of peace.

"Thank you for trusting me." Bear's voice was thick with emotion. "There are not enough words to express how sorry I am for all you've gone through."

She drew back far enough to see his glistening eyes, causing hers to tear up again. He brushed her hair from in front of her face and kissed her forehead. His gaze turned regretful.

"Everything I did last week, baby. *Jesus.* I'm so fucking sorry. What I said. The way I pushed. *Fuck.* I'm so sorry. You must have been terrified. Crystal, I'm not going anywhere, and I don't expect a thing from you. If you want *this*, if you want *me*, I will be the man you need me to be. I'll go with you to therapy. I'll talk. I'll listen—"

"Bear," she interrupted, unable to hold in her feelings any longer. "You *are* the man I want."

His jaw tightened again.

"I don't need to go back to therapy, but I love knowing that if I ever do, you'd be willing to go with me. That means more to me than you could ever imagine. The reason I went to see David was that I *do* want to explore whatever this is between us. I want it so much it's practically all I think about. *You're* all I think about. And in my head, I worried that I'd freak out if we got close, not out of fear of being intimate, because I'm not afraid to be intimate with you. I backed off out of nervousness. I had finally found someone I *wanted* to move on with, and I *worried* I'd freak out, even though I wasn't scared. That's why it took me so long. And it might have taken me even longer if you hadn't finally kissed me. I promise you, I've dealt with the actual . . . *incident*. It was all those months of wanting and worrying, *not* the assault, that made me freak out."

She swallowed hard, gathering the courage to tell him the rest of the truth.

"I haven't been intimate with a man since before the attack. I have a hard time trusting, and until you, I hadn't met anyone who made me feel *anything*."

His brows knitted, and guilt circled her like a vulture. In addition to tricking everyone into thinking she was some kind of biker chick, she'd led them to believe she was into meaningless flings with edgy men.

"I know none of it makes sense, given what I've led you to believe, but it does to me," she said, grasping for the right words to explain away her lies.

"When I was growing up, I was *Chrissy*, a girl who loved school and life, but when we moved to the mobile home, the neighborhood was rough, and I became hard around the edges. I learned to fight and talk back. A girl can take only so many catcalls before she snaps. Then, at college, I wanted to pretend that part of my life didn't exist, so I became *Chrystina*. The smart, sweet, slightly preppy, academically oriented *girl next door*. I had a few boyfriends and dated each of them for a while, but for one reason or another they didn't last. But after that night, I wasn't the same person anymore. I didn't want to be the girl everyone liked, because, well, look what *that* got me. And I didn't want to go back to being *Chrissy*, because that was a lost girl who missed her father, had a hot mess of a mother, and wanted to be someone else. So I became *Crystal*. All of this"—she waved toward her clothes—"and this." She lifted a lock of hair. "My hair, the attitude, all of it, including the stories about one-night stands, was meant to keep people *away*."

"Jesus, baby. You've been running or hiding for years."

She nodded, feeling the sting of tears simply because he understood and he was still right there. He wasn't judging her or telling her how she should have handled it. He was holding her and still looking at her like she was the gasoline to his engine—and she wanted to be.

"But even my best efforts at keeping people away didn't keep Gemma away, and they didn't keep *you* away."

"Or my brothers, or Dixie, or Tru and the babies," he pointed out. "You're part of us, and it doesn't matter what you call yourself or what color your hair is." He arched a brow and a soft laugh escaped.

God it felt good to laugh.

"Dirty blond." She tapped his chin. "You can make as many naughty remarks as you want about that, but not right now please."

A hint of a laugh fell from his lips, but she could see he wasn't taking this any lighter than she was.

"You never told Gemma?"

"No. And I feel horribly guilty about that. She's always been honest with me about everything. I feel bad about lying to you, too. I'm sorry, Bear. I'm sorry I led you and everyone else to believe that I was someone I wasn't. By the time I met you, I was in too deep. But you need to know, I didn't have one-night stands, and before we met there were a few boring first dates, but not a single one since you first put your arm around me and decided I was yours whether I liked it or not."

She smiled, and just as quickly her smile faded.

"And with Gemma, I had finally found a real friend. Every time I thought about telling her, I couldn't figure out how. But I want to. I need to. Just not yet. I know it puts you in a tough position, since you and Tru are so close, but I would really appreciate it if you could keep this between us."

He gritted his teeth and gently ran a hand down the side of her face. "Whatever you need. Whenever you need it."

She let out a sigh of relief. "Thank you."

"What happened to the asshole who did this to you?"

"Nothing. I had panic attacks for two days straight, so I packed up my stuff and left. I tried to tell my mother, but she was drunk, and basically made me feel like I'd somehow asked for it, and—"

"Wait. *Jesus*. First, your mother?"

"I know. Please, let's not talk about her."

"Okay, but, sugar, nothing happened to the guy? Didn't you go to the police?" His voice rose with anger, but she knew it wasn't aimed at her.

"No. I didn't go to the police. I didn't even know his real name. His friends called him *Cas*, but I heard one of them say it was for *Casanova*. All I wanted was to move on and to never, *ever* think about it again, which was ridiculous. I knew it even then, but at least I've done a damn good job of starting over."

Anger burned in her chest with the memories of how hard starting over had been. She'd spent weeks vacillating between bawling, screaming, and making it through each day like an automaton. She'd hated herself for being too weak to stick around and finish out her studies, but she'd been in no shape for classes. The fear she'd felt walking into David's office for the first time had been paralyzing. But the weight that had lifted from her when she'd finally told him the truth about the attack, her parents, and Jed's stealing had been equally healing.

"What about Jed?" he asked gruffly. "Did he do something to the guy?"

She felt his muscles tensing up. "He doesn't know."

"So this *asshole*, this *motherfucker*," he said through gritted teeth, "is still out there? He's never been punished for what he did?"

"Bear, listen to me, *please*. You have to let that anger go. You can't seek revenge. I want to have a normal life. I need to have a normal life. And I can't do that if I get all caught up in *him* again."

"*Caught up* in him?" he growled. "I'm going to make sure that you never feel unsafe again. I'm going to find that fucker and tear him apart."

She pushed back, anxiety climbing her spine. "No. I'm not one of the kids you can help by intimidating a bully. I'm a grown woman, and I've moved past that time of my life. I've got a new life—a *good* life—"

Bear shifted rage-filled eyes away.

"Look at me." She grabbed his face, pulling it back toward hers, and forced the calmest voice she could, which wasn't very calm at all. "I know you want revenge, or justice, but this is not about that. There is no revenge for what he did. Between losing my dad, my mom's alcoholism, and what happened, I don't have a pretty past. I've had no one to turn to since I was nine, and there was so much shit on my plate, I felt myself crumbling under the weight of it all. I made a choice. Rather than crash and burn, I left and I started over. I had to. I know there are people who will never understand my not going to the police. But they aren't me. I had no one I trusted enough to turn to. Not my parent, not a best friend, not a counselor. And by the time I met David and we'd worked through enough of the issues that I could have considered going to the police, it was too late. There were no witnesses, and honestly, I wanted to move on. I made the decision that was right *for me*, and I stand behind it. And now that's all in the past and none of it can be fixed with revenge. There's only what happened and how I've moved past it. And"—she softened her tone—"how I want to have a relationship with you. Please don't let your anger about what happened come between us, because it *will*."

"*Fuck*." He closed his eyes. Then he took her face in his hands, restrained rage present in the hard press of his fingers. "You're asking me to go against everything I believe. You're asking me to let a rapist walk free."

"Yes, I am. It was more than four years ago, Bear. There is no evidence. You said you would be what I needed. This is what I need."

BEAR ROLLED INTO the parking lot of Whiskey Bro's around midnight, surprised to see his father's car parked among the typical lineup of motorcycles and trucks. His father came by the bar often, but he didn't usually stick around that late. Bear checked his phone to see if he had missed a call from Bullet asking him to take a shift. He was scheduled to bartend Wednesday night, but sometimes they called him on the spur of the moment if the bar got busy. He'd been so blown away by what Crystal had told him, it wouldn't have surprised him if he had missed a text. Luckily, there were no missed messages from his brother.

To a passerby, the wooden building with rough, marred pillars, frequented by bikers and avoided by most others, didn't look like much more than a shady dive. The Dark Knights clubhouse, located behind the bar, was equally unimpressive. But to Bear, who'd practically been raised in the bar, walking into Whiskey's was like coming home, and with the way his insides were roiling and his mind was waging a full-on war, he needed as much stability as he could get.

He stepped into the bar, inhaling the scents of leather and alcohol, comfort and stability. There were only a handful of customers sitting at tables and around the bar, nodding their greeting as Bear walked past. His father was sitting at a table with two guys from the club, and Bear made a beeline for behind the bar, where Bullet was engrossed in something on his phone.

"What's up?" Bullet didn't look up from his phone. His thick dark brows were drawn down in concentration. At six five, he was the most intimidating of Bear's siblings. Bullet had a warrior inside him.

The deadly kind that could kill a man with a single punch. Bear had seen his eldest brother get the most formidable of challengers to back down with nothing more than the lethal stare he'd mastered during his years in the Special Forces. But Bear had also seen him bring women to their knees when those ice-cold, coal-black eyes smoldered with seduction.

What's up? I want to track down some motherfucker and torture him until he can't breathe, and then I want to help him breathe so I can torture him all over again.

Bear fixed himself a double shot of whiskey. Not trusting himself to give a more civilized answer, he ignored the question. "What's Pop talking to Viper and Bud about?"

Viper and Bud Redmond were brothers and members of the Dark Knights. They owned the Snake Pit, an upscale bar at the other end of town, as well as Petal Me Hard, a local flower shop.

"From what I can piece together, he's on another kick to expand Whiskey Bro's and they're giving him pointers."

Their father had talked about expanding the bar on and off for the past few years. It was a good idea, but a major undertaking that Bear knew would fall on his shoulders.

Bullet's eyes darted to Bear, and he shoved his phone in his pocket. "What the hell happened to you?"

Bear set the glass on the bar and went to the other side, climbing onto a stool, feeling the weight of Crystal's confession eating away at him. He stared at the amber liquid, which he'd been ready to down three seconds ago.

He pushed the painful reminder of what Crystal had endured across the bar. "Take this away, will ya?"

Bullet grabbed it and downed it in a single gulp and leaned his forearms on the bar, bringing him eye to eye with Bear. "Now I know some shit went down."

"Yeah, some shit went down all right, but . . ." *I can't talk about it.* His eyes skated around the bar as he replayed the night for the umpteenth time. After he and Crystal left the park, he'd driven her back to her car and then followed her home. He'd walked her up to the door, expecting to go inside and hold her, make her feel safe, but she'd said she just needed to sleep and had apologized profusely. He'd seen the fatigue in her eyes and in the drooping of her shoulders. Where her confession had gutted him and then filled the hole with a fireball of rage and sadness, it had depleted Crystal of all of her energy. It had killed him not to push her to let him stay, but he knew she'd taken a giant leap of faith by trusting him with her secrets, and he vowed to respect her wishes, no matter how hard it was for him.

"But . . . ?" Bullet leveled him with one of his glares. He had the patience of a saint when it came to Tru's kids, but he had a nose for bullshit and for trouble, and where family was concerned, Bullet didn't put up with either.

That threatening glare was almost enough to make Bear spill his guts. *Almost.* But he'd never betray Crystal's trust. Not even for Bullet.

"Nothing."

Bullet leaned so close Bear could smell the alcohol on his breath. "Either spill your shit, little brother, or wipe that look off your face. You look like you're either going to rip someone's head off, in which case I need to back you up, or you're going to start tearing shit apart, in which case I need to wrestle you to the ground."

Bear smirked. "I don't need backup. I just need advice."

His brother laughed and pushed off the bar, shaking his head. "That's a first. You're usually the armchair psychologist standing on this side of the bar, doling out advice the way hookers dole out blow jobs."

"No shit."

"What's got you so effed up?" Bullet filled a glass with ice water and pushed it across the bar, watching him like a hawk.

Bullet had a way of getting into people's heads. For that reason, Bear stared at the glass as he spoke. "Thanks. What would you do if someone you cared about was taken advantage of but wanted you to take a step back?"

Bullet laughed again, but in the next second his eyes cast daggers. "*No one* tells me to take a step back." He set his palms on the bar, leaning closer again. "You always do what's right, little brother. It's that simple."

"No, bro. It's that fucking complicated." He guzzled the water. "It's Crystal."

Bullet's brows slanted in disapproval.

"Some shit went down years ago, but . . . *Fuck*, B. I don't know what to do." Bear felt his father's hand grip his shoulder. He tipped his face up, taking in the familiar roadmap of wrinkles. His father's skin was like worn leather from his years of riding all day and partying all night. *Once a biker, always a biker.* It was in their blood. There was no mistaking the *biker* in Biggs, from his black leather vest with the Dark Knights patches to the leather boots he'd had since Bear was a kid, and every tattooed inch in between. His father looked as though he belonged on a mean machine, save for the cane and slight drooping of the left side of his face, which was hidden pretty well by his scruffy white beard and mustache.

"Hey, Pop."

"What's got your nuts in a knot, boy?" He sank down to the stool beside Bear and nodded to Bullet. "Mind getting me a water, son?"

His father hardly ever called them by their given names or their road names. It was always *boy*, *son*, or *kid*. Asking had never been his forte, either, until after his stroke. Still, it was a rare occurrence. Bear guessed that was where he'd learned to *do* or *take* or *tell*. His father had been demanding things from him for as long as he could remember. *Ride your bike over to the bar after school to help with inventory. Run up to the store and get [whatever he needed at the moment].* His father didn't dole out life lessons the way most parents did, with thoughtful discussions and kind conversation. No, sir. Biggs believed lessons were learned by *doing* not *listening*. From the time Bear had gotten his driver's license, his father would haul his ass out of bed with a phone call to drive drunken customers home. Bear would drive the customer's car and one of his brothers, or Dixie, when she learned to drive, would follow behind and drive him back home. When no one else was available, Bear would drive the customer to their house and then take a cab back. He'd minded those trips like nobody's business, until one day when he'd driven a drunken man home and the guy had rambled the whole way about his beautiful, smart little girl and his son who tried his patience at every turn. When he'd dropped the man off, he'd seen a little girl peering out the window. He'd known then that regardless of how tired he'd be the next day at school, his father had done the right thing. The image of that little girl's face pressed against the window had stuck with him.

"His girl's gone through some shit and she wants Bear to ignore it," Bullet explained.

"Jesus, B. Think you can let me speak?"

Bullet lifted his shoulder and went to help a customer at the other end of the bar.

"Shit you can fix?" his father asked.

"Shit someone should pay for."

"Always do what's right, son." His father took a drink of water. "Need to get the law involved?"

Bear's gut told him yes, but Crystal had told him no, leaving him in a hell of a position. He looked at his father, who was by no means perfect, but he'd lived a fairly clean life, and he'd helped a lot of people. He had accumulated a lot of wisdom in his sixty-nine years.

"The *right* thing? What if you found out a woman had"—*shit*, he had to be careful with his choice of words—"been hurt, but she doesn't want you to take care of it? Would you act on it or let it go? Is the right thing to respect her wishes or track down the asshole and get him off the streets?"

"There's a whole world of hurt out there, son. I guess it depends on what level of hurt you're talking about. You've seen a lot in your lifetime, so just ask yourself this: When we helped that little boy last week, was your goal to make him feel safe? Or was it to send a message to the bully so he'd never do that shit again?"

"Both." But it wasn't that easy, Bear didn't know who the enemy was other than a nickname used by probably hundreds of guys at college parties.

"Then I think you have your answer." His father stroked his beard, a sure sign that he also wanted to talk about something heavy.

It didn't matter that Bear didn't see any real answer in his father's response. He knew Crystal was right. Without evidence there would be no justice for what had happened to her. But he'd make damn sure that she was safe from now on.

"I've got something else for you to think about," his father said. "It's time we expand this place."

Bear gritted his teeth. His time was maxed out between covering shifts at the bar, handling the shop, and hopefully, spending more time with Crystal. And if he got his shit together and took the offer from Silver-Stone, he'd be working fewer hours at the bar, not more.

He glanced up at Bullet, who arched a brow. Bullet was already working more than sixty hours a week.

"What are you thinking?" Bear asked, considering telling his father about the offer and nipping the expansion in the bud.

"I'm *thinking* that we'll put our heads together and make it happen," his father said. "It's time to shake things up and bring in more customers. I want to leave you kids something of value. A Whiskey legacy."

Painful memories came rushing back. He'd never forget the devastation in his mother's voice when she'd called to tell him his father had suffered a stroke, or the fear that had consumed him at the possibility of losing the man who meant so much to him.

"Pop, you're not going anywhere anytime soon." He held his tongue about the offer. He couldn't take away his father's dream when all he was thinking about was his children.

"Actually, I'm leaving right now. I need to get going before your mother drives out here and hauls my ass home. Love you, boys." He pushed to his feet and patted Bear on the back. "Church Monday night. We can discuss it then. Start thinking about how you'll make it work." Meetings for the Dark Knights were called *church*.

When he left, Bear and Bullet exchanged a long, stressed look. It was no secret that their father loaded Bear up with responsibility like a Sherpa.

"Dude, you got this?" Bullet asked. "I'd offer, but I don't know shit about anything other than keeping the place in order and serving drinks."

"Yeah. I've got it. I won't let him down." He pulled out his phone and sent a quick message to Crystal in case she was lying awake and couldn't sleep. He hated the idea of her being alone tonight. *Thinking of you. You okay?*

"Need help closing up?" he asked Bullet.

"Nah. Get out of here. You look like shit." Bullet came around the bar and laid a hand on his shoulder. "Don't do anything stupid."

Bear shoved his phone in his pocket and headed for the door. "No promises, bro. No promises."

CHAPTER SIX

CRYSTAL'S APARTMENT WASN'T waterfront. It was barely water view. But if she went up on her toes and leaned just the right way over the railing, balancing with one hand against the brick wall, she could see the water, as she was doing now. She got a little thrill every time she did it, like she was stealing a glimpse of something sacred. Seeing the water helped clear her mind, and she needed that this morning. She lowered herself to her heels, phone in hand, thinking about texting Bear. Last night had been one of the hardest, most emotional nights of her life, but it had also been the most liberating. She'd woken up feeling lighter than ever before, and she knew she owed that to him. And probably to David, for not letting her use him as a crutch, but for supporting her in the very best way he could. By letting her know he was there for her and reminding her that she had done all the right things and had all the tools she needed to have a full life and an intimate relationship when she was ready. He didn't try to fool her into thinking it would be easy, but he reminded her that she was a smart, capable, emotional woman who could make her own decisions. She didn't need his permission to be intimate with Bear. She only needed her own.

She clutched the phone tighter. It was a strange feeling, wanting to call Bear and simply hear his voice. Wanting to rely on him. She'd always felt safe with him, but last night he'd taken that even further. He'd become her safe haven, and that made her feel good and a little scared. She hadn't had anyone in her life that she could truly rely on since her father died.

She scrolled through her messages, skipping the selfie Jed had sent her last night with the caption, *The new and improved Jed!* She hoped that was true, but she wasn't counting chickens just yet. She read the thoughtful text from Bear for the tenth time, and the warm and fuzzy feeling she'd gotten the first nine times returned. She'd responded this morning with, *I'm okay. Thank you.* It was a lame response, but she had no idea what was appropriate. Should she have said the bigger truth? *You make me feel happy and safe, and I want to be in your arms again. Can you please come over?* She wouldn't even know *how* to be the person who texted something like that. But she wanted to. God, she wanted to so badly.

She'd hated telling him she was too exhausted to invite him in last night, but she *had* been emotionally exhausted, and she was a little afraid to open another door. Getting on the back of his motorcycle had been a baby step, though it had felt enormous. Confessing her secret was like handing him her heart on a platter, and he'd handled it with tender, loving gloves. If she'd allowed him to come in and comfort her, she was afraid of where that might have led—by *her* doing, not his. And she didn't want to take that step until he'd had time to process what she'd been through.

But she wanted Bear.

And she wanted to hear his voice.

She sank down to the chair on the balcony, staring at her phone, as if it held her courage. *Why is this so hard? It's a text. Just ask him to come over.*

She told herself she wasn't relying on him; she only wanted to see him.

Exhaling loudly, she knew damn well why it was so hard. Because the people she should have been able to count on, who should have been there for her, had let her down. How could she rely on anyone other than herself?

She set her phone beside her and covered her face, groaning. She needed to think about telling Gemma, too. Gemma's wealthy parents had showered her with everything *other than* love and attention. Her dreams had revolved around having children of her own and giving them all the love she'd never experienced, but because of medical issues, she would never be able to bear her own children. When she'd met Truman, he'd had little more than the shirt on his back, two babies he'd rescued from a crack house, and a drug-addicted brother Truman had gone to prison to protect. She knew now what she hadn't known when they'd met. If anyone could handle her past, it was Gemma. The guilt of having lied to her weighed heavily on Crystal.

Baby steps.

She sat there for a long time, trying to clear her head. They only had two parties scheduled at the boutique today, and they didn't start until eleven. *Plenty of time to get out of my head before going to work.* A quick trip to the ice cream store was in order. Or maybe the bakery. Sugar, definitely sugar. She walked inside, grabbed her bag, and threw open her apartment door, nearly plowing into Bear.

"Hi," he said with a sexy smile.

Startled, she opened her mouth, but no words came. He was holding a box with two large milk shake cups from Luscious Licks ice cream shop in one hand and the cutest calico kitten she'd ever seen in the other. But it wasn't the sexiness of that smile, or even the adorable kitten in his hands, that had stolen her voice. It was that he had appeared moments after she'd been wishing for him. Like a miracle. It took her a few seconds to push past the void he was quickly filling up inside her and find her voice.

"You're here? I was just thinking about you. And . . ." She bit her lower lip to stop her overexcited self from rambling. How had he known she needed him? Her eyes dropped to the precious kitten in his hands. Was there anything hotter than a tiny kitten tucked against a strong, tatted-up arm? *Bear's* strong tatted-up arm? She was a little jealous of that cute kitten, allowing Bear to cuddle him so easily.

"Can I . . . ? Is he yours? Can I hold him?"

"*She's* yours, sugar. Her name is Harley." He leaned forward, handing her the snuggly little kitten.

She gasped. "Mine? You got me a kitten?" She rubbed her chin over the kitten's soft fur. "Bear . . . ?"

"I hated the idea of you being alone last night."

Chip, chip, chip. Down came more of her walls.

"That's . . ." She felt like she was going to cry. What the heck was going on? She wasn't a crier. She was a bold, in-your-face woman. But as she stood before the man who had drawn her tears last night and then held her through them, checked on her in the middle of the night, and now was standing right there with her, that bold woman refused to appear. She turned away so he wouldn't see her damp eyes, and blinked them dry.

"That's so nice, and this little girl is so freaking cute. Thank you." She looked down at the kitten and lowered her voice. "What do you think, cutie pie? Should we invite the sexy beast in?" Her stomach went six ways of crazy as she slid her gaze to Bear. This felt more like a jumbo leap than a baby step.

He held up the box with the cups. "I brought you a mango, pistachio, blueberry, lemon milk shake, but don't worry, no fries for dipping."

She laughed about the fries. "How do you know my favorite ice cream combination?"

"From the Easter parade with Tru and the kids. How could I forget?" His voice went deep. "I couldn't take my eyes off of you licking that four-decker cone."

The parade had been several weeks ago. How had he remembered something so trivial? *That now seems meaningful.* She remembered the lascivious looks he'd given her, and she turned away again, hoping to hide the heat burning her skin.

"I think I remember Dixie wiping drool from your mouth," she teased. "Today is like sweetness overload. Thank you." She kissed the top of Harley's head. "Where did you get her?"

"She's one of Big Mama's litter."

"Really?" Could her heart get any fuller? She hadn't been by his shop since Truman and Gemma had moved to their new house and Quincy, Truman's brother, had moved into their old apartment above the shop several weeks ago. But she'd seen Bear with Big Mama and knew how much he loved her.

"That makes her even more special," she said.

He followed her in and set the drinks on the distressed wooden trunk she used as a coffee table, beside the candles and the design magazine she'd been looking through earlier in the week.

"I got everything you'll need for her." He went back out and carried in a bag of kitty supplies and a cat box, which he must have left in the hall.

"Bear, you didn't have to do that, but thank you. You saved me a trip to the store before work. Oh gosh, I don't want to leave her. I'm going to take her with me."

"Think Gemma will be cool with that?"

"She loves kitties. I'll keep her in the office. I don't want her to be alone all day."

She watched him survey her eclectic, one-bedroom apartment. She'd never had a man in it before, and Bear was so big and broad, he made the space feel a little more confined, but in a good way. A very good way. She liked seeing him there among her things.

"I've thought about what your place might look like forever." He walked over to the bookshelves separating the kitchen from the living room. They were filled with books, plants, glass vases, and of course, a handful of the dolls her father had made for her. She kept her favorites in her bedroom, where she needed to feel safest.

He picked up one of the dolls, inspecting it closely, and the warmest smile appeared on his handsome face. "I love that you have so many of these." From where he stood, he couldn't see into the dining room, her design studio, where more worry dolls were lined up on the windowsill.

"Thank you. My father made me a lot of them. It shows how often he traveled." She watched him looking over her things and felt a bit exposed. But it wasn't a bad feeling. It was just *new*. "They're just yarn, fabric, and twigs, but they carry so many of my worries. They've pulled me through a lot."

"*You've* pulled you through a lot." He set the doll back on the shelf. "Was this the first apartment you rented here?"

"This is the only place that has ever been mine. I went from living with my parents, to college, then here. When I first rented the apartment, I had no money, and I lived with nothing more than a beach chair and a mattress on the floor for the first few weeks. I didn't mind, though, because it was *mine*. Every time I went to buy cheap furniture, I got a sick feeling in my stomach, because they reminded me of the person my mother had become."

"I'm sorry, babe."

"It's okay. Jogs and gaps and all that. I was working at the department store, making next to nothing. But when I started working with Gemma, I worked extra hours, and I hunted for bargains. I found pieces like the zebra-striped rug and that antique dresser at amazing prices." She pointed to the dresser by the balcony. "This was my new beginning. My *home*. I wanted to love coming home, and I do." It was her *first* safe haven.

"I can see why." He ran his hand over an antique chest, touching each of the colorful candles on top, and glanced outside. "You can almost see the beach. It's a great location."

She watched his gaze move over the gray, velvet-tufted couch, which reminded her of the local hipster coffee shop. The wall behind the sofa was red and black brick; the other walls were painted peach. On the opposite side of the room was an overstuffed red armchair with a worn indentation that fit her rear end perfectly, and a patchwork footstool from Pier One. She loved that stool. Behind the chair hung an enormous slate-blue clock that was six feet in circumference, surrounded by pictures she'd collected over the years.

"I like your place," he said after what felt like an hour but in reality was probably two minutes. "It's very cool. Very *you*."

He approached her with a tender look in his eyes. He was still worried about her, and that made her nervous. She was okay. At least she was okay *for now*, and she needed him to know that.

"I'm glad you want to take Harley with you. She's not used to being alone all day." He scratched the kitty's head. "She likes you."

"Of course she likes me. I'm pretty kick-ass. What's not to like?"

"I can't think of a damn thing." His eyes heated as he reached for her, and just as quickly, he gritted his teeth and stopped short of touching her. "Can I give you a kiss on your cheek?"

Her stomach sank. "Bear . . ."

He raised his brows with an apologetic expression.

"Don't do that, okay? Please don't treat me with kid gloves. I know you mean well, but that will only make me feel weird. I didn't tell you what happened so you would back off. I told you so we could get closer. I like who you are. And believe it or not, I like that you're presumptive. Just, maybe don't be too overly aggressive? At least until I'm able to deal with being intimate like a normal person, which I think I am, but after my reaction to our kiss, who knows."

He placed a gentle hand on her hip and smiled, a fiercely sexy smile that told her he might be treating her differently, but he didn't feel differently about her.

"Babe, you *are* a normal person. Normal people have shit to deal with. I do. Gemma and Tru did. Kennedy and Lincoln will. We all do. We may have different issues, but it's still there. I'll try not to be overly aggressive, but I worry that with you, I might get carried away. I'm only human, and being close to you, holding you in my arms. That's all I've dreamed about for months. So if, or *when*, I get carried away and kiss you too hard, or hold you too tight, or forget that I can't strip you naked, toss you down on that sofa, and love the hell out of you, please smack me in the head, or bite my tongue, or do something to tell me to back off." His eyes flamed again. "*Wait.* Don't bite my tongue. I might like that."

She laughed. "You're awful. Shouldn't you tell me that you'd *never* get too carried away or something?"

"Only if you want me to lie. I'll never push you past your comfort zone again, but if we're kissing and my hands wander, that's out of desire, not aggression. I'll need signals, like a flashing neon light that says, 'Today you may not go past second base.'"

She rubbed the kitty's back. "Bear?"

"Yeah?"

"I have no flashing lights, but please kiss me hello."

He touched his lips to hers in a feathery kiss, and she laughed. "A big-girl kiss, please."

His strong arms circled her, the kitten cradled between them. Her body tingled with anticipation as his mouth descended on hers in a smoldering kiss. She waited for panic to barge in, but the longer they kissed, the less she worried. Bear's kisses knocked the strength from her knees, caressed her mouth as much as he possessed it, and just when he eased the kiss and she thought he was going to pull away—*No, not yet*—he took it deeper, scrambling her ability to think. She'd kissed enough men to know that there were kisses— and then there were *kisses*. This was different from a sweet kiss, more powerful than a hot kiss. This was an intimate kiss that evoked trust *and* desire.

He lavished her with a series of tantalizing, shivery kisses, making her feel light-headed and swoony.

"Hello, sweet girl," he said in a gravelly voice that electrified her as much as their kisses did. His warm eyes moved over her face. "Was that okay?"

"Um. I'm not sure. I think we should try again."

GEMMA WAS BUSY rolling out the red-carpet runway for the first party when Crystal arrived at the boutique. She set Harley's cat carrier down inside the door. Another gift from Bear, which had been hiding in his truck.

"Did you see my text?" Crystal had texted to ask if it was okay if she brought a kitten into work, but Gemma hadn't responded.

"No. Sorry. My phone must be in my bag. I was running a little late. Tru and I were deciding on paint colors for the playroom. I still can't believe we're getting married in less than three months. And I'm so glad we're doing the wedding in the backyard. It feels right with the kids." Gemma smiled as she rose on tall, knee-high black boots. A black and red bodice hugged her curves, flaring out into a short black skirt. She wore long purple gloves and a black and red cape trimmed with gold.

"Whoa, mama. The Queen of Hearts princess has never looked so hot. Want me to handle the party so you can go surprise Tru for a little playtime?"

"No, but maybe I'll wear it home tonight." Gemma waggled her brows. "What did you text me about?"

Crystal picked up the kitty carrier.

"You got a kitten?" She came around the benches that separated the runway from the entrance of the store and took the kitten out of the carrier. "This looks just like Harley."

"It is Harley. Bear gave her to me."

"Bear *gave* her to you? He loves that kitty as much as he loves Lincoln and Kennedy." She gasped, her eyes wide. "Ohmygod. You've been holding out on me!"

"No. Maybe a little? But not on purpose." He loved the kitty as much as he loved the babies? *And he gave her to me?* Her heart filled up a little more.

"Crystal Moon, I tell you everything and you've been hooking up with Bear and keeping me in the dark?"

"No, no, no." Crystal waved her hand. "That's not what I meant. We haven't hooked up. I promise. We've only kissed. We're . . . *testing the waters.*"

"Testing the waters? That sounds like something *I* would say. I seem to remember you teasing me about *Princess Swallows* and *Prince Cunnilingus.*"

"You have to admit, that was funny." They'd always joked like that. Crystal had even made up jokes about the guys she'd pretended to go out with.

"It was hilarious, but come on. Bear might have a huge heart, but I cannot see him *testing* any waters. He's more of a dive-in-headfirst-and-come-up-for-air-later kind of guy. There's no way that man is going without."

Emotions Crystal didn't recognize pulled at her. Gemma was right. Bear was a dive-in-headfirst kind of guy. He could have any woman he wanted, and he definitely came across as *too* sexual to go without. The man emitted testosterone like cologne. Of course Gemma would think they were mattress bumping. Guilt wound through Crystal. Gemma deserved to know the truth about why they weren't playing *bone the biker*, but she wasn't ready to share her secret yet. Not on the heels of telling Bear. She could only handle one monumental confession at a time.

"Can we please not talk about Bear's sexual proclivities?" She took Harley from Gemma. "Do you mind if I keep her in the office? I have a cat box and everything she needs in the car."

"Of course. Hey." Gemma touched her arm. "I'm sorry. I didn't mean to upset you. I thought you were pulling the wool over my eyes. Honestly, I thought you and Bear had been hooking up for a long time. I never imagined that you hadn't been."

"You didn't upset me. I was just surprised that you thought we'd been hooking up. I would have told you if I'd boned the biker." Her typical snarkiness felt wrong when tied to sleeping with Bear. The truth was, if she didn't have the past she had, she probably would have jumped in the sack with Bear a long time ago, and she probably would have told Gemma.

She quickly added, "He's different than we thought, Gem. But then again, aren't we all? I'm going to put Harley in the office and get her stuff so I have time to change. I thought I'd be Pocahontas princess today."

"The sexiest Pocahontas ever," Gemma called after her.

As she headed toward the office, her mind slid down a dark path that led directly to a pool of awful thoughts about Bear and other women. She closed the office door behind her and sat on a chair with Harley in her lap. Anyone who knew Bear wouldn't believe he'd go without sex.

Would he?

The kitty purred loudly. It figured Bear's kitten had a monstrous engine. She looked down at the sweet, cuddly girl. He'd never give her away if he didn't know he could still be part of her life. She pressed a kiss to Harley's head, pushing away the fleeting worry.

For months Bear had been right there with her, even when she'd pushed him away. She thought about the night at Woody's, and the worried look in his eyes when she'd pulled away from their kiss. She could still feel his arms around her when he'd held her last night, could still hear his voice when he'd told her the truth and asked for flashing lights instead of lying about what he was capable of doing—or *not* doing.

Bear told her he hadn't been with another woman since the first week they'd met, and as astonishing as it might seem, she believed him.

CHAPTER SEVEN

BEAR HELD BIG Mama and peered over Dixie's shoulder, reviewing the accounting spreadsheets from last month for Whiskey Automotive and trying like hell to keep thoughts of Crystal's attack from consuming him. But they were as present as the fucking numbers on the computer screen.

"Earth to Bear." Dixie waved her hand in front of his face.

"Yeah. Sorry." He shoved those dark thoughts away and tried to focus on Dixie.

"Where were you all morning?"

"The bar. Bullet couldn't make it in time to get today's delivery." Bullet had called him shortly after he'd left Crystal. He'd had business in the next town over and had forgotten about the delivery. Bear had taken the delivery and then his father had shown up and wanted to discuss the expansion. He'd had to rush through the repairs he was slated to work on, skip lunch, and he still had to tell a customer their car would be done Monday morning instead of today. He hated letting customers down.

"I've been working on some of our suppliers. I think I can bring them down by a percent or two." She navigated to next year's budget. "Which will help for next year. When we had the building inspected, the guy said we'd need a new roof in the next five or six years. Next year it'll be five years, so I've budgeted for that."

When he'd taken over running the shop, it was barely turning a profit. But Bear was a master at networking and negotiations, and Dixie had an incredible knack for finances and business. Together they'd expanded their clientele beyond the biker community, which was where his uncle had found his niche. They were turning nice profits every month, but he was stretched to his limit time-wise. He had no idea where his father had gotten it in his head that he'd have time to manage the bar expansion.

Then again, his father had never worried about Bear's time. He took for granted that Bear would make it happen, the way Bear always had. He could hardly blame his father for his own inability to put up boundaries.

"I was thinking," Dixie added. "Maybe it's time to redo the kitchen in the apartment."

"Is Quincy complaining?"

"No, but we always said we'd make it nicer when we could. And now we can."

He'd completely forgotten about both the inspector's suggestion and the kitchen, but as always, Dixie kept them on target. "Dix, do you like what you do here at the shop?"

"Hell, yes. I love it." She crossed her arms, narrowing her catlike green eyes. "Why? You can't fire me. I'm part owner."

He laughed. "Like I'd ever *fire* you? Do you want to do more?"

"*Duh.* Always." She shuffled papers on her desk and put them in a drawer.

"Dad's talking about expanding the bar."

"I know. Mom told me, and she said he wants you to handle it."

"Yeah." He leaned his hip on the desk. "But if I'm going to put more time into anything, it'll be designing bikes, not revitalizing a floundering bar."

"The bar is not floundering. We turn a profit every month. Besides, you're amazing at turning businesses around and expanding the clientele, and I'll help you. I'd love to get my hands on Whiskey Bro's and bring in a cook and waitstaff and do the kinds of things they do at Mr. B's microbrewery, like the charity auctions for the community. It's totally in line with the Dark Knights and Dad's view of helping others. We could arrange a charity ride and have it end at the bar, raffle off free meals to bring in money for the community and bring in new customers."

She went on and on with one fantastic idea after another, driving home what Bear already knew. Dixie needed to *run* the bar.

"I'll talk to Dad about you handling the expansion. You're there half of the time anyway, and the planning and business oversight is where you shine. It makes sense."

"Save your energy," she said in a deflated voice. "I love him, but the man is ass backward when it comes to women. But I'll get financial projections together, because you know he'll want those next. You should get started on the expansion plan."

He should put something together, but he was in no hurry to perpetuate the inequities, and he couldn't commit to the project when he was still considering Silver-Stone's offer. "Thanks, Dix. But I can't help thinking that maybe it's time you went out and found another business to run. Something where you can get the credit for the work you're doing. You deserve more than playing second fiddle to me. I can find someone else to do the books and run the shop."

"Are you crazy? I love working with you and Tru and working at the bar with everyone. As ass backward as Dad is, I'd still rather work with family than work for some idiot who thinks he knows more than I do."

Bear wasn't surprised by her vehemence. "Then you need to handle the expansion." He thought about telling her about the offer from Silver-Stone, but he didn't want to put her in the middle of it. Dixie would get on his back about accepting it, and he needed to figure out things for himself first.

"I'm strapped for time, and with Crystal in the picture, I'm not exactly looking to fill my nights with managing a new project of that magnitude."

She gathered her hair over one shoulder and tapped a red fingernail on the counter, looking up at Bear. "She's it for you, isn't she?"

He petted the cat. "Big Mama and I are pretty close, but I'm not sure we're compatible in the sack." He smirked and lowered his voice. "Sorry, Big Mama."

"You're an idiot." Dixie laughed. "I mean *Crystal*. I still can't get over that you *gave her* Harley."

"She needed her more than I did."

The truth was, he wanted to *be* Harley, and be there for Crystal night and day. Holding back was killing him. Almost as much as it was eating away at him that she'd gone through so much between losing her father, dealing with her alcoholic mother, and having some asshole force himself on her.

"Why? Are you two a couple now?"

"Come on, Dix. You know as well as I do that we've been a couple for months, just not a conventional one."

Her eyes narrowed in speculation. "Then why does she suddenly need Harley?"

The door to the shop opened and Quincy walked in, saving Bear from having to come up with an answer. Quincy had come a long way from the strung-out junkie he'd become while Truman was in prison. His blue eyes were clear, and with his longish brown hair and few days' scruff, he was a dead ringer for Brad Pitt in *World War Z*. He was thickening out, and acting proud and confident.

"How's it going?" He strode across the floor and leaned over the desk.

"Hey, Quincy," Bear said. "What's up?" There had been a time when their relationship had been strained. When Truman had first gone to prison, leaving thirteen-year-old Quincy in the hands of their drug-addicted mother, Bear had tried to keep Quincy on a straight-and-narrow path. He'd taken Quincy to visit Truman every week until Quincy began disappearing, hanging with the wrong crowds, getting drunk and stoned. Bear had tried to get him help up until the day Quincy had gone missing for good, only to resurface years later, standing over his mother in the crack house where she'd overdosed.

But that was behind them now. Quincy had gone through intense rehab, passed his GED, and was now taking college courses and had a stable job at a local bookstore. He'd even cleared his brother's name for the crime he'd committed.

"Do y'all have any issue with me getting a roommate?" Quincy asked. "The community college doesn't offer some of the classes I want to take, and the bigger universities' online classes are more expensive."

Dixie exchanged a proud smile with Bear. "Why would we mind? But won't that hinder you with the ladies?"

"Why? There are two bedrooms. It's not like we'll both be staying in mine." He ran a hand through his hair. "Although, it could be interesting if I get a chick as a roomie."

Bear laughed. "No problem. You know the rules. No drugs, no troublemakers. We've got babies here all day, and their welfare has to come first."

"Dude, I know that better than anyone. Think I'd fuck up everything y'all and Tru have done for me?" He leaned further over the counter, and his expression turned serious. "Not a chance. Family first. I will *never* screw that up again."

He and Bear tapped fists.

"That's it, bro," Bear said.

"Before I forget, Tru told me to tell you you're helping him with kid duty and painting the playroom at the house next Tuesday while the girls are out shopping."

"We're getting Gemma's wedding dress fitted and picking out dresses for me and Crystal." Dixie poked Bear in the side. "That means you're free, because *your girl* will be busy."

Bear loved that Dixie referred to Crystal as *his* girl. "Sounds good. Where are you headed?"

"Tru's," Quincy said. "Dinner with my baby brother and sister, then out to Luscious Licks. One day Penny's going to realize I'm the best lick she'll ever get." Penny owned Luscious Licks, and Quincy had been crushing on her since they'd first met.

"*God*." Dixie rolled her eyes. "You really need to come up with something better than that to get that woman to notice you. Don't you guys know anything about romance?"

"Romance?" Bear scoffed. "This from the woman who nails guys' balls to the wall for every little thing."

She rose to her feet and flipped her hair over her shoulder. "Romance. Flowers and chocolates and all that stuff. I may be tough, but at least I know what I like."

Quincy headed for the door. "I'll be sure to let Crow know romance might get him in the door."

Bear glared at him. "Get the hell out of here before I shove that thought down your throat." Crow was a biker they'd grown up with, and he'd had a thing for Dixie since they were kids. He had the reputation of a snake, and he wasn't going anywhere near Bear's sister's grass.

Quincy's laughter followed him out the door.

Bear dropped his eyes to Dixie, who was smiling as she scrolled through her texts. "Wipe that grin off your face. Crow's not going near you."

"I ought to sleep with him just to show you that you're not the boss of me." She sauntered around the desk with a dramatic sway of her hips, underscoring her independence.

"That's one way to get a man killed." Bear took his vibrating phone from his pocket, happy to see a text from Crystal.

He opened it, and a picture popped up of Crystal dressed in the sexiest costume he'd ever set his eyes on. A leather choker with an aqua charm in the center circled her neck, and a fringed suede minidress with a sinfully short hemline rode high on her thighs. Harley was in her arms, sporting a silver-studded black collar with a pink bow. She'd taken the picture in the mirror, and she had a smirky, sexy smile. The text read, *Hey, biker boy. Want to come over and see your girls tonight?*

Hell yes.

After a quick shower, Bear stopped by Petal Me Hard. He'd be damned if any woman would be romanced better than his girl. The pungent floral scent cleared his senses after he'd spent the day in the auto shop.

"Hey, Bear," Isla, Bud's daughter, called from behind the counter, where she was arranging a bouquet. "I'll be right with you."

"Great. Thanks." He meandered through the shop, looking at all the flowers. He'd never bought a woman flowers before, and he had no idea there were so many to choose from.

"What brings you in?" She leaned over the vase of flowers, her thick blond hair curtaining her face.

"I'm looking for something special."

"For Crystal?" She popped up and arched a dark brow. Her flannel shirt was tied at the waist, revealing a sliver of skin above a tight pair of jeans.

"What do you know about me and Crystal?"

She wiped her hands on her jeans and folded her arms across her chest with a sassy smirk. "What does everyone in this town know about you and Crystal? Just that every time the Whiskey brothers are out and about, you've got your arm around her. Word around town is that you're taken. I assume that means something."

That was news to him, and he was thrilled by it.

"It means a hell of a lot."

"So you need something special. Like red-rose, I-love-you special?"

"You need a bigger hook than that to go fishing in my lake, little one."

Isla was twenty-two and rebellious as they came, and because of her father's relationship in the club, she was considered family. Like another nosy little sister.

"You're no fun." She came around the counter. "Any allergies?"

"I'm not sure, but I need something safe around kittens. And I'd like something that isn't common. She's unique, and the flowers should be, too."

"Now we're getting somewhere. I like a man on a mission. Tell me what she's like."

He thought about her question as he looked around, catching sight of the most gorgeous flowers he'd ever seen. *Perfect.* He pointed across the store. "Are those safe for kittens?"

What had started as a mission in romance competition ended up coming straight from his heart. Half an hour later he took the steps to Crystal's apartment two at a time, reminding himself not to overwhelm her and sweep her into his arms. But it felt like forever since he'd held her, and he knew the moment he saw her iridescent smile and those sharp blue eyes that challenged and seduced him at once, he'd have a hard time holding back.

He prayed for willpower as he knocked.

The apartment door swung open and his raven-haired goddess stood before him in a gray sweater that hung off one shoulder, revealing a black bra strap with purple skulls on it, a black miniskirt with tiny white diamonds sewn into the hem, knee-high boots, and passion brimming in her smoky eyes. *Holy fucking hell.*

Restraint. *Gone.*

He hauled her against him, breathing too hard, holding her too tight, and hating himself for it. *"Please* tell me to kiss you."

She narrowed her baby blues, pushing her hands into his hair, unraveling him with the possessive touch. "Stop talking and kiss me."

Hearing the desire in her voice set his body on fire. He crushed his mouth to hers, and she returned his efforts with reckless abandon, tugging his hair to the point of pain that pierced his skull and headed south. She went up on her toes, pressing her soft curves against him and making him hard as stone. Desire, lust, and greed wound together, coiling inside him like the devil, urging him on. One hand pressed flat against her back; the other still clutched the flowers. He should try not to crush them, but right that second he didn't give a damn about the flowers, or anything else other than finally—*God, finally*—having Crystal in his arms.

Fuck. He needed to slow down.

But how could he *ever* stop kissing her? She felt too good, tasted too sweet.

A tiny *meow* slipped through the war raging in his mind, and he felt Harley's tiny claws climbing up his jeans, reminding him they were still on the landing outside her apartment.

Crystal whimpered as he reluctantly broke away and scooped up the cockblocking kitty. He reclaimed his girl with an arm around her, keeping her close, and whispered, "I'm sorry."

CRYSTAL TRIED TO pull her lust-addled head together. She'd thought about Bear all day, and having Harley with her had only made her miss him more. Remembering his kisses, the sweet things he'd said, and receiving his thoughtful texts throughout the afternoon had made her even more anxious to see him.

"I hope you're referring to *stopping* and not the kiss itself, because I wanted that kiss," she assured him. "You can make it up to me later."

He chuckled, but she couldn't miss the relief washing over him. She didn't want him to worry, but she loved that he did.

"We don't want our little girl to go downstairs and get lost." As they walked into the apartment, her heart melting at his use of "our," he added, "Define *later*."

God, that pushy side was so *Bear*! She loved it! "That's to be determined."

She was a little surprised that even after all she'd revealed, and knowing she wasn't ready to jump in the sack, snarky, sexy comments still rolled off her tongue easily. She'd worried that the changes she was experiencing as she opened up to him might alter her personality, and she'd reinvented herself so many times, she wasn't entirely sure what her real personality was anymore. Maybe her snarkiness was part of the real her after all. She smiled with the thought, because despite going from blond hair to jet-black and having to adopt a new name, persona, and fake dating history, she thought she was a pretty cool chick.

He pressed a kiss to the top of Harley's head, making Crystal's insides melt a little more. He was wearing the leather vest with the Dark Knights emblem on the back she'd seen him wear often, but tonight it made him look even more badass. Or maybe that was just because she was finally allowing herself to really, truly see *all* of Bear instead of keeping him at arm's length. She'd even changed his contact name in her phone from *Him* to *Bear*, which felt really good.

She closed the door behind them and noticed he was holding a gorgeous bouquet of orchids. There must have been at least a dozen in varying colors. Awestruck, she said, "Biker boy, did you bring me *flowers?*"

He eyed the bouquet with a playful expression. "These were for Harley, but I guess you can have them." He set Harley on the couch. The kitty looked up at them with sad eyes.

"She knows you just gave away her flowers," Crystal teased. He handed her the flowers, and she inhaled their beautiful scent. Telling him about what had happened had brought out a softer side of both of them. She was surprised by how much she liked it, but her mounting emotions made her worry about how she'd come across. Too girly? Too weak? She went with what was comfortable and familiar, a tease.

"I've never been given flowers. Does this mean we're going *steady?* Boyfriend and girlfriend—"

"It means you're my *woman.*" He hauled her against him again hard enough that their chests bumped, making her laugh at his possessiveness. "Now you have to wear a choker with '*Property of Bear Whiskey*' printed on it."

"In your dreams." She sat on the couch taking a closer look at the flowers, and he sank down beside her. "These really are gorgeous. Thank you."

"How about a choker that says, *Bear's?*"

She laughed. "How about I admit that I'm your girlfriend and you know it *here.*" She touched his chest over his heart. "Can that be enough for a possessive guy like you?"

"Babe, after all this time, I think I deserve the choker. But hell, I'll take it."

He leaned in for a kiss, and she couldn't help but think he deserved a Boyfriend of the Year Award. He'd taken that role before she'd allowed him to, and yes, he was pushy, but he was also protective, and loving, and many more things that had kept her riveted by him for so long. Thank goodness he'd somehow known they were right for each other and had refused to give up. She wouldn't wear a choker, but she was proud to be *willingly* on his arm from now on.

She smelled the beautiful bouquet again. "I didn't even know orchids came in all these colors."

He draped an arm over her shoulder. "Neither did I, and honestly, I had no idea these were orchids. By the way, they're safe for cockblocker over there. I asked."

She laughed. "We are *not* calling her that."

"Maybe not out loud." He whispered, "I love her, but she is one."

Smiling, he pressed his lips to hers. "I wanted to get you something special." He took the bouquet from her and pointed to one of the flowers.

"These gorgeous babes are still finding their way. They're outgrowing their innocent yellow base, striking out on their own with the orange and dark red spots. They look tough, but a little unsure. Those say '*Chrissy*' all over them. The little girl whose life was turned upside down and forced to grow up too soon in a harsher world than she deserved."

Chrissy. He had listened to every word she'd said. She reached for Harley, trying to distract herself from the unexpected rush of emotions. She'd never stood a chance of resisting him. He might be cocky and possessive, but he was equally tender and loving, funny and sweet, and she couldn't believe that after all she'd been through,

Bear was turning out to be the man she'd thought he was, and so much more.

He held her tighter, pressing a kiss to the side of her head.

He pointed to the pink and white flowers. "These delicate ladies?" he said in a voice so full of love she wanted to wrap it around her and snuggle inside it. "They were so smart, they knew how to blend in and fly under the radar. Look at them, so feminine and strong. They blow me away. *Chrystina.*"

"And these pretty little gals are bold and captivating." He touched one of the blue and purple orchids. "They say, 'Don't fuck with me. I might be poisonous, but I'm too tempting to resist.'"

He paused long enough for her to forget how to breathe.

"Like you. *Crystal.*"

She pressed her lips together to keep her emotions from spilling out, but when he guided her face toward his with a gentle press of his finger beneath her chin, his serious gaze held her captive, and her eyes teared up.

"They say orchids are symbols of love and affection," he said softly. "And the harder they are to find, the more love and affection they hold. When you put all these magnificent beauties together, you get the most unique flower on earth."

He was looking at her as if he could see her innermost thoughts, and everything around them faded away. He was all she could see, smell, *hear.* When he took her hand in his, a familiar current traveled up her arm. Could it be possible to just live in this moment forever?

"Some people might see those bold colors and think they're too much," he said, bringing her back to earth. "They might see the dainty pink and white as too soft, or the others and think they're too rough. But when I see them. When I see *you.* I see the woman who stopped me cold the first time I saw her. And when you opened that incredibly sexy, snarky, and often too-adorable-for-words mouth of yours, I knew I was in big trouble."

For a long moment she didn't move, didn't breathe, didn't think, just sat beside him, numb from the honesty written all over his face. She didn't know how to handle this, and she turned away, overwhelmed and embarrassed by the feelings stacking up inside her. "I think I'm allergic to those saccharine lines."

He drew her face toward his again. "Don't do that."

"Move?" She hated herself for being snarky. She hadn't planned on reinventing herself ever again, but there was no denying the changes taking place inside her. She'd been hiding from herself, from the truth, from being judged, for so long, that the warmth and love he gave her made her feel vulnerable, and she didn't know how to handle it.

"Don't *deflect*." His tone was pure control, telling her what to do, not suggesting.

Pure instinct made her scoff, and just as quickly, she regretted it. This wasn't a reinvention born of fear or necessity. She wasn't in survival mode. She wasn't in any mode at all, and that was the most incredible feeling in the world. But it was also frightening, because she wasn't sure who she was anymore. But when she looked at Bear, she wanted to find out. *Desperately*.

"I'm sorry. It's—"

"Habit?" He lifted Harley from her lap and took her hand in his. "I get that. But if we're going to be together—and we are, so don't even pretend anything else is an option—I'm going to say what I feel. If I have to hold back my physical display of affection, my emotions have to come out in some way."

"So, that scorching-hot kiss was holding back? Holy shit, Bear. Now I'm building you up in my mind to epic proportions you can never live up to."

His eyes smoldered. "Wanna bet?"

She didn't want to bet; she wanted to find out. "Is this a ploy? I have to endure these types of embarrassing, in-my-face compliments or sleep with you? And when we sleep together, what then? The sweet stuff stops? Like a catch twenty-two?"

He laughed. "What goes on in that beautiful mind of yours?"

"You don't want to know. Trusting is a little hard, even when I don't want it to be." She pushed to her feet, her heart beating a mile a minute. "I'm going to put these in water."

He followed her into the kitchen. "You're wrong, Crystal. I want to know what you're thinking about and what you feel. I want to know everything about you."

He stood behind her as she filled a vase with water, and his arms snaked around her belly. He was gentle and comforting, wiping away the fear of the unknown.

But as he lowered his mouth beside her ear and whispered, "Talk to me, baby," the desire climbing up her limbs created anxiety all its own.

She set the vase on the counter and leaned her head back against his chest.

"I'm not used to hearing those things, and I don't know how to trust them. But I trust *you*. And the hardest part of all of this is that I'm not a weak person, and not knowing how to handle this makes me feel like I am. And that's frustrating, because what I really want to do is kiss you. I want to turn around and have you lift me up onto this counter and kiss me until I can't see straight like they do in movies. I want to wrap my legs around your waist without having to worry about if you're worried about me, or if *I'm* worried about me."

She turned around, her pulse racing, and said, "I just want to go with what I feel and stop thinking, and maybe that will help me accept the rest."

In the next second she was sitting on the counter, Bear's wide hips between her legs, his mouth swooping down over hers. The first touch of their lips was like jumping off a waterfall, and then she was soaring through the air. Her arms and legs circled him, embracing her freedom, her passion, her affection for the incredible man who was possessing more of her by the second. His hands moved like wind over her back, into her hair, down her arms, coming to rest on her hips. She felt his resistance, and she fell harder for him for holding back.

She grabbed his ass, letting him know she wasn't afraid, and *thank God*, he slid his hands to her butt and did the same, bringing their bodies together. She was barely breathing into their kisses, lost in the pleasure of allowing herself to feel their heat—and enjoy it. Damn, did she enjoy it. *I'm not broken.* A rush of titillating energy whooshed through her, like nothing she'd ever experienced. Not even in their kisses. She was breaking free. Really, truly allowing herself to leave the past behind. The realization slammed into her, and she drew back from the kiss, panting and smiling and laughing like a crazy person.

She was crazy. Crazy for Bear Whiskey.

"I want to kiss you forever" rushed from her lungs.

She grabbed his head, plastering her mouth to his again, and felt him smiling into their kiss. He lifted her off the counter, never breaking their connection as he took a few steps, slowing to deepen the kiss. Her back met the wall with a *thunk*, and lust spiked up her spine. Her eyes flew open, and he drew back so fast it filled her up with him even more.

"I liked it," she assured him, feeling as shocked as he looked. "That was intense and freaking *hot*. Like a shot of . . . *Whiskey*. I want more Whiskey, please."

The gratified smile staring back at her reached all the way up to his eyes, turning to liquid fire as he took her in another incredible kiss. He carried her through the living room and sank down on the couch with her knees straddling him. She'd expected him to lay her down, to dominate her without thinking, but she realized he was giving her an escape. Giving her control. And in doing so, it made her want to *give up* control.

He pushed his hands into her hair, his mouth moving along her jaw, to the tender spot beneath her ear. "Sweet as sugar," he whispered.

In the next moment he was devouring her neck, sending shivers of lust skittering through her entire body. She closed her eyes, reveling in the illicit pleasures she'd wanted for so long. Inhaling the heady scents of leather and potent *male*, she focused on the feel of his tongue, his lips pressing hard against her skin, the scintillating graze of his teeth. He was hard beneath her, and when his mouth moved along her bare shoulder, her nipples pebbled tighter, burning with anticipation.

Eyes still closed, she followed the length of his arm down to his hand and brought it to her breast, whispering, "Touch me."

He claimed her in another passionate kiss as he caressed her, teasing the sensitive peaks through her shirt. Tingling heat seared down the center of her body, pooling between her legs and drawing a long, low moan from her lungs. She moved his hand beneath her shirt, earning a groan from Bear that obliterated all her thoughts. His big, rough hand covered her breast, and she arched into him, wanting to feel his desire everywhere. He kissed her harder, rocking beneath her to the same rhythm she ground her hips, and when he took her nipple between his fingers and thumb, lust streaked all the way to the tips of her fingers and toes.

"Oh God that feels *good.*" She writhed against him, resting her forehead on his and using his shoulders for leverage.

He gathered her hair in his hand and sealed his mouth over her neck, sucking and kissing and driving her out of her mind. She'd dreamed of this—of *him*—but her dreams hadn't come close to how incredible he felt. He slanted his mouth over hers again, urgent and ravenous, thrusting his tongue to the same pulse as his hips rose beneath her. When he squeezed her nipple, she couldn't stop the stream of moaning, mewing noises coming from somewhere deep inside her. He caught her lower lip between his teeth and gave it a gentle tug.

"Ohgod" slipped out. "Again," she pleaded.

He did it again, and then dipped his head, reclaiming her neck in an act of divine torture. She panted, caught up in the overwhelming sensations coursing through her. His hand dropped from her hair to the top of her ass, applying more pressure to their exquisite friction. *Yes, yes, yes.* She rocked harder and lowered her mouth to his neck, getting her first taste of his salty skin. She was powerless to resist her desires as she licked and sucked, earning another hungry groan from Bear, and several uttered curses.

"I need my mouth on you, baby. But—"

No buts. Not now. Not ever. Not with you. "Yes. Yes."

She couldn't lift her shirt and unhook the front clasp on her bra fast enough. She guided his mouth to her breast and held him there, feeling triumphant in the depths of her trust in him. *This* was what she'd longed for. The ability to let go and the courage to allow herself to *feel* her desires, to *experience* the pent-up passion she'd been running from all these months. *This* was right.

His mouth ignited her entire body with each hard suck. She held on for dear life as bolts of pleasure tore through her. She rode him hard, the clothing between them amping up her desire. When he moaned, it vibrated through her chest, making her hotter, wetter, *greedier*. She was utterly lost in him, and she never wanted to be found. She wanted to live in this magical haven of Bear forever.

Heat climbed up her limbs, burrowing into her chest, burning deeper and deeper. Pressure mounted at the juncture of her thighs, taking her up, up, *up*. She hung on the edge of a cliff, barely breathing, her entire body throbbing, on the verge of exploding, and then he tightened his hold, possessing her so completely, she spiraled over the edge, free-falling into a world of *Bear*.

CHAPTER EIGHT

CRYSTAL COLLAPSED AGAINST Bear, whispering, "Wow, wow, *wow.*"

Bear held her tight, kissing her cheek as her heart calmed. "I've got you, baby." Watching her come, feeling her surrender to their passion, was so fucking hot he'd nearly lost it.

"That was amazing. *Intense.* How did you do that without . . . ?" She rested her cheek on his shoulder. "We're definitely doing that again."

"And again and again," he promised. "But you don't have to build me up, babe. It'll be even better as we get closer."

She mouthed, *Better?* Her eyes widened, and understanding dawned on him.

"Have you never . . . ?"

She shook her head, embarrassment pinking up her cheeks.

He kissed her again, tender and sweet, and hopefully reassuring. "Not even . . . *self*-pleasured?" he asked gently.

"God, this is so embarrassing. No, I haven't *flicked the bean*, and not because I'm screwed up. I've had sex before, in college, but it was never particularly enjoyable. And even though I know pleasurable things are possible, I just never wanted to try to do that by myself. And then I met you, and I thought about you so much, I *wanted* to try, but . . . Let's just say that every time I thought about it, like *really* thought about going there, I worried I wouldn't be able to, *you know.*

And I didn't want another bad thing associated with that part of my body. So I never tried."

"Oh, baby." He hugged her. "I promise we'll make up for all the orgasms you've missed."

She laughed. "You're *so* generous. I've missed *a lot*. Like, hours and hours' worth." She wiggled her bottom.

"Let's not do *that* right now." He lifted her off his lap, drinking in the curious and sultry look in her eyes. The combination made him want her to continue moving her fine body all over him, but he already felt like a volcano ready to erupt, and it would be torturous to have to stop again.

"Jesus, babe. Don't look at me like that." He rose to his feet, adjusting his painful erection.

She pushed from the couch and wound her arms around his waist. "I'm sorry. I'm not ready to, *you know*, but I can offer you a fashion magazine and the privacy of my bathroom to relieve that pressure."

"Christ," he uttered. "You're going to be the death of me, woman."

"I was being serious. It's not like I have recent experience to draw from. I've never even had a man in my apartment. I don't know what couples do at times like this, but I feel bad leaving you all revved up with no finish line in sight after the way you set my world on fire."

He kissed her again. "Baby, *you* don't have to do anything about it. I'm not an animal."

"Your name suggests otherwise."

He laughed softly. "I've waited eight months, and I'll wait eight more, or a *hundred* more, if that's what it takes for you to be ready."

She glanced at the bulge in his pants, brow wrinkled. "You sure you don't want that magazine?"

He slapped her ass.

"What?" She laughed. "I would offer to help, but I don't trust myself."

He ground his teeth together. "Baby, do *not* put images like that in my head, or I'll never calm down."

"Don't get too excited. I've never . . ." She made a circle with her hand and moved it like she was jerking him off.

"Great. Another image I'll never be able to forget."

Someone banged on the door.

"Saved by the knock. Expecting someone?" He untucked his shirt to cover his arousal as he headed for the door.

"No."

He answered the door and found a young guy holding a pizza box.

"Finally, dude. I was here fifteen minutes ago, but no one answered."

"Shoot." Crystal grabbed her purse from the table by the door and began digging around in it. "I forgot I ordered pizza for us before you got here."

"No worries, babe." He whipped out his wallet and paid the guy. "Sorry for the wait. Thanks for bringing it by again."

He closed the door and wrapped an arm around Crystal. "That was thoughtful, but I would have taken you out for dinner."

"I live off of pizza and Chinese. Oh, and I can burn toast, but that's about it."

He cocked a brow. "Seriously?"

"Don't judge." She went into the kitchen and grabbed two plates from a cabinet.

He made a mental note to cook her an amazing dinner sometime soon and headed for the dining room.

"Besides, this pizza rocks," she said as she came to his side. "You won't find room to eat in there."

"I see that." He set the pizza on a chair and stepped into the room.

Three long tables were lined up beneath the windows, covered by layers of colorful fabric with sketches strewn across them. Several more dolls that her father had made were on the windowsill. His chest constricted. Tins of buttons, spools of thread, and other sewing supplies littered every surface. In the corner of the room, a mannequin wore a black-and-white polka-dot skirt; a piece of bright pink fabric was draped over its shoulder. Hand-drawn fashion designs and swatches of fabric, along with pictures of costumes and clothing torn out of magazines and newspapers, were tacked to a large corkboard. Across the room, a shirt with one sleeve, a skirt with several pins securing lace to the hemline, and other pieces of clothing in various stages of design hung from a metal rack beside a sewing machine. He loved her colorful, creative chaos.

"It looks like something exploded in here."

"An explosion of my mind, maybe." She opened the pizza box. "Everyone needs a place to disappear. This is mine." She put a slice of pizza on each plate and handed him one.

"My girl has more secrets, and I want to know them all." He leaned in for a kiss and forced himself to focus on the glimpse into her world she was offering. "I knew you were making costumes, but I had no idea you were into designing clothes. Are these all yours?" He studied the sketches pinned to the corkboard while he ate.

"Mm-hm. I studied design in school. I *tinker*. I design, redesign, try to make a few things each year." She took a bite of her pizza.

"You're incredibly talented." He looked at the sketches spread across the tables, amazed at the complexity of the designs. "You and Gemma are going to do this all on your own? That's awesome."

"We're going to make a few and see if they sell. If they do, then we'll try to recruit a few design students to help."

"Is that what you'd like to do eventually? Fashion design?"

She shrugged. "I love working with Gemma, and if we can pull off selling our own costumes, that'll be enough for now. I'm not ready to go back to school, and I'd need to in order to really make a name in fashion design, not to mention interning in New York City and all of that. None of which I have any real interest in. Maybe someday that'll change, but right now I'm happy."

He pointed to a sketch on the sewing table, recognizing the diamond print. "Is that the skirt you have on?"

"Yes." She took another bite of her pizza. "I finished it a few weeks ago. Check this out." She finished her slice of pizza and lifted a big roll of fabric, pointing to the end of the cardboard that it was wound around. "This is called a *bolt* of fabric. You should know that in case you decide to frequent fabric stores to feed your satin and lace addiction."

"I think you mean my *Crystal* addiction." He leaned closer to read the tag on the bolt—*Black Bear*—and laughed.

"I couldn't resist," she said with a sexy smile. "I found it three months ago, and I had to buy all of it."

"Three months ago? You really were into me all this time."

She rolled her eyes. "You have no idea . . ."

He slipped an arm around her waist, holding her close. "See? Even the fabric gods want us to be together." He pressed his lips to hers. The taste of pizza and lust twined together with the unique taste of Crystal. "Damn, sugar. I'm never going to get enough of you."

"Good." She went up on her toes, pressing a kiss to the center of his lips. "Then we have a lot in common."

"That's a far cry from, 'I'm not your sugar.' You sure you want to claim me so blatantly? Because I might just enact a no-take-backs rule."

"As if I ever had a choice about claiming you?" A grin lifted her lips. "You made it impossible for me to think about anything *but* you."

"Babe, you are all I've thought about for so long, I can't remember what I thought about before you."

"That's a pretty awesome line."

"I'm a pretty awesome guy. See? I have even more in common with my kick-ass girl."

She laughed.

"We actually do have a lot in common," he said more seriously. "You design clothes. I design bikes."

"Get outta town." Surprise lifted her brows.

"Sorry, babe, but I'm in this town to stay. In fact, you might have trouble getting me to leave this apartment."

"You wish." The heated look in her eyes disputed her words. "How have I known you this long and not known that you design bikes?" She served them each another slice of pizza and carried the box into the living room.

"I could say the same about you designing clothes."

"I'm serious. That's huge. I mean, I design clothes in the privacy of my dining room. No one knows about it but Gemma and Dixie. But motorcycles? That's huge."

"It's just a hobby. I do it in my garage at home."

"What's stopping you from doing it as more than a hobby?"

"I need time to invest into the process to do it right, and I can't walk away from my family's businesses."

"But designing and building motorcycles? That's not something just anyone can do. I'm sure they'd understand if you wanted to break out on your own. Bones is a doctor, and Bullet went into the military."

He cleared his throat to try to push past the discomfort that came with this conversation. "I have an offer from Silver-Stone Cycles to work with them on a part-time basis designing bikes."

"*The* Silver-Stone Cycles? They're as big as Harley-Davidson. That would be amazing."

Amazing was right, but earth would have to shift to make that pipe dream become a reality.

"Are you going to take it?"

The excitement in her voice made him want to say he was, but he wasn't there yet.

"There's a lot to consider." He didn't want to get sidetracked with a long conversation about his dilemma right now, so he tried to shift the focus away from him. "How do you know about Silver-Stone Cycles?"

She teasingly wiggled her shoulders. "A girl has got to do something on weekend nights when she's pretending to live a tawdry life of hookups with hot bikers. I watch *Chop Shop* and *Sons of Anarchy*, and—"

He laughed. "I think you just got ten times sexier."

"All in the name of research. I love tattoos and scruffy beards and leather. *Mm, leather.* And seeing you on your bike? That's the best foreplay *ever.*"

"I'll remember that," he said as they sat on the couch. "And I'll remember *not* to bring you by the bar when the guys are there."

"You're the only biker boy I want. I started watching because I needed to learn the jargon, but the eye candy isn't bad." She said *eye candy* with a taunting tone.

He set their plates on the coffee table and tickled her ribs, making her squeal with laughter. "No more eye candy."

"You don't *own* me," she said between laughs. "*Eye candy, eye candy, eye candy.*"

He tickled her again, and she squealed louder.

"Okay, okay, okay," she panted out. "Only *Bear* candy."

His mouth came down over her laughing lips, taking her in a long, sensual kiss that turned those sweet laughs into lusty moans.

Harley climbed up Bear's leg, and he reluctantly pulled away to scoop her up and kiss her tiny pink nose. "Hey, little CB."

"You are *not* calling her that!" Crystal reached for Harley.

He held the kitty farther away. Crystal leaned across his lap trying to get her, and he snaked an arm around her middle and kissed her neck. "Now, that's more like it." He kissed a path along her shoulder. "*Mm-mm*. Sweet as sugar."

She laughed. "And you're wicked as a Cajun spice."

"Baby, you haven't *seen* wicked yet." He waggled his brows, cuddling the kitty. "I'm outnumbered by females. I should have gotten you a tomcat."

"I have one by the name of *Bear*." She bumped him with her shoulder and grabbed her pizza.

"I am not a tomcat anymore." He didn't regret his past experiences, but he needed her to know she was the only woman he wanted.

She tucked her feet beneath her. Her skirt inched up her thighs and his gaze followed.

"You're still a tomcat, even if I'm your only prey. I bet the guys in your big, bad motorcycle club would give you shit about being with only one woman."

"That's not how it works, babe."

"Then how *does* it work?"

"Depends who you talk to, and it's not just club guys. They're regular guys. Some are single; some have girlfriends or families. Guys are different. Some are all about sleeping around, and some are all about ownership, or possessing their women, while others—"

"Sounds like my guy," she mumbled.

"*No*, it doesn't. I might be possessive and protective *of* you, but I don't think I *own* you."

"Then you won't sell me to the highest bidder?" Her smile told him she was kidding.

"Not unless you misbehave." He set Harley on her lap. She'd known him and his siblings long enough to understand that their club was comprised of people who shared an interest in motorcycles and biker culture, as opposed to a motorcycle gang, whose members were typically known for engaging in illegal activities.

"There's no difference between going out with me and going out with a guy who's not in a motorcycle club except I'm better looking, tougher, smarter, and a million times hotter in bed."

"My biker boy is very arrogant, isn't he?" she whispered to Harley.

He laughed. "You're a strong woman, Crystal, and I'd imagine you're not going to like some things about how the club works." That brought serious eyes up to his.

"Dixie told me that she's not allowed to be a member, so you're not going to shock me with the no-women-allowed thing."

Relief swept through him. *Thanks, Dix.* "I know it sounds chauvinistic, but I respect the reasons behind what started as tradition and lives on as brotherhood among members. Think of it like a boys' club. Once you add women into the mix, romances between members start, breakups happen, and the brotherhood becomes divided."

"I love that *brotherhood*. The way you and your brothers are there for Tru and Gemma and the kids is amazing. And what you did for that little boy the other night? That's what real heroes are made of."

"No, sugar. That's what *humanity* should be made of." He was thrilled that after all these months she was finally admitting her feelings toward him instead of doling out snarky comments. "My father taught us well in that regard. I just wish there was more equity where Dixie is concerned."

"Where *does* Dixie fit in? She doesn't seem to mind the boys'-club mentality of the Dark Knights, or at least she doesn't let on that she does."

"Unfortunately, Dixie is stuck in the 'princess' slot in our father's old-school head."

Crystal laughed. "'Princess'? Your sister is *no* princess. She's the toughest woman I've ever met in my life. She doesn't take shit from anyone."

"I don't mean 'princess' as in she thinks she's a princess. She's the president of the club's daughter. She's relative *gold*. No one messes with the president's family. Especially the women. And my father adores her, but he's so frigging old-school that he holds her back. She works as hard as me and my brothers but has no say in any of the bigger business decisions. I respect my father, but that doesn't mean I agree with everything he does."

"But she runs your shop and she works at the bar. How is she held back? She loves working there."

"She's done great things for our shop because *I* put her in that position against my father's wishes. I gave her a shot and she proved herself. But her talents are wasted working at the shop and waitressing at the bar. If ever there was a person who should be *running* a business, it's Dix. If he let her take charge of the expansion, she could do great things. Asking me to do it with Dixie helping out behind the scenes is a slight to her."

Her eyes filled with challenge. "Then what are you going to do about it, Mr. I'll-Make-You-Want-Me Whiskey?"

"It doesn't work that way. It's all about respect, baby, and I respect the hell out of my father."

"And what about Dixie?"

Therein lay the issue. What about Dixie?

CRYSTAL SAW BEAR'S walls go up the minute he started talking about his family. She knew his brothers and Dixie well, but she only knew his parents in passing. She was a little worried now that she knew his father's true feelings about a woman's place in the world. She wasn't exactly good at biting her tongue.

"Let's get out of here." She pushed to her feet and carried the pizza box and her plate into the kitchen to wrap up the leftovers. Bear followed her in.

"Where to, gorgeous?"

She wound her arms around his waist and said, "Whispers."

Whispers was one of the busiest nightclubs in Peaceful Harbor. They'd been dealing with such heavy emotions the last few days, she hoped Whispers would be just the distraction they needed to get out of their heads for a little while.

He groaned, kissed the kitten's head, and set her down beside her food dish. "How about Whiskey Bro's instead?"

"If we go to Whiskey's, you'll stay in that place in your head that's got your face pinched tight." She slid a finger into the waist of his jeans. "I want to dance in your arms with no thoughts of anything other than you. And maybe that incredible feeling you gave me earlier."

His eyes darkened, and he grabbed her butt.

She guided his hands up to her waist. "Take me dancing, biker boy."

"You're not sitting on my bike in that skirt unless you want to witness me killing every man who takes an eyeful."

"Seriously? All my goodies will be pressed up against you. Nobody can see anything. But I'll change to calm your jealousy. Give me a sec."

She headed for her bedroom, feeling the heat of his stare on her back and loving it. She changed into a pair of black leather shorts she knew he'd love and took an extra minute to fix her hair and makeup and brush her teeth.

She strutted into the living room anticipating a hungry look in his eyes, but nothing could have prepared her for the naughty thoughts running through her mind when she found him standing with his back to her. His dark jeans clung to his powerful hips and stretched across muscular hamstrings. He'd tucked in his shirt, accentuating his broad shoulders and trim waist. She licked her lips as she approached and wrapped her arms around his middle, loving the way she was able to embrace those feelings.

He turned, a sinful grin lifting his lips, and her mind went straight to the gutter, racing through a maze of mattress dances. Their earlier make-out session had opened some sort of vortex to her inner vixen. Images of Bear in her bed flew through her mind at breakneck speed. *Gulp.* She wasn't ready for that yet. Was she?

She wanted to be.

She forced herself to take a step back and gain control of her runaway hormones. Motioning toward her shorts, she said, "Better?"

"Jesus, baby. You are the sexiest thing I've ever seen."

He leaned in for another kiss.

"*Dancing*," she said, a little dazed, and handed him her keys. "Pocket?"

He chuckled and pocketed her keys as they headed for the door.

The wind whipped over Crystal's thighs, and Bear's abs flexed beneath her hands as they rode down to Whispers. She felt liberated, like so many of the tethers that had bound her to her past had been severed. If she could only figure out how to handle the one tie that was becoming more strained the longer she held on to her secret. *Telling Gemma.*

CHAPTER NINE

IT HAD BEEN a long time since Bear had been in a trendy nightclub like Whispers, where sexual tension ran as freely as beer through a tap. He tightened his hold on Crystal, searching the face of every man as they weaved through the crowd and wondering if they were the asshole who had attacked her. He knew he had to let it go, but he could be anywhere. How had she moved past it when he fought the urge to find the fucker and kill him every minute?

Her fingers pressed into his side, bringing him back to the moment.

Women wearing too much makeup slithered against testosterone-laden men, bumping and grinding, groping and open-mouth kissing. Crystal pushed out from beneath his arm and turned to face him. Taking his hand, she walked backward, pulling him deeper into the crowd with a predatory stare that could get an impotent man hard. Her shoulders swayed to the beat as the sea of people parted for her, making Bear wonder if she frequented the club regularly. Jealousy clawed up his spine. She was sexy as sin in those tight shorts, which had nearly made him cream his pants, and the thought of her dancing with any other guy made his blood boil.

She stopped in the center of the dance floor, purple lights misting over her gorgeous face as she pulled him closer. Thigh to thigh, chest to chin, she moved with the fluidity of an asp and the sensual prowess of a panther in heat. Her hands slid beneath his vest, up his chest, and then over her head in a sensual dance. Her long, graceful fingers flexed with the beat as her hips rocked against him. Heat slicked down his torso, bringing the animal in his pants to the gate.

Holy hell. He scanned the crowd, catching several guys watching her erotic show, and gave them a back-off glare.

Bear wasn't a dancer, and at six three, with his leather vest and tattoos, he stood out among the upscale crowd. He'd be damned if he would be outdone by some nitwit in a button-down shirt. Focusing on Crystal, he matched her rhythm. His hands moved possessively around her, drawn in to her seductive dance. She shifted, bringing his thigh between her legs, heightening the sexual tension that had been simmering between them all evening. She wound her arms around his neck, and he lowered his mouth to hers, sinking into the kiss, devouring her sweetness.

They danced to every song, kissing and groping, the stress of their confessions pushed away. A dusky backdrop to their desires drumming with a beat all their own. Time passed in a blur of deep, sensual kisses, the oppressive heat, making their dirty dancing feel even more libidinous. He turned her in his arms, grinding against her ass, his hands moving down her ribs, over her hips, and coming to rest over her belly as he kissed her neck. Her skin was slick, salty. *Delicious.* She ground against his erection, her hands gripping the backs of his thighs. She turned her face, capturing his mouth with hers over her shoulder and driving him out of his fucking mind. He spun her in his arms, crushing her soft body against his hard frame.

He was lost in their heightened state of arousal. He buried his hand in her hair, cupping the base of her skull and angling her mouth so he could intensify their kisses. Somewhere beneath the lust, beneath the greediness pushing his hips harder against her, thrusting his tongue deeper, came a foggy warning.

He drew back, giving heed to the caution he needed to remember. Her dark eyes held him captive, full of disappointment and morphing quickly to a look of fierce determination. The music came into focus, and he recognized the provocative beat of "Way Down We Go" by Kaleo. Sensual beats climbed slowly, mounting to explosive crescendos, then dialing down to provocative vibrations before escalating again to a dominating thrum of electricity.

Crystal guided his hands tighter around her waist, rubbing her gorgeous body against him and wreaking havoc with his control.

She mouthed, *Don't let go*, and arched back, her arms falling limply to her sides, her shoulders swaying like branches in the wind. If he let go, she would fall, and he knew it was another show of trust.

CRYSTAL GAVE HERSELF over to the adrenaline coursing through her veins, the desire rising through her core. Bear's penetrating gaze heated up every inch of her, from her face to the juncture of their bodies, where his strong hands kept her anchored against him. He'd cast such threatening glares at the other men on the dance floor, she'd wondered if he'd loosen up enough to dance, but her attempt at drawing his *complete* attention had worked.

She'd begun letting the music take her over like this when she was alone at night in her apartment after she'd first moved back to Peaceful Harbor. The nights when she was so restless nothing would quiet her ghosts. She'd come to Whispers a few times with Gemma before Gemma and Tru had gotten together, but she'd never danced like this with a man. Now, as pieces of herself she'd thought she'd lost long ago sparked to life, she *needed* this dark, erotic release. It was another step in finding herself, trusting herself. And she knew she was safe to explore that realm with Bear.

She grabbed hold of his leather vest, feeling his power in the press of his hands on her back, soaking in his strength as she pulled herself upright. Led by the auditory seduction, their bodies came together like the sun melted into the horizon. The music faded to a whisper, the nearly silent beat pulsing beneath her skin. Bear's eyes blazed with desire.

"Kiss me again." She drew his mouth to hers, anticipating the dominant thrum of the chorus.

He kissed her with the force of rolling thunder. She returned his efforts with fervor, her body vibrating in memory of what they'd done earlier. Her hands moved down his biceps, feeling the ridges of his muscles as he tightened his grip on her.

When the song ended and their mouths parted, she said, "I want to keep kissing you." Her confession came unbidden, but it was as true as true could be.

"Not here." His rough voice thrilled her.

His arm circled her waist, holding her so tightly she thought he'd like to unzip his skin and tuck her inside. He plowed through the crowd, straight out the doors. Cool air rushed over her heated skin, bringing rise to goose bumps. When they stepped out of the dome of light thrown from the club, Bear hauled her against him, taking her in one toe-curling kiss after another. They stumbled, kissing their way across the pavement.

"Where'd you learn to dance like that?" he asked.

"Taught myself. I needed a way to destress. Just kiss me."

And he did. Urgent and rough, then slow and deep, in an intoxicating rhythm that made her want, and want, and *want*. Their hands were all over each other at once, and when they reached his motorcycle, they both stopped and stared at it. Getting on the bike meant no more kissing. She wanted to kiss! She stole a glance at Bear and knew by his grimace that he was wrestling with the same conundrum.

He touched his lips to hers in a kiss so sweet her insides melted.

"I love *those* kisses, too."

"Sugar, I've got months of kisses with your name on them." He hugged her, kissing her until she was light-headed.

She grabbed his vest. "You need to stop."

He did. *Immediately.*

She banged her forehead on his chest, hating that she had a past that interfered on any level, but especially on *this* level. "Do you have to listen so well?"

"Damn right I do." He lifted her chin and gazed into her eyes with a serious expression.

"I love that you're careful, and I want you to be. But I *meant* I needed you to stop because I was so caught up in you my knees were going weak."

His lips curved up in appreciation. "Yeah?"

"Yes. And I hate that the sexiness of what I meant gets lost in the worry of what you think I need. I must not know how to send the right signals. But I'll figure it out."

"Trust me, babe. You're sending all the right signals."

A group of guys piled out of a car a few parking spots away, and Bear pulled her closer. "Come on, let's go back to your place, where I don't have to watch guys leer at my woman."

"For a guy who says he knows he doesn't own me, that's a very ownerish thing to say."

He helped her onto the bike, ignoring her taunt.

"How fast can you *safely* get us to my place?"

"Less than ten minutes. Why?"

"Because I want to kiss you!" She pulled him down for another kiss, and he straddled the bike, facing her, and proceeded to kiss her until every inch of her body went nearly numb. When he leaned in for another, she planted her palm on the center of his chest and shook her head.

"One more kiss like that and I'll fall off the bike."

"No kisses, then, but a massive vibrating beast beneath you." He winked, and gave her one last quick peck. "Hold on tight, sweet girl."

After getting their helmets on and resituating themselves, Bear reached behind them and hauled her forward, as he'd done the other night. The engine rumbled to life, and her girly parts threw a little party. She wrapped her arms around him, feeling the waist of his jeans beneath her fingers as he pulled out of the parking lot. Her mind was still on their kisses, and her body was completely engrossed in the vibration happening down below. She wondered if it was affecting him, too, and the longer they rode, the more curious she became. As he turned into the parking lot at her apartment complex, she let her hand drift south, over his zipper. The big bulge of denim was warm. *So* warm. She glanced in the mirror and could tell he was smiling.

He parked, and as she moved her hand, he placed his over it, squeezing lightly so she could feel *all* of him. She buried her face in his back, like a kid caught with a firecracker who hadn't thought about the repercussions of being discovered. She felt him grow bigger beneath her palm, and her pulse sprinted, but she didn't try to pull away. She liked this silent descent into naughtiness. She felt his fingers lace with hers and he moved her hand from between his legs. Removing his helmet, he turned toward her with a wolfish grin. For a beat they didn't speak; she wasn't even sure she breathed.

He took off her helmet—because she was frozen stiff from being caught feeling him up—and said, "Want to settle any other curiosities?"

"Um." *Yes, please.* "Shall I make you a list?"

He climbed from the bike and locked up the helmets. Then he repositioned her so she was sitting sideways on the seat. He stood between her legs and pulled her forward. The position alone made her heart race in the very best of ways. He cradled her face in his hands, bringing their mouths so close she prepared for a kiss. *A hot one.* Her lips parted, and she felt light-headed from the anticipation, but he just held her there, searching her eyes as if he was waiting for her to say something. What, she wasn't sure, because all she wanted to do was plaster her mouth to his again.

"Do I make you nervous? Standing like this?" he asked just above a whisper.

"Only because I'm waiting for you to kiss me and you're not doing it."

That earned another sinful smile. "Oh, I'm going to kiss you, baby. I'm going to kiss you until you can't remember ever asking me to. And then I'm going to keep kissing you, until you're so hot and bothered you can't think straight."

It was all she could do to stare at him, imagining those kisses.

"But first I'm going to spend another minute standing right here. Not kissing you."

"Because you like torturing me?"

"No, sugar. Because that curiosity you're feeling is so fucking sexy, and I want you to be even more curious." He licked his lips, and she salivated at the sight of the slickness he left behind.

"It's working," she admitted. "I'm *super* curious."

What felt like an hour later, but in reality was probably a minute, she rose from the bike, trying to get closer, and he lifted her off her feet with one arm around her waist and began walking toward the apartment.

"Put me down," she said, laughing.

He eased his grip, and she slid down his body, her toes touching the ground. He tugged her up again. They laughed and kissed all the way up the stairs to the landing, where he took her in his arms and backed her up against the door, kissing her so deeply she felt it all over. She grabbed his pocket, searching for the keys and desperately wanting to feel the hard heat between his legs. He drew back long enough to dig out the keys and unlock the door. They stumbled into the apartment, and he kicked the door closed behind them. She was vaguely aware of the sound of keys hitting the floor as they tumbled down to the couch.

He moved off of her, and she instantly missed the weight of him. She pulled him closer, and he angled his hips so they were lying side by side, her knee between his, his thigh over hers.

"Is this okay?" he asked between kisses.

"Better than," she panted out, pulling him in for another kiss. They kissed for a long time. Slow, loving strokes of their tongues turned to a dance of domination, then dialed back to sweet and tender. It was enough to drive her mad. She tugged at his shirt, and he gently held her hand.

"Tell me, baby."

"I want to feel your skin."

He shrugged off his vest, tossed it on the coffee table, and untucked his shirt from his jeans. "Off?" he asked.

Oh, how she loved that he asked. And how she hated it. It gave her time to pause, time to think, and she shook her head. "Just untucked for now."

The warmest expression washed over his face. He lifted his shirt around his waist and guided her hand beneath the soft cotton. That first touch should probably feel no different from touching his arm or his cheek, but there was nothing familiar about exploring this part of his body without the cover of fabric. His skin was softer than his cheek or arms or hands. *Warmer.* The muscles beneath were temptingly hard. Pushing her hand up his back, she felt his muscles bunch and flattened her palm between his shoulder blades. Her fingers ran over deep grooves in his skin, rough and patchy in places and slick and smooth in others.

"Scars," he said softly.

She'd heard stories about how he'd gotten his biker name. "Then it's true? Tru said you got your nickname because you wrestled a black bear?"

"Yeah, but I don't want to talk about that now."

She knew a thing or two about not wanting to talk about certain memories, and she let it go.

He lowered his mouth beside her ear and whispered, "I'm yours, baby. No pressure, no expectations. You touch me when you want to touch me. You're in total control. I want you to get used to being close to me without thinking it has to be sexual."

"What if I want it to be sexual?" she asked softly.

He nipped at her lower lip. "There's nothing wrong with wanting to touch someone you're attracted to. We'll be as sexual as you want to be."

"Kiss me, Bear."

He grinned. "You do like kissing me."

"It's like a snack, tiding me over until I'm ready for more."

"Snack, baby. Snack."

His kisses consumed her. His hands moved over her hips, down her thighs, then back up again. His fingers slid along the hem of her shorts in a hypnotizing rhythm. Her hips picked up the beat, and his matched it. As they kissed, their bodies shifting against each other, his chest came down over her, and she relaxed onto her back. He kept his body half off of her, half on. When his hand touched her waist, he drew back from the kiss, asking her silently for permission. She moved his hand beneath her shirt, holding his gaze.

He lifted his chest from hers, dipping his head to kiss her belly. Shivers of pleasure raced up her chest. He continued kissing, loving her stomach and ribs, moving higher, caressing her breasts, slowing long enough to gain her visual approval before unclasping her bra and shifting the cups to the side.

He pressed a kiss to one nipple and lifted his eyes to hers again. "If you want me to stop, just say so. You're in control of everything we do."

"Will you take your shirt off? I want to feel your skin on mine."

As he tugged it off and tossed it to the floor, she maneuvered out of her bra, leaving her shirt on. A trick she'd learned in the middle school locker room, when she was too modest to change in front of everyone. Her hands came down on his shoulders, which felt bigger and stronger now than they did clothed.

"Keep touching me," she said, earning a low chuckle as he dipped his head again, teasing and taunting her into a writhing, needy mess.

He shifted his body between her legs, palming her breasts with both hands and kissing the center of her belly. She closed her eyes, allowing herself to get carried away by the pleasures washing through her. His tongue moved around her belly button, dipping inside, then around and around again. He dragged it along her waist, and her hips rose off the cushions. He kissed his way up again, between her breasts, to the very tip of each one, where he lingered long enough to draw several panting moans from her lungs.

When his mouth came down over hers, she wiggled and writhed beneath him. He was being careful. She felt his restraint in his fingers curling around her hip. She shifted, so her legs weren't trapped, and unhooked the snap on her shorts.

"Baby," he whispered.

"I want you to touch me." She waited for fear or embarrassment, or *something* to stop her, but she was so full of Bear, there was no room for anything else. She'd wanted him for so long, and her body was giving her the green light. There was nothing holding her back any longer, and she wanted to revel in him, to experience what she'd been dreaming about without regret and without her past hanging like a noose around her neck.

He kissed her lovingly as his hand moved over her belly and slipped beneath her panties. Her insides clenched and heated at once as his thick fingers cupped her sex, as if he were waiting again for a final sign of approval. She angled her hips, so the tips of his fingers touched her wetness, and as he dipped them between her legs, he groaned. The pleasure-filled sound vibrated down her throat and wrapped around her heart. Without breaking their kiss, she wiggled out of her shorts and kicked them off, leaving her panties on. His thick fingers moved between her slick lips, making her tremble with need.

"Bear," she finally begged, eyes closed. "Please touch more of me."

"Look at me, sugar. I need to know you're okay."

She opened her eyes, and he held her gaze as he slid his fingers into her. The heat of his gaze, the naughtiness of staring into his eyes while he pleasured her, made what they were doing that much hotter. Her eyes fluttered as he moved over the magical spot that sent shocks of heat racing through her.

"Still with me, baby?"

She opened her legs wider in response, and he lowered his mouth to hers, kissing her as he loved her down below. He used his thumb on her most sensitive nerves, sending shocks of heat racing up her torso. Tingling began in her thighs, traveling up her core and down her limbs, curling her toes under. Her breathing became shallow, and her head tipped back. Even through closed lids, she felt his gaze searing into her, heightening the thrill of it all. His whiskers brushed over her cheek—another scintillating sensation.

"I'm yours, baby," he said in a rough voice. "Let go for me."

Then his mouth was on her neck, and his fingers moved quicker, his thumb pressed harder, and his arousal rocked against her thigh. When he brought his mouth to her breast, the first tantalizing suck brought her climax crashing down on her.

"Bear, Bear, *Bear!*" An avalanche of pleasure tore through her. She squeezed her thighs together, trapping his hand. "Kiss me, kiss me, kiss me."

And he did. Deep, passionate kisses that went on and on, carrying her through the very last pulse of her orgasm, and then he kissed her some more.

SWAMPED BY EMOTIONS too big to climb out from under, Bear focused on the brave and beautiful woman he adored lying in his arms. He held Crystal through the shuddering aftershocks of her climax, through her blissful exhalations, until she began drifting off to sleep. He pressed a kiss to her temple, *I love you* hanging on the tip of his tongue.

"Stay," she whispered, snuggling closer and tucking her leg between his.

She didn't need to ask twice.

CHAPTER TEN

AS THE FOG of sleep lifted, Bear realized he was alone on Crystal's couch, save for a very loud purring kitty curled up on his chest. He opened his eyes, and Harley lifted her head and pushed to her paws, digging her claws into his chest as she stretched. She padded down his belly, across his leg, to the other side of the couch, where she curled up and closed her eyes.

"Nothing like a little clawing in the morning." He swiped at a dot of blood on his pec, turning toward Crystal, who was sitting on the old chest she used as a coffee table, wearing *his* T-shirt. She had a serious look in her eyes, and her gorgeous legs were crossed, her feet covered by fuzzy pink socks. She was leaning forward, elbow on knee, her chin resting in her palm, watching him as she popped jelly beans into her mouth. He'd worried that Crystal might wake up feeling differently than she had last night. He was prepared for the worst.

"Hi," she said, popping another candy into her mouth.

"Hey, babe. You okay?" He pushed up to a sitting position, stretching his arms out to his sides. He loved the lascivious look that appeared in her eyes when he positioned one leg on either side of her.

"Mm-hm." Her eyes moved along each of his arms, down his bare chest, to the bulge in his pants. "Doesn't *Little Bear* ever hibernate?"

He laughed. "First of all, there's nothing *little* about any part of me. Second, he needs sustenance before he can hibernate, and it's been a long, cold winter."

"*Hm*." She seemed to think about that for a minute. "Sorry. I've been kind of selfish in the orgasm department, huh?"

"Not at all. Don't you worry your beautiful self with that stuff."

She held out a palmful of jelly beans.

"No thanks, sugar. I like my mornings to start with hot, dark liquid."

"Shame." She popped another one in her mouth. "I thought you might want to start it with a hot, dark *female* who likes the taste of candy in the morning."

He snagged them from her hand and chewed them up, earning a playful smile.

"Fast learner." She rose to her feet, and he caught sight of a pair of pink panties before his shirt drifted down to the middle of her thighs. Her nipples poked against the soft cotton as she climbed onto his lap, her dark hair tumbling around their faces. "Is this too unfair?"

He gritted his teeth against the throbbing ache behind his zipper. "The only thing *unfair* about you is that your lips are too far away from mine." Inhaling the scents of candy and happiness, he buried his hands in her hair and pulled her in for a sweet, sugary good-morning kiss. "Mm, baby. I do like the taste of jelly beans in the morning after all."

She smiled down at him and ran her fingers over his whiskers.

"How long have you been watching me sleep?" He could sit like that all day, with Crystal looking at him like she never wanted him to leave and touching him like she truly believed he was hers.

"I woke up too wired to sleep about two and a half hours ago, and I *might* have watched you for a few minutes."

"So, you're okay with this. With us?"

"After eight months of being in a relationship without sex or kissing or anything else? I think you nailed it on the head, biker boy. I'm *not* panicking, and that tells me that you're already in here." She put her hand over her heart. "I just needed to give myself permission and get over the worry about panicking. Worry breeds anxiety, at least that's what David says. So, yes. I'm good with us."

He gathered her closer. "Baby, that makes me so happy."

"I liked waking up in your arms. And I especially liked that you *really* held me while you slept."

"As opposed to pretending to hold you?" he teased.

"Every time I moved, you held me tighter. It felt nice. *Safe.*" She flattened her hand on his cheek and pressed her lips to his. "It felt sexy, too. I tried to go back to sleep, but *Little Bear* kept rubbing against me, and my *cave* got a little too welcoming, so I got up and worked on the costumes."

He couldn't suppress his smile. Knowing she'd wanted him while he was sleeping made his chest feel full.

"Your *cave?*" He clutched her hips, wanting to *explore* that cave. *With his mouth.*

She dipped lower and kissed his cheek. "Every bear needs a cave." She kissed his other cheek, and then her warm lips touched his.

Was that an invitation? His mind sprinted down a hopeful path, while his hands moved to her bottom, pulling her closer as he took the kiss deeper. She stroked his arms in a series of seductive touches, lingering on his triceps, then sliding down to his elbow and back up again. He imagined those delicate fingers wrapped around his cock. Jesus, was she giving him hints? He fucking hoped so. But he couldn't afford to be wrong, so he held back and enjoyed the hell out of their kisses.

She touched his cheeks again, kissing the edges of his mouth and making his nerves flame. She kissed the center of his chest, and a tormented groan slipped out.

"Sorry," she whispered. "*Sort of.*"

He groaned again, and she laughed.

"Too unfair?" she asked with a spark of mischief in her eyes.

"Are you trying to be?" He grazed his teeth over the spots on her neck that had driven her wild last night and lifted her—*his*—shirt, bringing her breasts against his chest, testing the waters.

"I love seeing you in my shirt, but I think it would look even better on the floor."

She leaned back, fidgeting with the hem of the shirt, her eyes dark and curious. "I don't want to be a tease."

"You're not a tease, but don't do it if you are at all uncomfortable."

She nibbled on her lower lip, still fidgeting with that hem. And then she whipped the shirt over her head and it floated to the ground.

Holy fucking hell. She was hot as sin fully dressed, but Crystal Moon wearing nothing but a pair of pink lace panties and a confident smile? *Unfuckingbelievable.*

"I like being bare skinned with you, but being completely naked might be hard for both of us. Would it be too much to ask to keep my panties on?" She wrinkled her nose, looking adorable and hot, and it was enough to make him lose his fucking mind.

Nothing's too much, babe, was on the tip of his tongue. *Except this. This is too much.* His fingers curled around her hips. He was salivating at the prospect of devouring her.

"On . . ." he repeated, more to himself than to her.

Her smile widened, as if she were reading his mind. She dragged her finger down the center of his chest, all the way to the button on his jeans. "Well, since you're shirtless, but you have pants on—"

"I can fix that real fucking fast," came out before he could stop it, and he quickly added, "Sorry. I'm kidding."

She dragged her eyes down his chest, revving him up even more. *Visual torture*, she was too good at it.

"I'm not ready to do more yet, so I think my panties should stay *on*. And by *on*, I mean, um . . . covering the *Bear cave*."

"Pants and panties staying on. Got it." He lifted her off his lap and set her on the wooden chest faster than he could blink.

"You moved me?" She pushed out a pouty lower lip.

He dropped to his knees on the floor between her legs, running his hands up her thighs. "Just so I can reach you better."

He pressed a kiss to her inner thigh, and she curled her fingers around the edge of the chest. He kissed her other thigh, and she let out a long, slow breath. His pulse raced as he continued kissing, running his hands along her legs, nudging them open wider. She watched him with a hungry look in her eyes as he slicked his tongue along the crease between her thigh and her sex.

"Want me to stop?" he whispered.

She shook her head.

"I will if this makes you uncomfortable."

"It's the very best kind of uncomfortable."

He pulled her to the edge of the chest and went up on his knees, claiming her mouth in a ravenous kiss, like he wanted to take her down below, delving in deep. Tasting *all* of her. When their lips parted, her eyes remained closed, and he lowered his mouth to her breast, loving her the way he'd learned she liked it. She arched back, offering him more, and he laved his tongue over the tight peaks, then trailed kisses down her belly. When he reached her panties, he brushed his nose over her mound, inhaling the scent of her desire, and kissed her thighs again.

"*God* . . ." Her whisper lingered in his ears.

Their eyes met, the air between them sizzling.

"Don't stop," she urged.

He brought his mouth to her center, over her panties, tasting her essence through the thin material. He was so hard, so ready to make love to her, he felt like he was going to burst, but he wanted her to enjoy every second of their intimacy and decide how fast they moved without pressure. Forcing his desires down deep, he pressed his tongue to her panties, moving hard and slow along her center. She breathed harder, gripping the chest so tight her knuckles blanched. He reached up with one hand and pinched her nipple between his finger and thumb, determined to make her come. He ate at her through the thin material, careful not to break her rules, when what he really wanted to do was shred those sexy panties and bury his tongue deep inside her.

He rose again, slanting his mouth over hers and kissing her *hard*. One hand teased her nipple, while the other moved over her sex, rubbing and stroking and matching the beat of her rocking hips. She arched, moaning into their kisses, and just when he was ready to seek permission to slide his fingers inside her and give her what she needed, her hips rose and her head fell back, eyes slammed shut. She clutched at his biceps, and the sexiest noises he'd ever heard streamed from her lips. Her sex clenched against his hand, and he lowered his mouth to catch the beat, the taste, the love.

When the last thrill rolled through her, he took her trembling body in his arms.

"I'm addicted to orgasms," she panted out, her cheek resting on his shoulder.

He chuckled. "Like I said, babe. You've got years to catch up on."

"I don't want to catch up on anything." She gazed into his eyes with the hazy look of a satisfied lover. "I think it's because I feel so much for you. I wouldn't let anyone else do *that*. It takes a world of trust. It's too intimate."

The caveman in him loved that he was her one and only.

"I've gone out with guys since college. Not many. Just a few first dates here and there. I never panicked when I kissed them good night because there was nothing there. No desire for even a second date. And then you came along, and you burrowed into my life like you belonged there."

"I'm not about to apologize."

She laughed. "I don't want you to. I'm trying to say that it's not the orgasms I'm addicted to. It's the man who's giving them to me."

"Me too, babe. I've got a bad case of Crystal Moon addiction. Spend the day with me and we can try to fight our addictions together. We'll get cleaned up, grab some breakfast, and then we can go for a ride."

"Breakfast? I already ate the leftover pizza." She glanced at her kitchen. "I guess I can burn you some toast if you're feeling adventurous."

He reached for his shirt to help her dress. "Thanks, but I think I'll pass."

"I'll get my own shirt so you don't have to ride home shirtless." She hurried down the hall as she spoke. "I love pizza for breakfast. No judging, remember?"

He watched her pink panties disappear into her bedroom, and a minute later she came out wearing a fresh pair of black panties and pulling a T-shirt over her head.

"Okay, so no breakfast." He put on his shirt. "Tell me you're mine for the day and let me cook you a *real* dinner tonight."

"You cook? What other hidden talents do you have?" She wound her arms around his waist and gazed up at him with a sweet smile.

"Babe, I've got talents that will make your head spin."

"I bet you do, and I'm getting more curious by the minute." She hugged him tighter. "I promise not to torture Little Bear anymore. It's just that I had been thinking about you for *hours*, like ice cream when you're on a diet. You were all I could think about."

"I think I know a thing or two about wanting what you can't have." He arched a brow.

She buried her face in his chest. "Ohmygod. I'm a cocktease."

He lifted her chin. "A very beautiful cocktease, and worth the wait. How about our date?"

Her smile reached all the way up to her eyes. "I have to work on the costumes for a little while longer. Can we go later? Maybe around noon?"

"Perfect. I'll let you get back to work and see you around noon. Wear long pants and your leather jacket."

"It's going to be warm today," she complained.

"We're going on a long ride. I may not own you, but I damn well want to protect you. Leather, baby cakes. You want to bring a pair of your sexy shorts in your bag, be my guest." He leaned down and planted a hard kiss on her lips. "In fact, *please* bring your sexy shorts."

CRYSTAL WORKED ON the costumes for most of the morning, taking a short break to make a bedcover for Harley out of the red satin Bear had picked out. She added a few strips of black lace and fitted it over the kitty bed. Harley purred as she curled up on the luxurious fabric with one of her toy mice. Crystal picked up her phone to text Gemma, glancing at the beautiful orchids Bear had given her. She'd set them by the windows so she could enjoy them while she worked.

She startled when Jed's ringtone sounded in her hand. "Hey?"

"Hey, sis. You sound like you have way too much energy."

She paced. "Sorry. Big day planned."

"With . . . ?"

"Not sharing details," she said with a smile.

"I'd come over and torture it out of you, but I can't drive, which is why I'm calling."

She stared up at the ceiling. "Oh, Jed. What did you do now?"

"I brought Mom cigarettes, which unfortunately is not on my way *to* or *from* work. Dickhead McCarthy pulled me over."

"You're a few weeks from getting your license back. Why would you chance it for *her*?"

"Because she guilted me into it. But I'm taking the ticket to court to try to avoid points and hopefully still get my license back on time. My buddy referred me to a lawyer, but I need a ride a week from Tuesday around one. Any chance you can take me?"

She rolled her eyes. "Yeah. I'll have to clear it with Gemma, but she loves you, so I'm sure she won't mind."

"Thank you. And thank Gemma for me, too. I have another favor to ask."

"Jesus, do you need me to fight the ticket for you, too?"

"I figured it's better to lay all the shit on you at once. My buddy's wife is going in for surgery and I'm taking on more hours at work. Can you make dinner at Mom's two Sundays from today instead of during the week?"

"Sure. Do you need a ride to her house, too?"

"I'll let you know."

"Okay."

"Shrimp, you sure you don't want to tell me who you're going out with?"

His curiosity took her by surprise. He never pushed his way into her personal life. "I'm sure."

He tried to joke it out of her. Every joke was worse than the last.

"Jed, *please*. Why do you even care?"

"It's been a long time since we've really talked. I guess I just miss you."

She wanted to believe him, but she'd been let down so many times in her life, she was afraid to let him in. Because letting him in would make it that much harder when he let her down.

"Thanks, Jed. I miss you, too. We'll catch up when we have dinner."

After she ended the call, she opened and reread the text Bear had sent half an hour after he'd left.

Big Bear misses you. She'd returned the text with a playful one. *How can a text make me swoon?* His response had been immediate. *It's not the text. It's the memories of my paws all over you.* Feeling cheeky, she'd responded with, *I do like your paws, and your mouth, and your . . . Now let me work before my boyfriend catches you texting me and kicks your ass.* He'd responded with an emoticon of a bear and the word *growl.*

She loved the feelings he stirred and reveled in allowing herself to *finally* experience them. But what she loved most was sharing that newfound confidence with him.

Grinning like a fool, she snapped a picture of the costume she'd been working on and sent it to Gemma with the text *Warrior Princess is almost done!*

She went into her bedroom and grabbed her chunky, silver-studded black boots out of her closet. She'd chosen one of her favorite outfits for her date with Bear. A short, black lace dress with a studded leather belt, stud earrings, and a wristful of black and silver bracelets. She pulled on leather leggings beneath the dress for the ride.

Her phone vibrated, and she sat on the edge of the bed and opened Gemma's text while she laced up her boots. A stream of pictures of tattooed penises popped up, and she laughed out loud. They were the pictures she'd sent to Gemma when Gemma had first started dating Tru. Crystal had teasingly asked if Tru had ink below the belt.

An increasingly familiar wave of guilt washed through her as a second text rolled in from Gemma. *Well?*

Her smile faded as she typed her response—*Haven't explored that area yet*—worrying over how she'd ever be able to reveal her lies to her best friend without losing her. Her finger hovered over the send button as she contemplated texting something like, *Can we talk later?* But they were in the middle of planning Gemma's wedding. If she told her the truth now, she'd be hurt and angry, and . . .

Crystal's throat thickened at the thought of hurting her. She couldn't do it. Not until after the wedding. She'd waited this long, and it wasn't like Gemma knew she had anything to confess. At least after the wedding she wouldn't hurt her *and* ruin her big day. A knock at the door sent her thoughts scattering. She quickly transmitted the text and went to greet her man.

She pulled the door open and was immediately swept away by Bear, looking devilishly badass dressed in head-to-toe black. He'd trimmed his scruff, bringing out his chiseled chin and making him look even sexier. He raked his eyes from her face all the way to her toes, and like a leaf in a windstorm, her body quivered.

"Damn, baby cakes. You look good enough to eat."

She grabbed him by the shirt and yanked him forward, her stomach swirling with memories of him doing just that earlier. "If we're going to make it out of my apartment, you can't say stuff like that, because my newly unleashed hormones are like live wires desperately seeking a plug."

He cocked a brow.

Yes, please.

"No," she said firmly, and pressed her lips to his, pulling away quickly. "No long, lusty kisses, either. You make my insides feel like the Fourth of July."

"I'm totally digging this new Crystal who spills all her secrets." His arm circled her waist, and he kissed her so freaking deliciously she mentally debated throwing caution to the wind and forgetting their date.

Harley wound around Bear's feet.

"CB." He scooped up the kitty. "Did you miss me?"

"Her name is *Harley*." She grabbed her backpack and shoved her keys in the pocket where she'd tucked a worry doll. *A little extra courage never hurt anyone.* Her phone vibrated, and she checked the text message quickly. It was a picture of Jed holding up a paycheck with the caption *Told you I was really working.*

"Everything okay?" Bear asked.

"It's from Jed. I think he really is trying to clean up his act. He sent me a picture of his paycheck." She returned his text. *This makes me so happy! Love you!* Then she stuffed her phone in the backpack.

"That's great. When will you see him again?"

"Two weeks from Sunday, when we see my mom for dinner."

"Yeah? I'd love to meet the woman who raised you."

"No, you wouldn't. Trust me. She's a hot mess." She lifted her bag over her shoulder.

"I don't care. I'd still like to come along."

"Didn't your parents ever teach you it's rude to invite yourself places?"

"Not where you're concerned. I want to meet your mom so I know what you're dealing with. I want to hang out with Jed and hear all the embarrassing stories about when you were little. And I don't want to argue about any of it."

"You're a pain." As embarrassed as she was about her mother, she was still oddly pleased he was pushing so hard to meet her.

He kissed Harley and set her in her new satin bed with a surprised expression. "*That's* what you did with the satin and lace I picked out?"

"Some of it." She grabbed his vest and tugged him out the door. She wasn't about to tell him that she had a sexy idea for the rest. A girl needed a few surprises up her sleeve.

Twenty minutes later they rode over the bridge, leaving Peaceful Harbor behind. Riding on the back of Bear's bike on wide, open roads was completely different from the short stop-and-go trips they'd taken in town. As they passed long stretches of rural land, the air smelled fresher, and even though she was wearing her leather jacket and pants, she still sensed pockets of warmer and cooler air. She tried to tie them to the clouds, but it was impossible.

What other mysterious, wonderful things had she missed by riding in her car with the windows rolled up?

She held on tight, wondering where they were going. Bear had been secretive, but as time passed, the pungent scents of the sea crept back in, and the causeway came into view. She realized he was heading to Capshaw Island. She pressed her hands tighter on his stomach, excitement rushing through her. She'd never been to the island, even though it was only a little more than an hour away. Capshaw Island was a small fishing town, and she'd heard stories about wild ponies and the lack of commercialization there, and it had piqued her interest. She was surprised that her badass biker would want to go to such a quiet place. She'd imagined them hitting the highway and stopping at roadside biker bars. Then again, Bear knew how she'd lost her father, and he'd been so careful with her in every other way. This was another thoughtful gesture. And it made her first trip there even more special.

As he drove over the causeway, she wished she could whip off her helmet and let the air kiss her face. Long, marshy grasses sprouted up through the rippling water. Paddleboarders moved seamlessly across the water, and in the distance a powerboat motored along, leaving a trail of whitecaps.

They rode down the main drag, which looked old-fashioned compared to Peaceful Harbor. Painted brick and wood-sided storefronts boasted scalloped awnings shading wooden benches and planters full of summer flowers. From what she could see, there were only two blocks of businesses, just as she'd heard.

Bear parked on a side street. He was smiling as he chained the helmets, watching her taking it all in.

"Have you been here before?"

"No, but I've always wanted to."

"Then I'm glad we came. I've driven through with the club, but I've never stopped to walk around. A first for both of us—there's nothing cooler than that."

"Speaking of cool." She hooked her fingers in the top of her leather leggings and stripped them off. When she reached the top of her ankle boots, she laughed. "Oops. Not cool."

Bear was already bending down to unlace her boots. "Sexiness has a price." He flashed a wink as he pulled one off.

She steadied herself with his shoulder as he slipped the pants over her foot. "If you get bored down there, I can think of something to keep you busy."

Desire flared in his eyes. "Careful poking a hungry bear."

After he finished helping her out of her pants—and into her boots—he ran his hands up her outer thighs as he rose to his feet and rather blatantly adjusted the formidable bulge in his jeans.

"Sorry," she whispered, grinning from ear to ear.

"What was it you said to me last night? I'd make up for it later? Quid pro quo, baby." He kissed her again and tucked her pants into the backpack. She reached for it and he gave her a you-must-be-kidding look as he slung it over his shoulder.

She'd never had anyone take care of her the way he did, and even though she secretly loved it, she couldn't resist teasing him. "Sounds like ownership to me."

His arm darted around her shoulder, and she snuggled in to her favorite spot.

"Call it whatever you want," he said.

They walked to the main road, Bear's eyes scanning the faces of every man they passed, giving off that threatening vibe again, like he'd done in Whispers. She was coming to accept that being with him went hand in hand with being watched over like a hawk. Maybe that wasn't such a bad thing, but she had a feeling there was more behind his watchfulness than mere boyfriend-like protection. He hadn't said anything more about what happened in college, but she sensed it was eating him alive.

As they meandered through a gallery of nautical sculptures and paintings, she wrestled with what she was really asking of him. Was it fair of her to expect him to let her past go? She'd had years to deal with it, but she'd laid it on him and demanded he do nothing.

They left the gallery and visited a marine supply store, and as they walked around, she told herself that her decision was the right one. It was what she needed, and hopefully he'd eventually get past throwing off the killer vibe. On their way out, Bear bought a dark purple carabiner.

When they left the store, he opened the backpack and hooked the carabiner to her keys.

"What's that for? Are you going to buy a leash next?"

"If you're not careful, I might." The tease in his eyes tugged at her as he hooked the carabiner to a leather loop inside the backpack. "You can hook this to your keys, then on your jeans or inside your bag. That way you're not always digging for your keys. It's safer this way."

She snuggled up to him again, loving that he'd been noticing everything about her. "You really do care."

"Babe, if you're still figuring that out, you're miles behind."

Maybe so, but she was catching up quickly. "You watch over me so carefully, and I appreciate that. You were protective before I told you what happened, but ever since, you've been even more watchful."

He guided her out of the middle of the sidewalk to let another couple pass by, and his face went serious. "As long as that guy is out there, I'll worry."

Her stomach knotted up. "Bear, please. I know it's hard, and I'm sorry for asking you to let it go, but I wish you could just forget it ever happened. I left that part of my life behind."

"And all I want to do is make sure it stays there."

They visited a few more stores and stopped at a café for lunch. After Bear ordered fries, Crystal added a milk shake to her order.

Bear dunked a fry in her milk shake and fed it to her, watching her intently as her mouth closed around it. "You are totally into dipping my *fry* in your *milk shake*."

"If you're still figuring that out, you're miles behind," she teased.

They kissed for the millionth time, and she hoped they'd kiss a million more.

The waitress told them about the island's weekly Sunday market down by the water and an observation deck located off of Ocean Drive, where they could see the wild ponies in their natural habitat. When they were done eating, they walked down to the market, passing rows of small, weather-beaten cottages.

"It's nice getting out of town for something other than seeing my mother."

"We'll go on lots of rides together." He smiled and added, "Do you know how long I've wanted to take off on my bike with you?"

"I'm sorry it took me so long to come around. But you're a little intimidating—in a good way, not a scary way. Just being around you made my pulse go bonkers. There is no easing into Bear territory." She gazed up at the bright sun, enjoying the warmth on her cheeks.

"Don't be sorry, babe. I'd have waited longer. I might have gotten frustrated, but I wouldn't have given up until you told me I had no chance."

"What a load of bull that is." She laughed. "I told you dozens of times that nothing would happen between us."

"Verbally, yes. But your eyes told a different story."

She knew that was true. Gemma had told her as much. "I'm glad you were so perceptive."

When they reached the market, the road was blocked off with orange and white construction barriers. Helium balloons danced in the breeze, and a bright blue banner stretched across the road that read SUNDAY MARKET. Beyond the barriers, crowds of people milled about beneath a sea of white canopies. They joined the crowd passing booths selling fruits and vegetables, homemade jams and jellies, arts and crafts, and beaded jewelry. The scent of popcorn hung in the air from a vendor at the end of the street.

"Baby cakes, check this out." He nodded toward a T-shirt vendor, where a short, stocky man was talking with customers while a tall, thin woman worked an iron press. "I want to get Kennedy and Lincoln a little something."

They looked through the children's shirts.

"How about these?" she suggested, holding up T-shirts that said *I love Mommy* and *I love Daddy*.

"Those are always good choices," the man behind the table said, flashing a kind smile.

"Can I get something custom-made?" Bear asked.

"Sure." The man grabbed a pad of paper and a pen. "What would you like?"

"I'd like a girl's size-three pink T-shirt that says 'I love Uncle Bear,' but spell 'Bear' with an 'H' instead of an 'R.'" Bear lowered his voice and said to Crystal, "She needs something unique, like you." To the man, he said, "And I'll take a black T-shirt for a one-year-old boy that says, 'Future Dark Knight,' with a 'K.'"

"No one can say you aren't the best uncle ever," Crystal said as the man and woman began working on his order. "While you're waiting, I'm going to use the restroom." She pointed at a sign for the restrooms.

"I'll go with you as soon as he's done."

"Don't be silly. I'm a big girl." He kissed her like she was going off to war, and then he kissed her again until she laughed into the kiss. "I'll be back in a few minutes."

"Seems like a long time to me." He held her hand as she stepped away, his fingers slipping down to her fingertips and then finally breaking away.

She followed the signs to the public bathrooms and waited in line to use the facilities. Afterward, as she washed her hands, she took a long look at herself in the mirror. She felt different inside, but she was amazed at how different she looked, too. Her eyes seemed clearer, and even her skin seemed to glow. She wished her father could see her now. He'd be happy for her, and proud of her for doing so well. It was a good feeling, thinking of him, and she smiled all the way back to the market.

Bear was talking with a thickly bearded guy at another booth. The backpack was fuller than before, and she assumed he'd already gotten the kids' shirts. She asked the vendor to make her a shirt, and after she paid for it, she waited for Bear to finish his conversation. She held the shirt behind her back, bouncing on her toes, trying—and failing—to contain her excitement.

Bear turned, his eyes locking on her as he closed the distance between them. When he was a few steps away, she whipped the shirt from behind her back and held it up, watching as he read the gold letters. *Dip me in honey and feed me to Bear.*

He crushed her to him, kissing her hard, like a tsunami about to unleash its wrath.

"Careful, sugar," he said gruffly. "You're poking a starving bear."

"Maybe I don't want to be careful. Maybe I *like* poking my starving bear."

CHAPTER ELEVEN

BEAR HAD NEVER spent much time thinking about relationships, but as he and Crystal drove out to the observation deck to watch the wild ponies, all he could think about was that he never knew it was possible to fall harder for someone in just a few hours. He parked at the end of the road and helped Crystal off the bike. She'd put her leggings and jacket on for the ride, and she looked like she belonged on the cover of a Biker Babe calendar. But it wasn't just how sexy and beautiful she was that had him falling harder with every minute they were together. It was *her*. All of her. Her sweet, vulnerable side. Her sassy, snarky confidence. Her loving nature, which she'd covered so well for so long. He loved the way she was coming into her own, and there was no place he'd rather be than right there by her side. And it didn't matter if it took her a day, a week, or a year to embrace their relationship as fully as he had.

The fact that he felt that way and they hadn't even slept together yet didn't escape him. Neither did the realization that he'd felt that way long before they'd even kissed.

They followed a path to the observation deck, and he couldn't remember the last time he'd had such an enjoyable afternoon. Crystal leaned over the railing, peering through the trees.

"Look! There they are." She pointed through a gap in the branches at a band of wild horses grazing on the grass at the edge of the beach. They were sturdy and shaggy. "Aren't they beautiful?"

"Wild and free. Reminds me of a certain someone." He wrapped his arms around her from behind.

She pushed beneath his arm, moving beside him. "Thank you for today. The market reminded me of the ones I used to go to with my dad."

"I'm glad you enjoyed it. I can't remember the last time I've had such a great day. Thanks for letting me monopolize you. But I have some bad news."

Her brows knitted.

He brushed his lips over hers. "Today has done nothing to lessen my addiction. I think I need another hit."

"Lucky for you, I happen to have a huge supply of kisses." She went up on her toes, and he met her halfway to feed his addiction.

They watched the ponies until something spooked them and they bolted away, their muscular legs pounding the earth, kicking up dirt in their wake. They rode home as the sun dipped from the sky. In Peaceful Harbor, they passed Whiskey Bro's, where his brothers' and Dixie's bikes were parked out front, along with his mother's car. The bar wasn't open on Sundays, but Dixie went in to take care of the books, and a few family members usually ended up hanging out with her. Normally he'd stop by, but tonight all he wanted was to be with Crystal.

He drove through town and turned off the main drag toward the mountains, winding through tree-lined, narrow roads toward his home. One of the things Bear loved most about Peaceful Harbor was that in addition to all the benefits of the beach, just a few miles away it also offered the seclusion of lakeside living in the mountains.

He pulled into his driveway and stopped in front of the garage. The property was dark, save for the moonlight slicing through the trees and glistening off the lake down the hill to their right. His mother was always on his back about putting up solar-powered lights so he didn't come home to a dark house, but no one fucked with a Dark Knight.

He pushed the garage door button on his key fob and pulled his bike inside. As he climbed off, he imagined Crystal arriving there alone. He was getting miles ahead of himself, but even those few hours apart that morning had driven him crazy. He'd used the time to prepare what he hoped would be a nice surprise, but that hadn't taken away the longing to have her right there by his side. He made a mental note to put up a few solar lights.

"I didn't know you lived by the lake." Her eyes swept over his partially assembled bike and the metal shelves around the perimeter, which were littered with equipment, tools, and various vehicle parts. A motorcycle crane and old wooden tool chests sat against the back wall along with three workbenches. "And you thought my design studio looked like it exploded. What is all this stuff?"

"That's the bike I'm currently building. It doesn't look like much yet, but it's getting there."

She walked over to it, stepping around his tools and other para-phernalia lying on the floor. "It looks like *much*," she said with a smile. "How exciting. I can't wait to see how it looks when it's done."

She pointed up toward the bikes parked on the loft at the rear of the garage.

"And those bikes? Are they your *extras*?"

"I designed and built two of them."

"You should really take that offer with Silver-Stone. I mean, look at this place. Motorcycles are your life. You said you designed and built two of them. So are those other two extra bikes that you bought?"

"Those were my uncle Axel's. I bought this place from him before he passed away. A lot of this stuff was his." A familiar wave of emptiness pushed through him. "He taught me everything I know about . . ." He waved a hand. "We lost him to lung cancer when I was twenty-two."

She reached for his hand. "I'm so sorry."

"It was a long time ago."

She took another, longer look at the bikes, and then her gaze dropped to the pictures behind his workbench. She walked closer, her eyes latching on to the sexy pinup calendar that had been his uncle's. He wondered what she'd have to say about the side view of a naked brunette straddling a motorcycle, back arched, hair hanging over one shoulder, her sultry gaze and ruby-red lips seducing the camera.

Crystal glanced at him with a glimmer of heat in her eyes. "Maybe we can replace that naked girl with another"—she walked toward him—"more *familiar* girl."

"Sugar, if you think I'll hang a naked picture of you on my garage wall where my brothers can see it, you're sadly mistaken." He took her in his arms. "But I'll proudly hang that picture in my bedroom."

"Mm, the *real* Bear cave. I'm anxious to see what your house looks like. I picture a bearskin rug and lots of leather."

He chuckled and grabbed the backpack. "You have quite an imagination."

He led her down the mulched path toward the house, inhaling the scents of pine and fresh water, so different from the scents of the sea. His two-bedroom cedar and stone cabin sat on a ridge about thirty feet from the water's edge. It wasn't huge, but in addition to the bedrooms, he had a den and a loft, and the wide front porch and screened-in sleeping deck provided extra living space.

Crystal stood at the crest of the hill, flanked by tall trees, and gazed out over the lake. Her lace dress shifted with the breeze. He'd imagined her there so many times, he could hardly believe this was real.

"You wake up to this every morning?"

"Most, anyway. Today I woke up to a much more gorgeous view."

"Biker boy," she said as they headed up to the house. "You've got some pretty good lines."

"I've got *damn good* everything." He loved playing with her like that because it made her smile, and it wasn't her normal snarky smile or her warm, seductive smile. It was the smile of a girl who was always thinking, trying to process what he was saying. Was she coming up with snappy retorts? Trying to decide if he was really that cocky? He didn't know, but he loved that look.

He unlocked the heavy wooden door and pushed it open, following her inside the house he'd considered his second home when he was growing up, and set the backpack on the floor by the door.

Surprise lit her eyes. "Whoa, this is like the ultimate gearhead bachelor pad. You have a pool table instead of a dining room table? That's awesome." She ran her fingers along the polished wood edge, glancing up at the loft that overlooked the living room.

"Thanks. My uncle and grandfather built the cabin. My brothers and I updated the kitchen, repointed the fireplace, and refinished the hardwood floors a few years ago. No need for a dining room table. I usually eat there." He pointed to the bar separating the living room from the kitchen. The open living space suited his lifestyle, as did the *gearhead* furnishings, like the chandelier hanging over the pool table, made from leather, chains, and a wheel that came from a Silver-Stone motorcycle. And the side table his buddy made from old tools, nuts, and bolts.

"Wait until you get a look at the bathroom."

"The bathroom?"

"I have a feeling you'll get a kick out of my appliances."

She dragged her eyes down his body. "I do love your *appliances*." She eyed the sectional sofa. "Do I have to worry about catching a disease on your sex-pit?"

He cocked a smile at her brazen question. He'd bought the extra-large sectional because of its versatility. But he liked her idea a whole lot better. "That'd be hard, considering I've never had sex on it."

She gave him a disbelieving look.

"Sugar, you've got the wrong impression of me. My *escapades* ended a long time ago." He helped her off with her leather jacket and tossed it on the sofa, pulling her closer. "I don't want you to worry about my past, okay? You're the only woman I want, so whatever's going through your mind about anyone else, let it go. Okay?"

She nodded.

"I had a few girls here when I first bought the place, but when I renovated it, things changed. It went from being a hangout to a home, and no woman has been here with me since. Well, other than Dixie, my mom, the guys' girlfriends and wives, but not *with me*. Got it?"

She grabbed him by the vest. "Got it, biker boy."

WATCHING BEAR COOK should be like watching the abominable snowman walk through the desert. It shouldn't fit together. But it did, in a very sexy way. He sliced bell peppers, sausage, and chicken like a pro and threw the meat in a bowl with olive oil and a handful of seasonings without ever consulting a recipe. After covering it, he set the bowl in the fridge, which was full of healthy foods, putting her fridge to shame. He heated olive oil in a pan and stirred in garlic, rice, and red pepper flakes.

Crystal leaned against the counter beside him. They'd both taken off their boots, and she'd taken off her leggings amid kisses and gropes, and *I really did invite you here for dinner, not just to make out*. She loved being in his home, and the fact that he hadn't had a revolving bedroom door spoke volumes about him.

"You're really not going to let me help with your secret dish?" He wouldn't tell her what he was making.

"Nope." He gave her a chaste kiss and went back to stirring, mixing in chicken stock and a number of spices and other ingredients. He brought them to a boil, reduced the heat, and covered the pan. His hands circled her waist, and his mouth began a tantalizing exploration of her neck.

"*Mm*. I like helping you cook." She felt him laugh. "Who taught you how?"

"Same guy who taught me about bikes and cars. When I was growing up, my mom worked shifts as a nurse and my dad was always at the bar. I spent a lot of time at the shop. I'd go after school and follow my uncle around. Sometimes I'd stay with him until close to bedtime."

He placed one leg on either side of her. Even his stance was possessive, and she was no longer surprised by how much she liked it.

"I did my homework while he cooked dinner, and he'd walk me through the steps of whatever he was making. I guess his skills wore off on me. By the time I was a teenager, I was cooking dinners with him, and when he got sick, I cooked for him. Even in his last days, when he couldn't stomach a thing, he'd ask me to cook. I think he knew we both needed the distraction."

Her heart sliced open. "You were with him, here, at the end?"

He pulled out another skillet, poured in some olive oil and tossed in the ingredients he'd marinated. "My mother cared for him here. She'd pushed for him to go into hospice care, but he was a feisty bastard. Tough till the end." He cut up onions and put them in the skillet, blinking against damp eyes. Whether it was due to the onions or memories, she couldn't be sure.

She reached for him. "I'm sorry you lost someone so important to you. It sounds like you had a special relationship."

He hooked an arm around her neck, hugging her in the crook of it. "He was a heck of a guy. When I was in high school, he helped me apply for scholarships and fill out college applications."

He washed his hands, going silent while he stirred in the rest of the ingredients. "I wanted to go into industrial design and engineering. I won a scholarship, but then my old man got sick. Bones was in med school. Bullet was on tour with the military."

"So you never went," she said, realizing his loyalty ran even deeper than she'd thought.

He was quiet for a few minutes before answering. "My family needed me. And when we realized my uncle wasn't going to beat his cancer, I knew where I belonged."

He opened another cabinet and began mixing rum, lime juice, brown sugar, and water in a big pot. Then he stirred a bowl of shrimp into the other skillet, and she realized what he was making.

"You're making paella and hot grog." How could it have taken her so long to figure it out? And after everything she'd confessed that night on the hill, how had he remembered every little detail?

"For my girl. I hit the store while you were working this morning."

A lump lodged in her throat. "Bear," was all she could manage.

"That's my name, babe." He grabbed two plates from the cabinet and spread the rice onto them and topped them with the meat and seafood mixtures.

"Thank you." She opened the drawers in search of silverware. "It smells incredible."

"Hopefully it will taste even better." He reached around her and opened the silverware drawer, revealing utensils that looked like tools.

She lifted her brows.

"What? Your forks don't have box-wrench ends?" He picked up the utensils, showing each to her. "You don't have spoons with an open-end wrench or a knife with a plier for a handle?"

"No. I have a Bear with a toolbox."

He laughed. "That you do, babe. A very *large* toolbox."

"You should be careful building up the size of your junk." She lowered her voice to a whisper. "What if I'm disappointed?"

"You've felt it," he said, as arrogant as ever as he reached into a cabinet and withdrew two wineglasses. "I know you like to be careful about drinking, so if you want to skip the grog, that's cool with me."

He'd thought of everything. "No. I'd like some. It sounds perfect."

He pulled a shiny silver tray from a lower cabinet near the dishwasher and set it on the counter. There were two circles inside it, one read BLUE HAWK and the other read STAINLESS-STEEL MAGNETIC MECHANIC'S TRAY. He set the plates inside it, and when he put the utensils in, they *clink*ed.

"You're seriously using a mechanic's tray?"

"A good mechanic always has the right tools for the job." He swatted her butt and then ladled the grog into a big pitcher. "Do you mind carrying this?"

She carried the pitcher and he set the wineglasses on the tray. They went out of the kitchen to a hallway she hadn't noticed when they'd arrived. After standing for so long, she felt her muscles begin to ache.

"My legs and butt are sore from the ride."

"Don't worry, babe. I'll massage all your aches and pains away, and I promise to behave."

"Darn," slipped out before she could stop it. "I mean . . . Um. *Darn.*"

He laughed. "You lead, and I'm happy to follow."

"I like the sound of that." She stopped to look at a series of pictures on the wall. She studied a photograph of three adorable, long-haired shirtless young boys and a girl with tangled red hair. They were sitting on a concrete step. The little girl was leaning forward but looking back at the boys, like she didn't want to miss a thing. Crystal spotted Bear easily, all elbows and knees, holding a cat on his lap and watching the other boys.

"Is this you and your brothers and Dixie?" she asked.

"Yeah. Taken at my parents' house."

She moved to the next picture, where a honey-eyed boy with thick black hair, who could only be Bear, peered beneath the hood of a car. Beside him a thin, bearded man stood with one arm around Bear's shoulders, pointing to something on the engine.

"Me and my uncle Axel," Bear explained.

A pang of sadness swept through her as they moved on to the other pictures.

"This was my first bike." He nodded to a picture of him as a young man standing next to a shiny black motorcycle. His father stood beside him, hands on hips, looking at Bear, but Bear was grinning proudly at the camera.

He motioned toward another picture. "This is Bullet, as you can probably tell by his size, and that's me over his shoulder." Bullet faced the camera with an angry scowl, holding Bear's legs. Bear's fisted hands were caught midair, as if he were pounding on his brother's back.

"What did you do?"

"The jackass was dicking around. He dumped me in the lake. Not my proudest moment, but I love the asshole."

"I'm sure you didn't let him get away with it."

"Hell no. See that shaggy hair? I chopped it while he was sleeping. He nearly beat me to death the next day. We both ended up with shaved heads that summer." He grinned as they headed for the stairs, passing a bedroom, den, and bathroom.

She peeked into the bathroom, taking in the gas-pump faucet and the hand drill used as a toilet paper holder. "You weren't kidding about your bathroom. It's very *male*." As they climbed the stairs to the loft, she said, "You're lucky. Your childhood seems so normal. Mine was like that, until we moved."

"If you consider sitting in the back room of a bar, hanging out in an auto shop several nights a week, or being woken up at all hours as a teenager to drive drunk customers home normal, I guess so. But it's all good. We had good times."

When they reached the landing, he said, "My bedroom."

Pine walls and a high, exposed-beam ceiling gave the room a warm feel. A bay window, complete with a cushioned window seat, offered a spectacular view of the lake. She imagined curling up with him on that window seat and watching the sunset in the winter, when the lake was iced over, with Harley snuggled up at their feet. A leather recliner sat beside a driftwood and glass table, stacked four books high. In the center of the room was the largest bed she'd ever seen, draped in a maroon blanket.

"Your bed is *huge*."

"It's not the only thing about me that's huge. Come on, sugar." He shifted the tray against his hip.

"This might be a stupid question, but why is it so big?"

"Not stupid at all, and not for the reason you think. When I was little, we all used to pile into my parents' bed on weekend mornings to wake them up. All four of us. My father would grumble, but we'd end up wrestling and laughing. It's silly, but it's one of my best memories. When I went to buy a bed, I decided to get one made that was big enough for that."

The more she learned about him, the harder she fell. "So . . . you want a family?"

"Definitely, someday." His brows slanted. "You?"

She weighed her answer, wondering if the truth would scare him off, and quickly decided that with Bear, nothing but the truth would do.

"I gave up wanting a family after my mom fell into the bottle. I was afraid I'd end up like her, and I didn't want to do that to a child. But spending time with Kennedy and Lincoln, and seeing the love Gemma and Tru give them, has made me think about it again. People say you turn into your parents no matter how hard you try not to, but I don't think that's true. It might take effort, but I think we choose our own paths."

"I respect my father," Bear said with a serious edge to his voice. "But I'll be damned if I'll turn into him. I think Tru and Gemma are a testament to the fact that we aren't fated to turn into our parents, and *you* have proven that we choose our own paths. The only thing we're destined to be is what we decide we want to be. Everything else is temptation, bad and good. But in the end, we're in control."

He opened a door behind him, revealing a rustic screened porch with an old wooden table and four chairs that had seen better days and another bed, which sat low to the ground. A lantern stood atop the table. Like the walls, the ceiling was screened, offering the natural light and beauty of the night sky. Marred and scuffed rafters matched the knotted wood beneath their feet.

"I love this." She set the pitcher on the table and looked out at the lake. "Feel that breeze? Don't you wish you could have your whole house screened in and then somehow, just for winter, wrap it up tight?"

He set the tray on the table, and his arms circled her from behind. This was her second favorite place to be, the first being tucked against his side. "I spend nearly every night out here. I thought you might like it."

She turned in his arms, completely taken by this outdoorsy side of him. "I more than *like* it." He held her gaze for so long, she thought he must be reading between the lines, just as she hoped he would.

They ate dinner by the dim light of the lantern, sharing the grog and too many kisses to count. The paella was even more delicious than she remembered, but that could be because she knew the lengths Bear had gone to in order to prepare such a special night for her.

Now they lay on their backs on the bed, their fingers laced, gazing through the screen at the stars above and talking.

"Biggest dream?" she asked.

"That's a hard one. Other than you?" He squeezed her hand. "Probably making a name for myself in the motorcycle business. You?"

"My biggest dream is this. I've worked so hard to have a normal life, and I know that seems simplistic. But being here with you, like this? It's so big to me."

They lay in silence, listening to the sounds of nature. It was nice, not overthinking or being entertained. Just being there with Bear felt wonderful.

"Your name," he said softly. "Do you have a preference for what I call you?"

Her nerves prickled. She didn't want to get into a discussion about her past, but she liked that he was asking. "My real first name is Christine, but the only name that fits now is Crystal." She turned onto her side, and he did the same. "But what I like most is when you call me whatever you feel. *Sugar, baby cakes,* your *girl.*"

"I thought you weren't into ownership."

"I'm not. But you're not an asshole who treats me like a possession. If you were, I wouldn't be here with you."

He touched his lips to hers. "That's because I adore you, and if I turn into an asshole, I'm sure you will shut me down."

She ran her fingers over his whiskers, smiling at his response. "I've told you so much about myself. I got the impression you didn't want to talk about your nickname, or the scars, but I'd like to hear the story. If you'd rather not, I understand."

His face went serious. "Babe, the only reason I didn't want to talk about it was that I wanted to be close to you. Not because I didn't want to tell you about it." He pulled off his shirt and rolled onto his stomach, resting his cheek on his forearms.

Between his shoulder blades were long, swooping scars. Some were slick and paler than his skin, others puckered and dark. Three looked more prominent, wider and angrier than the others.

"You can touch them," he said, watching her.

She ran her fingers along the length of each one, silently counting as she went. *Five.* "It must have hurt a lot."

"I was too pumped up on adrenaline to notice the pain. We'd gone on a camping trip with a few of the families from the club. I went to take a piss away from the campsite, and when I came upon two bear cubs, I knew I was in trouble. The hair on the back of my neck stood up before I heard the mama bear growling, and as I turned, her claws came down on my back, knocking me to my knees. I remember shouting, but have no idea what I yelled. I *fought* with everything I had. Bullet had boxed from the time he was eight, and he was always on my ass about being tough. That's why he used to do shit to me like toss me in the lake. He was toughening me up. Anyway, he'd made it his job to teach us all how to fight. Even as a kid Bullet was giant. There was no arguing with him. So I learned to box and to street fight, which meant enduring *him* as my opponent."

He laughed a little, as if he were remembering those boxing matches. "I clocked that bear in the snout, which stunned her for a few seconds, giving me enough time to get to my feet. And long enough for Bullet to plow through the forest like a bat out of hell and put himself between me and the bear. The whole thing happened in seconds, and someone was watching out for us, because that bear roared again, then ambled off with its cubs."

She flattened her hand over the scars. "Your heart is going crazy."

"Adrenaline. It's like I'm right back there facing that beast. Man, Bullet didn't hesitate to put himself between us. I owe him my life."

"You're both so brave." She lay beside him again, and he pulled her close.

"I think you take the cake on bravery," he said gently. "I guess we both know a little about survival."

She lay in his arms, listening to the sounds of the lake and the leaves brushing in the breeze. Lying together, talking and sharing pieces of themselves felt like a whole new level of intimacy. She was surprised by how much time she'd wasted worrying about it.

"Do you ever wish you'd gone to the police?" he finally asked.

She closed her eyes. She'd sensed that he'd been stewing about what she'd gone through, but she'd hoped he wouldn't bring it up again.

"Not really, but I sometimes regret that I wasn't strong enough to stay in school, to have been in control enough to complete my degree. And paying back a portion of the Pell Grant sucked. But, you know, with time comes perspective," she admitted. "Sometimes I look back and I'm surprised I got out of the trailer park at all, and other times I somehow always knew I would. Do you ever regret not going away to college?"

"I'm not sure 'regret' is the right word. But do I wish I could have learned more? Sure. Who wouldn't? By the way, this week is going to suck. I've got a club meeting tomorrow night, and I'm helping Tru paint Tuesday night. I thought I could see you after, but he wants to paint the playroom as well as the rec room. I think he's nervous about the house being ready for the wedding. And Wednesday and Thursday I have to bartend until two in the morning." The muscles around his jaw tensed.

"It won't suck, and I'm glad you're helping Tru and Gemma. That gives me time to work on the costumes." *And time to miss you.*

"Can I see you Friday night? We can go on a walk down by the water, grab some dinner."

"I think I can manage that."

He ran his hand along her thigh. "How did you get so far under my skin that the thought of not seeing you for a night feels like my heart's being ripped out?"

"Don't tell Bullet that," she teased. "He'll want to man you up, and I like you just the way you are. And I can't answer you, because I'm still trying to figure out how you got me to tell you all my secrets and let down my guard so fast."

"Fast? It's been more than eight months. That is *not* fast."

She laughed. He had her there. "What's your real name? Fast Freddy?" She was teasing, but she realized she didn't know his real name. "What *is* your given name?"

"Bob. After my grandfather. Robert Whiskey."

"Bobby. I like that a lot. Maybe I'll call you that."

His eyes narrowed. "Babe, you can call me anything you want, as long as you do it often." He squeezed her butt, and she flinched. "What's wrong?"

"My butt is sore," she whispered. "I'm not used to riding for so long."

His eyes darkened, and it made her laugh.

"You are a *dirty* biker boy."

"You haven't even begun to get to know my dirty side, sweetheart."

His husky voice and the naughtiness of his words drew her in like a magnet. He massaged her butt and took her in a sweet kiss that quickly turned insistent. Their bodies touched, and she could feel every hard inch of him.

He brushed his lips over hers. "Let me soothe all your sore muscles. Lose the dress, babe. You can keep your panties on."

CHAPTER TWELVE

BEAR GAVE CRYSTAL privacy to undress and went into the bedroom to search for the body oil Dixie had given him last Christmas. He dug around in his nightstand, finding it beneath the rest of the crap in the drawer. When he returned to the porch, he stopped just inside the threshold. Seeing Crystal lying on her belly in the middle of his bed wearing only a pair of black lace panties was torture, but he was determined to keep his word and behave.

At least he'd try.

She blushed as he came to the side of the bed. "I'm more nervous than I was this morning when I was just as naked."

He lay beside her, brushing her hair from her shoulder and running his fingers along her cheek. He was so full of her; he wanted to reassure her as badly as he wanted to make love to her. "You don't have to be nervous. I made you a promise, and I'll honor it. I'm not going to touch you anywhere you don't want me to."

She trapped her lower lip between her teeth, then whispered, "I think that's the problem. I want you to touch me. And I want to touch you. I just don't know if I'm ready to—"

He kissed her slow and sweet to reassure her.

"Then we won't," he promised. "Do you trust me enough to let me get out of my jeans so they don't get oily?"

"Yes." She watched him strip them off, her fingers curling into the sheets as her eyes moved down his body, lingering on his erection.

He crouched beside the bed. "You sure you're cool with this?"

"Yeah."

His eyes drifted down her slender back, to the dip at the base of her spine and over the black lace. "Where does it hurt the worst?"

"My thighs and butt, a little on my lower back. And my shoulders from holding on to you so tight." Her smile widened. "I think I need a full-body massage."

He laughed and straddled her hips without putting any weight on her. He poured oil into his palm and rubbed his hands together to warm them up before massaging her shoulders. She let out a long sigh. He worked his way down each arm, kneading away the tension. He rubbed between her shoulder blades, easing the stress from her body, away from her spine and along her sides, feeling her breathing slow and then quicken as his fingers brushed her breasts. He lowered his mouth to her cheek and pressed a kiss there, on her jaw, her neck, and her shoulder. Her hips rocked up beneath him, and he went back to the promised massage.

Moving lower, he rubbed the tension from around her waist and hips. She moaned sweetly, and he saw a smile lift her lips. "Scoot up, babe."

She inched toward the head of the bed, giving him room to massage her foot. Kneading the tension from her sole earned another entrancing sound. He lavished the other foot with the same attention before working his way up her calves. He couldn't resist kissing the backs of her knees.

"Do that again."

He did, slicking his tongue along the sensitive skin. Her hips rose off the mattress.

"That's hot," she whispered.

She had no idea how hot.

His body blazed with an unquenchable thirst for her. He continued massaging her legs, and when he reached her thighs, he slowed, rubbing deep and sensually, knowing that was where most of her aches and pains were concentrated. She spread her legs wider, allowing his knees to fit between, and he caressed her hamstrings, moving up along the curve of her ass, gently stroking her cheeks. He pressed his lips to first one cheek and then the other. Her body was so relaxed, but with each press of his lips, he felt her stiffen a little, so he pulled back.

He poured more oil in his hands and gently stroked her inner thighs, but she was too alluring not to kiss. When his thumbs grazed her panties, he kissed the crease where her ass met her leg. She fisted her hands tighter in the sheets, turning him on even more. He ran his hands along her ribs, brushing over the sides of her breasts, to her arms, and all the way down to each one of her fingertips.

Coming down over her, he whispered, "Still okay?"

"Ohmygod, yes," she said in a heady voice.

"Can I take your panties off, baby? I don't want to get them oily."

"Yes." She lifted her hips off the bed.

When he'd asked to take off her panties, it had really been to keep them from getting oily. But as he moved to the side and took them off, he gritted his teeth against the dark thoughts going through his mind. And as he touched her, those thoughts came racing forward, testing his control. He was extra careful as he kneaded her bottom. His hands covered the supple globes, and she moved with him, widening her legs as his thumbs neared her sex, an open invitation. It was torture resisting the urge to touch her there, but he didn't want to assume he'd read her right.

"It's okay," she said softly. "Touch me."

He let out a breath he hadn't realized he was holding and continued massaging her bottom, teasing her sex with his thumbs. Each stroke earned a needful sound. He open-mouth kissed each cheek as he stroked between her legs. When she raised her ass, it was too much to resist. He spread her cheeks and slicked his tongue over her wet center, coating his tongue with her arousal. *Sheer bliss.* She moaned, lifting her ass higher, and he didn't hesitate to move one arm around her belly to tease her from the front as he licked her. His cock ached to get in on the sensual feast.

"Make me come," she begged. "I need to come."

Oh, hell yes. He moved one hand to her breast, using his other between her legs, and devoured her with his mouth, thrusting his tongue inside her sweet center to the same rhythm he wanted to use to make love to her. She writhed against his mouth, and he slid his fingers inside her, seeking the secret spot that would give her what she needed. She made a low crooning sound, writhing against him as she cried out his name. He wrapped his arm around her, kissing her back as she rode the waves of ecstasy.

Gently turning her onto her back, he positioned her legs on either side of his knees, and her eyelids fluttered.

"You okay, babe?" he asked, watching a smile lift her lips.

"I'm in a Bear coma. Don't stop."

He chuckled as he kissed the center of her chest and brought his mouth to her breast, his tongue circling her nipple. She bowed up, clutching the blanket tighter as he lowered his mouth over the taut peak.

"Bear," she pleaded. "My whole body feels like a live wire."

He rose onto his knees, noticing for the first time the tuft of blonde curls between her legs. His heart lurched. She'd changed her outward appearance, but she would have no need to change what people didn't see. A painful reminder of what she'd gone through and even more confirmation of how much she trusted him.

She opened her eyes. "Please don't stop. I need you."

Not half as much as I need you.

He lowered his mouth to hers, kissing her with all the love he felt building up inside him. He moved swiftly down her body, wanting her as much as she needed him, and brought his mouth to her slick heat, taking her up and over the edge again.

As she lay on the mattress trying to catch her breath, he lay beside her trying to ignore the pulsing heat inside him.

She opened her eyes and rolled over him, pressing her lips to his chest.

"I love when you touch me." Her fingers trailed up his sides as she kissed from his sternum to just above the edge of his briefs. "I love how careful you are with me." She pushed her fingers into the waistband of his briefs.

"Babe," he warned.

"*Don't.*" Her eyes narrowed, challenging his warning. "I'm a big girl. I can decide what I'm ready for. I want you to know how much you turn me on, not to weigh my answers or protect me from my own desires."

"I'm going to weigh your answers, because I'm falling so damn hard for you I can't see straight." The words fell forcefully from his lips. "I don't want to mess that up by overlooking something or pushing too hard."

"You never push me," she said so quietly he nearly missed it. Seduction sparked in her eyes. "I don't want you to back off, or to make me back off." She ran her finger along his lower lip, and he trapped it between his teeth. "I'm not ready for sex, but I'm ready for *more*. I *want* more with you."

He took her hand in his and pressed a kiss to the tips of her fingers. "I'm all for more."

"Good. Then lie there and let me . . ." She paused, and her cheeks flushed.

"Babe. You don't have to do *anything.*"

"Shush up, biker boy. I just realized that I may not be very good at this. All of my experience with this has been in my head." She wrinkled her nose, looking cute as hell. "Maybe I should go find someone to practice on." She turned away with a teasing smile, and he hauled her down on top of him, both of them laughing.

"Don't even joke about that."

"Thought you weren't possessive."

"Your mouth on some other guy? Fuck yeah, I'm possessive in that regard."

She giggled as she slithered down his body, kissing between laughs. "My biker boy has lots of jealous bones in his body."

"And you're torturing every last one of them. Come here, babe." He reached for her, and she pressed her finger over her lips, shushing him again.

"How hard can it be?" She laughed and dropped her face to his stomach, laughing harder. "I mean, how *difficult* can it be?"

He sat up, and she pressed her hand flat against his chest, pushing him back to the mattress. "Don't you dare move. What's that song? 'Candy Shop'? I'll just lick it like a lollipop."

"Christ," he mumbled. He grabbed her under the arms, and in one swift move she was under him and he was kissing her until her laughter turned to sexy, needful pleas.

She tugged at his briefs. "*Off,* Bear," she said between kisses. "Take them *off.*"

He pushed his briefs down and kicked them to the floor. Feeling her soft skin against him was almost too much to take. He knew what he had to do. To back off, to hand over the reins completely, but as he moved over her, her fingers grasping at his back, he was powerless to stop kissing her. He wanted to disappear into her.

Love bubbled up from deep inside him. "Baby." He kissed her again. "This is enough for me." He kissed her shoulder. "*You're enough for me. Just like this.*"

CRYSTAL STRUGGLED TO contain her emotions as she lay beneath Bear. He was falling for her. She wanted to hear him say it again and again.

"Then let me show you how hard I'm falling, too," she finally said.

She pushed him onto his back, drinking in his tempting physique. He was broad and hard-bodied, but the depth of emotions staring back at her softened all her biker boy's rough edges. As her eyes drifted to his hard length, rooted among a nest of dark hair and reaching up to his belly button, her heart thundered to an erratic rhythm. She was nervous, but not because of what she wanted to do, or even because of her lack of experience. She was pretty sure there wasn't any way her mouth would *not* feel good on him. Her nerves were born from the profound emotions she felt for him. The fact that she was sitting on his bed naked, *wanting* to love him with her mouth, was, in her mind, as intimate as intercourse.

He reached for her hand. "Sugar," he said softly, drawing her eyes to his.

Lord. She could drown in his loving eyes.

"No pressure, babe." He patted the bed beside him. "Lie here, and let me hold you."

His unconditional affection gave her the courage she needed to allow herself to grasp the brass ring. "I will. Soon."

She pressed her lips to his stomach and kissed her way lower, wrapping her fingers around his thickness. She didn't think about right or wrong, or the things she'd read about how to touch a man.

She didn't think at all. She let her heart lead as she slicked her tongue from base to tip, tasting his warmth, the salt of his skin, and reveling in the groans she elicited. She licked the broad head and around his swollen glans, feeling his restraint in the rigidity of his body, and slicked her tongue along the length of him again, getting him nice and wet so she could stroke him with her hand. When she took him in her mouth, he moaned, and his hips bucked off the mattress, but he stopped short, and she knew he caught himself for her benefit. She loved him with her hand and mouth, feeling him swell within her grasp. She was aware of everything: his potent male scent, the rigidity of his arousal, his quickening breaths.

"Baby, baby, baby," he pleaded.

She sped up her efforts and felt his hand cup the back of her thigh. His fingers brushed over her sex, sending electric currents racing through her. She was lost in their rhythm, vaguely aware of his body shifting, his hands lifting her.

"Straddle my face, baby," he said, and she did.

And then his mouth was on her and she was at the perfect angle to take him in even deeper. She explored, licking his shaft, around his sac, his inner thighs. He ate at her sex even more voraciously with every slick of her tongue.

"Squeeze me tighter," he said urgently. "Near the head."

She did, reaping the same benefits and loving that he told her what he liked. She squeezed and licked, sucked and stroked, writhing from the exquisite pleasure he was bringing her. Her legs tingled, and she worked him harder, faster, wanting more of him. Wanting him to come *with* her.

He groaned, a loud torturous noise that caused her to rear up.

"Did I hurt you?" *Oh God, how embarrassing.*

"No," he panted out. "You're going to make me come. Just use your hand. You don't have to . . ."

She was *not* going to miss out on experiencing *all* of his passion.

"Come with me," she said, grinning as she took him in her mouth again, so deep she felt him hit the back of her throat.

"Baby, baby—"

He clutched her thighs and did something with his tongue that sent her over the edge, oblivious to all sense of time and space as he let out a wild groan and the first salty jet of his release shot down her throat. She nearly choked, but she swallowed it down, feeling the warmth coat her throat with each thrust of his hips as her own orgasm tore through her in a series of earth-shattering quakes.

Her legs trembled as she shifted off of him. He gathered her close, easily turning her as if she were part of him, and wrapped his strong arms around her. He smelled like her, his beard still wet with her arousal. The taste of him lingered on her tongue, but nothing could stop the hypnotic pull between them. Their mouths fused together, their tastes mingled, salty, warm, and oddly satisfying. His thigh came over hers, and he took the kiss deeper, like he wanted to seal in the moment. To claim it and never let go.

She wanted that, too.

When their lips finally parted—a minute, or twenty, later—she longed for his to return.

"I was wrong." Her words pushed urgently from her lungs. "You *do* own me."

"No, baby. We don't *own*. We are *one*. We share, we love, we protect, but we don't *own*."

CHAPTER THIRTEEN

THE DARK KNIGHTS' clubhouse was located behind Whiskey Bro's in a similar building in need of updating. Bear sat at a table with Bullet and Bones Monday night at *church* as members discussed prospects, an upcoming charity ride slated for the fall, and the situation with Scooter, which seemed to have calmed down after they made their show of support. While Bear was glad to hear it, his mind wasn't on the meeting. After the weekend he'd had with Crystal, he wanted more time with her, not less, which was what he'd have if he helped with the bar expansion. If that wasn't enough of a distraction, he'd received a call earlier in the day from Jace Stone. He and his business partner, Maddox Silver, were ready to finalize their offer.

Bear stuck around after the meeting, waiting for his father to come over and discuss the bar. While the guys shot pool and played darts, talking about their last ride, or their next, Bear wrestled with his future.

Bones took a swig of his beer, eyeing him. His brother had come directly from doing rounds at the hospital. He'd changed into a Dark Knights shirt. His discarded dress shirt lay over the back of his chair. He was Dr. Wayne Whiskey by day, the epitome of the clean-cut professional, covering up his tats and careful with his language, and by night he became *Bones*, the die-hard biker Bear knew him to be.

"Bullet said you're having a hard time over something that went down with Crystal," Bones said. "Want to talk about it?"

Bullet leaned back in his chair, stroking his beard and giving Bear a look he knew too well. The one that said, *Spill your guts. We've got your back.*

"I made her a promise," Bear said, wishing he had been born with a better poker face. "I'm not breaking it to satisfy anyone's curiosity."

Bones tipped his chin down, giving Bear a serious stare. "Is she still in danger?"

That was the worst fucking part of this whole situation. The guy was still out there. Bear fisted his hands beneath the table. "Not imminent. Maybe not at all. But I still want to track down the motherfucker and kill him." He pushed from the table, needing air.

Bullet grabbed his arm. "Do *not* take vengeance, bro. You'll end up in prison, and Tru can tell you how fucking fun that is. And that pretty little filly of yours won't enjoy waiting for conjugal visits." He pushed to his feet, sliding a dark look to Bones and tightening his grip on Bear. "And whatever you do, you *don't* do it alone. You go down, we go down. Got it? You don't take care of whatever this is alone."

Yeah, he got it all right. Now he was on Bullet's *trouble radar,* which meant any move he made, his brother was keeping tabs. Gotta love the brotherhood.

Bear wrenched from his grip and stalked outside. Inhaling a lungful of cool night air, he paced, trying to calm his roiling gut, and sent a quick text to Crystal.

How's my girl?

Waking up with her in his arms had kept him going all day. He'd cooked her breakfast, which she'd reluctantly admitted she liked more than cold pizza. They'd had the hardest time saying goodbye when he'd dropped her off at her apartment this morning, but a text from Gemma reminding her to get to the shop early to discuss their schedule had pushed them along.

Her response came quickly. *Busy loving up Harley and working on the costumes.*

The door to the clubhouse opened and Bones stuck his head out. "Let's go. The old man's ready."

"I'll be right there." His phone vibrated again, and a picture of Crystal kissing Harley's nose popped up. Damn he missed them both. He sent another text, wishing he didn't need to hurry back inside. *Still have time for your boyfriend Friday night?*

His phone vibrated with a response before he even reached the clubhouse door. *Yes! Your fuzzy little girl misses you.*

He stepped into the clubhouse and made his way toward a table in the back, where his brothers and father were talking. The sounds of cue balls rolling, hearty laughter, and the dense *plunk* of darts hitting the dartboard were as comforting as a home-cooked meal. Or maybe a last meal, given the conversation they were about to have.

He pulled out a chair, ignoring the inquisitive glare Bullet was giving him. *Guess what, B. This one's not under your thumb.*

"Pop was just telling me about his plans to expand Whiskey Bro's," Bones explained.

"He's in," his father said in his slow drawl, as if there was anything Bones needed to be *in* with besides investing capital. Bones was the only one in the family who didn't work at the bar or the shop, but as an equal partner—and a male—he was included in major decisions. He'd attended medical school after college, and after graduating, he'd gone right into practicing medicine. Bear had no doubt Bones would give up everything to help his family, if need be, which was why he'd never made a big deal out of being the one to take over the bar after their father's stroke. There was no way he would have stolen either of his brothers' dreams out from under them.

His father sat back in his typical relaxed state, his cane hanging off of his chair. Bear wasn't fooled. His old man was a thinker, a planner. Bear knew that even after his stroke, if push came to shove, he wouldn't hesitate to throw his body in the middle of a fight to protect those he loved—or strangers who needed help.

Like the rest of us.

"I've been thinking about it," Bear said. "The kitchen will need renovating, and we'll have to hire staff. Offering food will make this place too big to be run as a family business. You've got to be cool with that before you do anything."

His father looked around the clubhouse. "Nothing's too big for family. We've got a damn big family."

"These guys have jobs," Bear reminded him. "And we're all working our asses off. We'll need a cook, a dishwasher, waitstaff . . . You can't expect Dixie, Bullet, Red, or me to handle it all." He'd called his mother Red since he was a little boy, when he'd heard her friends calling her *Wren*, her given name, and thought they'd said *Red*. The name had stuck.

His dad's mouth curved up in a crooked grin, the left side anchored low. "See? You know exactly what the bar needs. That's why you're going to manage it and make it a profitable endeavor."

Bear sat back, grinding his teeth together. "I'm running the shop and helping out at the bar a night or two a week. I'm maxed out. But Dixie can handle this. She's at the bar most evenings anyway, and she handled the renovations at the shop when we added the playroom. She could—"

"She'll be off and married and having babies before we know it," his father said. "Then what?"

"So you're just writing her off again?" Bear scoffed. He'd fought this battle before, and he knew damn well his father would win, because without his brothers' support, after he said his piece, respect would win out, and Bear would back down. Every. Damn. Time.

"She's doing a hell of a job at the shop, and she's a fine waitress," their father said. "She doesn't need to do more. She can help you out, like she did last time."

"*Help me out?* She came home weekends while she was away at college and worked just as hard as I did to turn Whiskey Bro's around. And after she graduated, she dug her heels in at the shop, too," Bear reminded him. "You pushed her in college to make sure she excelled. Wasn't that in preparation for this? Don't you think she's earned the right to run a business on her *own*? I assume you're going to have her buy in, like the rest of us."

Just once he'd like his brothers to open their mouths and stand up for Dixie. But while Bullet would give his own life to protect their sister, the same didn't go for standing up to their father. And Bones? He knew a losing battle when he saw one, and chose his wars carefully. Maybe Bear was driven by the anger coursing through his veins on the heels of learning about what happened to Crystal and not being able to do anything about it, or maybe it was just that he was sick of Dixie being denied what she deserved. *Or maybe it's that I have an offer for what I really want, and I can't seem to find the balls to take it.* For whatever reason, his patience for this bullshit was wearing thin.

"Of course she'll buy in." His father leaned his forearms on the table, his eyes moving slowly around the table, coming to rest on Bear and putting a silent end to the battle that hadn't really been fought. "The question is, how soon can you get a plan together?"

"I'll have to consult Dixie," Bear answered, full of piss and vinegar. "She's the one managing the budget."

His father grumbled something Bear couldn't make out.

They talked for another two hours about his ideas and what Biggs envisioned for the bar. Bear was itching to leave, but he was expected to stay, and even if his beliefs weren't on par with his father's, he stayed until Red texted their father shortly after midnight. Bear got up to follow his father out.

Bullet growled, "Sit down."

Bear lowered his ass to the chair, knowing better than to go head-to-head with Bullet at the end of a long night. "What?"

"Why are you giving him shit about Dix?" Bullet asked. "You know damn well he's not going to budge."

"Because someone has to."

"He's right, Bear," Bones said. "You know I don't agree with the old-school bullshit Dad pulls, but you're trying to change generations of hard-core old-fashioned beliefs. You can't teach that particular old man new tricks."

"Bullshit." Bear crossed his arms and sank back against the chair. "Has it ever occurred to you that *I* might want to do something other than give all of my time to the bar and the shop? Dixie's fully capable, and she deserves to manage the project—and get the kudos that goes along with it. *From Dad.* If the three of us stood together, he'd have to listen. He's only got one-fifth of the vote when it comes to the businesses."

"It's not about that. It's about respect. You don't go against the man who brought you into this world." Bullet sucked down his beer, clearly ignoring the idea that Bear might want to do something other than work with the family business. He probably couldn't fathom the idea, because to him, Bear was Bear, and it was Bear's own damn fault.

"Really, B? What kind of bullshit is that? You think it's cool for women to do the heavy lifting behind the scenes but not get the credit they deserve?"

Bullet leaned forward, his coal-black eyes as mean as a snake's. "I've got no issue with a woman doing anything. It's not about whether Dix is capable or deserves to do it. It's about respecting the decisions of the man who raised us."

Crystal's words came back to Bear with a vengeance.

"And what about Dixie? Who respects her?" When Bullet didn't respond, Bear pushed to his feet. "That's what I thought. Yeah, our father is *old-school*, and you're so fucking militaristic that you salute whatever the hell he does. But we have a sister, and she's got a fucking brilliant mind and just as strong of a work ethic as each of us."

Bullet scoffed. "You just don't want to give up more time now that you're finally getting a little pussy."

Bear grabbed him by the collar and got right in his face, gritting his teeth. "Respect her, B, or I swear I'll tear you to pieces."

"Bear," Bones warned.

"I might get my ass kicked because B's a fucking Sasquatch," Bear seethed. "But I'll get enough shots in to make my point. I learned from the best." He let go of Bullet's shirt and glared at Bones. "How about you man up for your sister?"

Conflicting emotions washed over Bones's face.

Bullet crossed his arms, his massive biceps flexing, but he had a fucking gratified look in his eyes, *trying* to rile Bear up. He lifted his beer as if he were going to toast and said, "I respect Crystal, and you fucking know it. You've got big balls, bro, which is why whatever you think you're going to do about her past, you are not doing it alone. Got it?"

"You've got my back when it comes to that shit and not when it comes to our sister? Yeah, B. I'm starting to *get it*. I'll see you for my shift Wednesday night." He turned to Bones. "See you around."

As he drove home, his thoughts returned to Crystal, where they remained for the rest of the long damn night.

CHAPTER FOURTEEN

"BONES IS ON his way to Tru's. We'll be painting for hours," Bear said.

He and Crystal were in the parking lot of Whiskey Automotive, waiting for Gemma and Truman to get the kids ready to leave. Crystal was meeting Gemma and Dixie to get Gemma's wedding dress fitted and to shop for Crystal and Dixie's dresses.

"I cannot wait until Friday," he said. "Still on for our date?"

"Yes. I'm counting down the lonely nights." Crystal's stomach flipped. She was looking forward to dinner and a walk on the beach, but she'd been hot and bothered last night thinking about what they'd done—and how much more she wanted to do. She'd stayed up late putting the finishing touches on two of the costumes she'd started last week, and then she'd tossed and turned all night, considering trying to take care of her neediness herself. But she knew that even if she could bring herself to orgasm, it would pale in comparison to the way Bear turned her inside out. Waiting had only served to make her more desperate for him. Even Gemma had noticed, teasing her about how she looked like *a girl in love*. Crystal hadn't corrected her. And now she was counting down the hours until she could be close to him again.

"If I had it my way, you'd never be lonely." He nuzzled against her cheek. "Why aren't you making your own dress for the wedding? Something black and lacy, with a splash of red satin?"

Even hearing him talk like that got her all revved up. How would she make it until Friday? "I'm too busy making costumes, and because we'd never make it to the wedding if you saw me in something like that."

"Damn right."

As he lowered his lips to hers, Dixie hollered, "Get a room."

"What does that mean?" Kennedy asked as she ran across the parking lot toward them, looking adorable in the new shirt Bear had bought her and a pair of purple shorts. She launched herself into his arms, and he kissed her cheek.

"I saw you kiss Cwystal," Kennedy said with a sweet smile. "Mommy says girls only kiss boys when they love them. So Cwystal loves you."

"Let's hope so," Bear said, winking at Crystal.

Dixie lowered her voice, for Crystal's ears only. "Mommy will be surprised when her little girl gets into high school."

"I love you, Uncle Be*ah*." Kennedy pressed her lips to his cheek.

"I love you, too, peanut." Bear's eyes warmed. He'd go to the ends of the earth trying to make Kennedy's dreams come true.

Crystal had a feeling he'd do the same for her.

Truman came out of the shop with Gemma under one arm and Lincoln in the other.

Lincoln looked cute in his new *Future Dark Knight* shirt. He held his arms out toward Bear. "Babababababa."

Bear reached for him as Kennedy wiggled out of his grasp. Crystal melted anew at the sight of Bear smothering Lincoln in kisses, earning the most adorable little-boy giggles.

Gemma kissed Kennedy. "Bye, sweetie. I love you."

"Bye, Mommy. Me and Uncle Be*ah* will paint weally pwetty."

"I know you will," Gemma said as Tru pulled her in for a kiss.

"Bye, princess," Tru said. "I'll see you in a few hours."

"I'll text you later, sugar." Bear kissed Crystal, giving her ass a swat as she walked away.

"Enough already!" Dixie pulled Crystal and Gemma toward Gemma's car. "I swear, when I get a boyfriend, he's calling me *Dixie*. I'm surprised you girls even remember what your names are. *Sugar, princess . . .*"

The girls laughed as they piled into Gemma's car. Dixie gave them a hard time the whole way to Chelsea's Boutique. They'd just arrived when Crystal's phone vibrated with a text.

"Ten bucks says that's my brother," Dixie said.

Crystal opened the text and held up her phone for Dixie to see. *Bear.*

"He's such a dork," Dixie said.

"He's not a *dork*, but if he were, he'd be *my* dork. So watch it."

"Whoa, someone's possessive." Dixie narrowed her eyes. "That means you're serious. Thank God, because all that dicking around was making me crazy. Please tell me you're *all in* with him. He's crazy about you."

"I think it's safe to say that I'm all in, Dix." She couldn't suppress her grin as she finished typing her text to Bear. *If you're good, maybe you can visit my Bear cave Friday night.*

Bear's response was immediate. *If? I'm better than good. But you know that, which means my girl knows what she wants.*

A little thrill rushed through her. She tucked her phone in her purse and they headed for the door.

"You *are* all in?" Gemma sidled up to her. "But I thought you two hadn't done the deed."

Walking ahead of them, Dixie covered her ears. "That's my brother you're talking about." She spun around with a disbelieving look in her eyes. "But that *cannot* be true."

Crystal opened her mouth to respond, and Dixie held her palm up, silencing her. "Forget it. Don't tell me. But . . . All this time?

Really? What the heck are you waiting for?" She waved her hand again. "Oh God. Don't tell me. I don't need to know those details about my brother. I'm going inside."

Dixie bolted into Chelsea's, and Gemma hung on Crystal's arm. "You're *all in*?"

"*All in*, Gem. We haven't done the deed, but I . . . *he* . . ." She inhaled quickly and blew it out hard. "I'm falling so hard for him. Or I've fallen. I'm *right there*. All this time, all these *months*. It was building and all the emotions were there, and I couldn't—"

Dixie pushed the door open and stuck her head outside. "Hurry up, sex kittens! Ew. Now I'm thinking about Bear again."

"I'm *so* happy for you," Gemma said as they walked inside. "We'll talk another time."

Crystal was excited to talk to Gemma about her new awareness and acceptance of her feelings, even if she wasn't ready to share all the details of her past just yet. She was a nervous wreck about that, especially the lies she'd told her about bad dates and one-night stands.

A beautiful blonde looked up from behind the counter where she was flipping through a magazine. "Hi. You must be Gemma." She smiled as she came around the counter. "I'm Tegan, your nip-and-tuck girl."

Gemma glanced at Dixie and Crystal. "How did you know who I am?"

"It has something to do with the starry-eyed, almost-a-bride look. And maybe because when you were walking up to the door, Jewel ran in the back and said, 'There's Gemma. I forgot to bring her dress up front.'" Tegan laughed.

"I'm sure I have the starry-eyed thing going on, too," Gemma said. "I cannot wait to get married."

Jewel hurried through the store carrying Gemma's dress. "Hi, Gemma." She gave her a quick hug. "I see you've met Tegan. She's amazing with a needle and thread."

"Don't let her fool you," Tegan said. "I'm amazing at *everything* I do. Using a needle and thread is just one of my many talents."

Crystal liked her already. She reminded her of a certain cocky male.

"Why does everything sound like it's about sex?" Dixie shook her head.

"Because you're lonely," Gemma teased. "Tegan, these are my besties, Dixie and Crystal. Jewel, they need dresses, too."

Dixie looked around the shop. "Gem, do you want us to wear a certain color?"

"No," Gemma answered. "I want you to be comfortable and be *you*."

"How could you forget that Gemma is all about being *free to be you and me*?" Crystal said. "That's why she loves my freaky side."

"I bet my brother likes your freaky side. Oh geez. Forget I said that." Dixie turned to Jewel. "Do you have a dress that says sexy and strong?"

"Do we ever." Jewel waved a hand around the store. "How about brown leather and floral lace?"

"Ohmygod," Dixie said. "Sounds heavenly."

"Leather and lace? That sounds like you and me," Gemma said to Crystal.

"True, but your man has brought out your wild side. Want me to hang with you while you get fitted?" Crystal asked.

"No. Look around. Maybe they have something for you, too."

"You'd look smokin' hot in the sexy little number I saw Jewel putting on the mannequin in the window earlier," Tegan suggested.

"Gemma, why don't you get changed, and I'll show Crystal that dress."

Tegan led her to the front of the store and pulled a sixties-inspired, blue-gray shift from a rack. "This dress is to die for. I love the crepe fabric, and the peekaboo cutout around the neck with that sewn-in choker? Girl, you are going to look hot as Hades."

Crystal took it from her, admiring the dress. The bare shoulders would drive her man out of his mind. He loved kissing her shoulders. "This is gorgeous. What about the color? And it's so feminine. I'm not used to wearing anything like this."

Tegan glanced at Crystal's Rolling Stones T-shirt. It was her favorite, with the big red lips. Her eyes dropped to her skinny jeans and ankle boots, then climbed back up to Crystal's face. Crystal had taken extra time with her makeup this morning, giving herself smoky eyes to go with the dark outfit.

"There are not many girls who can make the outfit you have on look like it belongs on a runway, but you definitely do. I think you can more than pull off this dress. If you put your hair up and leave some tendrils hanging down, you'll look *beyond* elegant. Throw in a pair of pretty heels, and no man will be able to resist you."

"I don't need every man, just one particular very hot one." Crystal fidgeted with the ends of her hair. She could count on one hand how many times she'd worn her hair up in the last few years. It was another layer of protection, something to hide behind. Maybe it was time to step out from behind that shield, too.

"Come on." Tegan walked toward the back of the store. "I'll show you the dressing rooms."

Dixie fell into step beside them. "I *love* that color." She held up a short, off-white lace dress with a wide brown leather belt. "What do you think?"

"That is totally you. It's perfect." Crystal stepped into a dressing room, pushing away the reality that the last time she'd bought something this feminine was when she was in college. She hung the dress on a hook and looked at herself in the mirror, feeling nervous and oddly proud of herself for even considering trying on the dress.

She'd had black hair for so long, she couldn't remember what she looked like with dirty-blond hair. How would Bear react if she ever went back to blond? Her heart squeezed with the memory of his silence when he'd seen her blond pubic hair, and she knew it wouldn't matter what color hair she had. Bear's affection was bone deep.

She changed into the minidress, instantly feeling prettier and even a little freer, though she was nervous about how feminine it was. The cutout beneath the choker, and the bare shoulders, made it super sexy. If she added one of her jeweled arm cuffs, she could take this dress from ultra feminine to edgy and *hot*. And Bear liked *hot*.

"Crys?" Gemma called out.

"In here." She ran her hands nervously over the dress, preparing for Gemma's reaction.

Gemma's head peeked through the curtains and she gasped. "Oh my gosh. You're gorgeous! Dixie, come see!"

Dixie's head appeared above Gemma's. "Holy smokes." She held up her phone and took a picture.

"Do not send that to Bear!" Crystal reached for Dixie's phone, but Dixie held it up over her head. "Please don't, Dixie. I want to surprise him."

Gemma grabbed Dixie's hand. "You can't ruin this surprise for her."

Dixie rolled her eyes. "Fine. But look how pretty you are. And he has to wait *weeks* to see you in it? Bear is going to lose his shit when he finally sees you."

"You really think so?" Crystal hoped she was right. "You guys look amazing, too. Gemma, you were made for that dress, other than the excessive amount of boob space that needs to be taken in."

They all laughed.

"I've got that covered," Tegan said, waving a pincushion.

"And, Dixie?" Crystal shook her head. "I've never seen you in anything but jeans. Talk about stunning. You should wear dresses more often."

"Yeah?" Dixie looked down at her dress. "For what? It's not like I need easy access for anything. If only I could find a guy who *isn't* afraid of my brothers." She'd told them that she'd hooked up with a few guys over the years, but finding a man who was alpha enough, sweet enough, *and* who flew under her brothers' radar was nearly impossible.

"Oh please," Jewel said. "There has to be some guy in town who isn't afraid of big biker guys."

"You are now on my Find-a-Man-For list," Crystal said.

"You have a Find-a-Man-For list?" Gemma asked.

Excited at the prospect of helping Dixie find a man, she said, "Well, I didn't. But now I do."

"I'll help," Gemma said. "Project Find a Man for Dixie. I like it."

Dixie rolled her eyes. "Might as well start the interviews with, 'Are you afraid of gnarly dudes on motorcycles?'"

"Yup," Gemma agreed. "That'll come right after, 'How fast can you run?'"

"Okay, ladies. Let's nip and tuck." Tegan waved to the three-way mirror. "Step right up here on this platform, Gemma, and I'll get you squared away. I've got to be out of here by nine. I'm making a clown costume for my niece, and she needs it by Friday."

Gemma and Crystal exchanged a curious glance.

"You make costumes?" Gemma asked.

"Just for Melody. She loves to dress up," Tegan said as she tucked and pinned the bust of Gemma's dress. "I've made my own clothes for years."

"Do you do seamstress work for other shops?" Gemma asked.

"No. I work here whenever Jewel needs me, and I do photo editing for my sister, Cici. She's a photographer. One day I'll figure out what I want to be when I grow up."

Gemma and Crystal told her about the costumes they were making for the boutique.

"I would love to get in on the ground floor of something like that," Tegan said. "When you're ready to hire, let me know."

They talked as she finished pinning Gemma's dress, and afterward, they exchanged phone numbers. Crystal picked out taupe open-toed slingbacks to go with her dress, and Dixie chose a pair of ankle boots, while Gemma went with jeweled white pumps.

"Crystal." Dixie held up a piece of copper and blue jewelry. "Have you ever worn an anklet bangle? It's totally *you*. They have a whole basket of them."

"I have ankle cuffs and bracelets." She took the pretty ankle jewelry and slipped it on. A thin rope of copper wound around her lower leg like a snake. Intricate swirls sprouted from the main branch of copper, and a hummingbird rested just above her ankle.

"Is there one with a bear?" Crystal asked.

The girls dug through the basket, and Crystal almost squealed when she found one with a bear standing on its hind legs. "Could this be more perfect?"

"He does like to show his dominance," Dixie said.

Crystal knew that was true, but he was also careful with her, and handed over control when he knew she needed it.

They paid for their purchases and piled back into Gemma's car, stopping at the bakery on their way home because Dixie needed a sugar fix. They peered into the glass displays, salivating at scrumptious éclairs, doughnuts, cakes, and cookies, while Cassie, the bakery owner, and her assistant, Anna, helped other customers.

"I liked Tegan," Crystal said. "I think she'd fit in well with us."

"Me too," Gemma agreed. "Let's see how the two costumes I've finished go over. We can put them on our website and wear them in the shop, letting people know we're taking orders."

"You should take orders for the ones you haven't made yet, too. Just put together sketches," Dixie suggested. "People want what's in limited supply."

"She's got a point," Crystal said.

Dixie tapped the glass with her fingernail. "Which of these is the best substitute for sex?"

Thinking about her night on the porch with Bear, she said, "Anything cream filled."

"She has a point," Gemma said. "It's all about the cream."

Cassie flashed a smile and planted her hands on her hips. Her light brown hair was piled on the top of her head in a messy bun, and she had streaks of white powder on her shorts. "Are we ready for the tasting this weekend?"

"Absolutely!" Gemma said. "I'm so excited to see what you've come up with."

"It'll be delish." Cassie crooked her finger. "Come with me. I made something for a bachelorette party, and I *know* you'll love them. I have extras."

"Sounds enticing," Crystal said as they followed her to the kitchen.

Cassie grabbed a tray from a counter and carried it over. "Penis pops!"

"Ohmygosh," Gemma said.

"That is *exactly* what I need," Dixie said.

"Hard up, huh, Dix?" Cassie frowned.

"You could say that," Dixie said. "I think I need to take a ride into another town or something."

"That would go over real well," Gemma said. "Date a biker from another club and you'll get him killed *and* end up like Rapunzel locked in a castle."

"No bikers," Dixie said with a determined look in her eyes. "I think I need to expand my horizons."

"Can we get back to *these* please? Is that cake?" Crystal looked over the puffy penis shapes with sticks poking out of the bottom.

"Of course," Cassie said proudly. "Watch." She put on a plastic glove and pushed on the spongy cake, and white cream came out the tip.

Giggles erupted from the group, and the taste of Bear filled Crystal's mouth. Butterflies took flight in her stomach, growing stronger with every passing minute as her special night with Bear neared. Three more days seemed like a lifetime and an instant at once.

CHAPTER FIFTEEN

BEAR CLIMBED THE steps to Crystal's apartment Friday night, anxious to disappear into her and lock the rest of the world out for a while. He didn't want to think about his impending meeting with Jace and how he was probably going to have to turn down the opportunity in order to help his family with the expansion of the bar. When he reached Crystal's floor, he stood outside, rubbing the tension from the back of his neck. He'd need a hell of a lot more than that to get rid of the weight of his family resting there.

Crystal answered the door wearing a sexy sleeveless black leather shirt that dipped in at the waist and flared over her hips, and a skimpy black skirt. Her feet were bare, and she looked sinful and adorable, making Bear's heart tug in ten different directions.

"You're early," she said happily, fisting her hands in his shirt and dragging him into the apartment. He fucking loved that show of possession.

"I couldn't wait to see you. You look beautiful."

He lowered his mouth to hers, and her arms wound around his neck. She made a sweet sound of surrender as they kissed, and his thoughts followed that needy noise all the way down to his greedy cock. He took the kiss deeper, earning another enticing moan. He wanted *all* of her. There was no stopping their passion. The other night had given him a taste of what their connection would amount to. Thoughts of skipping their plans for dinner and a walk tempted him.

"I missed you," she said. "This was the longest week in the history of the world." She slipped her feet into a pair of black sandals.

So much for skipping their plans.

"I missed you, too, babe." Harley brushed against his leg, and he picked her up. "Missed you, too, little one. Did you keep my girl company at night?"

"Every night. It was like sleeping with a running motor." She slipped the key to her apartment into his pocket and tugged him toward the door.

"In a hurry?"

Her stomach growled, and they both laughed. "Yes, but not just because I'm starved. Can we grab dinner at Jazzy Joe's and eat at the beach? I don't feel like sitting in a restaurant."

After picking up sandwiches, they drove to the beach. It was still early enough that there were a handful of couples and families milling around. They left their shoes in the truck and walked down by the water to eat. Crystal filled Bear in on her busy week, speaking so quickly he wondered what she was nervous about.

"We put the costumes on the website. I'm excited to see if they sell." She told him about meeting a woman named Tegan and how they'd met with her again last night to see some of her clothing designs. "Gemma's ready to hire her if the costume idea takes off." She pushed to her feet. "Can we take a walk?"

After he threw out their trash, they walked along the water's edge. It was a balmy evening, and the cool water felt good on his bare feet, but his gut was churning over whatever was going on in Crystal's head.

"What's happening with the expansion of the bar?" she asked.

He drew her into his arms and gazed into her troubled eyes. "How about you tell me what's really going on inside that beautiful head of yours?"

"I suck that badly at hiding it?"

"The question is, why are you hiding anything from me?"

She sighed, and a smile lifted her lips. "I lit and blew out candles in my apartment a dozen times before you got there."

Reality swamped him. His worries over his career were nothing compared to what must go through Crystal's mind when they were close.

"You're nervous about getting more intimate with me. That's understandable, and I meant what I said, that you're in control of how far we go in the bedroom." He held her tighter. "Just because we exchanged sexy texts all week doesn't mean we have to do anything. I'll never pressure you. I promise you that."

"It's not that. I'm more than ready. I wanted to drag you directly into the bedroom, which is why I hurried out of the apartment." She paused, and softened her tone. "I just need to make sure that you are."

He grinned, holding her closer. "Babe, I've been riding at half-mast for months. I'm more than ready."

Smiling, she said, "I know that, but can you stop looking at guys like you want to kill them and let us live our lives without my past hanging over our heads every time we're out in public?"

Well, hell. "It looks like I'm the one who sucks at hiding things."

She held up her finger and thumb and mouthed, *A little.*

"Sorry, babe. I'm not going to lie. All sorts of crazy shit has gone through my head. I want you to feel safe, and I don't know how you can knowing that guy is out there. But then I look at you, and you're living your life without looking over your shoulder, and I know I need to learn from that. I realize it's not my decision, but that doesn't make it any easier."

"Bear . . ." Her eyes teared up.

"Oh shit. I screwed up. I'm sorry. What did I say?"

"No, you didn't. You make me wonder if it's possible to care too much. You try to be everything for everyone, and I love that about you. And I love that you didn't go behind my back and try to do anything stupid."

"I thought about it way too many times, so I'm pretty sure I'm not done wanting to do the stupid part," he said honestly.

She wrapped her arms around him and he held her.

"I only know one way to live my life," he explained. "When it comes to one of our own, we fight together. I've never had to step back or ask for help. Not when my father suffered his stroke and I had to take over the bar, not when I lost my uncle and took over the shop, not when Tru and Quincy needed help. But, sweet girl, I want to do right by you, and to do that I think I need your help. I need you to be patient with me."

She smiled up at him with a relieved look in her eyes. "I think we both need to ask for patience. I've kept my secret for so long, there was no one to question my decision other than David, and he only wanted to understand my reasons. He didn't try to change my mind. I honestly don't know if it's too much to expect you to accept my decision without question. Maybe that's why I never told Gemma or Jed. Maybe I thought they'd push me to go to the police." She shrugged as if she had no answer. "All I know is that I did what I needed to do in order to move on, and I stand by that decision. But is it the right decision forever? I don't know."

"I'm not asking you to change it," Bear said. "But you need to know that I'm trying to put away that anger. It's just not easy to do when I want to slaughter the guy."

"You're offering to change who you are in order to give me what I need." She swallowed hard and pressed her lips to the center of his chest. She'd done that so often he should be used to it, but it still sent a streak of love through him every time. "You're offering yourself as an imperfect man, and it makes me fall even harder for you."

"I am sorry," he whispered. "I only know one way to be."

"So do I," she said softly. "It takes a bigger man to step back the way you are instead of trying to seek vengeance. When I lost my father, when my mom started drinking, and when I was attacked, I had no control. I have been fighting every minute of my life for control, and you, Mr. Control, have given it to me. I realize that it's killing you not being able to do anything, probably as much as it kills me to know that no matter how much I feel like I've moved past it all, it still slowed me down enough not to drag you into my bedroom, but to have this conversation instead."

"I'm sorry, babe," was all he could manage. He seemed to be saying it a lot tonight.

"It's not a bad thing. The best part of all of this is that I'm not terrified of losing control when I'm with you. I *want* to. But to be with me, you have to be okay with my choices, even if you don't like them."

Her voice was so serious the sea itself seemed to still.

"It's a little like swallowing broken glass," he admitted. "You know the Whiskey in me wants to give you those rules right back, but I'm not going to. What you want and what you need are what matter most. So instead, I'll ask only one thing of you."

She nodded, holding him a little tighter.

"Let me love you, sweetheart. Let me learn how to love you the way you need. Let *us* learn what we both need. There is nothing I won't do for you, but unlearning the visceral make-things-right part of me isn't easy. I'll need you to call me on it if it gets too bad, like you have been. Maybe that makes me a lesser man for needing your help, but if it means being with you, I'll take it."

IN ALL OF her years, there were only a handful of times Crystal had been one hundred percent certain that what she was doing was right. She'd known when she'd returned to Peaceful Harbor that the strength of her relationship with her father would help her regain her footing. She'd been sure that seeing a therapist would allow her to eventually live a full life without fear of intimacy, and she'd known the first time she'd met Gemma that it was kismet. As she led Bear into her bedroom, she felt as though the room itself had been waiting for him. Even as he turned her in his arms, her feelings for him were intensifying.

Slivers of moonlight sliced through the sheers that kept the rest of the world at bay, reflecting in his eyes.. She studied his face, seeing as much inherent strength and love as there was in his touch. She knew how hard it was for him to step back when he was used to barreling forward, and she sensed that their discussion had been freeing for both of them, even if it was a work in progress.

"Still okay, sweetheart?" He brushed his thumb over her jaw, watching her intently.

"Yes. I want this, Bear. I'm not afraid, not even a little, so please don't be afraid for me."

"All I want is for you to feel safe and loved." His hands moved down her arms, slow and gentle and somehow strong and reassuring.

Harley moved around their feet, her soft meow bringing a smile to both their faces. He picked her up and held her to his chest, kissing the top of her head. His eyes moved over the room, drifting to the windowsill where she'd set the orchids between an array of candles, separated into three vases.

His lips curved up in a soft smile. "Can I light them? I want to see you tonight."

"Sure." She was a little nervous, even though he'd already seen her naked. Seeing her naked while they were making love felt different. Exciting and intimate, but different.

Using the lighter she'd left on the sill, he brought shimmering light to the dark room. He petted Harley, looking around her room, taking in the shelves filled with books and a few of the dolls her father had made. Scarves and bags hung precariously off the ends. He walked over to the bed, touching the bongo drum she used as a bedside table. A tall brass lamp with a black-fringed shade sat beside her stereo.

He lifted a finger, as if he were going to turn on the music, and looked at her questioningly. She nodded, and seconds later, slow jazz filled the air.

"My girl," he said wistfully, crossing the black shag rug and setting Harley in the center of the dark purple armchair where Crystal liked to read.

"Stay here, little one," he said to the kitty, his gaze moving over the bed to the enormous white medallion headboard, which nearly reached the ceiling, and the string of colorful holiday lights draped unevenly over one side. His smile widened as he moved around the bed, finding the switch for the lights and bringing them to life.

Her pulse quickened with every move he made.

Watching her intently as he neared, he said, "Do you want me to *ask*, or do you want me to *take*?"

"*Take*," she said a little breathlessly. "Carefully."

His eyes flamed, pinning her in place as he lowered his mouth to hers, hard and insistent. *Claiming* her. His hands moved up her back and into her hair, hot and strong as he angled her head so he could take the kiss deeper. Adrenaline pushed through her veins, severing her inhibitions. His tongue teased over her lower lip, delving into her mouth, making her want, and need, and *crave*. She was lost in his touch, in the beat of the music, in the desire pulsing between them. His mouth left hers, and his finger trailed lightly over her lips. She tried to capture it, but she was too slow and opened her eyes as he stepped behind her.

His warm breath slithered over her skin as he gathered her hair over one shoulder. "Still with me, sugar?"

"Yes," she whispered. "*So* with you."

Her shirt zipped up the back, and she felt the leather loosening as he unzipped it painfully slowly. The first touch of his lips on her back sent rivers of heat to her core. She closed her eyes, reveling in the touch of his lips. She needed more shirts with zippers in the back. *Shirts, pants. An entire wardrobe of clothes that you have to help me out of.*

He slid his hands beneath the leather, caressing her shoulders as her shirt fell to the ground, landing heavily at her feet. His fingers moved over the black lace straps of the red satin camisole she'd made.

"Baby," he whispered. "You made this?"

"For you. Do you like it?"

His arms circled her waist, and as he spoke, his seductive tone slithered inside her. "Almost as much as I like what's in it."

His fingers trailed up her arms, playing over the black lace straps. The brush of his fingers brought goose bumps to her skin. He pressed kisses to her neck as he touched the hem of the camisole.

"My beautiful girl," he said as he lifted it off and it sailed to the floor.

"Kiss me more."

She bent her neck to the side, giving him better access to lavish her with the most sensual kisses she'd ever experienced. He sank his teeth into her shoulder just hard enough to cause her to gasp. She reached behind her and grabbed the back of his legs.

"Too hard, sweet girl?"

"No. *So* good."

He slicked his tongue over the tender spot. Then his hands moved down her belly. Anticipation built up inside her, agony and ecstasy at once. She closed her eyes as his mouth touched her neck, kissing and teasing until she was moaning, arching, desperately seeking more of him.

He pushed his fingers beneath the waist of her skirt. "Give me your mouth."

"*Yes.*"

Her body electrified as she turned her face, and he captured her mouth, pressing his hard length against her rear. His thick fingers went straight to her sex. *Sweet baby Jesus.* He held her so tight she felt his thundering heart against her back and reveled in his passionate, urgent kisses. Lust coiled deep inside her, pounding, burning, *begging* for release as he teased and taunted, gliding along her slick, swollen sex. She rocked, urging his talented fingers inside her, but he wouldn't obey.

When his mouth left hers, she couldn't stop a whimper from escaping.

"I've got you, baby."

His promise made her heart race even more. She wanted to turn around and tear off his clothes. To tackle him to the floor, to the bed, wherever she was able, and finally feel him buried deep inside her. But this heavenly foreplay was too good to miss a second of it.

He didn't speak as he unzipped her skirt, letting it drop to the floor. Then his mouth was on the back of her neck, her spine, kissing his way south. His hands moved down her torso, clutching her hips as he sank lower, kissing her bottom, the backs of her thighs. Cool air rushed over her skin, and his shirt fell to the floor beside her.

Heat radiated from his body as he rose to his full height and turned her in his arms. His lips hovered over hers, teasing, whispering,

"Even when you try to hide yourself in dark colors, your brightness shines through."

She was lost in his voice, his touch, and the way he was *worshipping* her. When his arms circled her waist, bringing their bare chests together, it was like coming home. Warm, safe. *Perfect.*

He dipped his head beside her ear. "Okay, beautiful?"

"Yes," came out with confidence.

He took his wallet from his pocket and tossed it on the bed. "Protection."

She didn't tell him she'd prepared, too. In her nightstand was an unopened box of condoms she'd purchased for tonight.

He guided her hand to the button on his jeans, silently seeking her approval. She worked it open quickly, and he stepped from his jeans, standing before her in only his tight briefs. This was the moment she'd dreamed about, the moment that had sent her scurrying back to her therapist to clear a path. But nothing could have prepared her for the way her heart expanded at the sight of Bear standing in her bedroom, ravenous for her.

When he lowered his mouth to hers again in a surprisingly gentle kiss, she went up on her toes, eager for more. He groaned into the kiss, and the raw passion in that sound unleashed the last of her tethers. Blood pounded through her veins as he lifted her leg to his hip, rocking his hard heat against her center. *Yes, yes.* She grasped at his back, but he was too broad, too big; she couldn't find purchase. And then she was in his arms, kissing him as he carried her to the bed, tossed the decorative pillows to the floor, and tore back the covers.

He lowered her to the bed, his big body coming down over hers. Lord he felt good. And then his mouth was on hers, kissing her deeply, lovingly, *masterfully*. She wanted to memorize every second, every touch, every noise slipping from his lungs. His hands pushed beneath her ass, lifting and angling her panty-covered hips beneath him. His hard length felt glorious pressed against her, moving to a beat all their own. But the kiss—*God, this kiss*—intensified, shattering her ability to think at all. Just when she thought she couldn't take another second of it, his mouth eased from hers, and he moved lower, kissing her breasts, her sternum, her belly. His hands hooked into the sides of her panties, and his eyes found hers again. That silent approval-seeking glance snagged her heart. She lifted her hips off the mattress, giving him the green light.

Flashing a devilish grin, he didn't hesitate to take them off. He kissed her thighs, and every touch of his lips made her wetter, needier. He knew just how to draw out her pleasure.

He dragged his tongue along her thigh, and she grabbed his shoulders. "It's insane how much I love your mouth."

Spreading her legs wider, he finally brought his tongue to where she needed it most, accompanied by a gratified, purely male groan. That sound soared through her, leaving a trail of sparks beneath her skin. She bowed up, digging her heels into the mattress as he licked and kissed and brought his hands into play, taking her right up to the verge of madness. Her orgasm was just out of reach, taunting at her with a tug deep inside her belly. She grabbed his head, rocking and shifting, trying to guide his mouth where she needed it most—though she couldn't be sure exactly where that magical spot was. Every slick of his tongue brought her closer to the edge. He countered her every move, taking her impossibly higher, until she was sure her body would shatter into a million little pieces.

"Please, Bear—"

As she said the words, he did something with his tongue, and his fingers, and her orgasm crashed over her in waves of exquisite pleasure. He sealed his mouth over her sex again, plunging his tongue inside her, and she rocketed to the peak again. And then he was tearing off his briefs, and gathered her in his arms. His wet beard crushed against her chin as he took her in another passionate kiss. She didn't care that he tasted like her. She wanted to climb inside his mouth and experience everything it had to give.

She grabbed at the back of his hips, arching up, slicking her wetness against his shaft and earning another heady groan. Their mouths parted, both of them panting as he reached for his wallet and retrieved a condom. He kissed her softly, and when he gazed into her eyes she heard his silent question loud and clear.

"Yes," she whispered confidently.

He sheathed himself and came down over her, kissing her cheeks, her forehead, her lips. His love for her seeped into her skin, burrowed deep in her bones, and when he said, "I love you, sweet girl," she was so caught up in him, it was all she could do to say, "I know."

He was smiling as their mouths came together, the head of his arousal pressing against her center. She wasn't scared, wasn't anxious, was only needful and wanting—and wishing her brain worked because *I know* didn't begin to cover what she felt.

"Wait," she panted out. He stopped so abruptly, she knew he thought she'd changed her mind. "I love you, too, Bear. So much. I just had to tell you."

The smile that crawled across his face was worth the momentary heart attack she was sure she'd given him. "I know you do, sugar. I see it in your eyes every time you look at me."

"You do?"

"I do, baby."

Her heart was so full, her body so alive, she didn't hesitate to pull him into another kiss. He entered her slowly, his strong arms cradling her as her body adjusted to the unfamiliar, and *welcome*, visitor. She could barely breathe as their bodies melded together for the very first time. He felt so good, so right. When he was buried to the hilt, they both stilled. His heart beat as crazily as hers. She opened her eyes and found him watching her, searching for that silent blessing he'd already so caringly sought time and time again. She couldn't speak, could only hope her smile conveyed how *very* okay she was. She lifted her hips, letting him know she was ready for more. Ready for *him*.

She expected to feel awkward, to wonder *if* or *how* they'd find the right rhythm, but there was no room for worry. There was only Bear taking control, finding their rhythm *for* them, holding her, loving her, kissing her, and whispering the sweetest, sexiest things she'd ever heard. His body was hard and insistent; his touch was loving and gentle. Too swept away to think, her body took over, rising to meet him.

Every thrust of his hips came with a whisper of love: "*Only you, baby. Feels so good. I'm yours, sweet girl.*"

His hardness electrified her, his tenderness made her melt, creating a storm of uncontrollable passion. Wanting to savor the excitement, their closeness, the newness of the heady scent of their lovemaking, she dug her fingers into his arms, trying to stave off her climax. But the harder she resisted, the more consuming it became. Every thrust brought a rush of new and overwhelming sensations, and her body betrayed her, yielding to the searing need that had been building for months. Her core flooded with fire seconds before his name burst from her lungs in a cry of sheer ecstasy.

"*Bear*—"

He tucked his face in the crook of her neck as her body pulsed around him. Thrusting once, *twice*, he reared up, his face contorted in the clutches of passion as he followed her over the edge.

"*Fuuck*, baby. *So* sweet. *So* good." He kissed her shoulder. "*So* right."

She clung to him, dizzy with emotions, as they fell limply to the mattress wrapped in each other's arms. He pressed his lips to hers, tucking her body tight against him.

"Hey, sweet girl," he said tenderly, bringing her eyes up to his.

He was searching again, needing confirmation that she was okay, and she loved him even more for it.

She touched her lips to his and whispered, "Perfect."

He took care of the condom, then rolled onto his back and pulled her on top of him, making her feel petite and special in his arms. She rested her cheek on his chest and closed her eyes. Her legs fell naturally between his, his sex nestled against hers. He curled one arm up behind her head, holding her as he pressed a kiss to her forehead. He pulled the blanket up over their waists, cocooning her in the safest, most loving position.

She snuggled in and closed her eyes, reveling in their intimate new world, and drifted off to the sure and steady beat of his heart.

CHAPTER SIXTEEN

BEAR LAY AWAKE with a purring kitty curled against one side and his beautiful girlfriend draped across the other. He'd thought of her that way for so long that as the sun crept in through the blinds, bringing her private world into focus, he wasn't surprised by the intensity of his feelings. He wanted to go to sleep with her in his arms every night and wake up with her every morning. He wanted to watch her creative mind at work, and cook with her, and take her on long motorcycle rides. He wanted to give her enough good memories to wipe away the bad. But tonight he had to bartend again, and if he honored his father's demands and took on the expansion, he'd have little to no free time in the foreseeable future.

As he looked around her bedroom, his thoughts returned to last night's conversation on the beach, and Bullet's words came back to him.

You always do what's right, little brother. It's that simple.

Right for who? That was the question.

Bullet stood behind his convictions even when it was clear to Bear that where Dixie was concerned, his brother's convictions were wrong. Did Bullet know something he didn't? Or was he just as hardheaded as his father? He'd fight for his brothers even if the odds were 50:1. Club brothers, Truman, Quincy, blood brothers. Brotherhood was brotherhood. The difference between Bear and Bullet was that for the sake of their sister, Bear would stand up to the one man

Bullet wouldn't. And though he had no concrete evidence of what Bullet would do in a situation like his and Crystal's, he had a feeling that in his brother's mind, doing the right thing meant nailing the fucker who had attacked her to the wall and dealing with the aftermath of Crystal's heartache later.

Crystal lifted her chin, smiling up at him with sleepy eyes, and his heart swelled. If that's what Bullet thought, he'd be wrong. Bear had made his choice and he intended to honor it. Crystal's well-being came before anything, or anyone, else.

They'd made love for a second time in the middle of the night after they'd woken tangled up in each other. He'd waited for her to take the initiative, not wanting to come across too pushy, and she had. Stepping back from the aggressive lover he'd always been had allowed him to feel more connected to Crystal and her needs. And that had deepened their connection and opened his eyes to other parts of his life that he'd been plowing through. It was time to figure out how to do the right thing where his father and Dixie were concerned. Had life always been this complicated and he hadn't seen it clearly until Crystal had opened his eyes?

He lifted Harley from the bed and kissed her before setting her on the floor.

"Mm." Crystal pressed her lips to his chest. "Does my Bear need sustenance?"

"Your Bear needs to hold you." He gathered her in his arms.

She pressed her hips to his. "Little Bear has other ideas."

He kissed her again, rolling her onto her back and deepening the kiss. "Don't feel pressured by my body's reactions to my beautiful girlfriend."

She touched her lips to his again. "Thank you, but finally being honest with you about why I held back for so long freed me from being under its thumb. I promise, if there are times that I need to slow down, I will let you know. But I have never felt happier, or more in control, in my entire life."

"Okay, then I won't ask again."

She smiled. "Yes, you will. You're my *pushy*, caring Bear. But hopefully you'll learn quickly and will let me own this decision sooner rather than later."

"You can own that one." He pressed a kiss to her chest, above her heart. "I only want to own this one."

"We don't own—we are *one*, remember? Now shut up and kiss me so I can see if my biker boy is as good in the morning as he is in the evening."

She pulled him into a scorching kiss, and he showed her just how incredible morning lovemaking could be.

Later that afternoon Bear was traipsing through the kitchen of Whiskey Bro's with Dixie, thinking about Crystal and Silver-Stone and wondering why he was wasting his time coming up with an expansion plan for the bar.

"I'll call Crow and get a handle on renovation costs." Bear leaned against the counter watching his sister take copious notes. She tucked her hair behind her ear, revealing the colorful tats on her shoulder. Her eyes were serious and focused, underscoring the differences in their interests for the project.

"I have ideas about how to reconfigure the kitchen, and I was thinking. Maybe we shouldn't offer dinner food. If we just offer things like sandwiches and fries, then we don't really need a chef. It'll keep expenses down while still offering more to the customers."

"I agree. Catering to a dinner crowd would turn Whiskey's into a different type of place altogether, and I'm not sure that's what any of us want."

Dixie closed her notebook, and he could practically hear the gears in her mind turning. After fourteen years of working in the bar, he had none of that excitement left in him, whereas every time he walked into the auto shop he got a rush of adrenaline. The shop wasn't just a job or just part of the family business he had to take over. It was the place he could see himself working thirty years down the line, and when he looked that far ahead, other than his family, there were only three other things he envisioned. Crystal, a family of their own, with snarky girls and badass boys, and his name attached to some of the most sought-after motorcycles in the world.

CHAPTER SEVENTEEN

IF ANYONE HAD told Crystal that one day she'd be happy and in love, she never would have believed them. Even during all those months when Bear was claiming her and she was unknowingly falling for him, she had still expected the floor to drop out from under her at any minute. But it had been a week since they'd first made love, and every day that passed had brought them closer together. Her legs weren't being kicked out from under her. They were becoming stronger, and she was learning that it was okay to take her trust to another level and rely on Bear.

Most mornings she woke up wrapped in Bear's arms, with a happy flutter in her chest. She'd noticed that Bear's need to throw threatening glances at every male they passed was easing, though it wasn't gone completely. It helped that every time he did it, Crystal threatened to withhold kisses. Her hungry Bear was a very fast learner.

Crystal had discovered other, unexpected pleasures of staying overnight with the man she loved, like how nice it was to be a real couple. Sharing their deepest worries and their dreams. She'd learned that lying in his arms talking until the wee hours of the morning could be as intimate as making love. She enjoyed listening to his stories about the uncle he'd admired and still missed, and her heart broke over how conflicted he was about the offer from Silver-Stone. The fact that he hadn't just walked away from his family's businesses when he'd gotten the original offer was proof of his loyalty, but she worried for him. If he went his whole life without doing what he really wanted, wouldn't he regret it? Maybe even blame his family? They talked about that, too, and it was clear that whatever decision Bear made would be what he thought was the right one.

On the nights Bear bartended, Crystal worked on the costumes for the boutique and went to sleep in a bed that felt too big, longing for him in ways she never imagined possible. Not for sex or the electricity that accompanied every kiss—although she missed those things, too—but for *him*. With the exception of a few of life's frustrations, such as Bear's dilemma over working with Silver-Stone Cycles or helping his family and her ongoing discomfort about visiting her mother, she felt happy and fulfilled.

Most of the time.

While she was no longer bearing the weight of her secret alone, there was no denying the stab of guilt she felt when she was with Gemma. Yesterday when she'd driven Jed to his attorney's office she'd felt guilty for keeping secrets from him, too. *One thing at a time.* She'd resolved to keep her past to herself until after the wedding, but the wedding was still weeks away. Even though they'd had fun last weekend with the wedding cake tasting and work was going well, Crystal couldn't fight the uncomfortable feelings building up inside her. How could she be Gemma's maid of honor knowing she'd deceived her? Knowing Gemma thought she'd been sleeping around before she got together with Bear? She wanted Gemma to understand just how special Bear was, and for that to happen, she needed to be honest.

Mentally debating that situation, she pushed through the doors to the stockroom Wednesday afternoon, pulling the costume rack for their next party. Despite a minor meltdown by a four-year-old, their first party of the day had gone off without a hitch, and the hours had flown by. Their new warrior princess costume had gone over well with both the parents and most of the little girls, although two of the girls had chosen the frilliest, laciest costumes they offered. That had prompted Gemma to ask Crystal to design a costume highlighting those two elements.

"I've got it," Gemma said from behind the counter. "We can design a pink and white costume like the old-time Victorian dresses. They have frills and lace. We can do entire themes and parties based on the Victorian era."

She was so excited about their recent success, and about Bear and Crystal, that Crystal's happy flutter was once again overridden by guilt. "Brilliant. Those dresses will take much longer to make than this." She waved at her warrior princess outfit. "But we can definitely make them."

She'd made two more costumes, and Gemma had begun spreading the word with an article in the boutique's newsletter. Tru had been making up fairy tales for the kids since the night he'd rescued them, and he made up a fantastic story to go along with each costume for the newsletter. They already had orders trickling in. It felt good to see their hard work growing into something bigger.

Crystal parked the rack by the dressing rooms, trying to muster the courage to talk with Gemma.

"You have that look on your face again," Gemma said.

"What look is that?" She joined her by the register and checked her cell phone for messages, smiling at the selfie Bear had sent of him and Lincoln.

"The cat-that-ate-the-canary look." She peered over Crystal's shoulder at the picture. "Our boys sure are cute."

"The cutest." Crystal shoved her phone beneath the counter as Gemma answered the boutique phone. Crystal motioned toward the back room and mouthed, *I'll get the other rack.*

Gemma held up her finger and shook her head, then spoke into the phone. "I'm so sorry to hear that. Okay. No problem. Sure. Let us know when you have a date. Thanks for calling." She hung up and said, "Our afternoon is clear. That was the Patricks. They had to cancel. The birthday girl fell and chipped her tooth. They're on their way to the dentist's office."

"Ouch. That poor girl." Crystal took it as a sign, and steeled herself to come clean to Gemma, at least about her supposed long list of one-night stands. "I'm glad we have the afternoon off. I wanted to talk to you."

Gemma's face grew serious. "I think I know what you want to say."

"You *know?*" Her heart sank. Could Bear have said something to Tru and he told Gemma? She'd cleaned out a dresser drawer for him to keep a few things at her apartment, and he'd done the same for her at his house. They'd also stocked his house with kitty paraphernalia, because where they slept, so did their little purring girl. Except for the nights when Bear bartended, they were practically living together. He and Tru could have gotten to talking about how much things had changed and something about her past might have slipped out. Although Bear was so careful about what had happened, she couldn't imagine him making that mistake.

"Well, I assumed," she said with a smile. "You and Bear really have been hooking up for longer than you wanted me to believe, right? I know you said that wasn't the case, but I've been over this so many times, and every time I see you two together, it feels like there's *a lot* more there."

"Nope." She took Gemma's hand and led her to the table in the back of the store. "Sit."

"Uh-oh," Gemma said as she sat down. "Crys, are you pregnant?"

"If only it were that simple." She sat across from Gemma. "You know all those times I said I was hooking up with guys?"

"You're pregnant and you don't know who the father is? Ohmygod." Gemma covered her mouth with her hand.

"Stop. I'm *not* pregnant. And up until last week, there would be no way for me to be pregnant." She was so nervous her words came too fast and too harsh, but she couldn't stop them. "I never had those one-night stands. I never had most of the dates, either."

"Come on," Gemma said with a half-smile, half-confused expression. "It's not like I'm going to tell Bear. Geez, is that why you've been looking so worried for the past few weeks? You're afraid I'll tell him about your trysts?"

Crystal rose to her feet and paced. "*No*, Gemma. I've never slept with *anyone* except Bear since before I left college."

"What?" Gemma pushed to her feet. "Why would you lie about that?"

The hurt and confusion in her eyes stopped Crystal cold. She'd only wanted to tell her about the fake hookups, but it was unfair to try to skirt around the truth. She should have waited until after the wedding, but there was no turning back now.

"Because I was afraid. When I met you I had been in Peaceful Harbor for only a few weeks, and I was afraid to tell you about my past." She turned away, crossing her arms over her chest, as emotions swamped her. "I was afraid *of* my past."

"Crystal," Gemma said gently. "I don't understand." She came to her side, as empathetic as ever, which made it that much harder for Crystal to tell her the truth.

"What happened that you were afraid to tell me?" Gemma asked.

"Not you specifically. *Anyone*." She wrung her hands together, trying to fight her mounting panic. This anxiety had nothing to do with what she had to reveal and everything to do with how hurt Gemma would be when she realized how much Crystal had kept from her. When she met Gemma's gaze, tears filled her eyes.

"I'm sorry. You're my best friend in the world, and I never should have lied to you about anything."

Gemma reached for her hand. "Crystal, *what* happened? I don't think I've ever seen you cry. How can I help?"

Her compassion only made Crystal cry harder. "I'm not crying because of what happened. Or maybe I am a little. I just hate that I lied to you. *You*, of all people. You know what it's like to have a messed-up family, and you loved me even when I was bitchy and you thought I was sleeping around." She laughed through her tears, because the whole thing was crazy. Who pretended to sleep around?

The answer stung as much as the lies. *The girl who doesn't want to get close to anyone.*

Gemma's arms came around her. "Of course I love you. You're my best friend."

"Not 'of course.'" She pulled back and swiped at her tears. "I've never had a friend like you before. And I was so afraid of the bottom dropping out from under me at any second, I screwed up. I lied to you about guys who never even existed. And now I can't stop crying because I kept the rest of it from you, which is also screwed up, because that's my *right*. But it still fucking hurts because you've shared everything with me and I should have trusted you with it." She squared her shoulders, desperately trying to escape the pain swelling inside her.

"I don't care about guys who never existed," Gemma said carefully. "I care about *you*. What happened?"

"Stop being so understanding!" She squeezed Gemma's hand and smiled through her tears. "Just tell me you're angry with me and get it over with."

"Fine, yes. I'm a little hurt. Who wouldn't be? We've been through so much together. But you're *crying*, and I know a little about perspective, so whatever you were afraid to tell me, I'm sure it outweighs my stupid hurt feelings. And if it doesn't? *Then* I'll give you a hard time." Between Gemma's childhood and Tru's history, she had enough perspective for a hundred people.

Crystal's hands dropped to her sides, nervously opening and closing. "I didn't leave college because of finances. I was raped, and I couldn't take being on campus." Her voice cracked, and she gulped in a ragged breath. "I tried, but two days after it happened, I gave up and came here. I never even reported it to the police."

Tears slid down Gemma's cheeks as she reached for Crystal again, hugging her so tight it was even harder for her to breathe.

"Crys," she said compassionately, holding her while they both cried. "I'm so sorry that happened to you and that you felt you had to hold it in all this time."

Crystal's mind spun. She was too overwhelmed to respond, wishing everything could have been different and knowing that all the wishing in the world couldn't change the past—or the future. Only *she* had the power to change her future, just as she'd done when she'd left the trailer park and when she'd come to Peaceful Harbor.

And when I let Bear into my life.

She drew back, feeling a little more confident. "I've wanted to talk to you about Bear for so long, but it's all been so confusing. You need to know the rest of the story." They sat at the table, and Crystal told her about how she'd reinvented herself time and time again. She told her about changing her hair and name, her mother's reaction, putting herself through years of therapy, and finally, she told her the truth about Bear.

"He was the reason I went back to my therapist. I was falling for him for so long, and I wanted him, Gem. I wanted him like I've never wanted a man in my life. When we finally kissed, I was so *afraid* I was going to fall apart, that I did. But I wasn't afraid of *him*, and I wasn't afraid of making out or having sex, or any of that. I mean, I was nervous about sex—don't get me wrong—because it had been years since I'd done that and because of what I'd been through. But I wasn't *afraid*. Not with Bear."

She paused, thinking about how much she loved him. It was that love that pushed her to explain the rest of the story to Gemma. "David, my therapist, explained that it's not uncommon in situations such as mine to worry about panicking. I had overcome the trauma and the fear of the rape, but I had built up being close to Bear to such epic proportions that it was no longer the situation itself that caused me to panic. It was the anxiety caused by worrying about it. It's confusing, and that's a very shortened and probably inaccurate description, but hopefully you get the idea."

"I get it. I really do. You were afraid you'd freak out, and that anxiety is what caused you to. I just wish I could have helped you."

"You *did* help me. Your friendship has been my saving grace. During those weekly sessions with David, when I'd see him at lunch or after work and I'd feel *off* for a few hours, or days, you were always there to cheer me up. Even when you didn't know the truth about what had happened."

Understanding shone in Gemma's eyes. "All those *bad dates*."

"Yes," Crystal said, feeling guilty all over again.

"Now that I know the truth, I can see it. You were much more standoffish when we first met. I've never thought about it, but now it's so clear. Those bad dates turned into—"

"*Assholes, guys who weren't good in bed*, and then . . ." Crystal paused, realizing that the most recent way she'd referred to men had showed her progression from victim to being in control. "I became a girl nobody would want to mess with and made up those guys. And then, when those bad dates turned into 'play toys to entertain me for a night,' it was all part of moving past what had happened. Obviously, I didn't want 'play toys,' but as I was healing and becoming more self-empowered, I wanted to tell you. I wasn't ready to lay it all out there, so using those stories was my way of sharing it with you. I did go on a few dates last year, but I never felt anything, not even when we kissed good night. And I thought I'd fooled myself into thinking I was healed. And then I met Bear, and sparks flew from the first time we set eyes on each other."

Gemma hugged her again. "*Fireworks. Volcanoes.* You two have had undeniable chemistry forever."

"I know, right? And things are good now. David was right. Telling Bear what I had been through helped tremendously. Not just because he could be more careful with me, but voicing my fears made me less afraid of them. And you know Bear. He's wonderful, Gemma. There's no room for fear when I'm with him. He's careful, and loving, and . . . if I'm being honest, he's had a hard time about my not going to the police."

"I was wondering about that." Gemma tucked her hair behind her ear. "He's so . . ."

"Pushy? Assumptive? Handsy? Aggressive?" She smiled, because she'd called him all those things since the day they'd met, when he'd first slung that massive arm over her shoulder and called her *sugar*.

"Protective," Gemma said.

"He's much better about it. But when I first told him, he looked like he wanted to throttle every man we passed," Crystal admitted.

"Does that change how you feel about your decision?"

"I did the right thing for *me*, and I can't change that. I feel bad that it's hard for him, but we're both on the same page now." Crystal looked at the office door, behind which her kitty was either sleeping or playing with her toys. She still couldn't stand to leave her alone during the day.

"Is that why he gave you Harley?"

She nodded. "The night I told him about what happened, I wanted to be alone afterward, and that killed him."

"I bet he wanted to stand guard over you."

Crystal laughed. "Hasn't he always? Even before he knew? He showed up the next morning with Harley and said he didn't like the idea of me being alone."

"He's so in love with you." Gemma smiled. "Tru said he has been for a long time."

She felt herself smiling. "I know. I think on some level, I've always known."

"How can I help you?"

"You already have. You don't hate me."

"I could never hate you." Gemma touched the ends of Crystal's hair. "Will you keep your dark hair?"

"I don't know. Right now I just want to enjoy not living behind a wall of secrets. I wondered if I'd change all over again, but I like who I am. Aside from lying to you, of course. That part of me sucked."

"No, it didn't. That part of you needed to protect yourself." Gemma pushed to her feet and pulled Crystal up to hug her. "Are you really okay?"

"Yes, and if you ask me that too many times, the bitchy Crystal will come out. I was a victim of rape, but that incident does not define me, and none of it—not losing my dad, or my alcoholic mother, or the rape—ruined me. I went through three years of therapy, Gem, about my dad, my mom, Jed, what happened at school. I didn't sweep it under the rug. I just didn't talk about it with anyone other than David. The only thing that I have been having a hard time with was not telling you, and I'm sorry."

"It's okay," Gemma said. "And I won't keep asking. Do you think Harley will be okay for a little while? I think you deserve to indulge in a multiflavored sundae."

Normalcy. That's exactly what Crystal needed, and she was beyond thankful that Gemma somehow knew that. "I'm in."

As they walked toward the front of the store, Gemma suddenly tugged Crystal against her. *Hard.* "I'm sorry. I'm just so fucking sorry. I hate that you went through something so horrible, and I hate that you lost your dad, and your mother was a jerk about what happened. And I hate that you thought you had to keep it to yourself. I just . . . *hate* right now. I'm trying not to cry, but . . ."

Tears poured from Crystal's eyes. "I know. Trust me, Gem. I know."

"I love you."

Crystal tried to speak through her tears, but it came out garbled. "I . . . love you . . . too."

"Sorry," Gemma said sheepishly, wiping her eyes. "I just had to get that out. I'm okay now, and I promise, no more tears."

Crystal wiped a streak of eyeliner from beneath Gemma's eye. "Penny's going to think we've both lost our minds. I know you can't keep this from Tru."

"I . . ." She bit her lower lip.

"It's okay. He loves me, too. I know that." They walked up front to get their bags. "Just tell him not to push me about not going to the police when it happened, and for the love of God, please tell him not to go all alpha crazy and try to get Bear to take revenge. That poor man is stuck between a rock and a hard place." She squeezed Gemma's hand. "Lucky for him, I like to rock his hard place."

Gemma's jaw dropped. "How can you tease about that after everything you've been through?"

"How can I not? I love my man." She grabbed her bag and put her arm around Gemma's shoulder. "Have I told you that I'm addicted to orgasms with Bear?"

Gemma covered her ears. "Don't tell me details." She dropped her hands. "*Wait.* Is his junk inked?"

Crystal laughed as she pushed open the door. "Wouldn't you like to know?"

"Ew. No." Gemma locked the door behind them. "That would hurt *so* bad. Why would any man do that?"

"Why do guys do anything?"

They looked at each other and said, "Because they can."

CHAPTER EIGHTEEN

BEAR SAT ACROSS from Jace Stone and Maddox Silver Thursday evening in Mr. B's, a microbrewery located down by the marina, far enough away from Whiskey Bro's that he didn't have to worry about his father stumbling upon them. Bullet must be wearing off on him. Even having a discussion about working with them felt disrespectful to his father. All his father wanted was to make Whiskey Bro's even more successful so he could leave his kids a valuable family legacy. And here Bear sat, possibly putting a wrench into his plans.

Where's the line between family loyalty and self-fulfillment?

Jace leaned heavily muscled, tatted-up forearms on the table, his dark eyes as serious as those of his silver-haired, thickly bearded business partner, Maddox Silver. While Jace rivaled Bullet in size and age, Maddox was just over six feet, and Bear guessed him to be around fifty. A *hard* fifty, with a strikingly handsome, weathered face and eyes that looked like they'd seen a world of pain.

"You were pretty clear about not wanting to give up working at the auto shop, and we respect that," Jace said. "The offer for a limited schedule stands, but we're running out of time. We need to get a handle on the level of commitment you're willing to make. Of course, there will be non-competes and such, given your profession."

"I understand. I'm working on figuring out what type of schedule I can commit to. I'm sorry it's taking me a bit longer than I had anticipated, but some things have come up with my family that I need to work through before I can make a firm commitment." As much as he enjoyed the time he got with his family at the bar, the hours sucked. Giving up those shifts was a no-brainer. He was slated to work until closing again tonight, which meant another night he'd be sleeping apart from Crystal. Giving up the hours from the shop, on the other hand, took more thought. He was still wrestling with that part.

"What we're offering," Maddox said in a voice as thick and slick as crude oil, "is a chance for you to make a name for yourself in the industry. You have a knack for concept designs that are a bit eclectic and graceful, while maintaining power—not at all what the public is used to seeing. We believe we can manufacture and market your designs in such a way that they become highly sought after. We'll limit production and use only the best materials, but success can only come with dedication. Even if you decide to commit to, say, sixty hours a month, there will be added travel time on top of that to consider, to meet with our engineers and attend design meetings. Some of that will be factored in, but there are always last-minute meetings that come up."

"I expected as much," Bear said. "Have you firmed up your timeline for opening this location?"

The two men exchanged a serious glance.

"We've decided to hold off on purchasing the building here in Peaceful Harbor. For now," Jace explained. "But we want to move forward with this collaboration. You've got a lot to offer, and conceptualizing can be done primarily off site. But we need a commitment. We've got a slot to fill, and we'd like to fill it with you. We'll need a decision within the next two weeks."

Bear knew a golden opportunity when he heard it, but he couldn't make a commitment to them until he made one to himself. And that meant preparing for another battle he might be waging alone.

WHISKEY BRO'S WAS busy for a Thursday night. Bear filled a pitcher with beer and set it on the counter for his mother, who was serving alongside Dixie tonight. She only worked a few hours a month, and Bear enjoyed when their schedules coincided.

"You're up, Red," he called out to her.

She hustled over in her black jeans and Whiskey Bro's shirt and leaned across the bar, lowering her voice. "How long do you think it will take Dix to give that blond guy a piece of her mind?" She glanced in the direction of the tall, blond man playing darts with two other guys. Bear had been keeping his eye on them, too.

"She likes the tips. When he crosses a line, she'll shut him down."

His mother patted his hand. "You're right. You doing okay, babe?"

Babe. His mother never used their road names and rarely used their real names. Bear was pretty sure it was because, when they were growing up and she had four hellions to care for, she'd had to run through all the names before she hit the right one. His name usually sounded something like, *Brandon, Wayne, Whateverthehellyournameis.*

"Yeah, I'm good," he said.

She pushed a hand into her short red hair and smirked. With her affinity for wearing black—shirt, pants, boots, jewelry—she looked an awful lot like a young Sharon Osbourne. "You can't fool your mother." She set the pitcher on the tray and said, "Next time you're down at Mr. B's, tell Maisy I said hello," and strutted away.

Damn. Maisy and Ace Braden owned the microbrewery. He'd been so worried about staying out of his father's sight that he hadn't thought about how closely knit the community was.

Bear was filling another drink order when Dixie sidled up to the bar, popping bubble gum and watching Bear like he was a halftime show.

"What's up, Dix?"

"I need two Jack and Cokes and a bottle of Bud." She glanced at their mother, who was standing with her hand on her hip, giving the blond dart-playing flirt a piece of her mind.

"She's going to ruin my tips," Dixie complained as Bear poured the drinks. "Did Dad reach you about the expansion plan?"

"He called, but I was busy." And by busy, he meant he'd let the call go to voicemail because he wasn't sure how he wanted to handle that situation yet.

"He asked if you'd spoken to me about it. I told him you had, and I gave him the financials and projected earnings with the expansion. I broke it all down, just as I did with the two-year projections a few months ago. He has all the numbers he could possibly need, whether he decides to move forward or not. But he's raring to go, so if you really don't want to do it, you should tell him. Let it fall on Bullet."

Bear scoffed, "He's got less time than me and no experience with this kind of thing. Plus, B's not exactly the most patient guy. Can you imagine him trying to negotiate prices for renovations?" He lowered his voice and narrowed his eyes, mocking Bullet. "*What the fuck do you mean you can't finish it by tomorrow? You'll finish the job or I'll use your head as a hammer and finish it myself.*"

She laughed. "Maybe it's time he learned since he's so gung-ho about following in Dad's footsteps. Thanks for the drinks. I need to go save my tips." She spun on her high heels and sauntered over to the guys playing darts.

A few hours later, when his mother was getting ready to leave, she pulled him aside. "Want to tell me about Jace and Maddox?"

"Not really," he said honestly.

She crossed her arms, her sharp green eyes telling him he wasn't going to get away with that answer. "Your uncle Axel used to say that you were going to be the next Harley designer. You were the kid everyone came to with their broken bicycles, skateboards, and toys. You've designed and built more motorcycles than you've purchased. Now, Robert, do you want to talk to me about Jace and Maddox?"

"Seriously? You're pulling *Robert* on me?"

"I'm pulling a mother talk on you. We don't do these often enough." She touched his cheek. "You're as stubborn as your father."

"Hardly," he said.

"I didn't say as 'rigid.' I said as 'stubborn.' There's a difference, sweetheart. I know better than to come between you and your father, so I'm going to say only this. You've done more for this family than a parent could ever hope for. You're a loyal, strong, intelligent young man, and I will forever be grateful for that enormous heart of yours. You saved this family, and you know how we Whiskeys work. When you're in trouble, *we're* in trouble and we have your back. You may not be in trouble right now, honey, but you need saving. Only this time you have to save yourself." She hugged him and whispered, "Bring that beautiful love of your life over sometime. It's time we do more than smile across the room."

Stunned by her support, Bear could do little more than watch her walk away.

By the time he rolled out of the parking lot at two thirty in the morning, he was beat. He'd received a call from Tru that had his gut tied in knots. Apparently Crystal had finally come clean to Gemma. As he drove up the dark mountain road, he cursed himself for taking the shift and not being there for her. It had been a long night. A group of rowdy guys had come in around eleven and stayed until after one, playing pool and hitting on every woman in the place. That shit got old quick, and tonight, when he wanted to be with Crystal and not babysitting horny guys, his patience had been hanging on by a thread.

He pulled up the long driveway, activating the solar lights he'd installed last weekend and bringing Crystal's car into focus. He cut the engine and jumped out.

"Crystal?" he called into the dark, peering into her car.

With his heart in his throat, he ran to the front porch and found her fast asleep, curled up on a chair with Harley in her lap, holding her car keys and clutching the little worry doll between her fingers. She wore a pair of plaid pajama pants and the shirt that read *Dip me in honey and feed me to Bear*. His heart squeezed. He dropped to his knees and wrapped his arms around her waist, a wave of relief washing over him.

She opened her eyes, a smile curving her lips.

"Hey, sugar. Are you okay?"

"Our bed felt empty," she said sleepily.

Our bed. Christ, she was every bit as *in* as he was. He picked up Harley and hugged Crystal. "I'm so glad you're here."

"I told Gemma," she whispered against his cheek.

"I know. Tru called to check up on you. Are you okay?" Tru had also wanted to check up on Bear and make sure he wasn't losing his mind, which he was, but he was keeping it under control.

"Yeah. She didn't hate me." Her eyes dampened, and another wave of guilt for not being there tonight hit him. "Tru called? Does that mean everyone knows?"

He helped her to her feet. "No. He just wanted to make sure you were okay. I'll make you a key tomorrow. I don't want you waiting outside for me. Why didn't you call? I would have come to you."

"I don't know. I missed you, so I packed up and came over." She glanced down at her backpack beside the chair, and he picked it up.

They went inside and headed upstairs. He was glad she was there, but Crystal sitting outside alone at night didn't sit well with him.

He took a quick shower and found Harley sleeping on his pillow. Leaving Harley where she was, he climbed into bed and cuddled up to Crystal.

She turned toward him. "Is it too presumptive that I came over?"

"I want you to be presumptive." He pulled her closer and pressed his lips to hers. "I hated the idea that you were alone tonight. I hate every night that we spend apart. I always want you with me."

"Me too." Her eyes turned serious. "I'm dreading seeing my mother this weekend. I know I didn't want you to meet her, but now that I'm not hiding anything from you, would you consider coming? Jed will be there, and we don't have to stay long."

"Of course. Whatever you want." He touched his lips to hers.

"I keep thinking about Gemma. She doesn't see her mother regularly because her mother is so awful. In a different way from mine, of course, but still. And seeing my mom . . . Well, you saw me that day we were supposed to paint Tru and Gemma's house. Every time I see my mother, I feel like I fall into a tar pit and I have to claw my way back out again afterward."

"Then why do you do it? I'm a loyal guy, but if it's that bad, why go? Are you helping her in some way by visiting?"

She shook her head. "She doesn't even seem like she wants me there. She's hateful and says horrible things about me and my father. She's even bitchy to Jed, who has always been there for her."

All his protective urges surged forward. "Then why put yourself through that?"

"Because I think my dad would have wanted someone to take care of her."

The sadness in her voice slayed him. "I think your dad would have been more concerned about taking care of *you*."

"Maybe. How did your meeting with the guys from Silver-Stone go?"

He didn't want to talk about Silver-Stone. He wanted to convince her not to visit her mother. But if there was one thing he'd learned, it was that Crystal did not like to be told what to do.

"They need a commitment, but it will mean hiring more staff at the bar and the auto shop, and the timing sucks, with my father's plans to expand the bar."

She snuggled in closer and pressed her lips to his. "Or maybe it's perfect timing. If you think my father would be concerned about me taking care of myself, don't you think the same goes for your father? That he'd be concerned about you taking care of yourself for once?"

I'm not even sure I know how to do that anymore. He rolled onto his back and draped his arm over his head, pulling her against his side. "I don't know, babe."

"I wonder if there's such thing as being *too* loyal."

"If there is, then we're both guilty of it."

CHAPTER NINETEEN

"BABE, YOU LOOK a little green." Bear pulled Crystal closer as they drove toward her mother's house Sunday evening.

"It's a special look I get just for my mother. You don't find it attractive?" She hadn't even been able to muster a smile when they'd picked up Jed. Nothing good ever came from visiting her mother.

"Our mother has that effect on people," Jed explained.

Bear squeezed her hand. "You seriously hate this."

"That's putting it mildly." She fiddled with the radio. "It was a mistake to ask you to come. You don't need to see what a mess our mother is."

"That's even more of a reason for me to be here with you. I don't want you going through that at all, much less going through it without me."

She pointed to the stoplight, her stomach knotting up tighter. "Turn right there. Then it's the second street on the right."

"I feel like I've been here before." Bear stopped at the light and glanced at her. "Are you sure you want to do this?"

"*No*," Crystal said. "But I have to. We'll stay just a few minutes, so I can feel like I've done my daughterly duty."

He turned the corner and followed her directions into a trailer park. "Now I know I've been here before."

"Really?" Jed pointed to their mother's trailer. "It's the yellow piece of shit."

"I know this trailer. You moved here when you were eight?" he asked as he parked.

"Yeah," she said.

"How do you know it?" Jed asked as he climbed from the truck.

Bear helped Crystal out. "I think I drove your father home. He was at the bar, too drunk to drive. I was a kid. Sixteen, maybe? I don't remember. But there was a little girl peeking out that window." He pointed to the window on the side of the trailer.

"That was my bedroom." Her pulse quickened. "But I don't remember that."

"Funny." Bear slung his arm over her shoulder. "I'll never forget it. Seeing you made me realize how much my dad cared about other people. He could have thrown customers into a cab and sent them on their way, but he never did. He said he didn't know how a cabbie would treat a guy who wasn't in his right mind, but he knew how the children he'd raised would."

It made her happy to think that Bear had met her father, even if it was under those circumstances. But if her father had been too drunk to drive then, had he also been drunk the night he died? Had he caused the accident that had killed him?

She looked at Jed, and he must have read the fear in her face, because he shook his head and said, "He was no longer drinking when he was killed. He wasn't at fault. He'd been sober for a while by then."

Tears of relief filled her eyes. "I'm so glad to hear that. I know your father has weird ideas about women and work, but I love him even more knowing that he took care of my father like that. Do you remember anything else about our father? What he was like?"

"Yeah, I remember. He looked like Jed, tall with dirty-blond hair, but older, of course. He talked about you guys the whole trip. His beautiful, smart little girl and the son who tried his patience at every turn."

It didn't matter that her father had been drunk. Bear had a memory of him that was new to her. "I love hearing that. Wait. Is this true, or are you trying to make me feel better because my mom is such a mess?"

"It's true, babe. I told you I don't lie."

"Thanks for driving him home," Jed said. "He was never a big drinker, but when he lost his job, it took a toll on both of them."

"You remember that?" she asked. "I only have vague memories, and I'm never sure if they're real or not."

"You were only eight, but I was eleven. He wasn't as bad as Mom. There were a few months when things were pretty fucked up, but then he sobered up. One night Crys looked at him and said she didn't like the way his breath smelled. That he didn't smell like her daddy anymore. And that was it. He stopped drinking that night. He was killed ten months later by a drunk driver."

Bear must have felt her knees weaken, because he held her tighter.

"I don't remember saying that to him, either," she said.

"It was you, Crys," Jed said. "You saved him from ending up like her. He loved you so damn much. He would have given his life for you."

"For you, too," Bear said to Jed. "I'm sure of it."

She looked back at the trailer, hating her mother even more. "I can't do this. I can't go in there. If he could sober up, why couldn't she?" She pushed from Bear's arms. "Do you have any idea, Jed? Do you remember anything?"

Sadness filled Jed's eyes, and he reached for her hand. "Listen, shrimp. There are some things you don't want to know."

She wrenched her hand free. "Bullshit. I can handle anything. Just tell me."

Jed hesitated, glancing at Bear.

"Don't look at him wondering if I can handle it," she snapped. "I have been to hell and back. There's nothing I can't handle."

Jed clenched his jaw. "Dad found out she'd had an affair, and he gave her an ultimatum. Stop drinking and clean up her act, or he was going to leave and take us with him. She didn't stop."

"Obviously. And . . . ?"

"He'd gone to Peaceful Harbor to see about renting a place there." Jed glanced at Bear, dropped his eyes, and finally met her gaze. "He was killed on the way home."

"He was *leaving* her?" She stumbled backward, unable to hear past the rush of blood in her ears. "He was *leaving* her? I have put myself through this every month because I thought he would want me to take care of her, and he was leaving her?"

"Babe." Bear reached for her, but she stepped away.

"No. This is . . . He died trying to save us. Because of *her.*"

"She turned me into a thief." Jed's hands fisted. "I'm not trying to dodge taking responsibility, but you should know the truth. I *stole* to make sure we had food on the table."

Crystal's jaw dropped. "You stole *for* her? That's why you did it? All this time, you told me it was who you were!"

"It was," he seethed. "What did you expect me to do? You had to eat. You needed clothes. Fuck, Chrissy. I did what I had to do. But I'm done. I've cleaned up my act, and I want to move away from here and find an apartment. Find a solid job. Forty hours a week instead of the part-time shit I'm doing now. I'm meeting with the attorney about my license this week, and hopefully I won't have issues getting it reinstated."

Crystal grabbed him by the shirt, still stuck on him throwing his life away for her, and hollered through angry tears, "You *stole* for us? For *me*? I did that to you?"

Jed wrapped his arms around her even as she struggled against him. "No, you didn't. *She* did. *I* did. But not you, Chrissy. Never you. You always did the right thing."

She crumpled against her brother, her arms falling limply by her sides as she cried. "He died saving us."

IT TOOK ALL of Bear's willpower not to storm into that trailer and give their mother a piece of his mind.

"I can't go in there," Crystal said.

"Never again, baby." Bear reached for her, and she came willingly into his arms. "Never again. And, Jed, you need an apartment? We can help you out. Quincy needs a roommate." This was what they did. They took care of family. Maybe Crystal was right. Maybe there was such a thing as being too loyal. Maybe it was time he made a change, too.

She pushed from his arms, her sad eyes turning fierce, her spine straightening with all the confidence and determination she'd always possessed.

"I have spent enough of my life being sad, or angry, or not understanding why she is the way she is." She swiped at her eyes and stormed toward the trailer with Bear and Jed on her heels. "I'm done with this once and for all."

"Babe." Bear touched her arm to slow her down. "You sure you want to do this and not calm down first?"

With a dark look in her eyes, she said, "Damn sure."

The harsh smell of smoke and wasted life hung in the air as they approached the trailer. Through the door Bear saw a bleached blonde sitting on a plaid sofa. She had a cigarette in one hand and was flipping through a magazine. A half-empty beer bottle sat on an old coffee table beside three empties.

She glanced up as Crystal stormed in, bloodshot eyes moving from her daughter to Bear and then to Jed. She returned her lazy gaze to the magazine. "I don't have enough food for an extra person."

Bear fought the urge to grab her by the collar and shake her.

Crystal was trembling, hands fisted, jaw clenched tight. "You drove him away."

Their mother's eyes lifted again, and she took a long drag of her cigarette. Jed stepped around Bear, but Crystal moved in front of him, focused on having this showdown. "How could we mean so little to you?" she accused. "How could you choose booze over us and Dad?"

Their mother slid a disgusted look to Jed. "You opened your big mouth, didn't you? Just like your father."

"I'd be lucky to be just like him." Jed stood tall and supportive beside Crystal.

Their mother scoffed.

"I am *done*," Crystal seethed. "Done feeling guilty about going off to college to save myself, done listening to you demean us." Tears brimmed in her eyes. "I don't know why you'd turn your back on us, on Dad, or what screwed you up so badly that you ended up like this. And frankly, I don't care. This is the last time I'm coming here."

"You think your father was so perfect?" Her mother pushed to her feet, wobbling on sky-high heels. "You have no idea what he was like."

Jed stepped between them. "Yes, she does. She knows all of it. I'm done protecting and enabling you. No more stealing, no more giving you money that you'll just drink away."

"You two think you're so special. You don't know what he was like. He promised me a good life, and look where I am!" their mother yelled. "He left *us*."

"No," Crystal said, sounding as though she'd simply given up trying to convince the woman of a damn thing. "He was *killed* trying to get us out of this hellhole. It was *you* who left *us*, long before we lost him."

"THIS HAS BEEN one of the longest days of my life," Crystal said as they drove toward home.

After they left her mother, they'd gone out for Chinese food, Crystal's go-to comfort food. But once their orders arrived at the table, even the thought of it turned her stomach. She knew that, like her mother, Chinese food was another thing she'd probably not want to see for a very long time. They dropped Jed at his friend's house, and he must have apologized a dozen more times. She should be miserable, given the events of the night, but as they drove over the bridge into Peaceful Harbor, she rested her head on Bear's shoulder and realized that although she was emotionally exhausted, she wasn't unhappy. She'd never understand why her mother had turned her back on them, but if she'd learned anything from her father's death, it was that life was unfair.

Bear tightened his grip around her shoulder. "I know, babe. I'm going to draw you a nice warm bubble bath when we get home. You must be hungry. Want me to stop for something?"

"No, thanks. I have everything I need right here."

"I'm proud of you," Bear said. "Sad about all of it, of course, but proud of you and Jed for realizing that it's time to put yourselves first. That's a really tough thing to do when it comes to family. Do you want to talk about it?"

"I'm still processing it. Thanks for calling Quincy about the apartment for Jed. I'm glad he'll be nearby. I'd like to spend more time with him. Do you really think you can hire him? Your father won't like that very much."

"My father and I are going to have a long talk, and Jed's your family. That makes him our family."

She smiled at his confidence. "You're pretty sure we'll stay together, aren't you?"

"Pretty sure? Babe, you're fooling yourself if you think we're ever breaking up."

"I don't think we will, but we haven't been together all that long." She loved poking her Bear, because—as he did now—it made him hold her tighter.

"When we're old and gray, someone will ask us how long we dated before we got married. No matter what you tell them, I'm tacking on eight months. So get used to it, sugar. You're stuck with me."

Married? As he turned into her apartment complex, she couldn't think of anyone she'd rather be stuck with.

When they got out of the car, she realized he'd parked in the exact same spot where they'd shared their first kiss the night when she'd panicked.

She wrapped her arms around Bear's neck and said, "Kiss me."

He lowered his mouth to hers, taking her in a kiss that rushed through her like fire and ice, awakening all the incredible sensations that had been trampled down by the difficult evening. She melted against him, reveling in their closeness and acknowledging in her mind, and in her heart, how free she felt.

She did this. She made the decision to walk away from the woman who had shamed her and continually demeaned her. Would she ever get over the feeling of wonderment, knowing she'd saved herself by putting herself *first*? That she'd done the right thing by finding a therapist? If she'd never taken that step, she may never have been able to be close to Bear, or even live the life she had. It was empowering knowing that every time life had kicked her legs out from under her, she was able to take control and find her footing again. And it felt equally good knowing that as long as Bear was with her, she'd never have to handle anything alone again.

When their lips parted, hers tingled with warmth.

"Kiss me like that again and we're going to give your neighbors quite a show." He nipped at her lower lip, holding her so tight she felt every inch of his arousal.

They went up to her apartment, and true to his word, after loving up Harley, Bear went to fill the tub. Crystal carried Harley into her sewing room, looking at all the dolls her father had made lined up on the windowsill. How could he have known she'd need them so badly?

Bear came out of the bathroom shirtless, his gorgeous chest on display. His thick dark hair was standing up on end, as if he'd just pushed his hand through it, the way she'd like to. His grin was all male, and it sent zings of heat ricocheting through her.

He wrapped his arms around her, kissing her shoulder. "Missing your dad?"

She cradled Harley between them. She loved the way he was looking at her, his eyes brimming with desire. She almost kept her thoughts about the dolls to herself, but she liked that she could finally share her innermost thoughts with him. It was another level of intimacy that she'd come to love.

"I always miss him, but I was just thinking about how much I counted on those dolls for all these years. It's not like they have magical powers. It's silly, really, but having them around gave me strength."

"That's not silly. That's love and trust. You believed in your father's love, and it gave you strength to become the incredible woman you are."

Embarrassed by his praise, she kissed Harley and set her on the floor. "Thank you. I'd like to think he would be proud of me. So much has changed since we've been together. Do you wish you had chosen an easier girl?"

He shook his head. "No, sugar. You're the only woman for me, and if you don't know that yet, then I'll just have to try a little harder."

"I know it." She touched her lips to his. "It's hard to believe that Jed kept all that stuff from me for all these years and I never told him about what happened to me. We suffered separately for so long, and despite living with a mother who did her best to ruin us, we both turned out okay."

"Better than okay, babe. You're amazing. Do you think you'll tell Jed about what happened in college?"

"Yeah, but I couldn't tonight. We've both been through enough today."

As he led her down the hall, she said, "You give me strength, Bear, the way you believe in me. Thank you, and thank you for being here for me."

"Don't thank me, babe. Just love me." He drew her into a delicious kiss. "Come on, let's get you in the tub."

He opened the bathroom door, and steam washed over her skin. He'd brought in the candles from the bedroom, and their flames danced in the romantically dim room.

She piled her hair on top of her head and secured it with a clip. Bear crouched before her, taking off her boots and running his hands up her legs. His touch made her whole body *want*. He lifted her dress over her head, and it sailed to the floor, followed by her bra and panties. He helped her into the warm bath, which felt luxurious, instantly relaxing her.

He pulled off his boots and socks and unbuttoned his jeans, never taking his eyes off her as he unzipped his jeans ever so slowly. She licked her lips at his provocative striptease as he worked them over his powerful thighs and kicked them to the side. Lord, she loved the way he looked in those black briefs. Visually devouring that formidable bulge, she scooped up bubbles and spread them over her chest, sinking lower in the warm water. She was slick between her legs, and she had the urge to touch herself while she watched him. It was the first time she'd experienced such a strong pull for the lascivious desire. He was watching her so intently, she wondered if he could tell. She couldn't resist brushing her fingers over her taut nipple, and inhaled sharply at the heat that seared down the center of her body.

He stripped off his briefs, exposing the part of his body she'd come to crave. She loved touching him, loving him with her mouth, her hands, her body. *My soul.* He knelt by the tub, kissing her as he dipped his hand beneath the bubbles and caressed her belly, moving his hand up as he took the kiss deeper, until it rested just beneath her breasts. She arched, wanting to feel that rough, strong hand caressing her, his fingers *inside* her. He feasted on her mouth while he moved his thumb lightly over the underside of her breast. When she tried to lean up, he slid his hand lower, teasing over her curls and dipping between her legs. She moaned into the kiss and felt him smile. He loved drawing out her pleasure, and she was learning to draw out his when they were making love, learning how to angle her hips, how to touch him and how to kiss him, how to suck on his neck when he was buried deep inside her and bring him right up to the cusp of release.

His fingers moved over her sex, without entering her. She broke the kiss, the anticipation overwhelming. He kissed her neck, dragging his tongue along her jaw, then nipping at it as he continued his relentless taunt down below. She grabbed the sides of the tub, raising her hips.

"Bear," she said breathlessly.

"I love hearing you say my name when you're so close to the edge. But I love hearing it even more when you come. Scooch forward, baby. Let me get behind you."

He climbed in behind her, and she leaned back, sighing with the warm, wonderful feel of his hard body. He wasted no time, sliding a hand between her legs and turning her face toward him, capturing all her needy noises in a penetrating kiss. There was something about being just out of reach that made their over-the-shoulder kisses scorching hot. His finger drifted over her sex, driving a path between her legs in a magnificent rhythm that brought her hips up and made her toes curl under. She soared with pleasure, and his free hand threaded into her hair, keeping their mouths fused together until she collapsed against him.

She turned, wanting—*needing*—to be closer. Straddling his hips, she took his face in her hands and kissed him deeply. She was conscious of all the places their bodies touched and of the water lapping at her belly, sloshing over the sides of the tub.

"Hold me," she whispered. Dropping her hands between them, she curled her fingers around his erection.

One of his arms circled her waist, and the other snuck into her hair, tugging it from its tether. It tumbled around their faces as they kissed, and she worked him with her hand. She stroked him hard and tight the way he liked, taking extra care to squeeze at the top. His kisses drew her in, turning her loving thoughts darker. Hearing his masculine groans made her want to feel more of him.

"Bear," she said feverishly. "I want to feel you inside me."

"We can't use a condom in the tub."

"I don't want to. Can I just feel you for one second inside of me without you coming? I need to be closer to you."

He ground his teeth together. "Baby, I'll do whatever you want, but seriously, that's playing with fire no matter how much control I have."

Adrenaline and passion burned through her, making her heart race and her breathing ragged. She kissed him again. "One second, that's all. I'm definitely going to see my doctor about getting on birth control. Jesus, how do people hold back? I want so much *more* of you."

He smiled as he kissed her, lifting her up and lowering her slowly onto his shaft. She wrapped her arms around his neck and buried her face in his shoulder.

"*Ohmygod.* You feel so big. This is heaven." She moved, and he gripped her hips, stilling her.

"No moving. Heaven *and* hell, sugar."

She whimpered as she forced herself to climb off the most glorious man on earth. "Come on."

He held on to her as they stepped from the tub. The second her feet were firmly planted on the bath mat, he plastered his body to hers, kissing her breathless.

She took his hand and ran toward the bedroom, not caring that they were dripping wet and sudsy. He tackled her on the bed in a fit of laughter, nearly crushing Harley, who scampered to the floor.

"Condom," she said urgently.

He sheathed himself in seconds, surprising her when he sat up against the headboard and reached for her, lifting and lowering her onto his shaft as he'd done in the tub. "Ride me, baby."

She put her hands on his shoulders, and he took her breast in his mouth. She was already so close to losing it, she held on tight, hoping to stave off her orgasm. Her head fell back as their bodies moved in perfect sync. He lavished her other breast with the same attention, circling her nipple with his tongue, then closing his mouth around it. Cool air rushed over her damp, heated skin, bringing even more titillating pleasure. Cupping her breast in one hand, he grazed his teeth over the sensitive tip, causing her whole body to clench.

"Bear," she panted out.

His hand slid down to her ass, squeezing as he pressed in deeper, stroking over the hidden spot that he seemed to find so easily, sending her spiraling into ecstasy. He pulled her into another mind-numbing kiss, capturing her cries. She could feel his body growing tense as hers gripped and pulsed around him, urging him toward release. She rode him faster, and his fingers tightened in her hair.

She could feel him holding back, knew he wanted to last for her. She loved that about him. "Let go," she said against his lips. "I love when you lose control."

A rough, male groan sailed from his lungs as he found his release. "Baby, baby, baby."

They lay on the damp sheets for a long while, until goose bumps covered her body and he insisted they change the sheets. After changing the sheets and cleaning up the trail of water they'd left from the bathroom to the bedroom, she was digging through her shirts looking for something soft to put on when Bear handed her a bundled-up shirt.

"What's this?" She looked down at the soft black material.

"Something I got you on the island."

She shook it out and read the silver letters. *Whiskey Loves Me.* She clutched it to her chest. "You made this for me?"

He tucked her hair behind her ear and kissed her. "I loved you then. I love you even more now." He took it from her and slipped it over her head. It fell to her thighs. "For those nights when you might forget."

"I could never forget, and not just because you text me your name, or because of this shirt, which I love. But because you have imprinted here." She covered her heart. "And that'll never go away."

"Good, baby, because I want you to always know that you can count on me. My love for you will only get stronger, no matter what we're going through."

Her stomach growled, and he touched his forehead to hers.

"Ice cream," she said. "I need it."

He pulled on a pair of jeans, and they went out on the balcony and shared a pint of ice cream from her freezer. The warm evening air brushed over her skin. She'd had one of the roughest nights of her life, and still, it was one of the best. She'd learned so much about her family, and herself, over the past few hours, she *almost* felt guilty for being so happy.

Bear stood beside her, leaning against the railing. "I want to be with you every night. Every morning. Every minute. Do you want that?"

"I'll ask Gemma if you can come to work with me, like Harley." Her heartbeat sped up. She missed him so much on the nights they were apart. She had to fight the urge to throw herself into his arms and say, "Yes!" This was a moment she'd never allowed herself to dream of, and she wanted to savor it. There were so many seemingly unattainable moments, but she realized that falling in love didn't count as one. Falling for Bear had been a massive number of moments woven together like an unbreakable web of love.

"Smart-ass." He patted her butt. "Move in with me."

"So you can have your way with me anytime you'd like?"

"That's a perk. You need to live with me," he said as she filled her spoon for the umpteenth time. "I'm worried about your eating habits."

She smiled around the spoon. "Mm. *Worried* or *jealous*? Not many people can live off sugar, pizza, and Chinese food and get away with it."

"Come on, babe. You know you want to take the next step."

She stuck her spoon into the ice cream again, unable to suppress her unstoppable smile.

"So . . . ?" he urged.

"Remember when we went to Woody's that first night?"

"Of course. I'll never forget. That was the night of our first almost kiss. That was the night you started to let me in."

She melted a little at the way he remembered it. "Yes," she said softly. "But how did you get me to go with you?"

His brows knitted, and that cocky smile she loved so much appeared.

"Sweet girl, I remember the day I *met* you. You were so full of snark and attitude, and more beautiful than anyone I'd ever seen. You snagged my attention that day, and you've captivated my heart ever since. Chrissy, Christine, Crystal, sugar, baby, baby cakes, sweetheart, will you please make me the happiest man on earth and move in with me?"

Overwhelmed with emotions, she let "Bear" out like a whisper as she fell into his arms. "Yes. Yes, yes, *yes.*"

CHAPTER TWENTY

THE NEXT WEEK blew in with a surge of happiness and passed in a whirlwind of busy days and busier nights. They spent the evenings packing up Crystal's apartment and fell into each other's arms at night with a second wind, making love until the wee hours of the morning. Bear wondered if a person could live on love. If not, he couldn't think of a better way to die than from too much *Crystal.* On Sunday, Bear's brothers, Tru, Gemma, and Dixie helped move Crystal's things into Bear's house. *Our house.* Damn, it felt good to think of it that way. They rearranged his den for Crystal to use as a design studio and moved the extra bed to Quincy's apartment for Jed, who they were helping move the weekend after next. It was amazing how the addition of her belongings transformed the cabin from what Crystal called a gearhead bachelor pad into a warm, welcoming *home.* She and Bear had taken extra care placing the dolls from her father around the house, setting a few in each room. He liked knowing a piece of the man who had cared enough to try to save her from her mother's deterioration was with her no matter where she was. Crystal had hung up pictures of her, Jed, and her father. She had no interest in including pictures of her mother, but for her sake, Bear hoped one day her mother would get sober and try to mend the broken fences.

Bear had spent months waiting for things to fall into place with Crystal, and it was worth every second. He'd never felt so complete, but he'd also learned a lot about strength and fortitude from her. As he paced behind the clubhouse Monday night with his cell phone pressed to his ear, waiting for the last of the members to drive away, he prepared to take his final stand in the battle he'd been waging for far too long.

"I just want to be sure that managing the bar is what you want before I make it happen," he said to Dixie. He'd put off this show-down for long enough, and at this point, it was as much about equality for Dixie in the family businesses as it was about him being able to lead the life he'd always dreamed of. And with Crystal by his side, he'd settle for nothing less.

"Hell, yes. If it weren't against the stupid club rules, I'd be there with you."

"I know you would. Did you meet with Dad this morning as we planned?" He'd tried to get an hour alone with his father earlier in the week, but their schedules hadn't meshed until tonight. With the Silver-Stone offer pending, he didn't have the luxury of waiting things out.

"Do I ever let anything slip through the cracks?" she challenged.

"Good point. I'll give you a ring when it's all said and done."

Dixie was quiet for a few seconds. "Bear, I just want you to know how much I appreciate what you're doing. Regardless of what Dad says or does, it means the world to me that you're willing to go to bat for me."

"For *us*, Dix. I want this to work out for my own reasons, too."

"I know, but you've been fighting with Dad on my behalf for longer than you've been trying to work with Jace or spend time with Crystal. That counts for something."

"Thanks. I'll let you know how it goes."

After they said goodbye, he called Crystal.

"How did it go?" she asked before he could say a word.

"I'm going in now, but I wanted to see how you were doing."

"I'm good. I called Jed and told him about what happened when I was in school. I figured since you were taking a big step, I should, too."

Bear closed his eyes for a beat, fighting the surge of aggression that came with talking about what she'd gone through and wishing he was with her right now. "How did he take it?"

"About like you did. He wanted to be sure I was okay, and then he went ballistic wanting to track down the man and kill him."

"Good man." Bear smiled and shook his head. "See, baby cakes? You've got more support than you ever imagined. I'm glad he's moving closer so the two of you can get acquainted with the people you've become. Sounds like you've both changed a lot since you lived under the same roof."

"I feel the same. Hey, Bear?"

"Yeah, babe?" He walked toward the clubhouse.

"Even if it doesn't go the way you want it to, I'm proud of you. And I'm rooting for you." He heard her moving the phone and then the rumbling purr of the kitty came through the line. "Harley is, too. We can't wait to see you afterward."

She'd insisted on waiting up for him tonight, and he loved knowing that they would be there when he got home. "Love you, babe."

He walked into the clubhouse even more determined to make tonight go the way he wanted.

Bones was leaning over the pool table, cue in hand. He lifted his eyes as Bear came through the door, and without a word, he made his shot. Bullet stood beside the pool table, tracking Bear across the floor to the table where their father sat talking on his phone. Going against his father was one thing. Taking on all three at once? Definitely not a walk in the park. He'd hoped they'd leave while he was outside.

Fuck.

"You guys taking off?" Bear sat across from his father.

Bullet took his shot and nodded to Bones. "Not a chance."

His father ended his call and set his cell phone on the table, looking at Bear expectantly.

Conflicting emotions pummeled him, from respect and love to anger and trepidation over whether he was making the right decision for himself and their family. One way or another, life as he knew it was about to be forever changed. He wiped his sweaty hands on his jeans and squared his shoulders, feeling as though he was preparing for Russian roulette.

"I want to talk to you about the bar." Bear was acutely aware his brothers were listening to his every word. Forcing himself not to look over, because it would only further piss him off, he remained vigilant in his effort to get his point across.

His father leaned back. "I'm listening."

"How serious are you about expanding the bar? You've talked about it in the past, but you never followed through."

"Dead serious," his father answered. "It's time. We've hit a plateau, and if we're not moving forward, we're going to shift in the wrong direction. There's only one way to make sure this place remains profitable enough to mean something for your kids' futures."

"And how do you know that?" Bear knew the answer, but he wanted to hear it from his father.

"Dixie's projections, of course."

"And you saw our outline for the expansion? Do you think it's solid?"

"Absolutely. I never doubted it would be."

"Then you know we're estimating it'll take roughly twenty hours per week of oversight during the expansion and hiring process."
Twenty hours I don't have.

"Yes." He stroked his beard. "I assume you'll manage the process and Dixie will step in when you can't be there."

"You're comfortable with that scenario?"

His father's lips curved up in a slow smile. "That's the scenario we've talked about since day one."

"Great. Then you have no issue with Dixie stepping in in my absence." Bear inhaled deeply, preparing to drop his bomb. "I'm cutting back my hours at the bar and the shop. Dixie will be overseeing the expansion."

His father's chest expanded.

"I'm committing to twenty-five hours a month working with Silver-Stone Cycles, and I'm selling my share of the bar ownership to Dixie. She's going to own two-fifths. I've given up a lot for our family, and I don't regret it, but it's time for me to take a step back."

Bear felt Bullet's presence before his father's eyes flicked up to meet him.

His father pressed both hands on the tabletop. The fingers on his left hand wouldn't follow his lead, curling up beneath the pressure. His icy stare chipped away at Bear's heart. "You can't sell your shares."

"What the fuck have you given up?" Bullet asked.

Without looking away from his father, Bear said, "I can sell, and I am." He lifted his eyes to Bullet. "You were away. Bones was in med school. I never left. You figure it out."

Bullet pulled out the chair beside Bear and straddled it. "You said you *wanted* to run the bar. I offered to take leave."

Bones put a hand on Bear's shoulder. "He's right. It's his turn regardless of what he said. I'm with Bear."

Bear's throat thickened. Bones was so careful about which battles he chose to fight, and having his support felt like the biggest gift on earth, despite how long it had taken him to get there. He gave Bones an appreciative nod and returned his attention to Bullet.

"You think I'd make you give up the only thing you talked about for as long as I can remember? Special Forces was to you what building bikes is to me and medicine is to Bones." He met his father's angry stare and said, "And what running this bar is to Dixie."

His father pointed at him. "You know your grandfather asked that the men in this family run the bar. You heard that with your own ears."

Bear shrugged. "You're right. I did. The same ears that heard Mom crying when you had your stroke, wondering how we were going to make it. The same ears that heard Dixie begging for more authority to run the bar on her own since she first got involved. And the same ears that hear your excuses for not giving it to her. She's capable. She wants it. And damn it, Dad. I'm sorry. You know I respect the hell out of you, but I respect her, too. I can't sit back and pretend this is okay." Thinking of Crystal's struggles with her family, her reason for leaving college, and even telling Gemma the truth pushed him to say more. "You're a good person and a loving father. Dixie knows that, but you don't want to be remembered as the guy who held her back. This control, or whatever it is you need to hold over her head. It's not worth it. She deserves the credit for her work, and honestly, Dad, you owe it to her."

Bullet pushed to his feet, and they all followed. Anger and nervous energy trailed them like shadows.

"I would have come back," Bullet said angrily, clearly still hung up on the earlier part of the conversation. He glared at Bear. "I wouldn't have saddled you with anything you didn't want. Damn it, bro. You should have said something."

"I made my choices, and I don't blame you." Bear squeezed his hands into fists, trying to keep calm. "There's no blame to be had. It's just time to fix this backward situation."

The sound of their father's uneven gait drew their attention. He stroked his beard with a distraught expression. "She's as stubborn as your mother."

"Dixie?" Bear asked, trying to catch up. "You raised us all to be stubborn."

His father's eyes moved between the three of them. "I raised you all to be *men*, and we raised Dixie to be a strong woman. But she's as stubborn as your mother. I want more for her. Don't you *see* that? Every damn time I tell her she can't do something, what does she do?"

"She blows it out of the water," Bear said.

"Exactly." He limped to within inches from Bear. "I respect your grandfather's wishes, but I also respect your sister, no matter what you believe. Do you *want* Dixie to spend the rest of her life in a bar? Around drunken men? Don't you want more for her?"

"More? Hell, yes. But Dix loves working at the bar *and* the shop. She doesn't want to work for anyone else. Have you ever asked *her* what she wants?"

Bullet stepped up beside Bear, arms crossed, face serious. "What do you want?"

"I want what's right," Bear answered. "I want Dixie to manage the project, and whatever else she wants to handle."

Bones came to Bear's other side. "No. What do *you* want? For yourself?"

The question slowed him down. He pushed away the guilt, forcing the truth. "I want to continue at the shop, and I want to work with Silver-Stone designing motorcycles. I've paid my dues. I've run the bar since I was barely eighteen. But I'm thirty-three, and I'm in love with Crystal. I don't want her sitting alone at night while I'm working at a bar. Family comes first. Always. She's my family now, too. That's what I want, and that's why I'm selling my shares of the bar to Dixie. The bar is her dream, not mine, and she has earned the right to manage it."

The muscles in Bullet's jaw clenched repeatedly. He stepped closer to Bear, and Bear held his breath, waiting for him to cut loose about how what he wanted didn't matter. But he refused to stand down. Not now, not ever again.

Bullet put a heavy hand on his back and faced their father. "He sells, I sell."

"Mine's already a done deal." Bones held up his phone, on which was a text he'd sent to Dixie ten minutes ago. *You can have my shares, too. Love you.*

Bear felt the earth tilt on its axis.

Their father scrubbed a hand down his face, eyeing his sons. "Stubborn motherfuckers. All four of you. No one's selling a damn thing. You think Dixie means it when she says she wants the bar? Then she'll have it. I thought I could push her toward something else without having to actually force her out of the family business, but not because she can't handle it."

"Right. Because she's a *woman*," Bear said with disgust.

"Damn right because she's a woman. She should work someplace where there are no drunk guys or late nights. She's my daughter. Would you want Crystal working at a bar until two in the morning?"

"Hell no."

"Well, son, maybe one day you'll understand why I've done what I've done. But she's your mother's daughter. I've been trying to get your mother to stop working at the bar for years."

"You don't want Red working at the bar?" Bear asked. "But you're all about family doing it *all*."

"Damn right I am." His father stood up taller. "I know you boys won't let anything happen to the girls when they're at the bar. But that doesn't mean I like them working there. Why do you think I pushed Dixie so hard in college?"

Bear shook his head. "I'm so fucking confused. Why didn't you just *tell* her?"

"Oh, yeah. That would go over well with little Miss I Can Do Anything My Brothers Can Do but Better." Their father tugged at his beard. "This was the only way I knew to get her to see the light. But she and your mother are two peas in a fucking pod."

"Pop, you let us believe you were a chauvinistic asshole."

"Hey." Bullet elbowed him.

"It's okay." His father gave Bear a hard look. "Better that you think I'm a chauvinistic asshole than Dixie think I don't want her in the family business at all. That girl's tough as nails, but she's also as sensitive as a hair trigger. She can see how I am about protecting our girls, and that fits in her mind as who I am. But hearing I don't want her in the family business for *any* reason? That would break her heart."

He rested his cane against his leg and set a hand on Bullet's and Bones's shoulders, staring at Bear. "Get your ass in here. I don't have three hands."

Bear stepped into the group hug.

"When your grandfather turns over in his grave," his father said, "that's on your shoulders."

"Thanks, Pop."

"No, Robert. Thank you. You held this family together for so long, I forgot it wasn't your job."

The recognition he'd spent years telling himself he didn't need made Bear's heart feel full to near bursting.

Bullet broke away from the embrace. "Don't tell him that shit. He's going to get a big-ass ego."

Bones cracked a smile. "Going to get?"

"I'll kick his ass and take care of that." Bullet slapped Bear on the back so hard he stumbled forward. Bear cocked a fist, and the three of them fell into a fake fight and ended up laughing.

When he walked out the door half an hour later, his father called after him, "Lunch, Sunday. Bring your little gal," and he knew life as he'd known it *had* changed.

For the better.

CHAPTER TWENTY-ONE

"COME ON, BABE. They're not going to care what you wear. We're just having lunch," Bear called into the bedroom.

"Just one more minute, promise," Crystal called to him. It was Sunday and they were meeting his parents at their house for lunch. She'd gone shopping with Gemma and Dixie Friday night and picked out a pretty wine-colored spaghetti-strap minidress with tiny off-white and black flowers. It was more feminine than she was used to, but she'd liked how she'd felt in the dress for Gemma's wedding, and she wanted to explore that side of herself a little more. She paired it with black biker boots, a few long silver necklaces on black strings, and silver bangles, making it look edgier, but she was still a nervous wreck. Of course, that had less to do with the dress than it did with having lunch with his parents.

"Babe?" Bear appeared in the doorway. His lips curved up and his eyes blazed a trail from her head to her toes. "Hot damn. You look gorgeous."

She fidgeted with the hem of the dress, thinking about how easy it was for guys to pick out their clothes. Bear always wore jeans and a T-shirt, with his leather vest thrown in most days. His tattoos were like permanent accessories. "Are you sure? Is it too girly?"

"*Too* girly? I don't know what that means, but if it's a bad thing, then hell no." His arms circled her waist and he began kissing her neck, sending shivers through her. "Why are you suddenly nervous about what you're wearing? You always look great."

"Because we're having lunch with your *parents.*" She hooked her finger into the waist of his jeans. They'd been through so much together, this should be easy, but it felt like another very big step. "Dixie will be there, right?"

"Yup, along with Bones and Bullet. But all that really matters is that I'm there, and I adore you. Have faith in me, and let's get out of here."

She grabbed her bag, and he draped an arm over her shoulder as they descended the steps. "You realize none of this matters, right?"

"Of course it matters. I'm a little nervous about talking with your dad."

"Don't be. Just be yourself."

She gave him a wry smile. "I'm not very good at holding my tongue. And I love Dixie, so I can't promise I won't say something he'll hate."

"Babe, I love you, and I won't ever ask you to be someone you're not. You say whatever you feel like saying. I'll always back you up."

After everything he'd been through lately, the last thing she wanted to do was say the wrong thing around his family. He couldn't know how much hearing that helped to tamp down her anxiety.

"Thank you, but I'm still a little nervous. Just keep in mind that if your father is as old-school, or club-driven, or whatever it is that causes him to think women aren't supposed to have certain jobs, then you'd better not begin taking after him. Because then I'd have to kick your ass."

He opened the passenger door of his truck. "Careful. I might enjoy *feisty* Crystal."

Between stolen kisses and lascivious comments, he kept her smiling the whole way to his parents' house on the outskirts of town.

Bear drove down a long tree-lined driveway and parked behind two motorcycles and Bullet's truck. Crystal took in the modest two-story brick home with a deep, welcoming front porch bordered by beautiful gardens. The house reminded her of the house in which she'd spent the early part of her childhood, giving her a sense of comfort.

At least that's what she told herself as they walked hand in hand toward the voices coming from the backyard.

A loud bark caught her attention as a large brown and black dog bounded toward them. Bear sank to one knee and opened his arms. The dog went paws on shoulders, nearly bowling him over, and covered Bear's face in slobbery kisses.

"Hey, Tink." Bear laughed, smiling up at Crystal. "This is Tinkerbell, Bullet's Rottweiler puppy."

"Bullet has a puppy named *Tinkerbell*? And are you sure she's a puppy? She's huge."

"She's definitely a puppy, and if you make one crack about her name, I'll make your boyfriend pay the price. Kennedy named her, and anything that little princess wants from her Uncle Bullet, she gets." Bear's brother pulled her into a hug. "How's it going, sweetheart?"

"Great, thanks. It's good to see you." Between Bullet's size, tatted-up body, and eyes that seemed to be in a constant state of *back off*, he was as intimidating as they came. But when it came to Kennedy and Lincoln, he was soft as butter, and he'd always been warm with Crystal.

Tinkerbell ran over to the garden and began digging.

"Tink." Bullet patted his leg, and the dog came to his side. He crouched and took the pup's face in his hands. "Don't you dig in Red's garden, sweetheart. I worked hard to make it pretty."

Crystal felt her eyes widen, and she tried to hide her surprise. "*You* garden?"

Bullet rose to his feet, hands on hips, scowling. "I suppose you're going to give me shit about that like Bear and Bones do?"

She held her hands up, unable to stifle a laugh. "I think it's adorable."

He growled.

Bear laughed.

"*Manly*," Crystal added. "That's what I meant."

"Come on, Tink." Bullet slapped his leg again, and the dog trotted alongside him toward the backyard.

"There they are." Bear's mother waved from across the yard. Her hair was a shade darker than Dixie's, cut above her shoulders in long layers. She pushed her sunglasses onto the top of her head as she approached and embraced Bear. "Hi, honey. I'm glad you two made it."

She smiled at Crystal, and in his mother's smile she saw Bear's warmth, and his mischief.

"Crystal, you look beautiful, honey." She embraced her.

"Thank you . . . ?" She wasn't sure what to call her. Wren? Mrs. Whiskey? Red?

"Call me Red, honey. Everyone else does." She winked at Bear and put an arm around each of their waists, heading for the backyard. It was easy to see where Bear got his loving nature.

The backyard was beautiful, all grassy lawn and mature trees, with lovely gardens surrounding a large patio. A glass table was set for seven with a vase of flowers in the center.

"I want to know everything Bear won't tell me," his mother said.

"Red." Bear gave her a *please don't* look.

"You finally meet the woman of your dreams, and you want me to back off?" She turned to Crystal with an amused expression. "You'd think after thirty-three years he'd know me. Honey, why don't you go see if they need help getting lunch ready?"

"I'm not leaving you alone with her. You'll give her the third degree."

Bullet tossed a ball for Tinkerbell and wrapped an arm around Bear from behind, putting him in a headlock and dragging him away. "Come on, bro. Help me play catch with Tink."

Crystal watched Bear maneuver out of the headlock and turn on Bullet. They began dancing around like they were boxing. "Should I be worried?"

"*Pfft.* If I worried every time they played like that, I'd be much grayer by now." Red pointed to a basketball hoop. "They'll take out their aggression playing ball. Give 'em five minutes. And don't worry. I'm not going to give you the third degree."

She breathed a little easier, although Red was so easygoing, she wouldn't have minded if she did.

"I know my big-hearted youngest son," Red said. "I've seen the way he looks at you, and Dixie tells me he's been trying to catch your eye for months. You're also the first woman he's brought home since high school. It seems to me, the boy who used to tumble into my bed at five o'clock Sunday mornings to cuddle, then wrestle with his brothers until they were sweaty from head to toe and starved for breakfast, has grown up and met his one and only."

Crystal felt herself blushing. "I love the man he is, and I'm happy to tell you whatever you'd like to know about me."

"Honey." Red smiled. "There's nothing you could say that would make me think you weren't right for him. I trust my boys, and of all of them, Bear is the most in tune with his feelings. He's with you, I'm with you."

Crystal's throat thickened with emotion, and a pang of sadness moved through her. Red offered the unconditional love she'd wanted so badly from her own mother. Before she could respond, Dixie and

Bones came out the back door carrying a tray of sandwiches and drinks. Dixie's eyes lit up as she set the tray on the table.

"Hey, Crystal." Dixie hugged her, looking over at Bear and Bullet, who were racing around with the puppy. Their father had agreed to let Dixie take over the renovations and manage the bar. But Dixie being Dixie, had insisted on remaining part-time at the shop as well. She was a loyal, stubborn Whiskey through and through. "Welcome to Testosterone Central."

"A little testosterone never hurt anyone." Bones embraced her. "Are you surviving my brother?" He gave her an assessing gaze.

Bear had told her that his brothers knew something had gone down a few years ago, but he hadn't told them what. She wasn't surprised. Her man didn't hide his emotions very well.

"Bones!" Bullet's deep voice sailed across the yard. "Get your ass over here. We're going to shoot some hoops."

She bent to pet Tinkerbell, who was carrying her ball in her mouth. "Doing much better than surviving him, thanks."

"Good. Glad to hear it." Bones pulled off his tank top, revealing a sculpted frame and a tattooed chest he kept well hidden behind those professional dress shirts she'd seen him in. He tossed his shirt on one of the chairs. "Sorry, but I have to go show my brothers who's boss."

"Told you," Red said. Tinkerbell trotted over to Red and dropped the ball at her feet. She picked it up and tossed it in the direction of a big weeping willow tree.

"If she digs up my gardens, I'm not going to be happy." Dixie crossed her arms, watching Tinkerbell.

"I was shocked to hear that Bullet gardened," Crystal admitted.

"His father taught him," Red explained.

"My dad planted that weeping willow for me when I was seven," Dixie explained. "He used to read me the story *The Wind in the Willows*. It was my favorite book. Do you know it?"

"Yes. I read it in grade school. It's a great story about friendship."

"Oh, honey," Red said. "It's so much more than that."

"'Independence is all very well, but we animals never allow our friends to make fools of themselves beyond a certain limit; and that limit you've reached,'" Dixie quoted. "It was the backbone of our youth. I loved it so much. I still do."

Bear's words came back to her from the night at Woody's when he'd told her about helping that little boy who had been bullied. *Love, loyalty, and respect for all runs as thick as blood through their veins. A blessing and a curse.* She hadn't understood what he'd meant about a curse, but as she'd seen him struggle with family loyalties and his desire to work for Silver-Stone, she'd figured it out. Still, she'd have given anything to have grappled with struggles of being *too* loved or *too* counted on, instead of the nightmare her mother had created. She took comfort in his family's closeness, and it was clear that his decision to stand up to his father and take the offer with Silver-Stone hadn't torn his family apart but seemed to have brought them closer together.

"He built the bench beneath it, too," Dixie said, bringing her back to the conversation. "And he planted the gardens around it. Now Bullet keeps them up, since Dad can't."

"That's really sweet," Crystal said, thinking of her own father and the projects she'd done with him.

"Before his stroke, my husband was a big gardener," Red explained. "When Bullet came back to civilian life, he had a rough time of it. He'd seen awful things, and he needed to get out of his own head."

"I know a little about needing to get out of my head," Crystal said.

Red's expression warmed. "Unfortunately, we all have our crosses to bear. Bullet pulled through, thanks to the support of his brothers and Dixie. And, of course, us."

Family. The one thing Crystal hadn't been able to rely on for so long. But they were helping Jed move next weekend, and she had high hopes of rebuilding at least that part of the family she'd lost.

"I'm surprised Bear didn't tell you," Dixie said. "He came over every night while my father and Bullet worked on the yard. He said it was because he wanted to learn how to garden, but you know that's not true. He'd rather be elbow deep in motor oil than garden soil."

Crystal looked across the yard at Bear, who was laughing with his brothers as they played basketball. They all had their shirts off now. Bear's arms were up, blocking Bones from making a shot. Normally she'd be lusting after her shirtless biker boy, but right then, all she saw was a caring brother who had spent evenings doing something he didn't really care about because he wanted to be sure the man who had taught him to fight, who had always had his back—the *man* he cared about—was okay.

Tinkerbell bounded across the yard toward the house as Bear's father came outside. Bear and his brothers headed for the patio. His father looked different than he did in the dimly lit bar. Older, and somehow kinder. Or maybe that was from the stories she'd been listening to. It sounded like he'd gone to great lengths to ensure his children grew up with strong morals, and to make Dixie happy.

He walked slowly across the patio, using his cane for balance. Crystal fidgeted with the edge of her dress, unable to calm her nerves as he approached.

He lowered his chin, looking at her with a stern gaze. Bear came to her side and put his arm over her shoulder. Tinkerbell stood by his feet, tail wagging, tongue hanging out.

"Pop. Don't give her the stare," Bones said as he pulled on his shirt.

Red patted her husband's butt, smiling at Crystal. "He's all bark, honey."

"Tinkerbell." Bullet's deep voice cut through the tension, and the pup trotted happily to his side.

Biggs's mouth curved up in a smile, lifting his thick gray mustache. His gaze softened and he reached for her with one arm, leaning on the cane with the other.

"I'm just trying to live up to my reputation." His speech was slow and slightly slurred. He leaned down and kissed her cheek, and she exhaled with relief.

"Now I see where Bullet learned it." Crystal smiled at Bullet. "You had me shaking in my boots."

"No, I didn't. You're a tough cookie. I can see it in your eyes. I'd bet it takes a lot more than a look to make you shake in your shoes." He winked at Bear and made his way over to the table.

Lunch was delicious, and they fell into easy conversation. Red told stories about Bear burying—and holding ceremonies for—everything from his pet goldfish to dead birds he'd found in the woods. Each of his siblings did their best to embarrass him, and by the time they'd finished eating, Crystal couldn't remember why she'd been nervous in the first place. She was drawn to his father, who took every chance he could to squeeze his wife's hand, wink at Dixie, or give his boys a hard time. He was a bit stern, and Crystal could see an underlying darkness in him, the way she could in Bullet, but the love he had for his family was palpable.

Bear's family was everything she'd always wished she'd had.

Crystal helped carry the dishes inside, and when she came back out, Biggs was sitting at the table petting Tinkerbell. He patted the seat beside him. "Sit with me a minute."

She heard Bear's hearty laughter, which she loved so much, and as she sat down, Bear and Bones came outside.

"Tell me about your family," Biggs said.

Bear sat beside her and pulled his chair so close their legs touched. He took her hand in his, watching her with a look that said he'd rescue her from the conversation, but she didn't need rescuing. She needed to cross this bridge at some point. It might as well be now.

"We lost my father when I was nine. My mother lives about an hour away, and honestly, she's a mess. A drinker," she said, surprised at how easily the truth came. "And my brother, Jed, is, well, he's a good guy, but he's been in some trouble. He's trying to clean up his act, though."

Biggs's gaze never left hers. He wasn't looking at her with a harsh glare or with tenderness. He was simply looking at her, without judgment. "I'm sorry about your parents. And glad to hear your brother is finding his way. Sometimes we have to fall before we learn to stand on our own." His eyes shifted to Bear. "And sometimes life throws us oceans of trouble, and it's all we can do to keep our heads above water."

She couldn't be sure if he was talking about her life, or theirs, but she lowered her eyes, feeling self-conscious. "Yes, that's true."

He tapped the side of her leg with his cane, and when she met his gaze, he was smiling again. "You keep that head up, darlin'. You're floating. Nothing can keep you down. But if life ever tries to drown you again, you've got Bear and all of us to pull you up. We take care of our own."

Tears welled in her eyes. She didn't think as she rose from her chair and hugged the father who had taught the man she adored about family, loyalty, and respect. He'd taught him how to *be* a man—and how to love.

CHAPTER TWENTY-TWO

CRYSTAL STOOD IN front of the bathroom mirror fixing her makeup and trying not to laugh at Bear, who was leaning on the doorframe watching her. His legs were crossed casually at the ankles, but there was nothing casual about the wolfish grin on his face.

"Don't you have something better to do?" She set down her eyeliner and smoothed her black tank top, giving her hips an extra shake for his benefit. She secretly loved that he was always lusting after her. They'd been together for more than a month, or by Bear's count, more than nine months. Either way, she was more in love with him than ever.

He stepped behind her, nibbling on her shoulder the way he *knew* drove her mad. "Better than this? Are you nuts, silly girl?"

"Bullet will be here in a few minutes. There's no time to fool around." They were helping Jed move into Quincy's apartment today. Crystal was so excited she could barely stand it. She and Jed had been talking more often since the incident with their mother, and they'd gotten even closer after she'd told him what had happened to her in college. It reminded her of how close they'd been when they were younger. She missed those times. She missed *him*.

She turned in Bear's arms, and he lifted her up on the counter, pushing her legs open and claiming his spot in between. She was glad he'd stopped being quite so careful with her.

"All I want is to touch you, sugar." He nipped at her lower lip, his hands gliding up her bare thighs to the fringe on her shorts.

Harley meowed as she came into the bathroom. She'd grown tall and slender, and Crystal swore she had developed a homing device for Bear's advances.

"There's our little cockblocker."

She felt him smiling against her neck. He loved Harley so much he let her have her own pillow on their bed.

She pushed off the counter and wound her arms around his neck. Guiding his mouth to hers, she kissed him until she felt him go hard.

He groaned against her mouth. God, she loved that. She loved everything about her naughty biker boy. He'd been a happier man since he'd agreed to work for Silver-Stone, and she was looking forward to the days when he was no longer working day and night. But she was even more excited to know his dreams were finally going to come true.

His hands roamed over her. "We just made love this morning, and I'm already having withdrawals."

She laughed as he kissed her, but she was already right there with him. She'd begun birth control shots, and not having to worry about condoms brought their intimacy and spontaneity to a whole new level. The other night she'd joked about making love on a motorcycle while it was running, and a few days later, in the privacy of their yard, they'd knocked it off her bucket list. *Oh, the vibrations!*

"Just let me make you come," he begged.

"Bea—" Her words were smothered in a kiss that lit her up like New Year's Eve. She'd never tire of the way he made her feel hot and weak at once. "God, your kisses unravel me every time. We have to be *fast*."

He kissed her again and pushed his hand into her shorts, teasing over her sex as he took the kiss deeper. She widened her legs, greedy for more. It never took him long to take her up to the edge, but he'd also learned to hold her at the peak until her legs went numb. He took great pleasure in making her come undone for lengths of time that should be illegal. If he did that now, there was no way she'd be able to help Jed move a darn thing.

"If you hurry, I'll make you come, too," she enticed.

"Jesus, baby. Like I'd say no to that?"

She unsnapped her shorts, letting them drop to the floor, and quickly undid his jeans, pushing them down his thighs. He quickened his pace.

She held her palm in front of his mouth. "Lick."

He did, and holy hell, that made her even hotter. She fisted his cock, going up on her toes as his fingers pushed in deep. He took her in a penetrating kiss, matching the rhythm of his fingers, and moments later she was soaring into the clouds. She squeezed him hard as she came, and his hips bucked. As she eased down from the peak, her body still pulsing, she took his hard length in her mouth. Bear buried his hands in her hair—another new and exciting addition to their incredible sex life—sending sparks of lightning sizzling through her. She sucked hard and fast until she felt him swell, and he found his release.

Thump, thump, thump.

Both of their eyes flew open at the sound of Bullet's heavy footsteps crossing the hardwood floor to the bottom of the stairs. "Bear? You up there?"

"Shit," Bear grumbled, helping Crystal to her feet. "Be down in a second," he yelled to Bullet.

Laughing and kissing, they washed up.

"Love you so much," he said, kissing her shoulder as she stepped into a clean pair of panties and pulled up her shorts.

"Me too, you, biker boy."

She hurried toward the stairs, and Bear hauled her against him with a serious expression. "Babe, you know I love everything about you. Not just the sex. Right?"

Oh, this man! He treated her like gold, had changed his whole life to spend more time with her, and he was worrying over their spontaneous sexy times? She bit back the playful response on the tip of her tongue. They'd come so far, she didn't want to make light of what was clearly worrying him. "I never doubted it for a minute."

He kissed her slow and tender. Then he slapped her ass, startling her out of her lustful state, and they hurried downstairs.

Bullet looked up from the sex-pit sofa—another bucket-list item they'd taken care of. *Quite a few times.* He pushed to his feet, shaking his head. "Get that look off your faces. I haven't gotten any in three days and you're pissing me off."

"Three whole days?" Crystal teased. "You poor thing."

Bullet pulled her into a hug. "Got any good-looking friends, sweetheart?"

"Tegan," she said on the way outside. They'd already received thirty orders for costumes, and Tegan had begun working part-time for the boutique. Crystal loved her, but she definitely wasn't Bullet's type. "You know I love you, but I think you'd probably scare the heck out of her. She's more Bones's type."

"She is *not* Bones's type." Bear unlocked the truck and helped Crystal in. Bullet climbed into the passenger side. "You think he's so clean-cut, but Bones has a definite dark side."

"Bro," Bullet scolded. Then to Crystal he said, "Chicks dig the dirty doctor."

Bear headed down the mountain. "You just chastised me for saying he had a dark side."

Bullet shrugged.

Crystal listened to their banter the whole way to Jed's friend's house, where he was staying in a basement apartment. It was only a few blocks from their mother's, and she got a sick feeling in the pit of her stomach, which remained with her while they packed up the trucks.

"You okay, sis?" Jed asked as he carried a box to the back of his truck. Thankfully, the attorney had not only been able to get the points dropped on his last ticket, but he had also proven that McCarthy had been targeting Jed. Jed's driver's license had been reinstated, and McCarthy was to be reprimanded. Jed was finally getting a chance to be the man he wanted to be, and Crystal could already see a difference in him.

"Yeah. I was just thinking about Mom. Is it weird that I feel guilty for not seeing her? I don't want to see her, but I kept hoping that one day I'd show up and she'd be the same person she'd been when we were younger."

"It's not weird, shrimp." Jed ran a hand through his hair and looked up toward the sky.

Crystal took a moment to study her brother, seeing even more of their father in him. She knew it was because he was no longer stealing or skirting the law.

"I think that's why Dad gave her so long to straighten out," Jed said. "I think he hoped for the same thing."

"Dad would be proud of you, Jed."

He leaned down and kissed her cheek. "You can't imagine how much it means to me to hear that."

Thinking of her father committing to taking her and Jed away from their mother brought a wave of sadness. It must have been so hard for him to make that decision. She wondered if he'd given her the worry dolls because of the person her mother had become, and not, as she'd thought, because he'd known she'd need them for the traumatic years ahead.

She watched Jed, and focused on the here and now, which was too damn good to be set aside for questions she'd never have answers to.

Bear blew her a kiss as he and Bullet carried a dresser to his truck. She couldn't have been happier than when she'd heard that Bullet and Bones had finally backed Bear in his confrontation with their father. He deserved everyone's support for all he'd done for his family over the years.

"I'm glad you're coming back to Peaceful Harbor," she said to Jed.

"Me too. It'll be like coming home. I owe Bear a lot, between hiring me thirty hours a week at the garage and ten at the bar and hooking me up with Quincy for the apartment." He stepped closer, his eyes warm and brotherly. She'd missed that look so much a lump rose in her throat. "But mostly I owe him for making you so happy. You deserve to be happy."

Bear winked as he headed back inside, full of badass swagger.

"I do love my biker boy."

She and Jed walked inside together to get another load of his belongings.

"I wish I could have been there for you when you left school. I know I said it before, but I can't stop thinking about it. I went back and gave Mom hell for what she said to you."

"You didn't have to do that." She grabbed a box from the counter. "What's in the past is in the past."

"I know." He hoisted a box into his arms. "I just wanted you to know that I may not have been there to have your back, but I do now, and I always will."

"Thanks, Jed."

"Hey, sugar," Bear said as he passed, carrying one end of a desk. "We're thinking of hitting a café for lunch on the way out of town. Sound good?"

"You know I'm always hungry."

"Some things never change," Jed teased.

An hour later they drove the loaded trucks to a café at the edge of town. Tucked against Bear's side, with Jed beside her and Bullet walking behind them like a bodyguard scanning the crowd, Crystal stifled her amusement. Going anywhere with Bullet, Bear, and Bones was like having three bodyguards. But she'd had no idea Jed had that much of a protective side. What else would she learn about him? She couldn't wait to find out.

The line was eight people deep, and her bladder was full of coffee. "I'm going to run to the ladies' room," Crystal said to Bear. "Would you mind getting me a turkey sandwich with lettuce?"

Bear scanned the café, his eyes landing on the sign for the ladies' room across the room. "Sure, babe."

He gave her a chaste kiss. She felt the heat of his gaze as she walked away, and she swore she felt Bullet and Jed's eyes on her, too. After using the bathroom, she read a text from Gemma as she headed back to the men.

Finlay just called. The catering is all set! Four more weeks!! How long until you get back with Jed?

They'd picked up their dresses and met with Finlay, the caterer, last week to go over the final menu for the wedding. Crystal wondered what syrupy-sweet Finlay might think of the tatted-up groomsmen. She stepped aside to let someone pass and sent Gemma a quick text.

You will be the most gorgeous bride EVER. We stopped for lunch. Will call when we get back.

When she looked up from her phone, Bear's eyes were trained on her, and her pulse went wild. His lips curved up in a loving smile, which was so different from his playful or seductive smiles. She adored every one of them. She moved through the people waiting to collect their food at the pickup counter. Bullet's ever-watchful eyes drifted over the shoulder of the guy he was talking with, to Crystal, then around her, before returning to the man in front of him. Jed was busy talking to a tall blonde. *Go Jed.*

The guy Bullet was talking to turned, and Crystal froze as the face from her past stole the air from her lungs. *No. No, no, no.*

Flashes of the attack slammed into her.

That face. Those cold, hard eyes.

She was slipping.

Going under.

His hands tore at her clothes.

She fought for clarity, refusing to let him win.

I'm not afraid of you.

She was breathing too fast, too hard.

Bear.

IN THE SPACE of a second the color drained from Crystal's face. Bear swept her shaking body against him, his heart racing. "Baby? What's wrong?"

Jed came to her side. "Crys?"

Her mouth was moving, but no words came. Bear put his ear close to her mouth, and her whisper sent fire through his veins: "It's *him.*"

He followed her gaze to the man standing in front of Bullet, rage clawing at him from the inside out. He thrust Crystal into Jed's arms and grabbed the asshole, slamming him against the wall, lifting him off his feet with the sheer force of his rage. The people around them scattered amid cries of fear.

"What the hell?" the guy yelled.

"I'm going to fucking kill you," Bear growled through gritted teeth.

Bullet moved in, a mountainous wall of strength beside him.

"Stop! Bear, no!" Crystal broke from Jed's grasp. "Don't! If you hit him, you'll get in trouble. I can't lose you!"

"Who the fuck are *you*?" The guy's eyes darted between all of them.

Her eyes turned fierce. "You don't remember me. *Christine*. The girl you *raped* at Lakeshore."

His face blanched. "Don't. Please. It was a frat party. We were both drunk. It was an accident."

Bear lifted the guy higher with the sheer force of his grip. "It was in an art building, motherfucker. How many women have you raped?" He cocked his arm back.

The guy's hands flew up in surrender. "Dude, you know how parties are—"

"Don't!" Crystal grabbed Bear's arm.

"Goddamn piece of shit," Bullet seethed, also cocking an arm.

"Bullet! Don't," Crystal begged. "This is *my* fight."

Bear was too angry to speak. His muscles flared, his heart hurt, and his arms shook with rage.

"Please, Bear." Tears filled her eyes—not when she saw the man who had raped her, but *now*, for Bear. "*Please* don't. You'll go to jail, and I can't lose you. I love you both for wanting to kill him. But killing him isn't punishment enough. I'm not afraid anymore." She glared at her attacker, her eyes throwing daggers. "An accident? I'll make sure you never 'accidentally' *rape* another woman." She pushed buttons on her phone and lifted it to her ear.

"Hi, this is Christine Moon. I'd like to report a rape."

EPILOGUE

THE SUN SHONE down on Gemma and Truman's wedding like a blessing. Pink and white paper lanterns were strung between the trees, giving the afternoon a festive feel. Gorgeous shades of pink and blue flowers decorated the yard and the center of the table. A long table draped in a pale pink tablecloth with graffiti art depicting Gemma, Tru, and the kids along the edge sat off to the side. Truman had painted it. He was so talented. Pink lace bows decorated the chairs, and pink and white rose petals were spread on the lawn, creating an aisle that led to a floral altar they'd rented.

It was *perfect*.

Crystal closed Gemma's bedroom curtain feeling as nervous as Gemma looked. "They're not out there yet. I only saw Red, Biggs, and Jed. And Finlay, of course. You look gorgeous, Gem." Gemma had worn her hair down, with a delicate tiara made of tiny white and blue flowers.

"Let's make sure you have everything," Dixie said. "Something old?"

Gemma held up a bracelet Red had given her. Red was like a surrogate mother to Tru, and a grandmother to the children. Crystal knew how much Gemma adored her. Crystal had a special place in her heart for Bear's mother, too.

"Something new? Your dress," Dixie said.

"Something borrowed," Crystal said with a smile, because she'd lent Gemma her only pair of pink earrings to wear.

Gemma brushed her hair over her shoulder, showing the dangling earrings. "And something blue, of course." She lifted her dress, revealing the blue garter they'd bought.

"I have something blue, too." Kennedy lifted her tiny wrist, showing off a silver and blue gemstone bracelet. "Tooman, I mean, Daddy, gave it to me."

Kennedy looked adorable in a white chiffon dress with flowers appliquéd across the chest and shoulders, and a pair of pink ballet slippers. She insisted on wearing the same hairstyle as Gemma, including the tiara.

"That's my *Tru Blue*," Gemma whispered. She crouched beside Kennedy. "Daddy loves you so much. Do you remember what you're supposed to do?"

Kennedy nodded. "After Uncle Bullet and Lincoln walk up to Daddy, then me and Uncle Boney walk together."

Crystal smiled at her nickname for Bones.

"That's right, sweetie," Gemma said. "And you'll hold Uncle Boney's hand while Mommy and Daddy get married?"

Kennedy nodded, twisting from side to side, her pretty dress swishing over her legs. "Just like we pwacticed."

Gemma rose to her feet, reaching for Dixie's and Crystal's hands. "Are you guys as nervous as I am?"

"Yes, and I'm not the one getting married." Crystal touched her hair. Gemma had put it up in a topknot, leaving a few tendrils hanging down, just as Tegan had suggested. She had never felt more feminine. She was still getting used to feeling free enough to wear things like that, and it was wreaking havoc with her nerves.

"I'm not nervous," Dixie said. "I just wish we had filled the yard with eligible bachelors." She lifted Kennedy into her arms. "Right, Ken? Auntie Dixie needs to find a nice boyfriend."

"So you can kiss him like Auntie Cwystal and Uncle Be*ah*?"

"Exactly." Dixie gave Gemma a one-armed hug. "Want me to take Kennedy out and get the men to speed it up?"

Gemma nodded. "Thank you." She rubbed noses with Kennedy. "See you in a few minutes, baby girl."

"I need to kiss Cwystal!" She leaned forward, her lips puckered up tight.

Crystal's heart warmed as she kissed her. "Love you, sweetie. You're the prettiest flower girl *ever*."

There was a time when she'd been afraid to become a mother, but she wasn't afraid anymore. As Gemma's wedding neared, she'd found herself thinking more and more about what it would be like to have a family. *With Bear.* She knew he'd be an incredible, loving father, even if overprotective, and she had a feeling she'd be a damn good mother.

"I can walk, Aunt Dixie," Kennedy said, wiggling out of her arms as they left the bedroom. "I'm a big girl."

Alone with Gemma, Crystal faced her best friend and held her hands. "You're getting *married* to a man you met in Walmart."

Their eyes teared up. Both of them fanned their faces.

"No crying," Crystal said. "We look too good to ruin our makeup. I'm so happy for you, Gem. You deserve all the happiness in the world, and Truman is so wonderful."

Gemma nodded, tears still brimming in her eyes.

"No crying," Crystal whispered, and embraced her. "I love you so much. Thank you for sticking with me even after you found out I wasn't the slutty girl you thought I was."

"You're the girl I always thought you were, and I have no doubt you and Bear are naughty, naughty, naughty. You're my sister from another mother."

A funny thing had happened when she'd tried to talk to Gemma about sex with Bear. It was too special to share. "Are you sure you want me to walk down the aisle with you? That's *your* moment."

"Yes. It's *our* soul sister moment. Besides, I need you to hold me up in case I get so nervous I can't walk."

Crystal peered out the window again, spotting the men in their matching dark slacks, short-sleeved white dress shirts, and black suspenders and ties. Her eyes were drawn to Bear, Truman's best man. She'd never seen him dressed up, and he was so handsome she couldn't stop staring at him. He'd been teasingly making comments about getting married all week, and as she watched him standing by the altar, she couldn't tamp down her emotions.

"Gemma," she whispered. "I love him so much my heart actually hurts. I'm not afraid to want it all with Bear, and I'm not afraid of the bottom dropping out from under me, because I know he'll be there to catch me." She held out her trembling hand. "Look at me. You're the bride, and I'm more nervous than you are."

Gemma took her hand. "Maybe that's because I'm the bride and you *want* to be."

BEAR STOOD BESIDE Truman as Dixie and Quincy walked down the rose-petal aisle. Dixie looked beautiful in a pretty lace dress. She had the rosy glow of a woman who had been given something she'd always wanted. Two nights ago, their father had told her the truth about why he had tried to dissuade her from working at the bar. Dixie told Bear that their father loving her *too much* was the best reason for his actions. He was glad Dixie was finally getting the credit she deserved.

Dixie took her place on the bride's side as Quincy took his place beside Bear, and they bumped fists. He and Jed got along well in their new living arrangement. They were already playing wingmen for each other.

Bear watched Bullet walk down the aisle at a snail's pace, holding Lincoln's hand, like the Jolly Green Giant and Tiny Tim. Bullet's eyes drifted to Finlay Wilson, and a smile lifted his lips. Boy was he barking up the wrong tree. Bear had spoken to Finlay earlier, and she was so sweet she could give a man cavities.

Lincoln looked adorable in his dark pants and suspenders. It was incredible, watching him grow from a gurgling baby to a walking, sort-of-talking little boy. The pang of wanting a family, which had been creeping in more and more over the last few months, slammed into him.

Bullet lifted Lincoln into his arms and took his place beside Quincy.

Bear's heart swelled as Bones led Kennedy down the aisle in her fluffy white dress. She tossed rose petals into the air, a sweet smile on her pretty face. That earlier pang became a thrum, and he pictured a little girl with Crystal's blue eyes and confidence. He felt a smile tugging at his lips.

"Uncle Boney!" Kennedy said, pulling him from his thoughts. "Look how handsome Daddy is." She waved at Truman, then turned that brilliant smile on the rest of them. "Hi, Uncle Quincy. Hi, Uncle Bea*h*! Hi, Uncle Bullet! Look at me! I'm a *flowah* girl!"

The three of them looked like grinning fools. Bear felt sorry for whoever tried to date that precious little girl when she grew up. She had a host of uncles who would fiercely protect her, and he was at the head of the line.

Kennedy yanked on Bullet's trousers. "Uncle Bullet, bend down so I can kiss Linc!"

He did, and Bear's insides turned to mush.

He clasped his hands in front of him, trying to calm his nerves as he awaited Crystal's arrival, but the second she and Gemma stepped out of the house, it was all he could do to stare. He knew he should be focused on the bride, but *sweet Jesus*. He'd never seen Crystal look more gorgeous. Her hair was swept up in a knot on top of her head, and a few wispy strands framed her face, making her blue eyes, which were currently locked on him, even more alluring. Her neck looked long and graceful. His mouth watered to kiss her there. Her bluish minidress brought out the shine on her cheeks and accentuated her bare shoulders. He had a definite thing for her shoulders, and he wondered if she'd chosen that dress, and that hairstyle, just to drive him out of his mind. She wore a pretty jeweled cuff around her upper arm and a sexy copper anklet that wound around her lower leg like a snake. She looked classy and feminine. *Exquisite.* His pulse went crazy. He wanted to step out of line and sweep her into his arms, but he forced himself to stand tall and blew her a kiss instead.

Her cheeks pinked up, making it that much harder for him to resist going to her.

She'd become so much more than the love of his life. She'd become his world. She'd told Bear that he'd given her the strength to make the call to the police and have her attacker arrested. But it was she who had given him the strength *not* to rip the guy apart. Love was a powerful thing. They had a long legal battle ahead, but they'd hired Logan Wild, a top-notch private investigator from New York City. Logan had already confirmed that the school had security video from the art building where Crystal had been assaulted, dating back to the attack. Crystal was nervous about the legal proceedings, but this was her journey for justice, and she wanted to take it. And she wasn't taking it alone. She had Bear's support and love, as well as that of everyone else who was with them today, and the members of the Dark Knights. Bear would spend the rest of his life doing everything within his power to ensure she was never hurt again.

Crystal and Gemma hugged when they reached the altar, and he noticed her ankle jewelry had a bear on the side. His heart turned over in his chest. Was love supposed to be so consuming? He felt like his world was standing still, and as Crystal and Gemma took their places, he saw tears in Crystal's eyes. She was his orchid. His symbol of love and affection. His wild filly. His *forever*.

Bear tried to listen to Truman and Gemma's vows and pay attention to the wedding taking place, but he wanted to be the groom, and he couldn't take his eyes off the woman who had captured his heart. She was right there with him, her beautiful eyes trained on him. *Isn't she always?*

He mouthed, *That could be us.*

Her eyes widened, and a radiant smile lifted her lips. She mouthed, *You want to get married?*

Yes, he mouthed, his pulse racing. *Do you?*

Truman and Gemma kissed, and everyone cheered, but Bear and Crystal were in a world of their own, stepping across the rose petals toward each other. He reached for her hand at the same time she reached for his.

"You waited months for me," she said with so much love in her eyes he wanted to dive in and drown in them.

"You're the only woman I will ever want."

"Then let's not wait." She bounced on her toes as she'd done at the market on the island. "Let's get married. Here. Now."

The silence of the others broke through the sound of his hammering heart, and he realized everyone was watching them. He stepped closer to the woman he adored. "Sugar, a man likes to be *asked*, not *told*."

Her smile told him she was tying his comment back to their first date at Woody's.

"Bobby Bear Whiskey," she said breathlessly, "I'm truly, madly, crazily in love with you. Will you marry me and make me the happiest woman in the world?"

Bobby Bear. God, he loved her.

"Yes, sugar, I will marry you. But the real question is." He dropped to one knee, reached into his pocket, and withdrew the engagement ring he'd been carrying since the day after she'd moved in with him, waiting for the right moment to pop the question. Maddox Silver's brother, Sterling, was a custom jeweler. Bear had designed the black-gold engagement ring with a diamond-encrusted floral design and a half-carat round diamond at its center, and Sterling had created it. It was complex and unique, just like his girl.

Taking her hand in his, he gazed into her eyes and said, "Sweet girl, you are strength and grace, beauty and intelligence. You're the woman I want to carry our babies, the lover I want to hold every night, and the badass biker chick I want wrapped around me on long road trips."

She covered her mouth as tears streamed down her cheeks.

"Most of all, you're the woman I want to be my wife. Sugar, will you please do me the honor of marrying me?"

"Yes. I want all those things with you. Every one of them. I want every day. I want *forever*."

He slipped the ring on her finger, and she leapt into his arms as he rose to his feet. Cheers rang out as his mouth came down over hers. They were passed from person to person, hugged and congratulated.

Crystal and Gemma were in an endless embrace.

"Are you sure it's okay?" Crystal asked. "We didn't mean to hijack your wedding."

"Yes. Yes, yes, yes," Gemma said, and more tears fell.

Bear elbowed Tru. "Dude, I should have asked. Sorry, man. I got caught up in the moment."

"About damn time," Tru said, and pulled him into a manly embrace.

When they finally ended up in each other's arms again, Bear couldn't resist stealing a few neck and shoulder kisses. "I think I found my new favorite hairstyle."

"They're all waiting for us," she whispered.

"Let them wait."

He gave her a chaste kiss, and they took their place before the officiator. He was quick to point out that they had no marriage license; therefore the marriage would not be legally binding.

Bear took Crystal's hand and pressed a kiss to the back of it. "It will be real to us. We'll get a license this week and go to a justice of the peace. But today will always be our wedding date."

"And I'll get you a matching ring. Because we both need to show that we're not owned, but *one*." Her arms circled his neck. "Kiss me as a single man one last time."

And he did, through whoops and whistles from their friends and family, until Kennedy tugged on his pants leg. Harley must have given her pointers.

"Uncle Be*ah*, can you ma*ww*y her now? I'm hung*w*y."

He scooped her into his arms, and with Kennedy on his hip, surrounded by the people they loved most, they took their vows. And he wouldn't want it any other way.

WANT MORE WHISKEYS?

Each of the Whiskey siblings will have their own novels. Sign up for Melissa's newsletter to be notified of the next Whiskey release!

www.MelissaFoster.com/Newsletter

If you haven't read Truman and Gemma's story yet, please enjoy this sneak peek of their love story, TRU BLUE, a sexy stand-alone romance. Available in paperback, digital, and audio formats.

www.MelissaFoster.com/TruBlue

CHAPTER ONE

TRUMAN GRITT LOCKED the door to Whiskey Automotive and stepped into the stormy September night. Sheets of rain blurred his vision, instantly drenching his jeans and T-shirt. A slow smile crept across his face as he tipped his chin up, soaking in the shower of *freedom.* He made his way around the dark building and climbed the wooden stairs to the deck outside his apartment. He could have used the interior door, but after being behind bars for six long years, Truman took advantage of the small pleasures he'd missed out on, like determining his own schedule, deciding when to eat and drink, and standing in the fucking rain if he wanted to. He leaned on the rough wooden railing, ignoring the splinters piercing his tattooed forearms, squinted against the wetness, and scanned the cars in the junkyard they used for parts—and he used to rid himself of frustrations. He rested his leather boot on the metal box where he kept his painting supplies. Truman didn't have much—his old extended-cab truck, which his friend Bear Whiskey had held on to for him while he was in prison, this apartment, and a solid job, both of which were compliments of the Whiskey family. The only family he had anymore.

Emotions he didn't want to deal with burned in his gut, causing his chest to constrict. He turned to go inside, hoping to outrun thoughts of his own fucked-up family, whom he'd tried—*and failed*—to save. His cell phone rang with his brother's ringtone, "A Beautiful Lie" by 30 Seconds to Mars.

"Fuck," he muttered, debating letting the call go to voicemail, but six months of silence from his brother was a long time. Rain pelleted his back as he pressed his palm to the door to steady himself. The ringing stopped, and he blew out a breath he hadn't realized he'd trapped inside. The phone rang again, and he froze.

He'd just freed himself from the dredges of hell that he'd been thrown into in an effort to *save* his brother. He didn't need to get wrapped up in whatever mess the drug-addicted fool had gotten himself into. The call went to voicemail, and Truman eyed the metal box containing his painting supplies. Breathing like he'd been in a fight, he wished he could paint the frustration out of his head. When the phone rang for the third time in as many minutes, the third time since he was released from prison six months ago, he reluctantly answered.

"Quincy." He hated the way his brother's name came out sounding like the enemy. Quincy had been just a kid when Truman went to prison. Heavy breathing filled the airwaves. The hairs on Truman's forearms and neck stood on end. He knew fear when he heard it. He could practically taste it as he ground his teeth together.

"I need you," his brother's tortured voice implored.

Need me? Truman had hunted down his brother after he was released from prison, and when he'd finally found him, Quincy was so high on crack he was nearly incoherent—but it didn't take much for *fuck off* to come through loud and clear. What Quincy needed was rehab, but Truman knew from his tone that wasn't the point of the call.

Before he could respond, his brother croaked out, "It's Mom. She's really bad."

Fuck. He hadn't had a mother since she turned her back on him more than six years ago, and he wasn't about to throw away the stability he'd finally found for the woman who'd sent him to prison and never looked back.

He scrubbed a hand down his rain-soaked face. "Take her to the hospital."

"No cops. No hospitals. *Please*, man."

A painful, high-pitched wail sounded through the phone.

"What have you done?" Truman growled, the pit of his stomach plummeting as memories of another dark night years earlier came rushing in. He paced the deck as thunder rumbled overhead like a warning. "Where are you?"

Quincy rattled off the address of a seedy area about thirty minutes outside of Peaceful Harbor, and then the line went dead.

Truman's thumb hovered over the cell phone screen. Three little numbers—*9-1-1*—would extricate him from whatever mess Quincy and their mother had gotten into. Images of his mother spewing lies that would send him away and of Quincy, a frightened boy of thirteen, looking devastated and childlike despite his near six-foot stature, assailed him.

Push the buttons.

Push the fucking buttons.

He remembered Quincy's wide blue eyes screaming silent apologies as Truman's sentence was revealed. It was those pleading eyes he saw now, fucked up or not, that had him trudging through the rain to his truck and driving over the bridge, leaving Peaceful Harbor and his safe, stable world behind.

THE STENCH OF urine and human waste filled the dark alley— not only *waste* as in feces, but *waste* as in drug dealers, whores, and other deviants. Mud and graffiti streaked cracked and mangled concrete. Somewhere above, shouts rang out. Truman had tunnel vision as he moved swiftly between the tall buildings in the downpour. A dog barked in the distance, followed by the unmistakable yelp of a wounded animal. Truman rolled his broad shoulders forward, his hands fisted by his sides as memories hammered him, but it was the incessant torturous wailing coming from behind the concrete walls that had him breathing harder, readying for a fight. It sounded like someone—or something—was suffering inside the building, and despite his loathing for the woman who had brought him into the world, he wouldn't wish that on her—or wish the wrath he'd bring down on whoever was doing it on anyone else.

The rusty green metal door brought the sounds of prison bars locking to the forefront of his mind, stopping him cold. He drew in a few deep breaths, pushing them out fast and hard as memories assailed him. The wailing intensified, and he forced himself to plow through the door. The rancid, pungent scents of garbage and drugs filled the smoky room, competing with the terrified cries. In the space of a few heart-pounding seconds, Truman took in the scene. He barely recognized the nearly toothless, rail-thin woman lying lifeless on the concrete floor, staring blankly up at the ceiling. Angry track marks like viper bites covered pin-thin arms. In the corner, a toddler sat on a dirty, torn mattress, wearing filthy clothes and sobbing. Her dark hair was tangled and matted, her skin covered in grit and dirt. Her cheeks were bright red, eyes swollen from crying. Beside her a baby lay on its back, its frail arms extended toward the ceiling, shaking as it cried so hard it went silent between wails. His eyes landed on Quincy, huddled beside the woman on the floor. Tears streaked his unshaven, sunken cheeks. Those big blue eyes Truman remembered were haunted and scared, their once vibrant color now deadened, bloodshot with the sheen of a soul-stealing high. His tattooed arms revealed the demons that had swooped in after Truman was incarcerated for the crime his brother had committed, preying on the one person he had wanted to protect. He hadn't been able to protect anyone from behind bars.

"She's . . ." Quincy's voice was nearly indiscernible. "Dead," he choked out.

Truman's heart slammed against his ribs. His mind reeled back to another stormy night, when he'd walked into his mother's house and found his brother with a bloody knife in his hands—and a dead man sprawled across their mother's half-naked body. He swallowed the bile rising in his throat, pain and anger warring for dominance. He crouched and checked for a pulse, first on her wrist, then on her neck. The pit of his stomach lurched. His mind reeled as he looked past his brother to the children on the mattress.

"Those your kids?" he ground out.

Quincy shook his head. "Mom's."

Truman stumbled backward, feeling cut open, flayed, and left to bleed. His siblings? Living like this?

"What the hell, Quincy?" He crossed the room and picked up the baby, holding its trembling body as it screamed. With his heart in his throat, he crouched beside the toddler and reached for her, too. She wrapped shaky arms around his neck and clung with all her tiny might. They were both featherlight. He hadn't held a baby since Quincy was born, when Truman was nine.

"I've been out for six months," he seethed. "You didn't think to tell me that Mom had more kids? That she was fucking up their lives, too? I could have helped."

Quincy scoffed. "You told me . . ." He coughed, wheezing like he was on his last lung. "To fuck off."

Truman glared at his brother, sure he was breathing fire. "I pulled you out of a fucking crack house the week I got out of prison and tried to get you help. I *destroyed* my life trying to protect you, you idiot. *You* told *me* to fuck off and then went underground. You never mentioned that I have a sister and—" He looked at the baby, having no idea if it was a boy or a girl. A thin spray of reddish hair covered its tiny head.

"Brother. Kennedy and Lincoln. Kennedy's, I don't know, two, three maybe? And Lincoln's . . . Lincoln's the boy."

Their fucking mother and her presidential names. She once told him that it was important to have an unforgettable name, since they'd have forgettable lives. Talk about self-fulfilling prophecies.

Rising to his feet, teeth gritted, his rain-drenched clothes now covered in urine from their saturated diapers, Truman didn't even try to mask his repulsion. "These are *babies*, you asshole. You couldn't clean up your act to take care of them?"

Quincy turned sullenly back to their mother, shoving Truman's disgust for his brother's pathetic life deeper. The baby's shrieks quieted as the toddler patted him. Kennedy blinked big, wet, brown eyes up at Truman, and in that instant, he knew what he had to do.

"Where's their stuff?" Truman looked around the filthy room. He spotted a few diapers peeking out from beneath a ratty blanket and picked them up.

"They were born on the streets. They don't even have birth certificates."

"Are you shitting me?" *How the fuck did they survive?* Truman grabbed the tattered blanket that smelled like death and wrapped it around the babies, heading for the door.

Quincy unfolded his thin body and rose to his feet, meeting his six-three brother eye to eye. "You can't leave me here with *her*."

"You made your choice long ago, little brother," Truman said in a lethal tone. "I begged you to get clean." He shifted his gaze to the woman on the floor, unable to think of her as his mother. "She fucked up my life, and she clearly fucked up yours, but I'll be damned if I'll let her fuck up *theirs*. The Gritt nightmare stops here and now."

He pulled the blanket over the children's heads to shield them from the rain and opened the door. Cold, wet air crashed over his arms.

"What am I supposed to do?" Quincy pleaded.

Truman took one last look around the room, guilt and anger consuming him. On some level, he'd always known it would come to this, though he'd hoped he was wrong. "Your mother's lying dead on the floor. You let your sister and brother live in squalor, and you're wondering what you should do? *Get. Clean.*"

Quincy turned away.

"And have her cremated." He juggled the babies and dug out his wallet, throwing a wad of cash on the floor, then took a step out the door. Hesitating, he turned back again, pissed with himself for not being strong enough to simply walk away and never look back. "When you're ready to get clean, you know where to find me. Until then, I don't want you anywhere near these kids."

TO CONTINUE READING, PLEASE PURCHASE TRU BLUE.

More Books by Melissa

THE REMINGTONS

Game of Love
Stroke of Love
Flames of Love
Slope of Love
Read, Write, Love
Touched by Love

SEASIDE SUMMERS

Seaside Dreams
Seaside Hearts
Seaside Sunsets
Seaside Secrets
Seaside Nights
Seaside Embrace
Seaside Lovers
Seaside Whispers

BAYSIDE SUMMERS

Bayside Desires

THE RYDERS

Seized by Love
Claimed by Love
Chased by Love
Rescued by Love

SEXY STAND-ALONE ROMANCE

Tru Blue
Truly, Madly, Whiskey

BILLIONAIRES AFTER DARK SERIES

WILD BOYS AFTER DARK

Logan
Heath
Jackson
Cooper

BAD BOYS AFTER DARK
Mick
Dylan
Carson
Brett

HARBORSIDE NIGHTS SERIES
Includes characters from the Love in Bloom series

Catching Cassidy
Discovering Delilah
Tempting Tristan

Other Fiction Books by Melissa
Chasing Amanda (mystery/suspense)
Come Back to Me (mystery/suspense)
Have No Shame (historical fiction/romance)
Love, Lies & Mystery (3-book bundle)
Megan's Way (literary fiction)
Traces of Kara (psychological thriller)
Where Petals Fall (suspense)

Acknowledgments

Thank you for reading Bear and Crystal's story. I hope you fell in love with them, as well as all their warm and wonderful family members and friends, each of whom will be getting their own happily ever after.

If you enjoyed this story and want to read more about the Whiskeys and about Peaceful Harbor, look for *Tru Blue* or *River of Love*. I hope you will also check out the rest of my alpha heroes and sassy heroines in my big-family romance collection, Love in Bloom. Every book can be read as a stand-alone novel, and characters appear in other family series, so you never miss out on an engagement, wedding, or birth. You can find information about the Love in Bloom series and my books here: www.melissafoster.com/melissas-books

I offer several free first-in-series ebooks. You can find them here: www.MelissaFoster.com/LIBFree

A special thank-you to Lisa Bardonski and Lisa Filipe for our multitude of conversations regarding this book. I chat with fans often in my fan club on Facebook. If you haven't joined my fan club yet, please do! www.facebook.com/groups/MelissaFosterFans

Follow my author page on Facebook for fun giveaways and updates of what's going on in our fictional boyfriends' worlds. www.Facebook.com/MelissaFosterAuthor

Thank you to my awesome editorial team: Kristen Weber and Penina Lopez, and my meticulous proofreaders: Elaini Caruso, Juliette Hill, Marlene Engel, Lynn Mullan, and Justinn Harrison. And last but never least, a huge thank-you to my family for their patience, support, and inspiration.

www.MelissaFoster.com

Melissa Foster is a New York Times and USA Today bestselling and award-winning author. Her books have been recommended by *USA Today's* book blog, *Hagerstown* magazine, *The Patriot*, and several other print venues. Melissa has also painted and donated several murals to the Hospital for Sick Children in Washington, DC.

Visit Melissa on her website or chat with her on social media. Melissa enjoys discussing her books with book clubs and reader groups and welcomes an invitation to your event. Melissa's books are available through most online retailers in paperback and digital formats.

WITHDRAWN

CPSIA information can be obtained
at www.ICGtesting.com
Printed in the USA
LVOW03s1511070417
530030LV00002B/3/P